Recruitment

Book 1 of The Faction

Kit Hanson

Book 1 of The Faction
Recruitment by Kit Hanson
https://jointhefaction.wordpress.com/
Twitter: @VitameatavegamN

Editor: C. D. Tavenor
Twitter: @tavenorcd

Published by Two Doctors Media Collaborative LLC
www.twodoctorsmedia.com

ISBN: 978-1-952706-23-3 (paperback)

Recruitment

Book 1 of The Faction

<u>Researcher Notes</u>

Location & Date Redacted

Every once in a while, a chill runs down my spine. It's random. Unplanned. But I know better.

See, I recently came upon some documents.

Documents that should not exist.

Not in the world we know, at least.

After review, I've realized these documents are too interesting, too important, not to share with the public. Properly organized, they'd make for a flashy movie, a dramatic television show, or, in my case, a mediocre book. I've come to love the people whose adventures I've reviewed—their strengths, their weaknesses, their nuances. If it were possible, I'd gather them together to hear their tales in a heartbeat.

Alas, it seems I am doomed to illustrate their journey from behind the screen of my computer, shifting files and folders around to make sense of a timeline refusing to behave.

So, I'll begin with the "who."

The journey I've discovered begins with five people, all at different points in history, all who eventually connect to make something bigger than themselves. I want to tell their stories, but to do so, I have to move beyond the boundaries of time and space. Therefore, it's paramount that you, the reader, pay close attention to the dates and locations I include. Things are not always what they seem . . . but, you'll soon find out for yourself.

I apologize if the structure of my shared files seems messy at times. I'm pressed to hurry, to get this out into the general public, before someone stops me.

See, every once in a while, a chill runs down my spine. It feels random. Unplanned. But I know better. It's no accident; it's a bit of sixth sense.

A sixth sense which warns me.

I'm already being watched.

Folder 1: Personnel

<u>Folder 1.1, File 1</u>
"Discovery"
<u>Reported by Battery</u>

Mississippi, United States
June 21, 1989-A

The warm summer air filled the train yard, providing a blanket of comfort for those willing to accept nature's embrace. For those who resisted, like the small girl crying on the edge of a detached caboose, it was nothing more than an uncomfortable, smothering heat. Her soft sobs echoed through the otherwise silent yard, bouncing between trains and buildings.

The girl reached up and massaged her face, where a dark purple bruise had swollen around her brown eyes. She sniffled, rubbing her small, button nose. After a moment she took a breath, straightened her shoulders, and slid from the caboose, her feet crunching gravel. The impact of her landing sent her curly brown hair splaying out in every direction like a palm tree. Her brow furrowed and she took a determined step forward, emitting another crunch.

Who cares that her parents don't share the same color, or go to church on Sunday?

Crunch.

Why does it matter if her darker skin stands out in the sea of white faces at school?

Crunch.

How's she supposed to deal with the way people treat her if they don't look past her outsides?

Crunch.

The girl stopped, inhaling deeply.

Crunch. Crunch. Crunch. Crunch.

The girl glanced over her shoulder to find the origin of the mirrored sounds. What she saw was a pale, gangly, red-haired boy approaching her. His fair skin sizzled in the heat, and his bright green eyes glimmered as they reflected the sun's rays. The boy always told her that his eyes were like ginger ale, while hers were like root beer.

He gave a shy half-wave and walked up to her.

Crunch. Crunch. Crunch. Crunch.

His voice, heavy with Southern twang, was the first to fill the empty air.

"Hey."

"Hi."

"Ar'ya okay?" he asked.

She shook her head. "No, but I will be."

"I heard about what the other ones did." He frowned. "Someone should've stepped in—"

The girl squeezed him tight, pushing the air from his lungs and halting his words. For her size, she was surprisingly strong, making today's loss against the other students that much more embittering. Still holding on, she whispered to him.

"It's okay. You know I'm stronger than them bullies in town. I'm better 'cause I know what's important. It's not about our looks or our folks." Brown eyes angled up toward his face. "It's about loving the people we have and doing what we can to live a good life."

He smiled at her. "I couldn't've said it better myself."

The day began to darken, shifting from a bright yellow to a dull grey. The girl looked up to see clouds moving to block out the sun, then peered across the tracks of the train yard to a shape in the distance. She squinted, remembering why she was even here.

"Come on. I want to show you something."

New York, United States
September 9, 2001-B

Water lapped against the pier, half-hearted in its tidal force; the loudness of the wet slaps was odd, considering how little effort the Hudson River seemed to exert. Birds cawed overhead, seeking food, shelter, and mates. The sun shone with its natural confidence, without a cloud in sight.

This would be a great spot to relax today, Zen thought. *Well, if it weren't for him.*

The bloated corpse of a pale, balding, middle-aged man lay on the edge of the pier. His eyes bulged from his skull, and it appeared that a fish had already begun to nibble on the edge of his ear before the body was scooped from the river. He was mostly covered in plastic by now, as CSI had come and gone earlier today.

Or later yesterday, depending on your curfew.

"What happened here?" she asked, turning to her fellow detective.

Phil was a short, plump, middle-aged Hispanic man with leathery skin, greasy black hair and a bushy mustache. He was quiet, as usual, but he had an aura of wisdom surrounding his silence. He might appear to others as gruff or unapproachable, but he remained an amicable, professional partner. Zen held a great deal of respect for his tenure and experience.

Phil surveyed the scene before him, rubbed the sleep from his eyes, and grumbled in response. "Some kids found him bumping against the edge of the pier in the water a few hours after midnight. Maybe around two or three? They claim he was already like this." He gestured at the man, naked on the ground. "So, if the killer took the time to strip him and take his IDs, we can assume that there is something important about his identity, or about the evidence left behind on his body."

He sighed, stuffing his hands into his coat pockets. He looked up at Zen. "Cause of death appears to be asphyxiation. That's what CSI is saying. They'll perform a more in-depth analysis back at the lab. That'll be a while, though. Let's split up and check nearby residences. Maybe someone around here saw something than can expedite catching a killer."

Zen nodded in agreement and stuck a thumb out behind her. "There's a skate park nearby. I'll start there."

The two tired detectives trekked off, their parting figures outlined by dawn's golden-orange glow.

Mississippi, United States
June 21, 1989-A

The hairs on the girl's arm rose as a chilling wind cut through the summer heat, leaving her with lasting goosebumps. There was so much *energy* here. She loved it.

The two children trotted up the grassy hill before them, letting their hands sway and touch occasionally as they moved side-by-side. They ascended to the top and stopped to admire the large tree now filling their view. It was a Nuttall oak, the girl had learned through research, and what made it so interesting was its location.

These oaks were more common in the wetter River Valley, and it was rare for one to grow so far from a significant water source. It was unique to the area; something that stood out.

Something she identified with.

A sigh sounded beside her. She glanced over to see the boy's eyes close, a slight smile on his face as he enjoyed the windier weather. She grabbed his hand and squeezed, and he opened his eyes in time to see her point at the oak.

"I always come when I'm sad or mad. It's a place for me to . . . *center myself.*" She mimicked her pa's voice. "But I love it 'cause I get to see the storms up-close."

She was referring to the many thunderstorms and tornadoes which frequented their town. In the heart of the Dixie Belt, storms were just a fact of life for residents.

"I want you to be here with me today," she added. "This is a special tree for me, an' I want to share it with you."

She uttered her words at the perfect time. Dark clouds formed overhead, and the low rumble of thunder chased intermittent flashes of blue light. The pair scrambled to the base of the tree and climbed the trunk, invigorated by the power and the chaos swirling around them. They were young and spry, and it took little time or effort to reach the highest branches of the sturdy oak. The boy and the girl rested on a thick branch, leaning against each other, their legs swinging in the air as the heavy storm clouds approached.

New York, United States
September 9, 2001-B

Nothing frustrated Zen the police officer more than trying to reason with teenagers; this only proved truer in low-income areas of the city. A small handful of kids were at the skate park this early in the morning, and every single brat was sarcastic and uncooperative. She'd reached her capacity for snark by the time she wrote down their statements. It wasn't until she wandered away from the park to a nearby apartment building that she reached a reprieve.

At the building, the grass outside was dying, the grounds littered with broken bottles and discarded clothing. A group of men in jeans and dark hoodies smoked in lawn chairs outside the apartment entrance, but they scattered when they saw Zen approaching.

She entered and made her door-to-door rounds.

"Yeah, you want Trevor," mumbled a middle-aged man near the building's entrance. "He's always got these annoying hood rats coming over and making a mess."

"My daughter saw him at her school, hustling some kind of drugs!" gossiped a young mother down the hall, a few minutes later.

An elderly lady who said she "most times goes by 'Mrs. Jackson,' but 'Mary' is just fine for police detectives" confided the most interesting memories with Zen.

"My neighbor, he was at it again last night. I heard him yelling through the walls. There was another man's voice, deeper, yelling back. It was such a loud commotion, Detective! I think they were destroying his furniture. I was getting scared and had walked out onto my porch, ready to call nine-one-one. That's when I saw him. The other man, he was tall with a heavy coat, and he had a knit cap hiding a lot of his face. He stormed out of the apartment and walked around the building. Not but a moment after, Trevor left, too, carrying a long, dark shape over his shoulder. I was scared and went back into my apartment. The last thing I saw was my neighbor walking toward the river. I had never seen the other man before."

Mary leaned away from her apartment doorway, her face telegraphing some relief for the opportunity to share her story. Zen leaned closer to hear her next words, and she realized that the woman was in tears, her bottom lip trembling. "Things are so different now; so much meaner. I can't tend my window garden anymore. I'm afraid to walk by the river at night. I just want my neighborhood to go back to the way it used to be. Can you help me?"

Zen reached out and covered Mary with a compassionate embrace. The detective was "awful strong for her size," as her momma would say, but she managed to avoid leaving her witness with any lasting discomfort. After a moment, they separated, and Zen turned toward the hallway.

Zen said, "I'll do my best, Mary."

She walked away, passing under the dirt-covered fluorescent ceiling lights, approaching Trevor's apartment.

"NYPD!" She punctuated her announcement with a few sharp raps against his wooden door.

From within the apartment came a loud crash and the sounds of something scurrying across wooden floorboards. A muffled "Fuck!" rang out.

Zen sighed. "Sir, I just have a few questions for you. That's all."

She heard furniture slamming and clattering, but when Zen heard the distinct *clack-clack* of a racked pistol slide, she stiffened, the small hairs lifting themselves from the nape of her neck. Zen reached for the sidearm on her hip, but reconsidered. She needed this man's information more than he needed to die. She could handle herself without lethal force, and she wouldn't be satisfied until she could share the fate of the corpse at the pier with its family.

Zen slid her hand from the holster of her gun to the pocket behind it, where her Taser rested.

No. You don't need that, either.

She took two steps back and struck out with her leg. Her heel slammed against the wooden door with enough force to splinter the edges away from the frame. She repositioned to finish her personal demolition project, but a loud *crack* from within the apartment interrupted her. Sprays of wood brushed against Zen's face as a small hole appeared in the door, punctuating the bullet that had traveled through it. She rolled past the door frame and looked behind her, relieved the bullet had only penetrated the nearby drywall. At times like this, she could never trust her body to tell her if she was injured.

Zen returned to the door. She lowered her body, shifting on the ground into a low, pouncing position, her right leg splayed behind her while her left foot and both hands were planted near her face, resembling an Olympic runner at the starting line. Not allowing a moment's hesitation, she sprinted forward with every ounce of force available. The wooden door cried in protest as Zen's shoulder made firm contact. With a short-lived, inanimate woe, it pushed away from the frame and propelled a few feet into the apartment, reaching its final resting place.

The detective planted one foot on the center of the fallen barrier and surveyed the room. It was filled with haze and smoke, evidence of the constant exposure to cigarettes and, Zen assumed, a variety of other airborne substances. The room itself was in disarray. Clothes, magazines, and power tools littered the floor. An old beige couch at the center of the room pointed toward a small grey television. In front of the couch was a brown coffee table supporting a glass surface and covered in a collage of drug paraphernalia, from silver razors to glass pipes to questionably opaque bags and jars. At first glance, there was no evidence of a violent crime, but the observation did little to deter Zen's suspicions.

More important was the one missing detail: The resident himself. Zen moved into the room, maintaining a balance between speed and silence, sticking close to the walls to avoid an ambush. She leaned into the kitchen and saw an open window to the grass-covered field outside. Curtains blew on either side from the slight breeze, and framed, in the center of the window, the shrinking figure of a man running toward the skate park.

Zen furrowed her brow and hurled herself into the kitchen, not hesitating for a moment to take a leaping step onto the counter. In a single, deft movement, she grasped the top of the window frame and used her momentum to swing her body outside. The rocking motion sent her legs above her head for just a moment as she hung in the air. Not one to be bested by physics, Zen shifted her weight so that she dropped to the ground in an arcing motion, landing feet-first onto the grass. Steadying herself, Zen reached for the Taser again.

No, Zen. You don't need it. Believe in yourself.

She sprinted forward, taking long, graceful strides.

The man ahead of her had a shaved head and pale skin, and he wore a white t-shirt with dark green cargo pants. The sun glinted off the metal pistol still in his hand. He was muscular, but awkward, and he seemed already a little winded from the minimal exercise. The man glanced over his shoulder as he lumbered into the skate park, and his eyes widened when he realized that Zen was no more than a dozen yards away.

Her quarry entered the concrete jungle and pushed through the still loitering teenagers. His body, and then his head, dropped below sight as he fell into the nearest bowl ramp; whether by intent or by accident, Zen couldn't be sure.

Zen accelerated as she approached the lip of the ramp. She rocketed over the edge and found herself airborne, the wind rushing through her splayed, curly hair and blowing past her ears. The detective surveyed the scene below her; the man had reached the far side of the bowl ramp and was beginning to climb out.

She landed with a dense *thud* about halfway into the depressed skating area, and the man—most likely Trevor—spun around in surprise. He raised his pistol, but she continued her dash, and he was only able to fire two wide shots before she was upon him. Zen lowered her body to strike him with her shoulder, and the force of the collision knocked him off his feet and into the wall of the ramp behind him.

His gun clattered to the ground as he slumped over in pain, and Zen kicked it away. She stood over her would-be attacker, surveying him for the briefest of moments. Satisfied that he was no longer a threat, she gripped his collarbone in one hand and shoulder in the other, lifting him to his feet. With one solid push, his back struck the wall again.

"Trevor, right?" she asked, her voice steady. "What happened last night?"

The man took a step forward, nodding slightly, but she shoved him against the wall a third time, much harder than before. His eyes teared up from the force of his collision, and she cringed a little.

Hold it back, Zen. There's no reason to stoop to his level.

She said, "No! You don't get to move. It's bad enough that you shot at a police detective, but you fired your gun, twice, in a skate park. A damn *skate park*. There's no one but kids here. Are you out of your mind?"

The man grinned at her, his teeth stained pink with blood.

Jesus, Zen; restrain yourself.

"Don't give me that face," she said. "I'm giving you a chance, here, to do the right thing *now*. Not tonight, not in seventy-two hours, *now*. Redeem yourself and tell me about the body at the pier. Or I can keep reintroducing you to that wall until you're ready to marry it." She took a threatening step forward.

"No!" Trevor spoke, raising his arms in self-defense. His voice was high and squeaky; a strange sound from the large man.

"I'll talk," he continued. "I didn't want to do this anyway. It's not my fault."

Zen raised her hand in a beckoning gesture, her voice friendlier than before. "Tell me what happened."

Mississippi, United States
June 21, 1989-A

The wind picked up speed, blowing the first flecks of rainwater into their faces. The boy rocked a little in the gust, but the girl held him tight, steadying herself against the tree with her other hand. The clouds reached them. She gazed in awe up at the storm, at its raw power and limitless energy, her attention rapt.

"Isn't it amazing?" she cried over the howling of air through tree limbs.

The boy nodded, a little dumbfounded himself.

"I can't believe that none of the people in town just stop and watch the storms," he yelled. "They're so beautiful, hiding in plain sight. You know, people choose to fear what they look at instead of trying to find the treasure beneath."

The girl looked at his face, baring a broad, unabashed grin as she mirrored his earlier words. "I couldn't've said it better myself."

She leaned toward him, and he responded in kind. Chills ran up her arms as their lips touched.

Wow . . . this is what kissin' feels like.

Their hands touched at each other's knees, awkward but unashamed. The girl closed her eyes and embraced the moment, letting her worries and fears fade away. The people at school didn't matter; the people in town didn't matter; shoot, this storm didn't matter. All that mattered was the way she felt in this moment.

Rain began to splatter against them as they pulled away, faces inches apart. The boy was grinning a stupid grin, his face flushed. He grabbed her and drew her tight, wrapping her into a new hug. Her head against his shoulder, their bodies pressed together once more. She smiled into his neck.

"I . . . I think I love you," she said, her words lost in the loud cracking of thunder.

The tree creaked, and the hair on her arms stood up once again. Lightning flashed in the air around them, their bodies illuminated by blue light. She was convinced he hadn't even heard her, but in the second of silence between two thunder cracks, his whisper made it to her ears.

"I *know* I love you," he said.

The blue glow around them grew brighter, the rumbling sounds louder, the humid air hotter.

The boy gasped, looking into the sky over the girl's shoulder. She smelled the rancid odor of burning hair. Buzzing, like the parade of a billion hornets, washed over the young couple in

waves—
 And their world exploded.

**New York, United States
September 9, 2001-B**

Why are you here?

Zen walked alone down the trail of Fort Tryon Park; the rest of the world was slow to awaken, though pre-work joggers and dog-walkers passed her on occasion.

During her interrogation with Trevor, he had been more than willing to share his own story with her. According to him, a man in a dark coat and knit cap entered his life a few weeks ago, making cocaine purchases from him in larger-than-normal amounts. It was difficult to acquire so much at once, but Trevor had some allies outside the country, and he was able to obtain what the man wanted.

A few days later, the man revealed recordings of their conversations and transactions, with enough evidence to incriminate Trevor for life. Under the pressure of blackmail, Trevor ran victimless errands for the man, stealing various electronics, chemicals, firearms, and explosives, all from untraceable sources. Trevor claimed he could see no meaningful connection between the items, so it gave him no reason to worry about his begrudged alliance with the mystery man.

Until last night.

Zen continued down the trail, looking for a stone archway, contemplating Trevor's words.

"He showed up with a body wrapped in a plastic bag," he'd said. "I told him no, dude, but the guy insisted that I cut up the body and 'dispose of it' in pieces. I asked him how, and this asshole throws some trash bags and a surgical saw onto the floor without saying anything. He started to leave; I tried to stop him, I swear I did, but he just vanished!"

Trevor's voice started to tremble as he continued. "Look, lady, I've done a lot of shit, but I'm no murderer. Sure, I mean people ended up dead if they messed with me sometimes, but I didn't do it. Swear to God. So, I'm like, I don't gotta listen to this prick. I carried the body to the nearby pier and dropped it in the river. I figured all the evidence would sink into the river and that'd be the end of it."

What piqued Zen's interest, though, and what brought her to the park, were the details of Trevor's meetings with the man. The mysterious stranger instructed Trevor to meet him beneath the "small grey bridge" at Fort Tryon Park. Once there, the man told him to face the underside of the bridge with a white "S" graffitied on it. After pressing his head against the wall and closing his eyes, he felt a gush of air and heard the man's voice. Only then would he receive directions from the man in the coat.

A gush of air, Trevor had described it. *Every time.*

Now, that made no sense. It hadn't been windy in the last few days, and he described it as a consistent, mechanical puff. It sounded like something pressurized; something sealed. Maybe there was something more to the bridge.

Something hidden.

Lost in her own head, Zen was surprised to find herself already at the bridge in question. She moved underneath, the shade basking her in cool darkness. A gesture and a *click* preceded a cone of light as she withdrew her flashlight from her belt. It took no more than a second to locate the side of the bridge with the "S." It was an amateur, watery graffiti job; someone had sprayed the large, uneven "S" across much of the wall, not even bothering to prevent the paint from dripping down the wall before it dried.

This wall wasn't what interested her, though, according to Trevor's story. She'd traveled to Fort Tryon for the stack of stones opposing the graffiti. Spinning around to face it, Zen walked until her nose almost touched the rocky surface. She traced her fingers along the cracks that separated the grey blocks, walking back and forth from one end of the support structure to the other. She peeked around the edge of the bridge, noting how the walls connected to grass-covered hills on either side.

Zen bent down, picked up a fallen branch, and turned back to the wall itself. Breaking the ends and shearing the leaves with her hands, she made quick work of the branch until she transformed it into a thick, wooden staff. She jabbed the end of the branch into the individual bricks. Each brick emitted a dulled *thud* as the stick struck.

Thud. Thud. Thud. Thud.

She worked her way up and down the wall, travelling inch-by-inch from one side to the other, attacking each brick along the way with her impromptu, yet determined, methodology.

Thud. Thud. Thud. Thud.

Zen's biceps burned, and she felt light sweat on her brow. She poked and prodded two-thirds of her way across the wall of the bridge, but each stab yielded the same result.

Thud. Thud. Thud. Thud.

Discouragement and doubt seeped into her consciousness, slowing her efforts.

You know what they say about the definition of insanity, Zen.

Thud. Thud. Chink. Thud.

Zen stopped jabbing and returned to the previous brick. The odd square wobbled when struck, and she offered it a closer examination. It was moving a little, though it was still pressed against the wall, snug within its cracks. She rested her hand against it, hesitated, and pushed.

The rock resisted, but with a spongy resistance, not the resistance of stone against stone. Despite its unique qualities, Zen's firm push did not depress it very far. She gritted her teeth, steadied her legs, and pushed again. It slid into the wall, emitting a solid *click* as it made contact with something behind it. A gush of air struck her face as a large, rectangular segment of the rock surface slid forward and drifted open.

"Well I'll be damned," she said to the secret doorway.

The secret door revealed a grey stone stairwell, lit by a line of glowing fluorescent orbs along the walls. The steps descended at least ten paces before curving at an angle, preventing Zen from seeing where it ended. She paused for a moment, considering whether to reach out to her partner.

No. You can take care of yourself. Because what about Phil? What about Jeff, with his new wife already worried sick about him every day? What about Nancy, with her two children in kindergarten? If you call this in now, the place may end up being rigged with traps. There might be a haven of armed criminals waiting to murder a wise detective, a new husband, or a mother of two. There's no reason for someone else to get hurt when you're already here. You know you can take it.

Zen moved down the first two steps, and a faint *beep* sounded. She looked behind her to see a motion sensor change its light from green to red. The secret door slid closed with a whisper and a burst of wind. To Zen's relief, the lights retained their glow, at least for now. She moved down the stairs, moving as fast as she could while also being aware of her surroundings. She reached a curve and passed it to continue her descent. The stairs ended with a flat stone floor, and an endless tunnel stretched before her. As if by instinct, Zen reached for the Taser on her belt.

Stop, Zen. You weren't claustrophobic before, and nothing has happened to change that.

She sighed and jogged forward. The orbs, still producing their white light, passed by in a blur as she picked up her pace. The walls never changed, never highlighting anything other than grey stone. Zen began to regret her decision as she approached what she estimated to be a mile into the tunnel.

As she considered turning back, she noticed that the walls ballooned ahead of her, opening out into a wide, pearl-white room. Zen's jogging pace slowed as she reached the room; skidding to a stop, she looked around. White plastic chairs haphazardly surrounded three white plastic tables. Crumpled junk food wrappers dotted the floor. Square monitors lined the wall to the right of Zen's entrance, each screen showing a black-and-white sea of cars and faces. Were they traffic cameras?

No. This doesn't seem like any kind of state facility.

With nothing more to glean from the room, Zen walked through the space to an opening on the opposite side. The tunnel continued ahead, so she gathered her energy and resumed her journey.

Zen ran through several more rooms on her journey, and it became clear that the tunnel made its transition at regular intervals. Each room was different; some contained surveillance equipment, like the first room, while others contained wardrobes full of clothing or tables covered in chemistry equipment. In one room, she uncovered wooden boxes filled with automatic rifles with filed off serial numbers. Uneasiness stirred within Zen, not just in response to the contents of the rooms, but also due to the lack of other people. Whatever this place was, it was clean, it was neat, and it was far too modernized—all signs of a well-staffed facility.

So where is all the staff?

After she reached the tenth or eleventh room, Zen was somewhat winded. She stopped in the next room, panting and wiping a hand across her glistening brow. As her arm fell back to her side, a shape caught the corner of her eye. Mounted against the right wall was a silver ladder, ascending into an unlit space above her head. The ladder was not what drew Zen's attention, however; rather, it was the dark coat draped over one of the ladder's rungs.

Why hello there, mysterious friend.

Zen stepped forward, reaching for the coat, but pieces of metal slid beneath her feet, disrupting her balance. She picked up one of a dozen industrial screws piled onto the floor, each a foot long and as thick as a Cuban cigar. Zen brushed the coat onto the floor and dropped the screw onto it, muffling any noise the fall would have created. Flexing her fingers, the detective gripped the rungs of the ladder, scaling it with the speed and grace of a Central Park squirrel.

She climbed for several minutes before she reached a steel porthole in the ceiling. Zen pushed the door open a few inches, aligning her eye with the crack. The window of visibility was too small, though, and she pressed her face forward to better view her surroundings.

Peering past the dim shadows cast by incandescent bulbs, Zen's eyes adjusted to reveal rows and rows of dust-covered shelves, each full of what appeared to be cleaning supplies. She saw containers of soaps and acids, rolls of paper towels, and an eclectic assortment of vacuum cleaners, brooms, mops and buckets. She couldn't see any signs of movement, nor could she hear any noise over the dull roar of a nearby fan or generator. Zen lifted the porthole door, wary of any creaking hinges, and slid onto the concrete floor.

The ground was cold and hard, and she could smell animal urine.

Or . . . is that ammonia?

She climbed to her feet, using a nearby wall to steady herself. Her hand touched something cold and metallic, and it offered a gentle, vibrating response as her skin made contact. Zen jerked her hand away as if she had touched a hot stove. Curious, she moved closer to examine the object.

It was a black, metal box about the size and shape of a luggage case. Someone had mounted it to the concrete wall with four long metal screws, each screw piercing one of its four corners. A thin panel covered the front face of the box. Maintaining a steady hand,

Zen reached out and opened it to reveal a keypad and screen underneath. The screen's display was an old-school LED, like an alarm clock, and it exhibited one word in bright yellow: PENDING.

Zen moved her gaze away from the box, past the shelves, and to the adjacent wall. Another box was mounted there, too. She crept over to it and peered behind the door.

PENDING.

A muffled noise drew Zen's focus from the device, and she whipped around. Past the racks of cleaning supplies that stood between her and the opposite side of the small room, she saw movement.

Zen unsnapped her holster and slid her gun from her belt, moving in silence. She held it in front of her, but kept it pointed toward the ground. It wasn't in her nature to use lethal force, but she suspected that she knew what the devices were. If she was correct, her moral code came secondary to the safety of New York's citizens. Zen held her breath as she reached the far side of a shelf stocked end-to-end with bleach. Once she felt ready, she poked her head around the corner.

A man in a loose-fitting white shirt and blue jeans quietly hummed, lost in his work. As Trevor had described, a black-knit cap covered his crown. His skin was not quite white; rather, it was a light grey, and its texture was almost fuzzy, like a down-feather blanket. He held a small black remote in one hand, typing on the keypad of a third wall-mounted box with the other. Zen recognized the tune he was humming, though she couldn't quite remember the words.

Hmmm hm-hm hm hm, hmmm hm-hm hm . . .

Realization struck. It was a children's nursery rhyme.

The man stiffened, the fur on his skin sticking into the air as if alerting him to danger. He looked over his shoulder toward Zen. Where human eyes should have been were only black orbs, dull and glassy like shark's eyes.

Zen seized the opportunity to level her pistol at him and take control. "NYPD. Step away from the bomb or I *will* shoot you."

He continued humming, and her brain filled in the words.

Rock-a-bye baby, on the tree top . . .

The man turned to face her, his movements slow and relaxed. For a brief moment, it seemed he might comply. Then he grinned, baring long, sharp teeth, as if he'd filed them into points. His hands lowered to his sides, palms facing Zen. Before her eyes, the ends of his fingers blackened and grew into claws. His loose-fitting shirt squirmed and tightened, as if it housed a pack of wild animals hungry for escape. All the while, he never stopped humming.

When the wind blows, the cradle will rock . . .

The white shirt split and ripped along his back, releasing two large, feathery wings. Spanning at least twenty feet across, they were a dirty grey color with two black stripes on each wingtip, much like the colors of a pigeon. They stretched and flexed, as if they had slept for decades, before resting half-open around the man's shoulders.

When the bough breaks, the cradle will fall . . .

Zen stepped back. "What the hell is this?"

The man curled his claws and took two short, menacing steps forward. The barrel of her gun twitched, still aimed at his chest.

She said, "Stop. Last chance!"

He either didn't understand her or he didn't care, because he stepped closer, the distance shortening enough to make Zen uncomfortable. She squeezed the trigger of her pistol four times in quick succession. The muzzle flashes lit the dim room, and the sound of gunfire bounced around the concrete walls.

The expended ammunition never reached his body, though. The moment her finger began to squeeze the trigger, his wings curled in front of him to create a shield. The bullets disappeared into the feathers, leaving no marks beyond a slight ruffle where they struck.

The man flicked his wings apart, and Zen could hear the faint tinkling of the spent rounds falling onto the floor. As the wings parted, he revealed a short, boxy gun with a long magazine.

Is that a MAC-10? If so, she needed to move. *Now.*

Flicking his arm toward her with the deftness and aim of a dueling cowboy, the man depressed the MAC-10's trigger. An immediate, deafening wasp's nest of machine-gun fire buzzed at her, and white-hot bullets sprayed across the room in a wide fan. Zen dropped to one knee and rolled to the left, behind a supply shelf, but it was too late. She felt the intense, burning impact in her chest, stomach, and right arm and leg. The pain spread until her whole body felt like one giant, open wound.

Zen collapsed behind the shelving. Her firearm clattered to the ground beside her.

Oh, shit. SHIT. This was such a mistake.

Her limbs already numbed from nerve damage, she struggled to move. Bullet holes riddled her appendages, their intrusions causing blood to pour onto the dirty concrete floor. Zen coughed, and more blood sprayed out in a mist.

That's a punctured lung.

Her chest heaved, but she couldn't inhale fresh air. She could feel the blood entering her lungs, and it felt as if she were drowning. Dull pains sharpened in her stomach as her adrenaline spiked. She fumbled for her relinquished pistol for a moment, but stopped.

Slow and shaking, Zen reached for her belt, gripping her Taser.

I guess you do *need it.*

**Mississippi, United States
June 21, 1989-A**

It took a few seconds for the girl to blink the light from her eyes, and even longer for her blurred vision to clear. She was on her back, the grass tickling her ears and arms and legs. She took a deep breath and felt a tightness in her right shoulder. She looked toward the sensation, but shadow darkened everything in her line of sight. Something burned, its smell as sweet and as bitter as a campfire. The rain had stopped, but the clouds remained.

Another minute passed before her head stopped spinning. A huge chunk of the tree, as big and heavy as a sedan, pinned her legs and chest to the ground. An extended branch pierced her right shoulder, nailing her to the burning hill.

The girl's instinct was to panic, but instead she only felt a strong, intimate mixture of soothing calm and buzzing joy. Her head was clear, and her skin felt . . . *purer* than before. It was as if she had just stepped from the shower and smothered her soft body with fresh lotion.

An epiphany struck: For her entire life, she had been running half-empty. She felt . . . no, she *knew* she had been missing something tangible, something important. Today she received something that left her feeling whole.

But what had she received?

The girl placed her small hands on the tree above. Her eyes widened; blue arcs of electricity jumped between her fingertips, running through her skin like a kaleidoscope of cyan fireflies. Cuts and scrapes covered her bare arms and knuckles, and she watched the arcs jump across her wounds, stitching each one closed. Deep injuries that should have taken weeks or months to heal evaporated in seconds.

She inhaled again and felt a sharp pain in her rib cage. Glancing down, she saw a blue, pulsating glow beneath her shirt and along her sides. The girl winced as something inside her body squirmed.

With an audible *snap*, the pain subsided. Blue light filled her peripheral vision as the bruise from earlier in the day faded to nothingness, fading away with the ease of wiping a stain from a kitchen countertop. The energy danced around her body, showcasing its beauty and its power; in less than thirty seconds, she felt as healthy as before.

No. Not *as* healthy. *Better.*

The girl pressed her palms against the tree bark and pushed. Her arms were under her brain's control, but they unfolded against the thick trunk with no effort, more mechanical than organic. The tree creaked and cracked, showering bits of wood down onto her face. The girl gripped it tighter, and the bark splintered as her fingers dug deep into the oak. The broken shards should have penetrated her hands, but they flecked away from her knuckles, falling to the grass all around her.

She let go with one hand and marveled at the tree, heavy as a car, balanced in her palm with little effort. Her free hand snapped away the thick branch that had punctured her shoulder, pulling it both from the ground and from her body. Even as she motioned to toss it to the side, electricity rushed to the hole, and her wound healed before the bloody stake landed in the grass.

All that remained on the patch of skin was a trickle of blood lost before the opening vanished. The girl grunted, heaving the rest of the tree away from her body. It flew into the air so fast that it was nothing more than a blur, landing almost thirty feet away with a loud crash. She jumped to her feet, expecting exhaustion or pain to strike, but she instead felt ecstatic.

She felt . . . complete.

No. That wasn't right. She felt *charged.*

New York, United States
September 9, 2001-B

Zen pulled the Taser from her belt with her working hand and jammed its metal prongs into her neck, activating it. The hot electricity crackled into the air, but it faded into silence as it poured into her body. Her cells drank the energy, ballooning and tightening into something stronger, something tougher. Deformed bullets were pushed from the wounds through which they had entered, and electricity circled around the holes as they closed. The scuffs and scrapes of today's earlier chase washed away, and her muscles, once as weak as papier-mâché, transformed into an alien material more akin to steel or marble. Zen's head buzzed from the ecstasy—from the familiar sensation of *wholeness*.

Indifferent to the gun lying on the ground, Zen re-holstered her Taser and climbed to her feet. The winged man moved around the shelves toward her, his large shadow announcing his imminent presence. Zen gripped the metal shelf that separated them and swung the entire unit at the man, striking a large birdie with an even-larger badminton racket. She felt the metal vibrate with a *CLANG* as it smacked against him, and he tumbled across the room.

As she entered her opponent's line of sight, her hands tightened into fists, electricity running under her skin and flowing through veins. The man, still on his hands and knees, lifted the machine pistol he had somehow managed to retain as he fell. Zen raised her arms to protect her face and upper body.

He pulled the trigger.

Once again, heated lead struck her flesh; this time, blue sparks flew from each point of contact, and the bullets flattened harmlessly against her skin.

"Don't waste your time," Zen said. Her voice had lowered an octave, and it now carried an almost mechanical tone, as if she were speaking through a voice-changing device. "You had one chance to handle this the right way, and that chance is gone. Start talking, *now*. Where are we? What are these explosives for?"

The winged man chuckled and rose to his feet with supernatural grace, pulled upward by an invisible force. For the first time, he spoke, saying, "You're one of them." His voice was low and rough, as if he had eaten gravel, but it wasn't abnormal; its regularity belied his unorthodox appearance. "I told them, I *told* them we should have snatched you people away at the first sign of any Refinement. I *said* this would come back to haunt us. And look, here you are." He looked around the shaded room. "Are you here alone, or did you bring more? Where did you even Bogeyman in from?"

Zen strode forward and firmly gripped his shoulder as she spoke. "I don't know who you think your 'Bogeyman' is, or who 'they' are. I don't think they're worth hurting people over, right? Come down to the precinct with me; maybe we can have a hospital take a look at you, and the two of us can figure this all out together. I promise I'll help however I can."

The man slashed at her with his claws, but the talons sparked off the exposed skin of her forearm. What would have left deep, permanent tissue damage instead left thin scratches, no worse than paper cuts. Even those disappeared into the air, leaving behind a short spray of blue sparks.

He followed up the attack with a kick to her stomach. The force of his blow sent her flying backward several yards. She managed to land on her feet, shaky but secure, and she grabbed her stomach, taken aback by his strength.

"What has happened to you?" Zen asked.

He flexed his wings and claws, his grin mischievous. "Happened? To *me*? Don't worry about that. I'm exactly what I'm supposed to be." The man sized her up. "*You* are the accident. The mistake."

Hot, uncontrollable rage seared its way into her brain, carried there by the euphoria of her electrified state. She charged, lowering herself as she ran to resemble a defensive lineman. She bridged the gap between them in a blink; he must not have anticipated her speed, because she struck him in the center of his chest with her shoulder before he could react. Blue sparks flew from the point of contact, jettisoning him across the room in a straight line, his body nothing more than a grey blur.

The man struck the far wall of the supply room with the force of a train engine, rattling cleaning supplies from the nearby shelves and leaving fine cracks along the concrete surface. He dropped to his knees, gripped a nearby vacuum cleaner to steady himself, and emitted a raspy cough. A black remote slipped from his pocket into the palm of his hand.

He looked up at her, uttering a low growl of annoyance. "I don't have time for this."

The man pressed a button on his remote, and the screens on all three boxes flashed from yellow to red, announcing their status change from PENDING to ARMED.

The winged man gripped the handle of his vacuum cleaner and flexed his wings in front of his body. When he pulled them behind him, pockets of air travelled with them, propelling him toward Zen. Dust formed a cloud around him, and he was back in Zen's face in a fraction of a second, swinging the cleaning instrument at her head.

Zen tried to stop it, but she couldn't raise her hands in time to prevent the device from striking her temple. Blue energy rose around her head and arm in defense, and the vacuum shattered in half at the point where it struck her. She slid sideways a little, almost tipping over before regaining her balance.

Bending her knees and twirling in a full circle, Zen built momentum. Her spinning back fist connected with his raised, blocking arms, and the force of the blow rattled the light fixtures overhead. Loose papers and debris flew by them, and more dust sprinkled onto their heads. But as a counter, he clutched her offending arm, using her body as an anchor to prevent her from launching him again.

The man raised a knee into her gut, knocking the wind out of her, pushing her body up and back. His wings surrounded her like a cocoon, pulling her toward him, and he followed with a flurry of hand strikes: Jaw, neck, chest. She could feel the unnatural force of his attacks, each one making her insides squirm.

Pushing past the brief pain, Zen took advantage of her proximity to the winged man. She raised both fists above her head and plummeted them down onto each side of his shoulders. Her strike forced his body down into the ground with a thunderous *crack*, like a hammer striking a nail into the concrete. Dirt and rock sprayed from the point of impact as his feet made craters in the floor, highlighted by a spider web of fissures.

He bent for a moment, as if injured by the blow, but he suddenly straightened, smacking the top of his skull against Zen's face. Warm blood ran down her lip while blue sparks rushed to repair the burst blood vessels. She stumbled, and the man capitalized on her disorientation to dart around her, disappearing toward a side of the room she hadn't yet explored.

Zen wiped her nose, shook her head to regain her senses, and renewed the chase. She skidded around the shelving to find him prying open a pair of silver elevator doors embedded in the wall. They slid back, revealing the emptiness of the shaft beyond. He took two steps inside and flapped his wings once upward.

"No!" Zen said, her voice warbling electronically.

She reached for the incandescent light fixture hanging above her. Her hand gripped and squeezed the warm bulb, shattering the glass, and she fumbled to insert her fingers into the open socket. The lights in the room flickered, spastic and urgent. She diverted power from their circuits, the pull as irresistible as earth's gravity, and electricity cascaded into her body. Her muscles grew stronger, the ecstasy more intense; her heart pounded like a rabbit's foot, and her breath quickened. After three seconds she released the broken fixture, and the room's flickering returned to a warm, steady glow.

The man flapped his wings a second time, this time lifting him into the shaft, out of her sight. Zen leapt forward; the shelves around her dissolved into a blur, and her hair flattened against her scalp from the force of her jump. She flew past the open elevator doors faster than intended, denting the inner wall of the shaft before landing on the floor.

Inspired, she turned and jumped upward, rocketing twenty feet into the air. Her foot connected with the other side of the shaft, and her heel bit into the metal, holding her aloft for the millisecond it took to crouch and jump again, back to the inner wall. She bounced back and forth up the elevator shaft, carefully avoiding the metal suspension cable.

To Zen's frustration, the winged man flew further and further away. His flight path was much faster than her ricochet method of climbing, and he was fading into the darkness of the shaft above.

She had almost despaired when the man stopped and hovered in the air, just a speck in the shadows above. It seemed as if he was forcing himself into one of the closed doors sealing the building from the shaft. As he broke through the doors into the building, his arms and wings pushed behind him, sending the two pieces of the elevator door flying down toward Zen. She pirouetted in midair, her shirt skimming against the chunks of metal plummeting past her, no more than a hair's breadth away. Gritting her teeth, she continued her ascent, ignoring her anguished muscles and heightening vertigo.

The detective reached the fractured opening; with a cry and a final shove, she tumbled out of the shaft, her skin rubbing against carpet. Zen looked up and saw a sea of desks, computers, and telephones. A cluster of frightened faces, connected to white-collared shirts and black ties, surrounded her. She heard strained and panicked voices murmur about her appearance.

Zen rolled onto her back and saw the elevator label above the gaping entrance.

FLOOR 105.

You traveled, what, a thousand feet? Straight into the air? Wow, girl. That's impressive.

She climbed to her feet and glanced to the left, where, beyond a half-open door, she could hear shrill screams in the distance. Gathering her composure, the detective resumed her chase.

Mississippi, United States
June 21, 1989-A

Rejuvenated, the girl looked around. "David?"

No reply.

She scanned the charred landscape. "DAYYY-UHVID!"

Her eyes located a pair of smoldering shoes a few yards away. She tried to run to him, but her recalibrated legs launched her high into the air. She shifted her weight to better control her fall, landing next to the boy with a heavy *thud*.

The girl scrambled closer, anxiety knotting her stomach.

The boy's left arm and neck bent at an unnatural angle, making the girl queasy. Plumes of smoke rose from a charred, black crust covering the boy's chest. Small flames danced along his burned flesh, and his bloodshot eyes stared, sightless, at the dark sky. Worse still, despite the girl's despair, she shoved down pangs of hunger introduced by the aroma of barbecue drifting from his body.

The girl held out a finger and traced the outlines of the boy's burns. It took her a second, the longest second of her life, to realize why she was drawn to them.

They were the exact places her body had touched his when the lightning struck.

"No . . ." she gasped, her voice weak. The girl expected no answer, and she received none. Instead, tears arrived, rolling down her cheeks like raindrops. "Don't . . . please . . . don't go."

Sobbing, the girl slumped over her first victim.

New York, United States
September 9, 2001-B

The winged man rushed down the hallway, slashing his claws into any civilians within reach. Blood spurted from tears opened in arms, chests, necks, and faces, pooling onto the floor and splattering against the walls.

By the time he reached the end of the hall, a dozen people were lying still, their bodies underscoring a grotesque Jackson Pollock exhibit. Zen was close behind, vaulting over the fallen bystanders, urging herself to catch up and put an end to this madness.

The man burst through a pair of doors into a room devoid of furniture. The sun burned into Zen's eyes through the windows on her right. The grey assailant skidded to a stop, backlit by a row of floor-to-ceiling windowpanes. He turned around, his black eyes piercing her.

"You don't understand what you're doing," he said. "The moment you followed me here, you were already dead."

Something began to beep, its pitch high. The man pulled a small, rectangular device from his pocket and pressed a button, dismissing what Zen assumed to be an alarm. She checked the mounted analog clock on the wall to the left.

8:45AM.

Zen stepped forward to apprehend him, but she stopped at the sight of movement behind his silhouette, outside the window. Barreling toward them was an enormous passenger plane. Zen couldn't see into the cockpit, but it really didn't matter what was happening inside; by the time her brain registered it, the plane passed below her line of sight.

The entire building shook from the impact. Glass sprayed from the window frames, and flame and smoke coiled through the sky around Zen. The floor collapsed beneath her, a hot explosion rocking through her body. The shock wave drilled her into the walls, and she crashed to a stop on an unknown floor.

Powdered plaster filled Zen's lungs. She coughed as electricity flashed around her, attempting to keep pace with the damage inflicted upon her body. Her vision hazed, and the only sounds she heard were distant cries of terror mixing low, ominous rumblings.

Zen's movements slowed, her thoughts muddied. She wasn't sure how much time passed before she regained her composure. One minute? Two? Ten? The walls burned, the structure unstable and crumbling with every passing second. The dead littered the floor, motionless, while the living screamed and fled as fire consumed them. Sprinklers activated, but they did little to extinguish the flames from the jet fuel somewhere below.

Zen took a single step forward, but the floor caved beneath her, and the detective fell several stories before she came to rest again.

She looked up, her sight blurred by the heat and the smoke. Flames crept onto her skin; the energy inside of her released itself to keep her burns at bay. A dislocated shoulder retracted back into place with an audible *snap*. Gashes along her forehead sealed shut, punctuated by blue sparks.

Where did the winged man go?

Zen wandered through the chaos and the cries, navigating the inflamed deathtraps that were once simple offices. She passed a crater in the wall, revealing the outside sky, high above Manhattan's paved streets. Screams transformed into whimpers behind her, and she turned in time to see people fall from open windows, their fingers interlocked.

A beam creaked above. Two grey-haired men in suits were trying to escape down a nearby hallway. The side of the beam closest to Zen fell, crushing one of the men with a sickening *splat*. The other side of the beam remained suspended for a heartbeat, but it started to creak again as it, too, relinquished its battle with gravity.

In a dash, Zen moved between the other man and the falling beam.

"Go!" she yelled, wincing as the red-hot metal blistered her bare hands.

The man nodded his wordless thanks and ran past her. He survived six more steps before the floor opened and swallowed him, sending him spiraling into jets of flame.

Zen growled in frustration and dropped the beam. Her patience was fraying.

She shouldered her way through the drywall to her left and into a new room. A gigantic piece of metal, likely part of the airplane, lay burning. Its surface bubbled from the heat of the burning fuel around it. Emblazoned on the jagged debris were disfigured letters, spelling the word "MERIC."

Before she could continue her hunt for an escape route, a hand grabbed her hair from behind, its grip a steel vice.

"Still alive?" a gravelly voice whispered into her ear.

Black claws curled around her neck. She tried to react, to fight back, but the damage she'd taken had sapped much of the energy left in her cells. The winged man lifted her into the air and tossed her through a burning wall. Hot ash sprayed from the collision, but its erratic movement softened into snowflakes as it was exposed to the air from a gaping hole in the outer wall. Smoke swirled around the building and obscured the sky. Heavy footsteps sounded behind Zen, and an object dropped next to her face.

The black remote.

A small LED light near the top flashed with urgency. The time between blinks grew shorter and shorter as it picked up speed.

The winged man strode past Zen and jumped through the window, disappearing into the smoke, humming his tune.

And down will come baby, cradle and all.

Zen clutched at the remote, trying to find a way to stop the blinking, but nothing she pressed produced a response. She clutched at a nearby desk to pull herself to her feet.

The device blinked so rapidly that the light seemed static. A severed power cable hung from the ceiling near the desk, emitting intermittent sparks. Zen reached for the ragged end and clutched at it, drinking its energy.

Her muscles clenched and tightened. She could feel cramps forming throughout her body, but it wouldn't make a difference how far she pushed herself if she didn't survive. She *had* to survive. That's who she was.

The survivor.

The air crackled around her as electrical energy escaped her body, tracing black lines into the walls, floor and ceiling. Her ears filled with roars and screams; her mouth and nose filled with blood and oil. Zen closed her eyes, seeking some semblance of inner peace.

"I'm sorry, David," she whispered, her old Southern accent creeping back into her voice.

The remote at her feet reached a steady red before it flickered off, bathing the room in silence.

Then the rumbling began, far beneath her feet. From the basement.

Vibrations traveled up the floor and walls, rattling Zen's bones. Her stomach dropped from the sudden shift in gravity as the building began to plummet. She tried to escape via the same route as the winged man, but she tripped and fell in her hurry. The building imploded toward the center, and the outer floors slanted inwards, sending her sliding into the nucleus of her new hell.

The wind howled. Debris piled on top of her, its weight and pressure barely withheld by the blue energy encircling her body. Sirens wailed far in the distance, but they grew louder with each passing second. As the world faded under rubble, Zen heard another voice scream in terror.

This time, it was her own.

Karnataka, India
April 15, 2006-B

"You'll be fine," Ananya said in Hindi, straightening Nadi's necktie. "You can do this in your sleep."

"Ananya, I'm always fine," he responded with a toothy grin. "I'm just not used to sharing my life's work with the people who can take it away from me. Isn't that what marriage is for?"

"Like you'd know," Reyansh called out from his chair, spinning on its swivel several meters away. "Girls have to like you before you marry them."

Nadi pulled a pen from the breast pocket of his black suit and flung it behind him, smacking Reyansh in the ear.

"Ow!"

Nadi cinched his tie with a smirk. "Whoops, slipped out of my hand." He glanced at Ananya. "How do I look?"

Ananya waved her hand at the nearby restroom door, and he wandered inside. The mirrors against the sink ran from the ceiling to waist-height, but Nadi could see enough to assess his dress. The reflection that stared back at him was a thin, lanky man in a black suit with a corresponding black tie. He had bronze skin and professional, well-parted black hair. His face was clean-shaven, an aesthetic choice that emphasized his youthful awkwardness.

Still, that was just part of his charm.

He exited the restroom and said, "Even better than I expected." Ananya nodded in agreement, brushing back her dark brown hair.

"Eh, I've seen worse," came Reyansh's voice.

Nadi turned toward the mustachioed man, meeting his glasses-framed eyes.

Holding up the offending pen from earlier, Reyansh asked, "Can I keep this, then?"

Nadi chuckled, the shudder in his voice betraying his nervousness. "You two should be out there with me. Your hard work has been just as essential to this project. I couldn't have gotten as far as I did without the knowledge and expertise of my friends and coworkers."

Ananya smiled. "The sponsors like your face, for whatever reason. They feel like you can best"—she made a frustrated gesture with her hands, trying to find the right words—"*encapsulate* the scope and value of this project."

"Basically, the smart people are too smart to explain it to anyone," Reyansh chimed in. "You're dumb enough to spell it out for everyone else . . . it's a *compliment*!" He raised a hand to brush aside Nadi and Ananya's glares.

A notification on the far wall of the room chimed. Reyansh slid from his chair and trotted to a row of computers and monitors along the wall.

"Time's up." He shot Nadi a smile. "They're here."

The three gathered around the monitors and watched the scene far above their heads unfold.

A convoy of black cars traveled along the dirt roads of Western Gurur, kicking clouds of earth behind them as they moved. Surrounded on three sides by kilometers of flat, empty fields, their destination was clear: a compound composed of clusters of white buildings. A row of the structures pressed together to form steps; from each of those steps flowed a thin layer of running water. Metal railings surrounded the individual buildings along with the entrance to the compound itself.

Their journey complete, the vehicles entered Gurur's Waste Water Treatment Plant.

The line of cars pulled into side-by-side parking spaces, one after another. Security guards in suits and sunglasses emerged from the passenger's seat of each car and circled to the back. Five doors opened in unison, and five very different individuals stepped out.

They grouped together in stark contrast to the others beside them, surrounded by their security teams, and chatted amongst themselves as they walked into the compound. Their voices only carried above the flowing water by a few decibels, and they found themselves yelling to be heard by the time they were inside the largest of the buildings. Workers on catwalks surrounded the posse as they crossed the warehouse floor.

The group stopped near the center of the facility; before them was a small, box-shaped office with nothing on the outside but a plain metal door. One of the guards stepped forward and used a key to unlock the door; opening it, he gestured for the others to go inside. They complied with kind nods and pleasantries.

Inside the office was a wooden desk and metal chair, but nothing else. Part of the back wall bulged inward to form a rectangle. The same guard stepped up and waved a key card in front of the metal protrusion. A gracious *beep* alerted them to a large panel, which swung forward, revealing an elevator door. The guard pressed the "down" button and the door slid aside, providing access to a spacious, rectangular elevator car.

The group piled in, continuing their idle conversations as the elevator descended. The engine connected to the device whispered, and they would have been hard-pressed to notice its movement. A panel indicated they had begun on floor "G," and a speaker emitted a distinct tone with each new level they passed.

1 . . . 2 . . . 3 . . . 4.

The car halted and the doors opened once more, revealing a pearl-white laboratory as large as an airplane hangar. The laboratory hosted the examination and assembly of various mechanisms, including a green device resembling a jet engine and a series of floating, revolving discs which were held aloft by a man gesturing with a white glove. Near the center, a tarp laid beneath a smooth white box the size of a car engine, sandwiched between two empty glass, trough-shaped containers.

In front of this final display, the strange cabal lined themselves, standing still. Their chatter ceased, patient yet expectant.

"Let's do this," Nadi proclaimed, and turned toward an exit behind him.

The white, seamless door opened from the wall close to where the five guests and their security staff waited. He exited, beaming with confidence as he approached the group.

"Nǐ hǎo," he said as he bowed to a short, plump Chinese man, who returned the gesture. The man wore a stylish suit with a red tie, as well as circular red glasses. His hair was full, but stringy, and it came together as a black messy bundle on his head.

"Guten morgen," he said to a pale white man with piercing blue eyes, firmly shaking his hand. The man was dressed in crisp military attire; the decorations identified him as a German military officer.

Nadi paused in front of a dark-skinned Ethiopian woman in a gold and black dress, waiting for her response. As soon as she extended her hand, he offered a gentle grip and moved it up and down.

"Inidçti nehi," he said.

He moved to stand before a tall, older Indian man wearing a navy-blue suit and sporting a light grey beard. Nadi formed the Añjali Mudrâ, placing his palms together with his fingers pointing upward and his thumbs close to his chest. The man responded in kind.

"Namaste," Nadi greeted him, and they both bowed.

Nadi turned to the final person, a young Israeli man in loose-fitting white cotton pants and a flowing white cotton shirt. "Shalom." He offered his hand, but with a wry grin the man stepped forward and squeezed him into a tight hug.

"I told you that you'd make it here," the man whispered with glee in Hindi. They pulled away, and the Israeli man stepped back to join the others. "Show them what you told me," he continued in English.

Nadi addressed the group with a smile, also switching to English. "When I was a child, I was obsessed with the American *Ray Bradbury Theater* television series. It flirted on the edge between magic and technology, and while it was sometimes bleak, its creative uses of science in seemingly impossible ways inspired me."

He began to pace in front of them, exuding his mounting anxiety. "See, I grew up Kerala. For those of you unfamiliar, it's a small coastal city south of here. I was a child who grew up wanting to see change, to see progress, but I only ever saw people leaving for better places. Even as my friends fluttered off for new cities and countries, the loudest stories that made it back to my ears were ones of poverty, disease, and famine . . ."

Nadi paused for a moment, taking a breath to calm back down. "I found this unacceptable. What I began to strive after, more than anything, was a future where the benefits of new technologies could be shared with all. I wanted such advancements to result in better living, better health, and better communication. And then I wanted to put those projects in the hands of every world leader to give to their citizens. At the risk of sounding cliché, I thought such a world could be considered a utopia."

He shook his head. "But the real world impedes progress. Law, licensure, funding and politics get in the way. I moved from university straight into Technopark, but the company was too restrictive. Much to my good fortune, my university friend Noam introduced me to this private facility reserved for unconventional technologies." Nadi nodded to the Israeli man. "Thank you for that, Noam."

Noam grinned in response.

"As you all know," Nadi continued, "the caveat to working here is convincing investors that your project merits enough value to the world's governments to warrant its cost. If the project fails, it only wastes money from private coffers, so no government's budget is negatively affected."

He scanned the group, aware of the length of his monologue. They didn't seem particularly interested in his personal history. Most were making polite eye contact, though they telegraphed subtle glances toward the white box on the tarp.

"But you aren't here to hear about me. You're here to see if the report that I sent you was true. Why don't we get to it?" Nadi reached a hand into his inner jacket pocket and retrieved a white wireless keyboard. "This won't reach the public market for a few more years, but our scientists are happy to share the technology if it allows for refinements."

He typed with one hand, holding the keyboard with the other. "Consider the countries you find yourselves most attached to or responsible for. Whether they be areas like East Africa, rural China, or vast stretches of the Middle East, the one factor to which they most often must adapt is drought. Even self-proclaimed 'civilized' countries like the United States find themselves at a loss when dry spells strike the West."

Nadi tapped a final button on the keyboard. The pearl-white box expanded to reveal a grid on each visible surface, the lines formed by thin cracks. Beneath the open spaces was a white mesh, similar in design to the mesh that covers industrial speakers. The box began to make a low hiss, like a leaking gas stove. Nadi ignored it, continuing.

"Imagine walking into impoverished regions of your country, areas without any realistic resources to spare, and placing this box near a dried-up river, tributary, or water tower. Where the citizens could once fish and drink and play, everything has died. Now they rely on government handouts to survive. What if you could press a button"—He extended his hand to the clear trough to his left—"And give it all back?"

The hissing stopped, and a gush of displaced air blew upward from the tank, rustling the spectators' hair and clothes. The previously bone-dry container was filled to the brim with crystal-clear water.

The audience murmured with surprise. The Indian benefactor looked at Nadi. "How did you manage this?" he asked.

Nadi bent down and set his keyboard on top of the box. It lay there at a haphazard angle, darkened by the scientist's shadow as he stood to reply.

"The device takes advantage of a process called 'pair production.' Are you familiar with it?" The older man shook his head, so Nadi continued. "Boiled down to its simplest concepts, pair production is the creation of new particles from radiation, pulling apart the core components of energy itself and stitching it together to make something more tangible. Thanks to the funding and resources we've received from your generosity, we've learned to translate the photons within light. Trial and error allowed us to piece together the equation required to take those photons and convert them into the most basic particles that form water."

Nadi pointed both of his index fingers to the box at his feet. "The PAUS in front of you emits a broad electromagnetic field. When activated, we can program three-dimensional coordinates into the onboard computer. The shapes created from those coordinates, such as the shape of the trough, are then isolated within the EM field. Every photon in range of the field is translated into pure water like *that*."

He snapped his fingers to emphasize his point. The group stared at him with blank faces.

Tone down the tech talk, he thought. *They aren't here for a physics lesson.*

"Basically, it turns light into water," he clarified.

"Ohhhhhh," the group replied.

The Ethiopian woman nodded at Nadi.

"Excuse me; my English is not the best," she apologized. "Did you call the device *paws*? Like . . ." She held her arms up, bending her wrists so that her hands formed cartoonish kitty-cat paws.

Nadi grinned. "No, 'PAUS' is an acronym," he replied. "It stands for 'Photon And Ultrasound System.' Though I won't deny that I may have been biased when I named it. Who doesn't love a cute nickname?"

The group chuckled, their good spirits at odds with the stoic security guards surrounding them. The German officer raised his hand, and his accent sharpened his consonants as he spoke.

"You referenced ultrasound. Does that mean you completed phase two?"

Nadi sighed, offering a tight smile. Stepping back into the center of the demonstration, he retrieved his keyboard. Once the device was in his hands, Nadi said, "Zugführer Kalt is referencing a request he made several years ago. Back then, I was entirely focused on the pair production process, creating fresh water and placing it into areas in need. However, Kalt argued the additional value of *transporting* the water after it was created. He wanted us to research some way to reposition the fluid, post-production. I, of course, was completely on board with the idea."

Nadi shook his head and sighed again, running his fingers through his hair. "Before I had the opportunity to perfect it, though, my hometown was crippled by the Indian Ocean Tsunami. My family died under the crushing waves." He took a breath, wiping his eyes. "But the tsunami didn't stop at Kerala. The entire coast of Southwest India, as well as several other neighboring countries, were buried by the Indian Ocean. Almost three-hundred thousand people perished."

The group lowered their heads in solemn remembrance, and Nadi continued, anger biting into his words. "I was *so* close to completing Zugführer Kalt's request. The wasted time and unnecessary delays haunt me to this day."

Nadi's agitation manifested in a sharp, sweeping gesture toward the water-filled trough. His voice grew louder as he spoke. "See, any field that could control the movement of water would have to have hydrophobic properties to contain the fluid; that is, the force must repel water *from* it in order to *move* it. Therefore, any field manufactured on a large enough scale could be repurposed as, for lack of better words, a 'force field' against oceanic disasters."

He picked up the keyboard and entered a few keystrokes. There was a low hum, barely noticeable, despite the fact that it reverberated all around the laboratory. The edges of the trough shimmered like a mirage; then the water raised into the air, as if weightless. The liquid mass maintained its form from the trough, leaving it a sharp-edged, hovering prism of clear water.

"Imagine deploying PAUS along major cities of your countries' coasts," the scientist said. Drifting toward the benefactors, the prism morphed into a large sphere. "Another earthquake or hurricane stirs the waters, and your citizens watch in terror as a wall of aquatic death sweeps toward them." Nadi was practically yelling now. "But you, their fearless leader, push a button on the PAUS. The wave *strikes*!"

The sphere plummeted toward the group, and there was a frantic rush of security guards diving to protect their employers. Nadi cackled as the projectile collapsed a meter above their heads, flowing around them. The investors gasped in awe at the bubble of water which now swirled around them, leaving a pocket of air in the center where they stood.

"An invisible force covers the cities in a dome of safety," Nadi shouted through the bubble. "The ocean swims across the sky, though it never comes close enough to touch anyone. Your citizens see the power you wield and the way you've chosen to use it, restoring their faith in your leadership."

The security guards were reaching for their weapons, so Nadi dropped the bubble with the press of a button. Water splattered around them on the floor, and applause erupted, the crowd emphatically showing their approval. Begrudged, the guards' hands dropped back to their sides.

The Indian man looked at Nadi, his eyes almost daring him to guess the question on his mind.

Nadi chuckled. "Ultrasound, as the device's name suggests. A series of sound waves beyond the range of human hearing, broadcasting an infinite number of frequencies. Some have been found to create physical pressure. Inspired, I hunted for a similar frequency; one with hydrophobic properties."

He tapped on the keyboard again, and the water on the floor collected itself as small globules, merging together until they returned to one large prism.

"Once we found a wave range that would work for our needs, we programmed the PAUS computer with 3D mapping capabilities," he murmured, continuing to type.

The prism lifted into the air.

"Now, we can create an ultrasound field around a body of water to control its movement," he said. "All we had to do was outfit PAUS with some specialized directional microphones."

The water shimmered a little, emphasizing his point. The prism floated above the unused trough on the other side of Nadi's machine, then lowered itself into the container, a final puzzle piece fitting into its jigsaw frame. Nadi turned back toward his audience. "Both sides of the project, of course, can be formatted to meet any environmental or geometric needs you may have."

Eagerness had overtaken his investors, and he knew they were done with conversation for the moment. Nadi had come to expect a degree of rudeness from people in such positions of power, though; he understood how important their time was. The group began to dissolve. Some poked at the trough of water, while others examined the PAUS.

The German officer, however, approached Nadi directly. "I'm glad you reconsidered the request, mein freund. I would like to know more about your project, now that our friends are distracted. Okay?"

Nadi offered a polite smile and walked further from the crowd, the Zugführer in tow.

"Danke," Kalt continued. "So, what is the range of the device? How much water can you make at once?"

Nadi shrugged. "In theory? An infinite amount. It all depend on the size of the PAUS."

The German man smiled. "Excellent. Sehr gut. Also, what is your highest programmed velocity for moving the water?"

"Well . . . we haven't really tested for a speed," Nadi said, placing a finger on his chin. "I can't say for certain what our current limitations are. I supposed our limit would be the speed at which the ultrasound waves travel, so let's say about 340 meters per second?"

Giddy laughter erupted from Kalt. "That is spectacular! I will have my associates reach out to your marketers for an official order, but I will be very interested in a device with a range of at least thirty kilometers, programmed for your highest speed."

Nadi shifted, uncomfortable. "Yeah, I wouldn't really be involved with . . ."

"I can't thank you enough, mein freund. The U.N. has been so critical of our avoidance of surmounting terror threats. It's time that we introduce something new, something powerful. You and I, we can change the playing field. Terrorists around the world won't know what struck them!"

There was a disquieting pause as realization sunk into Nadi. "Sir, with all due respect, this is a humanitarian project. I have no intention of weaponizing PAUS for you, nor for anyone else."

Another pause. The Zugführer grazed Nadi with his cold blue eyes, as if to size him up.

"War will continue whether you like it or not," Kalt said. "Your device has the ability to create a quick and efficient response to terrorism, without lasting consequences."

Nadi shook his head. "But there *will* be lasting consequences, Zugführer. Consequences for those at the receiving end of your military force. I cannot stop the wars you wage, but I will not allow them to be my personal legacy."

He took a breath before continuing, plastering across his face the most flattering smile he could manage. "We received your funding in order to build the device. We added the features you requested. We were *not*, however, paid to weaponize it. Therefore, I will personally ensure your PAUS models are equipped with the appropriate safety features. I expect you will use them solely for their *intended* purposes. That is the end of this conversation."

Nadi turned heel on the glowering officer and addressed the rest of the crowd. "I believe we have representatives who will reach out to you to negotiate purchase agreements. As we wrap up development here, we plan to outsource manufacturing in the near future. You, our loyal investors, will of course receive enormous discounts on your orders."

He winked at the East African woman. She reciprocated, her lips curling into a flirtatious grin. The group chattered, swirling with positivity, and even the security guards seemed more relaxed. Everyone but Nadi began to file toward the elevator.

Before he could turn away, Nadi felt a firm grip on his shoulder.

"Danke for the demonstration, Herr Acharya." The name escaped Kalt's lips in a cold, biting tone. He continued his passage and joined the rest of the group in the elevator. Before the doors closed, he caught Nadi's eyes one more time. "We will be in touch soon."

––––––––––

"WE DID IT!"

Reyansh uncorked a bottle of champagne. It released its foam with a great *pop,* and the other scientists surrounding him cheered.

Ananya sidled over to Nadi, who was laughing at the commotion.

"Your presentation was unbelievable," she said. "I wouldn't be surprised if they signed a ten-year blank check for this facility."

Nadi chuckled and placed an arm around her shoulders. "Hey, I just told them what they wanted to hear."

Reyansh wandered closer to them, pushing through the throngs of partying coworkers.

"Bullshit!" he yelled. "You made googly eyes at Miss Zala until she was swooning. Don't think your good looks and charm will last forever!"

Everyone around him chortled.

Nadi peeked over at Ananya. "I don't know. They're working now, aren't they?"

She responded with a quick kiss on his cheek, and they both blushed.

"Oooooooh," crooned the tipsy crowd.

<u>Folder 1.2, File 2</u>
<u>"Massacre"</u>
<u>Reported by Aquifer</u>

Karnataka, India
April 18, 2006-B

Nadi walked along the first floor of the laboratory, chatting with other scientists. The air buzzed with ingenuity, yet it managed to retain a certain casual charm that he had grown to love.

"Hey Nadi, what brings you all the way up here?"

A man in a lab coat approached, yelling to drown out the ratcheting noises coming from a nearby project. The scientist appended a jovial smile to his question.

"Oh, I just needed to stretch my legs," Nadi replied in Hindi with an aura of nonchalance. "The PAUS is reaching the production phase and some fresh air—"

He was interrupted by a deafening roar.

In the far corner of the room, the emergency doors connecting the first floor of the facility to the ground floor of the Waste Water Treatment Plant exploded from their hinges, surrounded by fire and smoke. The pearl-white metal barriers made a tremendous crash as they landed, wobbling, halfway across the room.

Through the smoke entered a swarm of men, dressed in black riot gear and holding large, imposing rifles. Nadi counted at least ten of them even as they rushed inward, but he had to stop.

He had to stop because they opened fire on the scientists.

The intruders aimed their rifles toward each of the four corners of the large, hangar-like room, releasing bursts of flame and death. The scientists scurried like cockroaches under a kitchen light, but they had few places to go. Bullets riddled their bodies, spraying warm red blood over the pearl-white walls and floors.

As Nadi turned to run, a nearby intruder fired at him. He ducked and felt warm liquid splash against his back. Rolling on the floor, he saw the man he had been speaking to had received the bullets meant for him. His decapitated body fell to the ground in an awkward heap, sprinkling red across the floor. Nadi crawled to his feet and ran, panicked, searching for an escape.

A woman in front of him sobbed as she crawled beneath a project table, her right arm stained red from an open wound. Moments later, her cries ceased when one of the intruders, hearing her voice over the cacophony, knelt down and dispatched her with the squeeze of his trigger. The intruder turned to Nadi, but Nadi scrambled away, his heart pounding in his chest.

He made his way to the elevator and pressed the down button. The button did not glow, intonate, or respond in any other way.

They must have disconnected the power to the elevator.

A scientist pushed past him, trying the exact same thing he had done. He turned to Nadi and yelled, "THEY MUST HAVE DISC—"

Rifle fire sounded, and a series of holes appeared in the man's neck and chest. His blood splattered across Nadi's shirt and face, producing a sweet, metallic aroma. Nadi recoiled and turned toward the wall furthest from the hostile men in black—toward the service ramp.

The service ramp created a smooth, gradual decline into the outer walls of the facility. It began at floor-height on the first floor and spiraled through the other floors like a giant corkscrew, stopping down on the fourth floor. It opened up for access to every floor, facilitating the convenient transport of materials too large to fit in the elevator.

Today, however, it might just save Nadi's life.

He reached the entrance to the ramp, but he tripped over the small curb at the top of the descent. Crying out, he collapsed against the wall. Mid-fall he heard more machine-gun fire close to him, and bullets peppered the metal wall above his head. Nadi felt a chill as realization struck him: If he hadn't tripped, he'd be dead.

He could see two men advancing in his direction, rifle barrels smoking. They made a gesture to the dozens of other armed figures in the room, who were finishing off the few remaining survivors on the floor. As they completed their kills, they each migrated in Nadi's direction.

Nadi scrambled to his feet and fled down the ramp. Even with its long, winding path, his adrenaline allowed him to reach the second floor at record-speed. The wall opened up, revealing a cluster of confused and worried scientists.

"RUN! COME WITH ME NOW!" Nadi cried, motioning with a panicked gesture. Even as he spoke, he could hear heavy, militant boots stomping close behind him.

The group on the second floor approached him, but they were too late. As Nadi sprinted down the ramp, he heard machine-gun fire behind him. Cries of anguish and the splatter of bullet-ridden bodies filled the air, and he pressed his hands against his ears to drown them out.

Footsteps slapped behind him, and he was overtaken by a blood-soaked man.

"FASTER!" Nadi yelled at him.

They reached the third floor, and this time Nadi chose not to mince his words.

"COME WITH ME NOW OR THEY WILL MURDER YOU."

The workers on the third floor already seemed aware of the commotion above, though, as a group tried to repair the elevator through a panel on the wall. Those not near the elevator shivered, wearing frightened faces. Everyone on the floor looked toward Nadi as he yelled, dropped their work, and stampeded toward the ramp.

They moved with such speed and panic that they began to trip over each other near the ramp's edge. The few who made it there shoved against each other to squeeze through the opening, creating a bottleneck congestion. Two short, scared women in lab coats joined Nadi and his blood-soaked friend only moments before the intruders reached the third floor. They heard screaming, begging, and gunfire. The blood-soaked man wept as he ran, and Nadi swallowed a lump in his throat.

The squad of survivors made it to the end of the ramp. It opened into a donut-shaped entryway that encircled the elevator chamber. That entryway had a few meters of separation before it flared wide into the giant, hangar-shaped fourth floor.

The Special Projects floor.

The hangar was nearly empty; the room had very few projects compared to the other floors. Today, the only researchers on staff were Reyansh and Ananya, who were finishing some software updates for the PAUS, and an older, grey-haired scientist named Indra, who was working on his floating disc project in the back corner of the room. They all looked up with horrified expressions at the sight of their coworkers' conditions.

"The blast door!" Nadi yelled. "Close it! Now!"

Reyansh stood in alarm. "What happened?"

A sharp crack of gunfire exploded from above the ramp, and bullets rained into the lab. Sparks flew from the metal table and equipment all around Reyansh.

"Okay, got it," Reyansh squeaked, sprinting into the security room. Even as the door closed behind him, an alarm sounded. The opening to the hangar area released hydraulic steam, and two thick metal doors began to inch together from the left and right sides. It had closed halfway by the time Nadi and the three other survivors managed to cross its threshold.

The four runners dove to the floor, under the giant green jet engine structure. Nadi gestured for Ananya and Indra to join them, but neither of them moved, as if fear glued them to the ground.

The first few intruders on their warpath down the ramp appeared, and they shot through the shrinking gap of the hangar entrance. The rattle of bullets against metal deafened Nadi, and more blood splashed him, though he wasn't sure whose.

One of the attackers near the front of the party dropped his heavy rifle and sprinted toward the closing doors, now barely shoulder-width apart. He turned sideways to slip through; he would have made it, too, if a Frisbee-sized metal disc didn't whiz through the air and strike him directly in the forehead. The man in black gear fell onto his back, with his left foot and ankle still poking through the doorway. Nadi looked to the left and saw Indra with his white-gloved hand extended, dozens of hovering discs surrounding him.

The blast doors completed their closure with a sickening *crunch,* and blood gushed from the center of the entryway as the crushing force of the thick, dull metal severed the leg in its path. Even through the near-impenetrable barrier and over the sound of the alarm, Nadi heard the crippled man's frantic cries of pain.

The group hiding under the jet engine dispersed from their refuge. As they did, the taller of the two women from the third floor collapsed to the ground, lifeless. Blood covered the front of her chest.

She must have taken the brunt of the intruders' final assault, Nadi thought.

Reyansh exited the security room. Indra ran to join Ananya and the three survivors, his hand still clad in his white glove. The discs at his station clattered to the floor.

Nadi doubled over, retching. His stomach churned from the smell of his blood-soaked face and clothes.

"What are we going to do?" Indra asked.

"Come look," was Reyansh's reply.

The six scientists crowded into the security area, near the camera monitors. What they saw horrified them. They saw men in black, sporting machine guns, littering all four floors of the building like an infestation of ants. They saw scientists in white, hiding beneath tables and the bodies of their fallen peers. The few still alive were pulled from their shelters and gunned down on the spot. Most disconcerting, they saw a huddle of the intruders near the blast doors, adhering brick-shaped packages, probably some kind of explosive. The man with the recently amputated leg lay still on the floor, encircled by a pool of blood.

Indra looked around the room. "Like I said . . . what are we going to do?"

Ananya chimed in, a quiver in her voice. "What do we know about the other projects? Can we defend ourselves in here?"

"You've seen the extent of my project's defensive capabilities," responded Indra. "Those devices are made for data collection in hostile environments, not for combat maneuvers."

The blood-covered scientist, a short, pudgy man with square glasses, said, "I'm from the second floor. We didn't have access to the projects on this floor."

"Neither did we," said the woman from the third floor. She was shorter, like the other unfamiliar scientist, but with a small frame and brown hair that curled into a bun on her head. She paused as she looked over at her dead friend beneath the table, and solemnly corrected herself. "Neither do *I*."

Nadi looked at the monitors once more as he considered his options. *Everyone beyond this room is already dead. There's no way to help them from here. Meanwhile, they're about to blow a hole in the blast doors, the only thing keeping us safe.*

"I know what we can do," he said aloud, his voice stern.

He pushed past the others and left the security room, toward his PAUS prototype.

Ananya rushed to catch up with him. By her expression, she knew his intent. "What if there are survivors, Nadi?" she said. "Are you willing to bear that responsibility?"

He turned to her and raised his voice. "How am I supposed to know, Ananya? Our friends are outside, already dying!" She jumped in fright at his sharp tone. He continued, tears forming in the corners of his eyes. "We can gamble on some of them just being injured, for now. We can wait and see what they do, and risk *everything*. But that's not the pragmatic decision, and you know it. The pragmatic decision is to protect those of us who are still alive, to get them out safely, and then prevent this from happening ever again." Nadi placed his hands over his eyes and clenched his jaw, sucking air through his teeth. "This is a tough choice either way, which is why I'm not letting anyone else make it."

They both reached the PAUS, and Nadi furiously typed commands into the device.

"Does our local drive include the building's floor plans?" he asked aloud, swallowing the lump in his throat.

"Yes," said a voice behind him, and Nadi looked over his shoulder. The scientist in glasses had followed him to the PAUS. "I uploaded them for my project last year. You should have access, too."

"Thank you so much." Nadi looked at him. "I'm so sorry, but what is your name?"

The man stopped wiping the blood from his eyes. "Aarav. It's fine. Let's just hurry with whatever you're planning on doing."

Nadi continued programming as Ananya moved to the PAUS and prepared it for broadcast.

A few minutes passed before Reyansh yelled, "It looks like they're almost ready to breach!"

"Almost done!" Nadi and Ananya called back at the same time.

"What are you doing?" The woman from the third floor inquired, poking her head out of the security room.

"These people made a fatal mistake," Nadi muttered, entering the last few keystrokes.

She furrowed her brow. "A mistake? What mistake?"

Nadi looked up from the keyboard. "They didn't turn off the lights." He pressed ENTER.

The PAUS made a short hiss for just a fraction of a second. A heavy groan echoed from all directions. The floor and walls wailed and creaked, as if they had experienced an exponential weight increase. Through the cracks of the blast door, droplets of water formed and fell. Somewhere far above their heads, they could hear the twang of metal, reverberating throughout the hangar.

"Raand ka jamai!" cried Reyansh from the security room.

The woman near the security room widened her eyes and looked at Nadi. "What the hell did you do?" she demanded.

Nadi, Ananya, and Aarav rejoined the other three scientists in the security room to observe Nadi's handiwork.

Most of the video feeds blurred, their apertures unable to adjust immediately to the sudden environmental transformation. As the cameras began to focus, they revealed water filling the first three floors to the brim, while their current floor had only filled the space on the opposite side of the blast door. The struggling attackers and murdered scientists floated in a jumbled mixture of blood and water.

Reyansh cried out and pointed at some of the individual intruders on his monitors. They swam upwards, trying to find an exit, but there was too much distance and too much water pressure. Bubbles escaped their mouths and, one by one, they each stopped moving, adding themselves to the pool of corpses.

"Fuck them," Reyansh spat.

Nadi sighed and sat down in a nearby chair, relieved to be free from immediate danger. "Okay, this was as far as my plan went. Now how do we get out?"

**Karnataka, India
April 18, 2006-B**

The group spent the next hour or so in a series of frantic arguments amongst each other, debating on where the men came from, why they were there, and whose projects would warrant such a response. They bickered about what technologies were available to them in the moment, and what possible uses they might have in escaping their underwater lair. Eventually, Ananya ended the charade.

"This is getting us nowhere," she said, exasperated. "Look at the facts. They brought heavy breaching equipment, when the top three floors don't have security features that necessitate it. They knew our building design, and they had access to elevator controls. They were looking for something *here*, on *this* floor."

Reyansh said, "She's right. They knew what they were looking for. I doubt it was Indra's project; no offense."

Indra held a hand up. "None taken. I'm much too early in development to generate attention toward my project. Besides, I designed the drones to collect topographical and atmospheric data, these men probably want equipment capable of proper surveillance."

Nadi was only half-listening to their conversation. *Could he really have gone this far?* He looked up and gestured at the green jet engine. "What do we know about Varsha's equipment?"
Reyansh shrugged, while Indra shook his head. Aarav, who had finally cleaned the gore from his face, and Priya, the third-floor scientist, traded uncomfortable glances.

Ananya furrowed her brow and rose to her feet. "Let's not pretend like we don't know what's happening."

Nadi sighed. It was only a matter of time before she said something. "We don't know that it's Kalt, Ananya. He has the resources, and he clearly wants to misappropriate PAUS, but there are so many legitimate ways for him to obtain it. There's nothing to gain from this wanton violence and destruction."

The walls and ceiling creaked out another awful, haunting

moan. The group halted their conversation and looked to the blast doors. The leaking water had intensified over the last hour, and a thin puddle spread a quarter of the way across the room.

"We need to deal with that later, and leave *now*," Priya said, the urgency creating a tremor in her voice. She looked over to the body of her fallen friend.

Nadi and Ananya met each other's eyes, but Ananya was the one to speak.

"Well . . . maybe the device that trapped us here can also get us out," she said.

"By . . . adding more water?" Aarav raised an eyebrow.

Indra sighed. "No, their PAUS can also create hydrophobic fields. They're going to make one for us."

Nadi and Ananya nodded.

"The control system isn't flat, though," Reyansh responded. "The computer is one of the thickest and heaviest parts of the device. We can control it with the wireless keyboard, but even then, we'll have to heft it around."

Nadi stared at the PAUS, then over at the blast doors. The severed foot still lay there, blood diluted throughout the water puddle. His eyes drifted over to the drones at Indra's table, and he was struck by an idea. "I know what to do. Grab your tools and follow my lead."

They toiled for almost two hours before a shrill tone chirped from the security room, muffled by the closed door. Reyansh dropped what he was doing and sprinted inside. There was a long pause.

"Nadi! Ananya! Come here!" he yelled.

The pair left their stations while their project partners looked on with worried faces. Nadi and Ananya entered the security area to see Reyansh hunched over the monitors, his brow twisting with concern.

"The proximity alert that I set sounded." His index finger reached for the screen. "What am I seeing here?"

The cameras for the first floor showed movement near the archway of the emergency doors, where the original intruders had first blasted into the lab. Two shadowy figures dove down from the ground floor of the Waste Water Treatment Plant, but they stopped themselves from travelling very far into the facility. Flashlights flickered on, their beams cutting through the murky water. They examined the first set of floating bodies and machinery before reaching into some sort of container, retrieving a capsule.

Whatever it was, the capsule appeared to be about the size and shape of an American football. They released the object into the first-floor entrance way and retreated in the direction they had appeared. The capsule floated for a few seconds, lazy and still, before it bubbled with violent intensity. The bubbling permeated throughout the water of the first floor, as if boiling the space. As the effect reached the cameras, a frothy haze obstructed their view.

Ananya shook her head while Nadi pinched the bridge of his nose, exasperated.

"I don't know what I just saw, but I know that we need to leave *immediately*," he said.

The trio returned to finalize their separate projects. They used a ribbon of wires, bundled into a thick cable, to connect Indra's drone gloves to two pearl-white vests. Nadi and Indra strapped the gear to their chests, donned the left-handed control gloves, and faced the blast doors with the other four survivors. Ananya and Aarav paired up near Nadi, while Reyansh and Priya gathered next to Indra.

"Reyansh, when you open them, make sure there is a delay," Nadi instructed, priming the cannibalized PAUS pieces interspersed along his vest. "We need to move a safe distance away beforehand. The ultrasound's hydrophobic frequency keeps the water away, but it won't protect us from the solid debris that's right outside."

Reyansh nodded, disappearing into the security room. He rejoined Indra and Priya seconds later, just as the blast door alarms sounded.

Nadi took a deep breath.

I really hope this works.

The blast doors parted, and water gushed into the last bastion of dry air. Bodies, guns and equipment tumbled in with the flood. They struck the tables piled in front of the doors, and the loose debris rushed in a wave toward the scientists.

Excited shouts erupted from Indra's group, and Nadi looked at them. All three chattered to each other, pointing at their feet. The water halted several meters ahead of them, continuing its path around them, forming a dry circle. As the room filled up, the circle grew into a sphere large enough to comfortably fit at least twice as many people.

Glancing down, Nadi saw the same process occurring around his group. Aarav watched the water rise in front of him with an expression of awe on his face. He reached his fingers out to penetrate the suspended fluid; as he pulled back, the water rose over their heads, completing their ultrasound bubble.

"Okay, just a reminder," Nadi spoke, his tone authoritative. "There is no reason to move forward quickly, nor is there a reason to panic. We have limited oxygen inside these bubbles, but we should have enough to last us until we reach our exit." He met Ananya and Aarav's eyes. "Let me be very clear. The bubble is following *me*. You will only stay inside of it if you stay close to *me*. Understood?" The two scientists nodded. "Then let's get the hell out of—"

GLP-GLP-GLP. GLP-GLP-GLP.

"It's only the ultrasound reverberations," Nadi lied to his passengers. *What the hell is that?*

The noise had a wet thickness to it; he'd never heard such a sound so loud before. It was reminiscent of the sound a thirsty person makes when gulping a glass of water, yet infinitely more chilling. For Nadi, it was impossible to identify the source or of the sound, or determine its proximity.

Ananya and Aarav slowly turned to Nadi, their faces skeptical.

"Let's . . . let's just go," Nadi said.

GLP-GLP-GLP. GLP-GLP-GLP.

The two groups moved forward in tandem, careful to avoid the floating debris. As they passed a body, the man's head drifted into their bubble from the side. Aarav made a disgusted noise and pushed the head away, sending it floating off behind them.

GLP-GLP-GLP. GLP-GLP-GLP.

They reached the service ramp beyond the blast doors, pushing past the cluster of hovering corpses to make their way into floor three.

GLP-GLP-GLP. GLP-GLP-GLP.

The group rounded the corner to the third floor, illuminated by off-kilter lighting. Nadi's PAUS had sapped most of the photons in the building to fill it with water, but the electricity powering the facility quickly revitalized the artificial lights.

GLP-GLP-GLP. GLP-GLP-GLP.

A shadow appeared ahead of them on the ramp, descending from the second floor, and they all paused. It seemed cylindrical, and it moved in a wriggling, serpentine motion. They could not glean much from the silhouette, however, as its caster was large enough to block out almost all light coming from the second-floor emergency lamps.

There was a brief moment of silence, but the noise returned in full force, almost deafening Nadi.

GLP-GLP-GLP. GLP-GLP-GLP.

Nadi inched close to Indra's group so that their two bubbles merged into one shared space.

"We need to hide, at least for a moment," he whispered to the other five escapees.

"Why? The longer we stay, the more likely we're found," Priya said, her hushed voice cracking under the stress.

"But he's right," Ananya rebutted, pointing at the ramp. "That's our only active way to the second floor, so if that shadow is standing between us and escape . . ."

"Moving forward right now would be suicide," Indra finished.

"It's all we can do," Nadi replied.

Reyansh eyed the second-floor entrance nervously. "This thing seems to be heading down the ramp toward us."

"Over here, then," Priya whispered, gesturing toward a table across the room. "We'll hide behind my workstation."

"Let's go, before it sees us," Aarav said, exasperated.

The two groups moved through the mass of floating corpses and metal on the third floor, their footsteps quick yet careful. They reached Priya's former workstation, covered in pearl-white metal boards. Shaped like large, flat tombstones, their design was similar to coastal body boards.

The scientists moved around the workstation, and the gap between it and the far wall left just enough space for all six to cram together, crouched and panting. The proximity allowed the entire party to stay dry under the same ultrasound space. The boards on the table caught Nadi's eye, and he poked at one of them. "Is this what I think it is?"

Priya grimaced. "Yeah, some hack contracted me to design hydraulic personal transporters."

"So . . ." Nadi leaned closer. "Hoverboards?"

She sighed. "Spare me your *Back to the Future* comments."

"Can this wait?" Reyansh hissed at them, pointing toward the ramp. Everyone craned to see, either under or around the sides of the table.

From the opening to the corkscrew ramp slid a giant, purple, cylindrical mass. It had a slimy, round body as thick as a bus and at least twice as long. With no distinguishing features anywhere, its skin was a smooth, spotless, deep purple from one end all the way to the other. Nadi looked at his peers' concerned faces for answers.

"What is that?"

GLP-GLP-GLP.

The other scientists gasped. Nadi whipped his head back around, but he missed whatever had happened. The slunk further into the room, making slow, squirming motions.

Some kind of worm?

A scientists' corpse drifted by, only a few feet from the creature. Suddenly, the tip of the corpse's shoe touched the creature's skin, near the area that seemed to be the front side of its body. In a startling, whip-like motion, the worm writhed upward toward the floating former scientist. The smooth purple flesh at the tip peeled back, the skin wrinkling and pulling in an oddly phallic way. All Nadi could see inside the nightmarish monster was a dark hole. The creature sucked the corpse into its "mouth," pulling the feet and legs in with one swift motion.

GLP . . .

It twitched and contracted a second time, pulling the corpse's waist and chest inward. The arms bounced off the mouth's edge and floated upwards, limp.

GLP . . .

It made one final movement, and like soda through a straw, it pulled the rest of the corpse completely inside.

GLP.

Nadi and the rest of the group stared in horror, stunned by the thing's terrifying grace.

GLP-GLP-GLP.

The worm consumed another body, closer to the group this time. Nadi watched the worm slither around, eating corpses, while a pit formed in his stomach.

"I don't think this was sent here for PAUS," he whispered. "I think they sent it here to clean up evidence . . . dead *or* living."

"We can worry about that later," Ananya said. "Let's focus on surviving for now."

GLP-GLP-GLP.

The worm drifted toward a cluster of bodies near the far-right side. There would be no better opportunity to escape unscathed.

"Now's our chance," Reyansh said, vocalizing Nadi's thoughts.

Nadi, Ananya, and Aarav walked forward, taking slow, soft steps. Nadi looked behind him to see Indra's group stop for a moment before following. It seemed Priya had noticed the drone still tucked under Indra's arm, so she leaned over to pick up one of the hoverboards from the pile on her station.

GLP-GLP-GLP.

They crept across the third floor, edging closer and closer to the ramp. The tension from the worm's movements and the aching of their stiffened muscles created beads of sweat on their skin, which dissolved under exposure to the ultrasound and to the mounting carbon dioxide in the air.

GLP-GLP-GLP.

There was a sharp, scraping noise behind the two bubbled groups, muffled by the borders of Nadi's PAUS barrier. They froze, craning their heads to see what had made it. Nadi watched Indra's group through his bubble, about five long paces behind them, quivering. Looking past the three, his eyes fell on Priya's workstation. The pile of hoverboard prototypes began to stir, its weight seemingly imbalanced.

Oh Priya, why did you have to take one?

Indra, Reyansh and Priya's eyes widened into perfect circles, betraying their horror.

A tremendous screech grated against Nadi's ears, and the whole setup collapsed, its weight bringing the pieces crashing to the floor and attracting the worm's attention. The creature whipped its body around toward the chaos, sucking in a hoverboard that drifted too close to it.

GLP.

Nadi held his breath and watched the creature devour the board, too transfixed to notice anything else in their immediate environment. He winced when Ananya pinched his arm, and he followed her gaze. The body of one of the black-clad intruders floated above their bubble, directly toward Indra's group.

"Indra!" He whispered, but it was pointless. With their fields separated, a thick wall of water prevented any recognizable sound from reaching the other group.

The body floated into the other ultrasound bubble, feet-first. Reyansh saw the intrusion and appeared to say something, but before Priya or Indra could react, the entire corpse was ensnared by the shift in air pressure and pulled down, directly on top of Indra.

The other bubble blurred into chaos, as far as Nadi could see through his distorted window of water. Indra had collapsed in panic, possibly thinking another worm had attacked. He leapt back to his feet into a posture that indicated he was yelling. Reyansh and Priya tried to calm him down, but it was too late.

The worm saw them.

The pile of hoverboards near the back of the room flew in every direction as the worm changed direction, snapping to face Indra's group with the speed of a tripped mousetrap. Instead of getting closer, it lurched with the upper half of its body, as if it were about to vomit.

"Oh, no," Aarav said quietly.

Time seemed to slow as Nadi tore his attention away from the scene, looking down at the glove on his left hand. As he began to gesture, his mind drifted back to a few hours earlier.

"The control system isn't flat, though," Reyansh said. "The computer is one of the thickest and heaviest parts of the device. We can control it with the wireless keyboard, but even then, we'll have to heft it around."

Nadi stared at the PAUS, then over at the blast doors. The severed foot still laid there, the blood circling it diluted throughout the water puddle. His eyes drifted over to the drones at Indra's table, and he widened them as he was struck by an idea.

"I know what to do. Grab your tools and follow my lead." They assembled around the workstations while Nadi approached Indra. "Indra, what operating system is your drone control based on?"

Indra's put his hands to his head in realization. "Oh, we both use BOSS Linux, right?"

Nadi looked at him. "Right. And just like mine, you have it designed to map and navigate three-dimensional space, don't you?"

"That's how my drones know where to fly," Indra replied, smiling. "You want to merge PAUS with my gesture controls, don't you?"

Nadi grimaced. "It'd be a hell of a lot safer than typing on a keyboard while we're in imminent danger. But it won't be easy to program."

Indra extended his hand to shake Nadi's. "Leave that to me, project partner."

Now it's my turn to help you, project partner, Nadi thought.

He waved his gloved hand in short, frantic motions, tracing a rectangle in the air.

Okay, that's about six meters tall . . .

Priya and Reyansh, realizing what would soon occur, dove away from Indra. He turned toward Nadi's group and tried to flatten himself against the ground. Nadi splayed his fingers, waving them in a horizontal line across his face.

By ten meters wide . . .

The worm released a white, slimy substance from its mouth. It began its journey as one solid mass, but quickly dissipated into hundreds of interwoven strands, very much resembling the root system of a large tree. At the tip of each of the strands was an open, suctioning tube.

Nadi clenched his fist and twisted his wrist twice, beads of sweat forming on his brow.

Two meters is a stable thickness.

The tubular strands of the worm's proboscis latched themselves across Indra's entire body, and though Nadi couldn't hear it, he saw the man screaming in terror and pain. As quickly as the proboscis released, it retracted, faster than a bullet. In transit to the worm's mouth, the tubes compressed back into a narrower, solid mass, and the collapse compressed Indra, too. The water carried the muffled sounds of his cracking bones to Nadi's ears while Indra folded in half, his arms and legs balled together to fit into the worm's mouth. Blue sparks lit up the water as Indra's PAUS crumbled to pieces and his ultrasound field disappeared.

GLP-GLP-GLP.

"Indra!" Nadi and Ananya cried at the same time. The former gritted his teeth, shoving down the bitter sensation of hopelessness.

Focus. There's two more out there.

As the worm pulled Indra away from Priya and Reyansh, it also stole their bubble of air. They floated in place, five paces from Nadi's bubble. Nadi crept at a snail's pace toward them with Ananya and Aarav in tow. He worked on new PAUS coordinates as they moved, and the two floating scientists tried their hardest to maneuver a gentle, calm path into the remaining bubble.

Nadi punched out in a series of one-handed symbols.

Distance . . . twelve meters.

The worm reared back and scooted across the floor in a serpentine motion, barreling toward the spot Indra had been. At the rate they were traveling, Priya and Reyansh would collide right with the creature. Priya must have also realized this; while still clutching her hoverboard, she wrapped her legs around Reyansh's waist and draped the prototype over his back, the propulsion end facing the charging worm.

Nadi raised his glove. *4,000 PSI in-field. Okay.*

Priya activated her board, and the air intakes on each side pulled the water around it. A jet of concentrated water kicked the two scientists across the room like a torpedo. The worm noticed this and turned to pursue them.

As soon as they traveled past the point Nadi had targeted, he activated his final PAUS command. A two-meter-thick expanse of water, running floor-to-ceiling and wall-to-wall, shimmered between the worm and the five surviving humans. The worm ran into the barrier and bounced off, sending waves of force to stir up its side of the room. The worm reared up and spat out its proboscis once more, but the tendrils glanced away from the space Nadi had affected, jerking backward as a scolded child jerks his hand from a cookie jar.

Priya and Reyansh rocketed into Nadi's bubble, their curled forms entering about a meter up from the ultrasound wall, so they fell to the ground with a heavy thud. The ultrasound field had stripped all water from them as they passed through it, so despite their brief swim, the two stood up to find their clothes and hair as dry as desert air.

Reyansh hugged Ananya.

Priya hugged Aarav.

Nadi stood with his gloved hand extended, entering a few more commands into PAUS.

"What the hell happened?" Aarav asked.

Nadi glanced his way. "The short answer? The PAUS uses ultrasound to modify water pressure, too. I created a high-pressure area between us and that thing. Imagine a hundred fire hoses constantly firing in a small space."

Aarav shook his head. He seemed relieved, but exhausted. "My goodness. You saved our lives."

Nadi turned to the worm, watching Indra's drone drop from its mouth and drift to the floor. His face fell back into despair. "I should have saved Indra, too," he mumbled.

Reyansh fell to the ground, quivering. "I don't feel so good."

Priya turned to Nadi. "We'll mourn later. How long do you think it will hold?"

Nadi examined his PAUS. It was humming from the increased ultrasound output. "It's not a physical wall; it's made of energy waves. The worm can't *break* through. The PSI is set to four thousand, so the worm would shred itself to pieces trying to push into the barrier. As long as the wall is within the PAUS's broadcasting range, it will remain stable; once it's out of that range, though, the weak signal will collapse. That being said, we should be able to make it out of the facility before that happens." He turned to Aarav. "The tunnel you told me about. It's on the next floor?"

The scientist nodded.

"Good," Nadi said. "They're surely guarding the Waste Water Treatment Plant above."

Ananya and Priya helped Reyansh to his feet, draping his limp arms around their shoulders.

"Move, people," Ananya demanded.

Huddled securely inside the ultrasound bubble, they quickly strode onto the ramp. They circled the corkscrew corridor and found themselves emerging onto the second floor. The view was more of the same: Floating corpses, disheveled machinery, and murky gloom. Aarav turned to the other four and pointed down a side corridor. "This way."

They marched around to the wall adjacent to the ramp, across from the now-worthless elevator. Aarav pulled back a table to reveal a pearl-white paneled door, and Nadi moved closer so that the space around them would remain dry as they opened it. Aarav pulled it open, revealing cylindrical pipes and other large containers, all leading into the floor, ceiling and walls.

Against the back wall was a circular, dirty, copper-colored porthole. It was about the size and shape of a bank vault door, though it didn't seem locked, and it appeared to have a pressure gauge embedded within its frame.

Aarav walked up to the door and pulled a series of bolts from the side. "This waste outflow system runs underground at the same level as this floor's lab. The maintenance tunnel leads to the collection chamber for the lab's waste before joining the outflow system beneath the Varuna Canal."

He was interrupted by the telltale hissing of depressurization. Pulling against the mounted handle, Aarav slowly opened the heavy sliding door. Inside was nothing but darkness.

Nadi felt a squeeze against his left shoulder, and glanced toward it to see Reyansh's shaking hand resting there. He heard a soft clicking noise, and then a circle of white light beamed out from the PAUS into the blackness ahead.

"I added it back in the lab, just in case," Reyansh said, offering a thin, weak smile. His face was pale.

New sounds reached their ears, accompanied by a loud grinding of metal beneath their feet. Nadi heard glass break, the noise more closely resembling snapping twigs in this underwater hellscape. More metal screeched and tore, louder than before. The group craned their heads toward the ramp, their confidence shaken, but they couldn't see anything. Aarav turned back to the door, opening it enough for people to squeeze through.

"No water will enter the tunnel if you stay close enough to the entrance," Aarav said to Nadi, gesturing for him to stay where he was. "You go last."

Nadi nodded and leaned against the wall, keeping an ear out for more noises. Reyansh extended his arm toward the exit, looking at Ananya and Priya.

Priya walked into the dark tunnel with her hoverboard still clutched to her chest. She patted Aarav on the arm as he stood there, holding the door open. Ananya was quick to follow, but as she crossed the threshold, she stopped, straightening her spine.

She rotated back to Nadi and met his eyes, speaking in a loud, worried tone. "Nadi . . . was your barrier placed in *front* of the elevator or *behind* it?"

Nadi's eyes began to widen in terror. "ANANYA, RU—"

The elevator doors behind them exploded.

From the wreckage of floating glass and metal emerged the worm's enormous, purple head. It thrashed around in jerky, violent movements, and despite having no facial features, it seemed focused entirely on their escape attempt.

"GO, GO, GO!" Aarav yelled, shoving Ananya into the tunnel.

Reyansh began to run toward the door. As soon as he moved, the worm aimed itself at him and reared back. Its bottom half seemed stuck in the elevator shaft, but it didn't need complete freedom to catch its prey. The sticky, white proboscis emerged from its mouth and snagged Reyansh by the upper torso and head mid-step. The attack altered his momentum, and he flipped into the air. Before he ever had a chance to land back on the ground, the proboscis retracted.

GLP . . .

"Reyansh!" Nadi cried.

GLP . . .

"Fucking get in this tunnel now!" Aarav replied, horror and anger filling his voice.

GLP.

Nadi dove through the door's opening, rolling into a thin sheet of waste. Behind him, there was another, much louder, metallic tearing. Aarav quickly followed him, working his way around the outer side of the door as he pulled it closed.

"It's all the way out of the elevator now," Aarav said, his voice strangely calm.

Nadi jumped to his feet to support the door's weight so Aarav could squeeze through. As soon as he touched it, though, there was a mighty *SLAM*, and the door pushed against him. Something warm sprinkled against Nadi's left cheek.

"It . . . has . . . me . . ." Aarav managed to wheeze, his voice wet and strained.

"Oh no," Priya whispered.

Aiming his shoulder flashlight at Aarav, Nadi saw the man

trapped, his upper torso diagonally bisected by the pressure of the door against the frame. Blood oozed from his nose and mouth, his eyes pink and bloodshot. Nadi could hear the slow cracking of Aarav's spine and rib cage, like thick branches pulled from a tree.

Eyes welling up with frustrated tears, Nadi slammed his shoulder against the door. "No! You're so close!"

The metal didn't budge. In trying to catch Aarav, the worm must have slithered against the door, and the pressure and weight was keeping him trapped there. Nadi pounded against the metal, trying to scare away the creature, but nothing happened. He looked back over at Aarav and, through his tears, saw the man go limp, his eyes unblinking.

Nadi stepped away from the tunnel door, his body numb. A rustling noise came from the other side of the door, and some pressure must have relieved, because Aarav's body slid all the way to the ground. Before long, Aarav was pulled through the crack back into the laboratory.

GLP . . .

The distance between the PAUS field and the tunnel entrance left a little room for water to begin pooling into their side. Nadi strode back to the vault-like door.

GLP . . .

He clutched its handles and slammed it closed. Through the metal, he heard the worm one last time.

GLP.

Then, deafening silence.

Nadi's face contorted in anger, and he punched his knuckles against the door. "He bhagavaan! Madarchod ke aulaad!"

He kept punching the door, over and over, ignoring the blood that began to drip from his hand.

Something wrapped around his arm and Nadi yelped, jumping. He whipped around to see Ananya standing there. He leaned his head on her shoulder and wept into her hair. They huddled there for a moment, while Priya stood close by, her head hung in sorrow.

Slowly, quietly, Nadi's sobs petered out. He looked up the two women. "I'm fine. Let's go."

The three trekked onward, forging into the darkness ahead.

**Karnataka, India
April 18, 2006-B**

The next hour passed uneventfully, and Nadi was grateful for the solace. The PAUS was no longer protecting them, so he deactivated the device, keeping it in standby just in case. A strange mix of energies filled the air, and he suspected that Ananya and Priya felt similarly. They should be happy to be alive and proud of their tenacity, but he also felt the poignant loss of their friends and . . . guilt. Others died while they still lived.

We will deal with this together, once we are safe.

After miles of travel, sunlight burned his eyes, announcing their emergence from the tunnels. Looking down, he could see the trickling water of the Varuna Canal at their feet. The group crawled up the grass-covered bank and reached level ground. Standing to his feet, Nadi observed their surroundings.

Dirt and patchy grass filled most of the horizon. Ahead of them, to the West, he could see the outline of the Waste Water Treatment Plant over some green trees a few kilometers away. To the right and behind them—the North and the East—they could make out small grey homes and businesses. A small mining town. To the South, all he could see was kilometers and kilometers of grass and trees, with Ennehole Lake near the horizon. Finally, to the Southeast, he saw the Mysore Airport runway stretch out like a welcoming arm.

"That's where we're going," Nadi said, pointing toward the runway. "I have a friend there can help us get somewhere safe." As the trio shuffled in the direction of the airport, he looked over at Ananya and nudged her. "Thank you. Thank you for everything."

"It was a group effort," came her retort, and they pulled together into a walking embrace.

"Hey, don't leave me out of this!" Priya merged into Ananya's left side, joining the hug. The whole group stood still for a moment, their hot breath on each other's necks. Nadi recognized the delirium of their state, brought upon them by the carnage left behind; once his brain processed their reality, he doubted he would be able to laugh again for a very long time.

They stepped across the grass onto the tarmac, angling themselves toward the airport entrance.

"Well, you managed to save your hoverboard," Nadi said to Priya. "What's next?"

Priya looked at the device in her hands. "Well now that you mention it, I've had a few ideas about introducing—"

A loud pop, like a cork bursting from a champagne bottle, interrupted her. Priya's right eye exploded into a fountain of blood, and she tumbled to the runway, revealing a large crater in the back of her head. The hoverboard prototype struck the ground with enough force to crack the outer frame. It skidded a few meters away, only a dozen strides from the airport door.

Something whizzed past Nadi's ear, making it itch. The glass windows of the airport ahead made sharp slapping sounds as holes appeared in them.

Ananya looked at him. "Nadi? What—" Three holes burst from Ananya's chest, spraying the tarmac red. She twisted like a rag doll onto the ground, her eyes glassy, forever staring at the clouds.

"NO!" Nadi screamed, his voice hoarse. Projectiles slipped past him, the sound of their travels buzzing through the air. He had been thrust into the center of a hornet's nest.

Nadi sprinted toward the airport, leaving his last two friends behind. Something sparked off the metal shoulder of his PAUS vest, the pressure pinching his skin. The windows of the airport entrance had shattered, raining sharp fragments onto the floor inside. Beyond the window frames, the airport looked deserted, as if someone had ordered an evacuation.

He looked over his shoulder to see ten men rising from a patch of tall grass near the corner of the tarmac. They were dressed in the same black armor and equipment he'd seen back at the laboratory. Their rifles flashed small bursts of fire, but the sounds of their shots were strangely muffled. The pavement around him emitted sharp crackles, and hard pellets of rock flicked against his legs.

Nadi was only a few strides from the entrance when something moved above him, a shadow passing between him and the sun. He looked up in time to catch something launching itself from the roof of the airport. With little more than a soft whoosh, it flew over his head.

He glanced back at the ten men. The object landed in the middle of them with the mighty thud of a mortar shell, sending plumes of dirt and pavement into the air like smoke. The men flew away from the point of impact in every direction, each one landing prone a dozen meters away.

Grateful for the respite, he barged through the airport doors into an open, empty building. It was a wide, spacious area, punctuated only by patches of red seating chairs and black ropes shaped to form customer queues. The walls around him were made of small windows of glass, held together by a metal grid, and they stood several stories tall. Past the small, white attendants' booths and red seating areas were some boxy, enclosed partitions that were likely offices for security or management.

Beyond those areas were ten more men in black, rifles raised.

They aimed their weapons at Nadi, and the muffled roar of suppressed machine-gun fire bounced around the walls. The noise grated against Nadi's ears even as he rolled to his knees behind the nearest attendant's booth. Bullets splattered into the opposing side of his booth as he closed his eyes, lonely and afraid, tears rolling down his cheeks. After a few seconds, his fists clenched.

No. No more. Everyone else died running. I won't run, too.

He gestured with his PAUS glove, the anger making the movements jittery. Bullets created pockmarks on the tiled ground around him, and the edges of the booth exploded into frayed chunks.

Ten-meter diameter . . .

Boots stomped against the airport floor as the unit advanced in Nadi's direction.

2,000 PSI . . .

In front of Nadi, past the broken window frames, he saw the first ten men back on their feet, firing into the smoke at the mysterious object that had attacked them. For a fraction of a second, a flash of blue electricity arced from the cloud.

And . . . 1,000 kilometers per hour. Is that fast enough for you, Kalt?

He stood to his feet, keeping his head low to avoid the bullets. As it primed, the PAUS simultaneously hissed and hummed. He extended his gloved hand, fingers splayed apart.

All other coordinates track real-time hand gesture and motion. Let's go.

Nadi swirled to face his attackers, clustered in their tight formation. As his covered palm pointed at them, a massive sphere of water formed in front of him. It stretched from wall-to-wall and floor-to-ceiling, shimmering with untold violence from the pressure inside.

The tremendous construct blurred his view of the men, but he could see pinpoints of light form within the sphere as it swallowed their bullets. Before the attackers could react, he pinched his fingers together, pointing directly at them. The titanic ball of liquid zipped forward at barely subsonic speed. It struck the cluster of murderers, and they collapsed into the airport floor with a splash loud enough to rattle the remaining glass windows.

The weapon contained more power than Nadi could have imagined. Red clouds of blood, surrounding chunks of skin and bone, mixed with the water and sprayed against the walls. The sphere collapsed as Nadi dropped his hand and reactivated his ultrasound bubble. Dry air encircled him while excess water, chairs, and body parts flowed out of the airport through the broken windows.

The water leveled out after a moment, dropping to knee-height. Satisfied that none of his attackers survived the retaliation, he moved further into the airport. After reaching the end of the next hallway, a new sound reached his ears.

The noise of a helicopter.

Wind whipped around Nadi through the open windows, stirring the receding floodwaters. He ran as quickly as his legs could carry him to the closest office unit. Flinging the door open, he saw a beige-carpeted floor, a small metal desk, a filing cabinet, and another door near the back.

He closed the office door and looked around, but he couldn't see anything of use. Much to his good fortune, there were no windows, so he had a moment to move around without anyone seeing him. He ran to the back of the room and opened the second door. The revealed space was nothing more than a tiny, cramped coat closet. It was empty, save one tan, hanging raincoat. Nadi closed the door. He saw no benefit to cramming himself into a space so small.

"Find him!" A muffled voice yelled somewhere from within the airport.

Dozens of footsteps splashed through the water. They moved with considerable speed, based on the intensity of their footsteps.

Nadi began to program new coordinates into his PAUS. As he worked, he thought he heard a quiet vibration behind him, near the closet.

It's just the helicopter.

"Check the offices!" The same voice sounded outside.

Wet footsteps splashed louder, closer to where Nadi had holed up. He began to raise his glove, backing against the far wall, closer to the closet. The quiet vibration stopped. Nadi took a deep, shuddering breath, preparing for a final conflict with the men outside. New tears rolled down his cheeks as fear, sadness, and anger created a tight ball in his chest.

The entrance to the office rattled as the men tested the lock.

"It won't open!" Someone yelled.

"Breach it!" Came a reply.

There was a creak and a rush of air, and Nadi felt the closet door open behind him.

"Three!"

He spun, glove still raised, and gasped.

"Two!"

Standing in the closet was some amorphous phantom, a living shadow wrapped in black shroud. *Has Yama come for my soul?*

"One!"

In the same moment the entrance to the office exploded, a black-gloved hand clutched Nadi's shoulder and jerked him forward, into the closet. The door slammed shut, enveloping him in darkness.

**La Encarnación, Colombia
November 13, 1999-A**

Monsters.

Catalina took another sip of her Cuba Libre, watching the men yell and swear at their table over her shoulder. They wore cotton pants and colorful, short-sleeved collared shirts with the buttons left undone, exposing far too much chest hair. Their bodies had a sturdy, athletic quality while somehow remaining slightly pudgy. The round faces of all four men sported bushy mustaches and beady eyes. Catalina recognized the stench of Medellin Cartel members anywhere.

Why were they in such a small town, "en la media de la nada?" Their operations were far, far away, according to Catalina's father. He always referred to them as weak, lazy competition. Hardly competition at all. Maybe these men were on some sort of vacation.

Whatever the case, they had invaded Catalina's peaceful drink at the tiny, otherwise-unoccupied bar attached to the equally tiny inn. She sat on a stool at the counter, facing a middle-aged bartender wearing a frumpy burgundy dress and sporting a grey bun atop her head. Behind Catalina were three wooden, circular tables and a scattered handful of wooden chairs, the only amenities a bar so far in the wilderness needed. Not a criticism—she rather liked the place.

The four men in question were at the table closest to the entrance, making loud, lewd jokes and sharing stories of their sexual conquests. They even directed some of their comments at Catalina, but she paid no attention as she drank her Cuba Libre.

"It's rare that we get visitors, you know," the bartender said to Catalina in Spanish, punctuating her introduction with a smile. "I know the environment here is less than hospitable, but you're welcome to talk to me if you want some company. Jesus knows I could use it."

Catalina stared at the woman for five silent, awkward seconds.

Before the talkative woman could open her mouth again, Catalina raised a hand to a black silk scarf tied around her neck, wrapped as tight as a vice. She pulled it down halfway, revealing a thick, knotted scar running across the entire front half of her neck, drawing a grotesque line beneath her Adam's apple.

The woman blushed, embarrassed. "I'm sorry, I didn't—"

Catalina raised a hand to stop her before making a few gestures in LSC—Lengua de Señas Colombiana. [Do you speak sign language?] She always tried to learn the sign language specific to the areas she visited, just in case.

The bartender lifted her arms into an exaggerated shrug. "I don't understand, I'm sorry. How's this?"

She produced a pen and pad of paper from under the counter.

Catalina slid it to her side of the bar top, took another sip of her drink, and wrote in blocky Spanish letters. IT'S OK.

"What's brought you this far into the wilderness? You aren't planning on hiking, are you?"

Catalina reached into her pocket, wincing as the men behind her loudened. She wasn't quick to anger, but she wasn't brimming with patience, either. Right now, the men tested hers.

Besides, there's no tolerance for monsters like these.

Catalina produced from her pocket an envelope and unfolded the letter within. She offered the paper to the bartender, who shook her head, tears forming in her eyes.

"I know what it says," the woman said. "I helped write it, along with most of the other parents in this town. You're the hunter? I think we all expected you to be a man." She laughed and gestured to her own face. "A big, burly man with battle scars across his face. Serves us right for jumping to conclusions!" The bartender waved in Catalina's direction. "But look at you! You're petite and pretty. I'm jealous that you're able to handle something so tough while being so slight."

Catalina offered a tight smile, but the woman's words only chilled her heart. She was small, thin and pretty; that much was accurate. Her olive skin, green eyes and shoulder-length brown hair were true to her mother's Chilean heritage. However, her mother was nothing more than a "fantasma" now.

Her father had seen to that.

Catalina wrote, WHAT IS THIS MAN YOU MENTION IN THE

LETTER? A "LEAN" MAN?

The bartender shifted again, her discomfort apparent. "I wouldn't call him 'lean.' Maybe a better word would be sle—"

She was interrupted by the sudden appearance of one of the men from the table. He lurched against Catalina's back, using her shoulders to steady himself. His breath reeked of alcohol, and Catalina scrunched her nose. She took another sip of her drink.

"Whass a burtifal lady doin' in a shithole 'ike this?" he drawled in Spanish, and he spun her stool around to face him. The other three men at the table howled with abandon. "Come'n up to my room an' I'll give ya the best fuck you'll ever get."

He put his hands around her waist and pulled her off the stool and onto her feet. Her black boots clacked on the wooden tavern floor. She held eye contact with him for a moment, but he was too drunk—or brave, or stupid—to back down. He reached for her waist again, and she dodged his advance. Not one to quit so easily, he leaned in to kiss her. Huffing, she leaned toward him as well . . . and spit rum into his eyes.

In disgust, he cried and stepped back, startled. Catalina took advantage of his confusion by taking two deliberate stomps forward and punching him in the throat with a speed and force that she knew her slight stature belied. The man let out a gurgled, choking noise, reaching for his throat with both hands. He dropped to his knees, and Catalina reared back her arm. Before he could react, she delivered an open-handed slap across the face with a thunderous *crack*. He fell sideways to the floor, stunned.

Whether his temporary paralysis was from surprise or from pain, Catalina wasn't sure. She hoped it was both.

Good. Fuck the Medellin. Fucking monsters.

The boisterousness of the table near the bar's entrance subsided. All three men sat in silence, staring at Catarina. Their surprise broke when one stood and pulled out a long hunting knife.

"You fucking bitch," he said. "I'm gonna feed you to my dogs."

The bartender reached for something under the bar counter, but Catalina raised a hand to stop her. *Guns won't be necessary.*

Flanking Mr. Knife on the right, one of his friends grabbed his liquor bottle by the neck, wielding it like a club. His other buddy simply raised his fists to fight.

Oh, so you're willing to get your hands dirty. Catalina pointed at

Mr. Fist. *I respect that. You're first.*

The three men must not have understood her gesture, because they all rushed at once.

Catalina's chest thudded, her heartbeat quickening from a rush of adrenaline. She felt the pulling, painful sensation of her pupils dilating, accompanied by a slight pressure against the side of her temple. Time slowed to a crawl as the men approached.

Mr. Bottle reached her first by a split second, swinging the weapon of his namesake in a downward arc. As the bottle descended, Mr. Knife thrust his weapon out and forward, toward her stomach. Catalina turned sideways, dodging the knife thrust, and kicked him in the back. Mr. Knife's momentum carried him into the bar, and he tripped over the would-be sex offender sprawled on the ground.

In the process of turning, she grabbed Mr. Bottle's wrist and stepped into his attack, bringing their bodies closer together while halting his strike. She lashed out with an upward palm strike beneath his elbow, fracturing his forearm with a crisp snap. As it bent at an awkward angle, he cried in agony, the bottle falling.

Catalina released Mr. Bottle's arm and grabbed the bottle as it fell, all while continuing her body's turn. She now faced Mr. Fist, his arm in mid-swing with a haymaker. She ducked beneath the swing, and he struck Mr. Bottle in the face, exactly as she'd positioned him when releasing his injured arm.

Even as Mr. Fist's hand was connecting with Mr. Bottle, Catalina gripped the appropriated bottle with both hands and rammed the circular glass bottom into Mr. Fist's solar plexus. He doubled over in pain and vomited onto the floor. Mr. Bottle was still rearing back from his friend's punch, nose bloody and arm askew.

Catalina took advantage of Mr. Fist's bent position to swing her leg into a stern kick, striking him directly in the face with her shin. Some part of his face popped, he went white, and he collapsed face-first into the ground, seemingly unconscious.

I stay true to my word.

By now, Catalina was sure Mr. Knife had recovered from his fall. She turned just in time to see him rushing forward with another straight attack to her abdomen. The bottle in her hand swung down and connected with the metacarpal bones in his wrist. They snapped, his hand crumpled, the knife clattering to the tavern floor.

Mr. Knife screamed, wildly swinging with his good hand. She raised her forearm to block his punch; even as their limbs connected, she brought up her other fist as a counter. It found a home under his chin, and blood spurted from his mouth as his jaw fractured against her knuckles. His eyes rolled upward, and he fell to the ground on his back.

Catalina placed the glass bottle onto the closest table and turned to face its original owner. His eyes were already swelling—*impressive punch, Mr. Fist*—and he held his injured arm with his free hand. Catalina took a few steps toward him before she heard the distinct sound of a revolver's hammer.

Her pupils twitched.

The fourth man. Behind me and to the left, around my seven o'clock. He's shaken but still cocky. He's a Medellin, after all. He wants to shoot the head, but his fear will encourage a safer torso shot. That means it will end up somewhere in the middle, close to my neck or shoulder blade area. He's a pussy, which means he won't give a warning shot. He'll shoot to kill and tell a grand tale to his cartel friends afterward.

The hammer pulled. The trigger depressed. She'd forget the details of her rushing thoughts later, like always. After all, she never really *thought* in times like these.

She *reacted*.

Catalina bent her knees and swayed slightly to the left, cocking her head even further in that direction. With the deafening crack of gunfire, the bullet ruffled her hair as it passed over her shoulder.

Unfortunately, Mr. Bottle was in the path of the gunshot. The bullet traveled past Catalina and struck him in the collarbone opposite the arm she had fractured. He spun around and collapsed onto the table where he had been drinking. The table tilted with his weight and crashed to the floor.

One more.

Catalina peered behind her, finding the final man still lying on the ground, propped against the bar where she had slapped him. He had a silver revolver with a brown handle in his hand. She thought it might be a Smith & Wesson Model 10, chambered for .38 caliber rounds. He was already thumbing back the hammer for a second shot. Catalina scanned the room. There was nothing strong or sturdy enough within reach to deflect the bullets.

She'd need to cross the room. Unprotected.

He fired his second round. Catalina took two steps forward, jerking her body away from the incoming bullet. Her eyes tracked the bullet as it passed, verifying she was free from harm.

"La Mirada Del Diablo," her father had called it.

The Gaze of the Devil.

She may have received her appearance and stature from her mother, but she shared this particular trait with a long line of men and women on her father's side. His bloodline of protectors and assassins used the Gaze for generations to hold aloft their Venezuelan cartel.

While most in her family happily served the cartel with their Gaze, Catalina resisted. Sure, they fought terrible men, but they worked for men just as horrific, if not worse. Nonetheless, her father had insisted she train as a bodyguard for the cartel.

And whenever her father insisted, it was dangerous to say no.

The second bullet passed Catalina. She tilted her head and upper body backward about forty-five degrees, dropped to her knees, and slid across the floor. The third bullet passed above her face and embedded itself into the ceiling.

Her momentum carried her back to a running position. She skipped her feet off the ground as if she were playing a game of "rayuela," and the fourth bullet slipped beneath her boots, spraying splinters up from the floor.

Catalina was almost upon Mr. Gun as he chambered his fifth round and pointed his weapon at her center mass. Unfortunately for him, she was also close enough to the bar to reach her drink. As he raised his revolver to track her new position, she slammed the glass into his eyes, upside-down. It smashed into pieces, cutting into his face, and the liquor splashed with burning force. He cried in pain, twitching his arm as he fired. The shot went wild.

Catalina clutched the barrel of the revolver and twisted the trigger guard around his finger, breaking the bone like a fresh carrot. The man whimpered, retreating his hand. The revolver now in her possession, she aimed the barrel at his head, tempted to pull the trigger.

Monsters.

Mr. Gun wiped the liquor and glass away from his face to look up at her. Rather than staring at the gun barrel, however, he met her eyes, mouth agape. She knew what he saw: A small woman with large, black pupils, like the eyes of a cat on the prowl.

Catalina sighed and opened the cylinder of the gun. Five spent shells and one live round fell to the tavern floor, rolling in different directions across the wooden surface. She snapped the cylinder back into place, gripped the gun by the barrel, and clubbed the man across the face with the handle. He slumped over, limp as a rag doll.

As she felt her pupils reduce to a normal size, she glanced at the bartender. The woman seemed a little shaken, but she maintained her composure.

Catalina felt some guilt for the destruction she had caused, but the satisfaction of engaging these assholes overwhelmed that sensation. Still . . . She moved to the counter and scratched on the pad. I'M SO SORRY FOR THE DAMAGE. THIS FIGHT GOT OUT OF HAND. HOW MUCH WILL IT COST TO REPLACE EVERY-THING?

The bartender leaned over the counter and surveyed the men, sprawled across the floor. She reached out and placed her hand on top of Catalina's. "All we need from you is to find it. Find it and put a stop to this nightmare. We just want our children to feel safe again." She gestured at the four men. "We've dealt with men like these since the beginning of time. This new thing, whatever it is that's taking our families? We don't know what to do. Please just help us."

Catalina nodded, clasping her other hand over the woman's. They smiled at each before releasing their grasp. Catalina turned and walked across the tavern floor, kicking one of the men in the rib cage as she exited.

––––––––––––

Sunsets in rural Colombia were something to behold. La Encarnación bordered Natural Las Orquídeas, a tremendous forest thick with leafy green trees and other plant life. The bloody orange sun hugged the tips of the tree line, and the colors painted a somber melody as the ball of light sank out of sight. Catalina stared at it from the window of her inn, appreciating her moment of peaceful silence.

But it was time to hunt.

She turned on her heel from the window and went to the pile of black duffel bags she had brought with her to the village. Unzipping the first bag, she revealed an outfit made of tough black cloth. The suit came in three sections: A top half, a bottom half, and a hooded cloak. Tucked inside strategically placed pockets of the outfit were thick metal plates, collectively creating a layer of armor.

Next, Catalina opened the other two duffle bags, surveying the contents. Each bag was filled with various firearms—bladed weapons and explosives. She pondered, for a moment, before reaching into the bags, pulling out her weapons of choice for the evening and fastening their holsters, straps, or bandoliers to various parts of her suit. Saving the best for last, she retrieved a pair of flattened cylindrical devices, slipping them into her sleeves with a hefty *click*.

Catalina snapped together the thick black outfit and attached her protective cloak to her neck and shoulders. The weight of the armor pressed against her body, but she had trained for years to withstand such heavy burdens. She pulled the hood up and over the back of her head, leaving enough room around the sides of her face to keep her peripheral vision intact. The cloak crested over her shoulders and fell around her arms and side. The whole ensemble left her looking like a formless, black phantom.

Satisfied, Catalina turned to the window and opened it. She climbed outside and scaled the roof of the inn, carrying a long, black rifle behind her. With great care and precision, she walked across the shingles and laid the rifle onto a flat part of the surface, flicking out a v-shaped stand to keep it at the correct angle. She peered through the large magnifying sight atop the body of the gun, ensuring she had optimal view of the forest.

The message Catalina had received said the creature arrived almost every night. It didn't always claim a victim, but it always tried. They said it offered some sort of call, like a siren of Greek mythology. In the worst way possible, the village had learned its most susceptible victims were children.

Catalina's frustration stemmed from the fact that the village struggled to *describe* the goddamn thing. She'd need to be attentive tonight.

Her vigilance, however, wasn't necessary. Less than an hour passed before Catalina felt what she could only describe as a buzzing sensation. It started as a cerebral itch; at first, she swatted at her face, under the impression a mosquito was in her ear. It increased in intensity, as if someone were broadcasting radio static right into her brain. Within the static, she heard—or felt, or thought—a series of words.

"Co . . ."

"St . . ."

"Ki . . ."

"Lo . . ."

Though the sensation wasn't *pleasant*, at least not in a way Catalina would jump from the roof and run into the forest, it had a sedating effect. She could understand why children, with their impulsivities, would be so susceptible to this creature if it approached them.

She saw movement below her and to the left; a flash of white, moving at a steady pace toward the woods. She focused her rifle's sight toward the motion and saw a little girl in a white nightgown, walking rapidly toward the border of foliage. She couldn't have been older than eight. Her long brown hair blew in the evening's breeze, but she seemed unfazed by the disruption.

Her focus was on a dark shape, emerging from the forest.

"Co . . . me."

"St . . . me."

"Ki . . . me."

"Lo . . . me."

Catalina refocused her rifle toward the trees and saw a man. Except, it *wasn't* a man. Instead, it was a pale imitation, in the most unsettling ways.

It was maybe three or four meters tall, and it had spindly, almost skeletal features. The arms, legs and torso were as thin as broomsticks, and every joint ended at a sharp angle. Its "skin" was a pale white, but its exposed head revealed . . . nothing.

There were simply no facial features. Nothing but a smooth, white, empty canvas.

"Com . . . o me."

"Sta . . . th me."

"Kil . . . r me."

"Lov . . . me."

Most peculiar, though—it wore a suit. A goddamn *suit*. Black slacks and shoes, a black suit jacket, and a white collared shirt with a black tie.

What kind of monster dresses in business attire?

Catalina tried to draw a bead on the creature with her rifle, but its movements were jerky and unnatural, as if its limbs were bent in the wrong directions. She couldn't line up a proper shot at this distance, and she didn't want a missed attempt to put the girl in more danger.

The girl reached the forest, and the Man extended a long, sharp hand toward her in a welcoming gesture. The girl placed her hand into his, and Catalina felt another burst of static in her head.

"Come to me."

"Stay with me."

"Kill for me."

"Love me."

Together, the two disappeared into the shadows of the forest.

Catalina stood and grabbed her rifle, running to the roof's edge. She was on the second story, and a tiled awning extended from the separation between the two floors. In the blink of an eye, Catalina stepped from the edge of the roof and landed on the awning, her momentum sliding her down the perch and onto the grass below. As she sprinted into the forest, a cry came from the village behind her.

"Sofía? *Sofía!*"

The panicked cries continued. Windows glowed with yellow light as other members of the town awoke to the screams. Catalina gritted her teeth and pursued the girl, Sofía, into the forest.

Entering Natural Las Orquídeas, Catalina expected the sounds of chittering animals and chirping insects to be louder than in the village. Instead, the forest was as silent as death itself. Catalina only heard the pounding of her boots on the ground, the rushing of blood in her ears, and the whisper of her cloak rummaging through the thick leaves behind her.

A breeze blew past, and the branches above rustled with what Catalina would describe as "emoción." A girl's voice echoed from somewhere ahead. She slowed and took measured breaths, careful not to make too much noise. Crouched, she inched past the trees, cradling her rifle. The shapes of two figures, one very tall and one very small, meandered away from her at a casual pace.

Sofía chattered away in Spanish about her friends and family. Every so often she would pause, and the Man's head would vibrate, the movement almost imperceptible. No sound would emerge, but

Catalina could feel the static burst in her head each time it happened. Once the Man "responded," the girl continued her conversation.

When they began to slow, Catalina took advantage of the opportunity and descended from her crouched position, pressing her stomach against the grass. She pushed her face through the leaves at the edge of the small clearing the pair occupied, placing her rifle onto the forest floor. Once settled, Catalina held her breath and peered into the rifle sight.

Another gust of wind blew into her face, and the trees above rustled with fervor once more.

The gigantic weapon in her hands was, for the most part, just two long, black pipes adjacent to one other. The back portion included a handle, a padded shoulder rest, and an angled magazine protruding from the top. The front portion was just a long barrel ending in a flat muzzle brake, as if a hockey puck were glued to the tip of her rifle.

The device was once called the Boys Anti-Tank Rifle, but the British soldiers who used in during World War II aptly nicknamed it the "elephant gun" due to its appearance. It fired modified .55 caliber Boys rounds which, though ironically not very effective against tanks, worked quite well against living objects with uncertain physical properties. Catalina aligned her crosshairs in the center of the Man's chest area.

It wasn't *wearing* a suit at all. That was its *skin*.

It had animal patterning, not unlike an arctic penguin's "tuxedo." Her mind recalled Venus flytraps, and how they used their innocuous appearances to lure insects into their maw. The disguise didn't need to be perfect; it just needed to bring its prey within reach.

Catalina's pupils dilated.

Time slowed to a crawl as her finger squeezed the trigger of her rifle. In the split second between the depression of the trigger and the firing of the bullet, the gun creaked. She perceived, with her Gaze, the Man cocking its head in her direction.

Fuck. It's fast.

As the bullet exited the barrel, the Man was already moving to the side. It must not have understood or accounted for the elephant gun's power and velocity, though, because it didn't escape in time.

Instead of striking the chest, the bullet struck the creature's right shoulder, the impact as heavy as a tank shell. With a dull *thump*, the Man's entire arm flew from its body and into the shadows of the foliage behind it. The wound produced a substance similar to wet, stringy cotton; it oozed from the hole and stuck in clumps to the side of the creature's torso.

The Man faced the space where Catalina hid.

It hunched over and emitted a sickening crackle, as if the bones within it were tearing apart. Three more arms emerged on each side of its body, coming from points on its back instead of its shoulders. The blank white face of the Man split down the middle in a vertical line, revealing endless rows of sharp teeth, furthering its Venus flytrap similarities. It lurched, as if roaring, though no sound emerged. Instead, the familiar static filled Catalina's head with unexpected intensity. She collapsed.

"KILL FOR ME."

The trees above her rustled with the emoción she had noticed before.

This time, there was no wind.

Catalina rolled onto her back, trying to regain her coordination, and looked into the branches. Hanging from various parts of the treetops all around her were dozens of heads, each about the size of a basketball, seemingly identical to the head of the Man.

As she watched, they split open like the Man's head, revealing rows of teeth. They vibrated, rustling the trees, and Catalina could feel new static buzzing in her head, much fainter than the Man's, but with a new message.

"Feed me."

"Feed me."

"Feed me."

They're babies, thought Catalina. *It's bringing food to its babies.*

La Encarnación, Colombia
November 13, 1999-A

The babies shook, sprouting stumpy versions of the Man's humanoid arms and hands, four on each side of their head-like bodies. They continued their silent, static screeches as they descended from the trees in unison, held aloft by thick, white, wet strands.

Behind Catalina, the Man abandoned its focus on Sofía and fled into the trees beyond the clearing, scrambling with its awkward, inverse run.

Catalina had little time to lose.

She rolled to her feet and hurled her elephant gun into the clearing, sending it skidding to a rest at the far edge. Her hands reached into her cloak and retrieved a pair of automatic Glock pistols. Fitted with extended magazines, together they gave her sixty-six rounds. She surveyed the scene above her and worked her jaw, calculating. Sixty-six probably wasn't going to be enough.

Catalina raised her arms, firing short bursts from her pistols and separating her arms to strike multiple targets at once. The pistols chattered as they expended their ammunition, and the resulting fire cut into the descending creatures one-by-one, cracking them open like piñatas. Catalina maintained her steady fire rate as she backed into the clearing, watching the bodies fall to the forest floor.

Even with her accurate shots, she couldn't counter the overwhelming number of small, spidery monsters. Some of them reached the ground and crawled with the same jarring gait as the Man. Most charged Catalina, but a select few branched off in Sofía's direction. The girl rubbed her eyes in confusion.

No!

Catalina turned her Glocks and mowed down the babies headed toward the girl. She rushed toward Sofía, scooped her up, and looped her arms around her neck and onto the back of her cloak.

I wish I could tell her to cover her ears.

Her magazines ran low, but it seemed as if there were more spidery babies approaching now than ever before. She ejected her almost-spent magazines into a collection pouch on her suit and reached behind her back, feeling for two canteen-shaped devices. Catalina found the end pieces and inserted them into the handles of her Glocks, bringing the guns back to an attack position. Hanging onto the bottom of each pistol was a flat, circular drum magazine, designed to hold fifty rounds apiece.

Catalina dropped to her knees in the clearing and faced the incoming horde, Sofía still maintaining a death-grip around her neck. As the white, teeth-filled faces appeared, she fired again, burning through her ammunition as she fanned her arms back and forth. The hot lead cut a destructive swathe through monsters and shrubbery alike, and bursts of static appeared in Catalina's head as each creature released its death knell. They continued their assault, but the distance between the humans and the creatures increased.

The tide's changing. Time to finish this.

Seizing the opportunity, Catalina shrugged Sofía off her back onto the grass before dropping the pistols and retrieving two canisters from a bandolier around her torso. She squeezed the handles on the side of each one and released their safety pins. One after another, she arced the canisters into the incoming wave of monsters. A few seconds passed before she heard two successive *whumps*, following by the rapid spread of flames.

It's a shame to damage the forest, but sometimes tough choices have to be made.

The thermite in her grenades spread at a frightening pace, engulfing the spider creatures and the surrounding trees. Green plants turned brown and dissolved into ash so quickly that only Catalina's Gaze could see the progression. She retrieved a third canister and one of her Glock pistols, moving toward the flames.

The babies were burning and dying to Catalina's satisfaction. Still, she saw a few trying to escape from one side of the fire; she cut them down with her Glock before tossing her third canister into the middle of the inferno, spreading the destruction. As she turned away, one of the babies hopped from the flames in front of her, still on fire, and bit her arm.

Catalina staggered back. The creature hadn't penetrated her armor, but it had tremendous bite force. If it didn't let go soon, she'd have a shattered humerus and a useless right arm. She aimed her

Glock at the creature and pulled the trigger, but the gun was empty. Reloading would take too long; she could already feel her arm bruising from the pressure.

She released the pistol and withdrew a thick metal rod from her belt. It was a dark, silver, Maglite-sized device whose only notable features were an opening on one end and a small lever on the side.

Often used to euthanize farm animals, the captive bolt device was just as helpful in combat. She placed the tip of the device on the top-center of the creature's head, which was not yet in flames. When she squeezed the lever on the side, a long metal bolt drove into the center of the monster, releasing a metallic hiss. Thick, cottony material spurted from the new hole; the creature went limp, releasing Catalina's arm.

She stepped back to ensure no one else escaped her flames. Not a thing stirred except the crackling of burning, supernatural fauna.

Satisfied, she reset her captive bolt device and returned it to its holster. She reloaded her Glocks with standard, more portable magazines before returning them to their proper locations on her person. Fiddling with one hand for a weapon strapped to her back, Catalina gestured to Sofía with the other.

Go home. Please understand me. Go home.

Sofía seemed to pick up on Catalina's silent signals. Her eyes lit up, and she pointed in the direction of the path that left the forest. Catalina nodded, pulling a rifle from beneath her cloak. The girl turned to leave, but then looked back. After a moment, she ran to Catalina and hugged her waist. Gripping the new rifle by the handle, Catalina leaned down with her free hand to hug her back, though only for a few seconds.

"Gracias," Sofía whispered into Catalina's ear.

Then she was gone, rushing down the forest pathway back toward her home.

Catalina offered her first genuine smile in a while as she examined the weapon in her hands. The Russian revolving shotgun's wooden frame was punctuated by a large silver ammunition cylinder, not unlike the cylinders found in revolver pistols. She swung open the cylinder and verified she'd preloaded slug rounds. They would ensure maximum damage if they hit her target.

When they hit her target. She wouldn't miss again.

With Sofía safe and her arsenal ready, Catalina forged down the path left behind by the fleeing monster. The raging fire roared at her back, but its glow and its crackling petered out as she moved further into the forest. She was relieved to see there was no more movement in the trees above. Darkness enveloped her, and her cloak blended into the environment.

She was nothing but a floating silhouette.

Catalina traveled a quarter of a kilometer without incident before the soft leaves, once fluttering in the breeze, became sticky and heavy. Leaning forward, she reached out and touched one of the flat green plants. When she pulled away, some of the cotton-like substance followed her in strands. She rubbed it on the grass below, leveled her shotgun, and stepped through a cluster of branches into a new clearing.

As Catalina passed through the barrier, it ripped, the leaves pulling apart like Velcro. The shadows around her darkened, and the temperature noticeably dropped. She began to adjust her cloak, but she stopped when she registered what was around her.

Surrounding the clearing was a white dome, about a hundred meters in diameter, comprised of the same white substance that spilled from the Man when Catalina removed its arm. The cottony film spread from the ground to the tree trunks, stretching between trees and climbing along branches. A canopy stitched together the treetops, forming a "ceiling."

Catalina looked closer at the walls of the dome and squinted at the shapes suspended there. Her cat-like eyes widened.

She'd found the missing people.

Cocooned throughout the dome, some hung a meter or two from the ground, while others dotted the top of the canopy. Altogether, she identified about twenty people, an estimated five adults and fifteen children. Most were still, yet others twitched, and one of the girls on the far wall seemed to be crying. Around each of them squirmed white shapes that Catalina couldn't quite identify.

To the left of where Catalina entered the dome, she noticed a heavyset man hanging. He sported a short-sleeved collared shirt and a bushy mustache.

That's why the Medellin Cartel is here. They lost some of their people to this creature, too.

The man stirred and opened his eyes. As soon as he saw Catalina standing nearby, he panicked, struggling against his cocoon. She turned to face him.

"Mátame," he whispered. "Kill me."

She shook her head, shifted her shotgun to one hand, and produced a knife, gesturing the blade in the direction of his cocoon.

He shook his head. "No . . . I'm not—"

Before he could say more, he wheezed. The short disruption grew into a sickening hack, as if something blocked his throat. With a final wet, guttural noise, he leaned forward and vomited a white orb the size of a golf ball. Before it could fall from his tongue, the orb shook and sprouted eight tiny arm-legs, just like its larger counterparts earlier in the forest.

The man whimpered as the tiny creature crawled around to the left side of face, which Catalina couldn't see. He turned his head in protest—it was stripped of its flesh and muscle, down to the bone. The little monster opened its vertical mouth and wrestled free a bite-sized chunk of flesh as the man continued to struggle. It carried its prize behind the man and onto the cottony canvas behind him. Its gait almost triumphant, it joined at least a hundred others like it.

"I'm not . . . alive . . . anymore," the man continued, his voice weaker now. "Everything inside me . . . it's all gone. Now . . . all that keeps me healthy . . . keeps me awake . . . it's only because of *the nest*." He coughed again. She could see the weariness in his tortured eyes. "It's going to . . . keep me alive . . . until they . . . Until they take all of me . . . all of *us*."

His eyes traced the dome, finding the other people. Hacking coughs surrounded them, resounding mostly in the higher octaves of children, many of them likely Sofía's age or younger. They all vomited out the baby creatures at intervals, a small piece of their body taken away each time.

"We can't . . . we can't stay like this," the man wheezed. "It's worse . . . than death. Please . . . end it." A few small children cocooned nearby nodded in fervent agreement.

Catalina's head spun. Yes, she had already assumed these people were dead and eaten, but this was much more complicated. Could the doctors in town, or even further in the large cities, keep them supported without their major organs?

As she considered the option, a rapid rustle came from overhead. She looked up—the Man, the creature she hunted, crawled along the canopy of the dome with its seven arms and two angular legs. It didn't seem to notice her, its attention focused on the stomach of a young girl. Blood dripped onto the grass below, the red droplets nearly falling onto Catalina.

Catalina lifted her shotgun and fired, wasting no time to engage the monster. A deep, thunderous roll filled the nest, and the slug struck its target while it fed. The large bullet smashed into the Man's lower back, leaving a gaping wound leaking white fluid. The creature screamed, sending static careening through Catalina's mind, and released the canopy. It slapped into the ground, sprawled on its back.

She released the trigger of the shotgun and the cylinder rotated, preparing the next round. In her brief moment of preparation, the Man reached its feet, dripping cottony fluid onto the grass around it. Its blank face was covered in the young girl's blood. Raising its seven arms, it charged toward Catalina.

She aimed and fired once more, but the creature was prepared. Her pupils twitched, but she watched helplessly as the Man shifted with ease to dodge the bullet. Aware of the imminent impact, Catalina held the rifle out with both hands, creating a makeshift shield.

Catalina's Gaze registered the Man's presence in front of her, a sharp crack and sudden vibration blurring her vision. The wind rushed in her ears, and she struggled to focus.

Before her sight cleared, agony filled her body. With the telltale sensation of arrested motion, she smashed into an obstacle before striking the forest floor, landing on her face and stomach.

Pushing through her pain, Catalina assessed her predicament. The creature had thrown her from its nest, and the entrance to the dome now lay twenty meters ahead of her. A rough indentation had formed in the tree behind her, several meters in the air, where her body had struck it. She could see the pieces of her shotgun scattered throughout the clearing.

This is how much damage it can do with one swipe. There's no way I'll survive more hits like that.

Catalina coughed, wincing. The padding of the armor and cloak had protected her from most of the impact with the tree, but she could feel the pang of a broken rib when she breathed.

Static filled her head, and she looked up in time to see the Man emerging from the dome. He sprinted toward her without hesitation, lurching through the trees with its unnatural, crooked gait.

She poised, waiting for it. It appeared beside her, slashing out with four of its hands, extending those pointed fingers toward her face. Catalina tumbled beneath its attack with the grace of a gymnast, retrieving her Grizzly pistol from her thigh holster mid-roll. As she halted into a crouch, she pivoted and took aim with both arms.

The black handgun housed .50 caliber rounds, packing a serious punch. Catalina graciously shared those punches now, pulling the trigger in quick succession while panning a diagonal line across the Man's body. Three bullets emerged with thunderous roars, one striking the creature's bottom left hip, another hitting it in the center of its chest, and the final round piercing the top right shoulder, near the neck. Each strike produced a baseball-sized hole through its body, and it screamed in response.

The recoil numbed Catalina's fingers, compounding the pain in her already sore wrists. She wasn't often interested in using the Grizzly for this exact reason, but it was a fantastic resource when she was in need of immediate stopping power. That fact proved true once more with the Man, seemingly weakened by the trio of holes in its torso. Still, she couldn't fire it many more times without compromising her combat competence. She holstered the firearm as a backup plan and reached behind her cloak.

The Man, still reeling from the Grizzly shots, stumbled forward to slash at Catalina, slowing by a noticeable degree. Catalina took advantage of its weakness to withdraw two batons, each tipped with a curved blade running perpendicular to the handle.

Kamas, the Japanese called them. Shaped to be miniature, hand-held scythes, they were once nothing more than farming tools. The Shogunate era, however, transformed them into makeshift weapons, and several countries throughout Southeast Asia discovered they were perfect for disarming enemies.

And this enemy had plenty of arms to spare.

Catalina raised the kamas, one in each hand, resembling a viper's maw. Poised in her fighting stance, she awaited the monster's reply.

It opened its mouth, head vibrating, and Catalina's head fuzzed.

"Come to me."

"Stay with me."

"Kill for me."

"Love me."

She squinted to maintain focus, and saw a white, angular hand centimeters from her face. Her left cheek burned even as she moved to the side. The creature had drawn her blood.

Catalina took advantage of the attack, wrapping her two kamas around the offending arm. The sharp underside of one scythe blade pressed against the arm between the shoulder and its spindly elbow, while the other blade pressed in the opposite direction between the elbow and wrist. She pulled with as much force as she could muster, and like a cigar in its cutter, she snipped away the entire left forearm from its roots. Now the Man stood with a stump leaking white fluid from each shoulder, shadowed by the three remaining arms angled out of each side of its back.

Apparently less phased by the second amputation, though, the Man continued its relentless assault. Catalina rolled and dodged, avoiding its strikes or parrying them with her scythes. Splinters sprayed from tree trunks as the two sparred along the darkened forest trail. After what felt like an eternity, they came to a momentary respite. The creature shuddered as if ill, while Catalina struggled to catch her breath.

The Man had landed some solid blows on Catalina's arms and chest, but she had returned the favor with deep, leaking cuts along its body. They were both tired and slowed, but her strength and stamina was dropping more quickly than her opponent's. Even with the creature riddled with bullet holes and missing two arms, one wrong step or misplaced strike would spell her immediate death.

Then again, personal risk for the sake of the community was always a respectable compromise. One of the few lessons taught by her father she still honored.

Catalina moved a few steps back from the Man and sheathed a kama. The creature made another move and she pivoted away, reaching for her hood. Built into the sides of the hood were rubber plugs connected to thin, mechanical strips. She depressed the sides of the hood, flipping the strips' hinges and sealing her ears.

With her free hand, Catalina snatched a new grenade from her bandolier. Pulling the pin but keeping the lever depressed, she paused, waiting for the right moment.

The Man lowered itself into the grass and crawled toward her, more spider-like than before. It reached the edge of her boots in a heartbeat and reared up above her, mouth open, ready to take its first bite. Catalina released the grenade's lever and tossed it into the air, its path level with the monster's head. She rolled low—toward the creature. As she passed under its legs, the grenade exploded.

Catalina's ears were sealed and her vision obfuscated by the hood and cloak, but the flashbang's assault still demanded the attention of her senses. Bright light filled her peripheral vision, and the shock of the blast rattled her bones.

This monster uses some sort of subsonic organ to communicate and manipulate. Hopefully I can fight fire with fire, in this case.

She turned and surveyed her results. The Man reeled, its mouth closed, its head vibrating in a wild, chaotic pattern.

"Love . . . Kill . . . Me . . . With . . . Kill . . ."

It pressed its six attached arms against its head to create a shield. As Catalina had hoped, its back remained turned to her.

Now's the best chance.

Catalina unholstered the Grizzly with her available hand and leapt onto the creature's back. The moment she made contact, it jerked away as if by reflex, but she buried the scythe blade still gripped in her other hand into its shoulder blade. She rode the bucking bronco, fighting to maintain her footing.

As she jolted back and forth, she pointed the Grizzly pistol at the back of the Man's head. In the last moment before pulling the trigger, she noticed the shadow of six arms descending upon her. She tried to fire off a killing shot before the incoming assault struck, but the fingers clutching for her body shifted her aim. The .50 caliber bullet missed the creature's head by mere centimeters.

With that, the monster unceremoniously lifted Catalina into the air and slammed her onto the unforgiving forest floor for a second time. Her breath left her lungs, as if an elephant stepped on her chest. Her head rocked from the sudden shift in motion, and her neck tensed from the whiplash. The sharp sensation in her side worsened; in her excitement, she had almost forgotten about the rib.

The impact had loosened her grasp on the Grizzly. It was on the ground, next to her fingertips. As she strained to grasp it, the shadow of the Man blocked out the moonlight filtering through the trees overhead. After a second or two, her expanded pupils adjusted to the ambient light, revealing the monster's features once more.

It was in rough shape, to say the least. It had two armless

stumps from the elephant gun and the kamas, three holes along its torso from the Grizzly, a large crater in its back from the shotgun blast, and a kama embedded near the shoulder. Its body was covered in dozens of deep lacerations, and cottony fluid coated its skin. It twitched violently, as if agitated.

Catalina flashed it a menacing smile.

The Man's head buzzed and looked down at Catalina, then at the Grizzly beside her. Its mouth split open as it reached for Catalina, and she was airborne again. Her journey was short but unpleasant; the monster used its arms to pin her by the chest and shoulders to a nearby tree trunk. The shock of the impact left Catalina wheezing, and she spat out a little blood.

The creature leaned up to her eye level, daring to open its mouth wide, seeming to telegraph its awareness that the Grizzly had been left behind on the grass.

"FEED THEM."

From within the recesses of its head sprung a curved, white spike, resembling the horn of a rhinoceros. The appearance was sudden and alarming, like a sharp blade flicking from the handle of an organic knife. The creature aimed its head toward her stomach.

It wanted to add her to its collection. She had to end this. Now.

Catalina raised her right arm forward as if to give the creature a high-five, her fingertips almost touching its impregnation spike. Her thumb pressed a small mechanical button that rested on the side of her glove, close to the knuckle of her index finger. The response was the faint *click* of a mechanism beneath Catalina's sleeve springing forward. Two silver tubes protruded from her sleeve, extending a little past her wrist.

As the tubes emerged, a latch resembling a tiny stop sign flipped up. The pedestal portion formed a hinge with the tube mechanism under her arm, while the more circular pedal landed in the center of Catalina's palm. She curled her fingers down into a fist and depressed the pedal.

With an unflattering hollow *crack*, the left tube fired a triple-aught buckshot spread straight into the spike and the back of the Man's open mouth. The force of the blast, the proximity of the shot, and the size of the pellets created a destructive trinity that disintegrated the entire back of the monster's head. The tooth-riddled remnants of its skull left behind after the blast quivered, weak and defeated.

Catalina took no chances, though. She shifted her arm down to point at the neck area and depressed the pedal once more. The second spray from the right barrel sheared off the rest of the creature's head and carved a crescent-shaped crater into its neck stump.

The remainder of the Man went limp, collapsing to the forest floor like fallen tree branches, its arms releasing Catalina. She fell with it, managing a shaky landing on her feet. She curled an arm around her body, the injured rib sending ripples of pain up her side. The wind caught her cloak in the breeze and sent it fluttering.

The moonlight exposed her fallen weapons. She retrieved those still functioning, storing them in their proper holsters. When finished, Catalina glanced at the sprawled corpse one last time before looking behind her, in the direction of the nest.

It's not over yet.

She approached the dome, assessing her conditions. It was difficult to overlook the rib. She had taken several forceful blows to the spine and neck, which would need examination. There were the shallow slices on her cheek and a busted lip. Bruises were forming in patches along the front of her body. Noticing a sharp sting in her hand, she realized the heat from the emergency shotgun contraption had burned her fingers, too.

Alive is alive, she thought, taking a moment to retract the now-unloaded device back into its waiting position within her sleeve.

She entered the dome and turned to the Medellin cartel member who had addressed her before. He saw her and opened his mouth to speak. Nothing but a whistling noise emerged. While she was gone, the baby spider creatures had begun to tear away at his neck, leaving behind a hole leaking both breath and words.

Catalina grimaced, reaching for her waist. *There's no practical solution to this. The only way to transport everyone is to ask for the help of their friends and family back in the town, which would put them all in danger in this dome. Even then, disconnecting them from the nest would surely cause immediate death. There's no reason for these children's parents to watch them die like this, surrounded by these monsters. Hesitating any longer just drags this tragedy out for everyone. Sofía is safe. At least I saved one life today.*

Catalina withdrew a Glock, aimed, and fired; the man went limp. The baby monsters buzzed in agitation at the loud noise.

She turned her pistol to the young boy next to the dead man. The boy's eyes fluttered, barely conscious. Two other nearby children weakly turned their heads, their gazes delirious.

Pop. Pop. Pop.

Catalina's shoulders felt heavier with each shot fired. She moved around the wall of the dome, pulling the trigger as she encountered a new child or adult. Most were quiet, and those still awake found a way to avert their gaze, allowing a swift end to their hell.

Eventually, Catalina reached the young, sobbing girl she'd seen when first entering the dome.

The girl trembled within her cocoon, adhered to the wall. Everything below the girl's waist was already gone. The spider creatures crawled in a line from holes along her torso, carrying out what appeared to be bits of intestine. The girl's cheeks, while still untouched by the monsters, streaked with tears.

"Please . . . don't . . ." She choked out in Spanish between sobs. "I'll be okay. Please."

Catalina shook her head and gestured for the girl to close her eyes. The girl pursed her lips and shook her head back, the movement vicious enough to disturb the spider creatures above her head.

"Don't kill me. Please."

Catalina lowered her head and sighed.

"Please don't, miss. You don't want to do this."

Catalina lifted her gun.

"Miss, I'm not ready to d—"

Pop.

The girl's head fell forward, lifeless.

Catalina turned away, dropping her Glock as she buried her head in her hands. Blinded by her black gloves, she wandered in the direction of the nest's entrance. After a moment, she looked back up, turning to face the interior. Blood splattered the cottony walls behind each victim. The baby monsters squirmed on top of each other, at war over the corpses.

Removing her bandolier, she examined it. She had three thermite canisters remaining, and she reached for them. The cool metal pressed against her burned fingers as she pulled the pins.

The bandolier curved from her outstretched arm into the center of the nest. A massive spiral of flame splashed across the bodies of the children and the cartel men, setting them ablaze. The spider creatures withered away, eradicating what she hoped was the last living traces of the monster that plagued the village of La Encarnación.

Catalina made her way back through the forest, retracing her steps past the torn leaves and broken branches the Man had created. It wasn't long before she could see the orange light of the blaze she kindled earlier in the evening. She drew abreast of the fire, stopped at the edge of the clearing of her first battle, and picked up the elephant gun she had tossed. Continuing around the flaming trees and scorched earth, Catalina maintained a steady pace back toward town.

With proper direction, the townspeople can dig a dirt trench around the flames before they spread too far. Moist as the vegetation is around here, it won't be long until the fire begins to dissipate. Considering the weather—

Catalina's thoughts were arrested at the edge of the forest.

Through the last few trees, she saw the bright light of a third fire. One she hadn't started.

In the town.

The tavern and inn she occupied only hours ago was in flames. Ash floated around the buildings while the fingers of flame reached into the starry night sky. Smoke floated through the streets, highlighting the muzzle flashes of intermittent gunfire. Catalina squinted and stepped forward.

Medellín.

Men in street clothes with bandanas over their mouths ran around the building, firing automatic rifles into the neighboring homes. They pulled people from doors and windows, throwing them to the ground before continuing their warpath. In the dirt near the tavern, a woman in a burgundy dress lay motionless.

Is this a response to the fight earlier? Is this because of me? Catalina stepped forward once more, clearing the tree line. Her boot met a soft resistance, and she pulled back. Beneath her heel was a small leg connected to a body in a white nightgown.

Sofía.

The girl lay face down in a pool of blood. The red stained her dress, leaving it a sickening pink shade. As Catalina bent down, more gunfire erupted from the town. A few stray bullets flew past, splintering against the trees, ruffling the forest foliage.

Catalina looked back at the new bullet holes in the bark, down at Sofía, then forward at the muzzle flashes in the smoke, piecing together what had happened. She clenched her jaw hard enough to create a grinding noise with her teeth, and she formed fists tight enough to evoke droplets of blood from her open wounds.

Monsters.

Catalina rose, her black cloak billowing around her shaded form. The darkness changed her into a fantasma, much like her mother. Unlike her mother, though, *this* fantasma was corporeal.

Corporeal and vengeful.

Punctuating the thought, her hand reached down to her thigh and withdrew the Grizzly pistol. The wind ruffled the cloak around her as she moved, as if she floated toward the town, rather than walked. Screams and gunfire grew louder, the smell of smoke more potent. She racked the slide of her gun, chambering a new round.

Catalina melted into and out of the shadows, the smoke obscuring the moonlight and leaving her invisible. From within the darkness there was movement, and the cold steel of a gun barrel was the first part of the shadow that crossed the town's border.

Her hunt was far from over.

Alberta, Canada
May 1, 2011-B

Stacey opened his eyes to the sound of birds chirping outside his window. Their music made him smile, but the sounds of honking traffic came into focus as well, and he rolled his eyes. He turned over in bed, but Sam was still asleep. He shuffled under the covers, wrapping his arms around the man.

"Good morning, handsome," he whispered.

Sam's eyes fluttered open, and he leaned in to kiss Stacey. "Hey there."

The pair rose from the bed, shedding their blankets. As Stacey's feet hit the floor, a small migraine headache formed behind his eyes. He rubbed his temple.

"Headaches coming back?" Sam asked.

Stacey turned. Sam stood there in his white t-shirt and baby-blue pajama pants. He yawned, highlighting the dark stubble on his jaw. Every day, Sam's hair got a little greyer, though it contrasted nicely against his naturally black hair.

"Yeah, just a little bit. It's no big deal." Stacey shrugged it off.

"Well," Sam said, a tinge of concern creeping into his voice, "let me know if you change your mind about going to the doctor. I worry about you."

Sam wandered into the bathroom, the shower squeaking to life. Stacey went to the window and looked outside. The birds had since flown away, and fifteen stories below, he could see the mesh of cars forming the morning's traffic. Stacey tapped on the window before turning to dress.

He opened his closet and pulled out a sharply-creased brown-and-green uniform, the shower stopping as he began to don it. There was a pause while Sam dried himself off. Stacey reached for a thick folder filled with documents on top of the dresser. The bathroom door opened, and Sam emerged wrapped in a towel.

"Is it time already?" Sam asked.

Stacey sighed. "Yeah, it was extremely last minute. Less time to drag out good-byes than I usually get."

Sam started to dress himself as well, throwing on jeans and a blue cotton t-shirt. "They didn't say anything about where you were going this time?"

By "they," his husband referred to the Canadian Special Operations Forces Command, or CANSOFCOM. Stacey's job.

"Nope," Stacey replied. "I'll be briefed on the details in-transit. I already have a private plane waiting at the airport."

"Let me take you, then! It's my day off anyway. That way I see you a little longer before you're gone for who-knows-how-long."

Stacey noted Sam's eagerness and gave a wide grin. "Hell yeah. Let me just go be vain for a second."

He walked into the bathroom, wiped the steam from Sam's shower off the mirror, and stood at attention. In front of him stood a crisply-dressed black man in military attire. His hair was buzzed all the way down to his scalp. He admired how the uniform clung to his body; muscular from his training, but slender, like a swimmer.

Satisfied, Stacey turned to leave, but the sunlight glinted from the bedroom windowsill. He immediately felt a searing pain behind his eyes, and even as he backed away, the fluorescent bathroom lights seemed as bright as the center of a bonfire. He covered his face with his arm, drowning out the bombardment of lights, small tears forming in the corners of his eyes. The pain subsided after a few seconds, and he wiped at his face.

Stacey walked back into the bedroom to see Sam pulling a jacket from the closet.

"Oh, don't put that on," Stacey chided. "It's so tacky."

Sam smiled at Stacey's criticism and shrugged on a thick nylon bomber jacket. Dark green stripes—Sam's self-proclaimed "racing stripes"—ran down the arms and sides of the jacket, breaking up its otherwise burnt orange. It ended at the top with a tapered collar. "But it's my favorite."

Stacey sighed. "Fine, fine. But I'm still going to give you so much shit for wearing it."

Sam chuckled. "Fair enough."

Abbottabad, Pakistan
May 2, 2011-B

The military transport rumbled along the dirt roads on the outskirts of the small town of Abbottabad. Inside was a spacious, canopy-covered compartment with a series of seats lined along the two wider walls. Stacey, adorned in full tactical military gear, gripped his service rifle and his black, boxy toolkit in his lap. The vehicle was losing momentum, and Stacey looked up at the other five operatives sitting on either side of him. The truck came to a stop.

The four men and one woman all wore their green, battle-ready ensembles. Each carried their own assault equipment, though the specifications of their loadout varied in minor ways. Stacey had been relatively friendly with every one of them at different points in his CANSOFCOM history.

Ben and Adam, stocky, rugged Québécois, were snickering to one another in the corner opposite Stacey. Stacey looked away. He didn't want to be involved in another one of their practical jokes.

Xavier sat silent across from Stacey, reading a pocket-sized novel.

"What'cha reading?" Stacey asked him in a friendly tone.

Xavier didn't respond, and Stacey shrugged. The British Columbian was one of those withdrawn, aloof, artist types. Not an uncommon attitude.

Daanis, sitting to Stacey's left, nudged him in the ribs, smiling. "Don't worry about him. He's channeling the spirit of Glooscap. I told you about Glooscap, right?"

Stacey smiled back at the Nova Scotian Mi'kmaq native. "Yes, Daanis. That's one of your most popular stories."

She chuckled. "Well, it's not *my* story, of course. It's much older than me."

Stacey rolled his eyes at her attempts to be mysterious. "All the same . . ."

The giant, burly, bearded man to Stacey's right grumbled, interrupting them. Stacey shot him a side-glance.

"Did you say something, Lincoln?" he asked.

Lincoln shook his head. Stacey turned away; as impressive as the man was in combat, his relentless irascibility outshone his skill.

The sound of another vehicle approaching caught his attention. It was the middle of the night, so the headlights outlined the back canopy of Stacey's transport as they pulled up to the rear. Boots landed on dirt and rock, and a series of footsteps traipsed in the CANSOFCOM operatives' direction.

The curtain flung open, sending the headlight beams shining into their truck. Heat burned in Stacey's temple, as if the lights were growing brighter and brighter. Through the pain, the beam turned a shade of orange. He held up his hand, barely able to make out the shadows of people standing a few paces away.

"Hey! Can you turn those off?" Stacey demanded.

"Is this the CANSOFCOM unit that was requested?" came a deep, rasping reply.

Stacey glanced back at the other members of his current team. Though each of their personalities were normally different in wild and noticeable ways, everyone suddenly carried the same calm, quiet demeanor. Was it nerves?

Adam looked up. "Yeah, that's us."

"Okay." The shadow signaled behind him, and the headlights turned off, much to Stacey's relief.

Six men in black body armor, carrying automatic rifles, clambered up onto the CANSOFCOM transport vehicle and filed into the available seats not occupied by Stacey's team. Between the bulk of their equipment and the rags around their mouths to keep out dirt, Stacey couldn't notice any distinguishing features of their new friends. One of the men, sitting in the other back corner of the truck, leaned, forward, offering his hand to Adam. They exchanged a brief, cordial handshake.

"This is DEVGRU," the man said. "We're sorry for the smoke and mirrors, but we have reason to believe there are eyes and ears close to this mission who don't share our best interest. That's why you're here; the five men with me are the only ones attached to this that I can trust right now in U.S. ground forces. Outsourcing firepower from Canada's sharpest Spec Ops men and women seemed like a wise alternative, and your superior officer agreed."

Stacey furrowed his brow. "So, this isn't an official JSOC mission?"

The man looked at him. "What's your name?"

"Private Fields, sir."

"Private?" The man glanced toward Adam. "What happened to Major Edwards?"

Daanis waved her hand dismissively. "He grew ill a few days

ago, sir. Private Fields was our alternative EOD; he's a damn fine explosives tech, though."

The man nodded. "Well, Fields, welcome to Operation Neptune Spear."

Lincoln grumbled, "What exactly does this operation entail, mister . . ."

"Johnson. Captain Johnson." The captain gestured at the other five DEVGRU members sitting with him. "You'll find that they all answer to Johnson tonight. Got it?"

Lincoln rolled his shoulders. "Okay. Sure."

Captain Johnson pulled the dust rag from his face so he could be heard more clearly. "And what we're doing tonight, ladies and gentlemen, is ending the reign of Osama Bin Laden."

He slammed his fist against the wall that separated the operatives from the driver, and the vehicle bucked before moving forward.

"Originally the goal was capture if possible, kill if necessary. However, we've had far too many unexpected setbacks along the way to afford that distinction anymore. His allies have provided him with intelligence and resources that, quite frankly, leaves me scared shitless."

"Go in, shoot, leave, get a medal," Ben summarized. "I assume you found him?"

"Yeah, he has a compound here in Abbottabad, just south of the military academy. But it won't be that easy. The compound is likely wired with traps, hence our need for a competent EOD." He gestured at Stacey. "Our intelligence team, if they can be fully trusted, tells us that the compound is filled with other people, not just Bin Laden. We're looking at two, maybe three dozen potential hostiles."

Johnson paused, glancing throughout the cramped space. "Let me be *absolutely* clear. Stopping Bin Laden takes precedence over all other lives in this town. Yours, mine, or the possible toddlers strapped in dynamite and AK-47s. DEVGRU doesn't generally operate alongside CANSOFCOM, and I want to make sure we're on the same page. Are we?"

The six Canadian operatives nodded, almost in unison.

"Good. We have the element of surprise. It's clear now that someone is leaking our information to the enemy. So, all official records will state a planned attack by helicopter, set for tomorrow night. I pray this is all the edge we'll need."

The transport vehicle shuddered to a stop. The captain checked his watch. "We're a little after midnight. Let's make this quick."

The dozen operatives quickly, but quietly, hefted themselves from the truck. It waited, idling. Stacey took in the surroundings. There were flat expanses of dirt in every direction. The only object visible was the tall, tan building in front of him, surrounded by high walls of the same color and composition. Strangely, all the lights appeared to be off.

Maybe they don't run night security to avoid suspicion, Stacey guessed.

The twelve men fanned out, rifles raised, green laser sights pointed to the compound gate. Stacey moved ahead of the pack to investigate. There was patterning in the dirt that made it clear where mines were buried around the entrance. He gestured for the group to gather around him.

"See those rings? Avoid them. I could blow them with the laser I packed," he patted the box on his hip, "But then we'll lose the element of surprise. Just be careful."

They nodded and filed behind him in a line to avoid any unfriendly ordinances. When Stacey reached the gate, he paused. There was nothing other than iron bars, but the door itself swung inward. He retrieved a small flashlight and shined it through the bars at the ground. There, glinting in the light, was a thin wire. He traced the wiring up to where it embedded itself into the walls at head-height on either side of the gate.

"Okay, so . . ." Stacey paused, surveying the walls above him, but they were too high to climb by hand. "We have an issue. Explosives are set to trigger once the gate opens enough to upset the trip wire. We aren't equipped to climb around it. I can set a controlled charge to detonate the explosives. Thoughts?"

Captain Johnson stood solemnly. Stacey felt the small pinch of his migraine return.

"This isn't my preference," Johnson replied, "But I say we blow it and enter loud and fast. I'm not as close to Bin Laden as I'd like to be before alerting everyone, but we'll make it work. Won't we, soldiers?"

"HOO-YAH," the other five DEVGRU members whispered at once.

"Alright, then," Stacey said. He retrieved a breaching explosive and some putty from his bag and adhered it to the gate, entering something into the device as he worked. Stepping back, he unspooled a long red wire, motioning for the others to follow him to a safe distance. Once they were out of the assumed blast radius, he opened his hand to the group with all five fingers showing.

5 . . .

He dropped one finger per second, visualizing the countdown.

4 . . .

3 . . .

2 . . .

1 . . .

Stacey squeezed the detonator in his hand.

The gate exploded from its hinges, and as it did so, the wire-activated traps in the walls shattered the concrete with their own fire and fury. Stacey and Xander rushed in, followed by four of the Johnsons, then Lincoln and Daanis, the last two Johnsons, and finally Ben and Adam. They filed into the courtyard like ants into a colony while Stacey searched in the dark for more mines or traps.

It only took a few seconds to pass safely from the gate to the side door of the house. Stacey tried to examine the frame and knob, but one of the Johnsons pushed him aside and blasted the entire locking mechanism from its hinges with a shotgun, sending the door freely swinging open. They rushed forward.

What awaited inside was nothing like what Stacey had expected.

Moving into the large, multi-story home, he discovered an open living-room-style floor area filled with cots and mattresses. Blankets, pillows and various knick-knacks indicated it as a sleeping area.

But why so many people? And where were they all right now?

The thought had no more than crossed Stacey's mind when his vision adjusted a little better. Along the back of the room, from one side of the wall to the other, were ten to fifteen shadows of varying heights. As he raised his flashlight to see them better, a loud alarm sounded throughout the compound, and searing white floodlights clicked on all around him. The intense pain from behind his eyes caused him to drop to one knee, the rifle shaking in his hands. Heavy boots stomped from the floor above Stacey's head, approaching a staircase on his left.

The DEVGRU and CANSOFCOM operatives opened fire on the group in front of them.

His eyes refocused, and Stacey could see three children, four adolescents, and eight adults scrambling in front of him. They were not all Pakistani, however. In fact, most did not even look Middle Eastern. He saw a relative rainbow of skin tones and a mix of differing physical features. One of the children looked Inuit, and the man gripping their shoulder had very dark skin, his clothing similar to what Stacey had seen on a mission in Botswana. The mixtures of tattered clothing gave Stacey the impression of refugees, not terrorists.

One of the Johnsons on Stacey's right muttered, "Who they hell are *they*?"

Stacey barely heard the words over the gunfire. It was too late to ponder, anyway. They'd already engaged the "enemy."

The possible Tswana stepped in front of the incoming bullets, shielding the child from harm. Instead of penetrating his torso, though, they ricocheted off his skin with an awkward wobbling sound, flying into the walls and furniture around him. He extended both arms, and much to Stacey's surprise, they stretched out like taffy to strike both Lincoln and the Johnson next to Stacey. The two men yelped in shock and pain as they flew out of Stacey's field of vision. He moved to help them, but he didn't have a chance.

The footsteps from above reached the staircase.

He and two of the DEVGRU operatives turned their rifles to address the incoming threat. Nothing appeared within their line of sight for several seconds, though the footsteps did not cease. Like a ghost, a white-haired albino man in jeans and a white t-shirt suddenly popped into reality a few centimeters from Stacey's face. Before Stacey could let out a startled cry, the albino man punched him in the gut with one fist and the chin with the other, sending him reeling backward and collapsing to the floor. The two men with Stacey released bursts of machine-gun fire, but he vanished. The bullets passed through air, striking the staircase banister instead.

The albino man reappeared behind one of the Johnsons with a dagger in his hand. He jabbed it into his side, and the DEVGRU operative cried out in pain, stumbling a little. Stacey crawled to his feet, but the attacker noticed, disappearing and reappearing in front of Stacey to kick him in the face. Stars filled Stacey's vision, and everything grew blurry. He collapsed to the floor and felt wetness on his upper lip as his nose began bleeding.

Gunfire raged all around him, bullets whizzing over his head, and he could hear the slick swishing noise of the albino man's knife slicing into the operatives. He wiped his face and rolled to his shaky feet just in time to avoid the pattering of stray projectiles exploding into the space where he laid. The albino man stood over one of the DEVGRU men with his knife raised, about to strike a final blow.

Stacey screamed, leaving his rifle behind in the heat of the moment, and leapt at the attacker. He tackled the albino man to the ground, knocking the knife from his hand, but the man vanished, leaving him alone on the ground. The man reappeared a few steps away, reaching for his knife.

Before the albino man could retrieve his weapon, a cluster of bullets buzzed past Stacey and pattered into the assailant's chest like raindrops on a tin roof. The man fell over, bloodied and dead. Stacey looked behind him to see Xander approaching with an expressionless face, smoke pouring from his rifle barrel.

Stacey rolled to his feet and ran to pick up his own rifle. Around him was a blur of motion, a violent dance of maddening proportions. Some of the hostiles in the house were already dead or incapacitated. Lincoln, Adam, and two of the DEVGRU operatives fought the seemingly elastic Tswana, rolling and hopping to avoid his long, serpentine strikes. A woman in silk pajamas rushed past Stacey to attack Ben. As she drew close, her hands glowed with a purple light. Before she could use the light, Stacey and his comrade fired into her face, stopping her permanently.

More footsteps pounded above his head, and he turned to read-dress the staircase. A woman, in some kind of robe and sporting a pink-and-black pixie haircut, ran into view, preceding a gust of wind. She rocketed over the banister, landing feet-first on the far wall. She pushed away in a blur, now only a few paces from Stacey. She reached behind her back and withdrew a short, wide sword with a decorative handle.

Oh, shit, Stacey thought, snatching his rifle from the floor.

The woman raised her sword, but Stacey unloaded the rest of his magazine in her direction; he was taking no chances, considering the situation. Instead of dodging or being struck by the bullets, though, her body separated in a dozen different directions. Multiple transparent torsos split away from her in the milliseconds of her attack, each one carrying her head and arms to a unique location, though all remained rooted to her at the waist. Each version of the woman had one of those swords, all using the flat side of the weapon as a shield against the bullets.

The grinding noise of lead striking metal filled the room, and the bullets flew away from the woman's unearthly form, burying themselves into the walls, floor and ceiling. With another gust of air, the woman appeared before Stacey, swinging her sword down toward his head. Instinctively, he extended his hands to defend himself, but his vision blurred. Before he could register what happened, he was standing halfway across the room. The woman's blade dug into the floor, and she looked up at him, a bewildered expression on her face.

Her eyes drifted to his hands.

Stacey looked down as well, turning his palms upward. They were smoking, but they didn't feel much warmer than normal. He realized his rifle was gone, so he searched the room and found it lying close to the woman with the sword. The grip of the weapon, where he had last held it, was red-hot.

His headache returned, stronger than ever. The floodlights intensified, focusing like lasers into his eyes.

The pixie-haired woman lifted her sword in time to smack the flat of it against one of the passing DEVGRU operatives, knocking him to the ground. Gunfire erupted, and she split into her multiple selves again, deflecting the approaching bullets. All the while, she studied Stacey, observant of his confusion and distress. The woman took a few slow, nonthreatening steps in his direction, and she opened her mouth to speak in English.

"Do you know what you're—"

Small-arms fire cracked nearby, and a hole appeared in her forehead, spraying faint red mist. She fell face-down onto the floor, revealing Captain Johnson holding a pistol. Blood pooled around her head, and Stacey saw the red silhouette of a giant butterfly embroidered on the back of her robe.

"Good work, Private," Captain Johnson yelled over the gunfire. "Where's your—"

More heavy noises above them sounded just seconds before a wide hole exploded from the ceiling. Four people dropped into the chaos, the largest of them landing directly on top of two DEVGRU men. The three smaller people wore hoodies, jeans, and scarves over their mouth. It was difficult to tell the exact size, build, or appearance of the three newcomers due to their clothing. They sported machine pistols aimed at Stacey's and Johnson's teams.

The fourth person, the larger one, wore long, grey sweatpants and nothing else. As the smoke cleared, Stacey realized his inhuman nature. Instead of skin, muscle, hair and bone, his body appeared to be made of thousands of small, pastel-colored pieces of glass all pressed together.

If Stacey squinted, he could see through the person's chest to the other side of the room, albeit distorted by the refracted, colored light. As he moved—his motions just as fluid as anyone else's—the floodlights sparkled colorfully across his body. It reminded Stacey of the sun passing through the mosaic windows of the ornate church he visited once or twice as a young boy.

The three hoodie-wearing assailants opened fire on Stacey's teams, and the teams returned the favor. The mosaic man stepped off the two unconscious—*hopefully*, Stacey thought—DEVGRU men and wrapped one hand around Lincoln's neck. The burly man choked out some words Stacey couldn't hear and drew his sidearm. Lincoln fired his pistol directly at the mosaic man's forehead, but the bullets just bounced away. The glass giant tossed Lincoln across the room, and he limply struck the wall.

The pressure and heat behind Stacey's eyes nearly overwhelmed his focus, but he pushed past the pain to take advantage of an opportunity. He retrieved a grenade from his vest and pulled the pin. "Live one out!"

He lobbed it at the mosaic man's torso, intending for it to land at his feet, but the grenade never reached its destination. Swift as a striking cobra, the inhuman assailant plucked the explosive from the air with one hand and clenched it in their fist. There was a flash of light and a muffled vibration, and the mosaic pieces all along the thing's body glowed their pastel colors with even brighter intensity. He opened his hand, and smoking bits of metal fell from his palm.

That last flash of light was too much for Stacey. It propelled his migraine beyond the point of reconciliation. Faint, orange light filled his peripheral vision; the floodlights were so intense that he could *hear* them in his mind. The inside of his skull felt like a hot iron seared his brain. He had struggled with milder headaches like this for years, but nothing so incapacitating ever occurred before.

Maybe I should have listened to Sam.

He stumbled across the floor, tears in his eyes, almost tripping over the Tswana's dead body. There was a giant, bloodless hole in the man's chest, and Stacey felt a lump in his throat when he noticed the Inuit child lying on their stomach nearby, lifeless arms still reaching out for the man. *What did we do?*

As he collapsed to the floor, pressing his back against the nearest wall, he heard something strange . . .

"We should use it!" Adam yelled, laying down cover fire against the mosaic person near the staircase.

"We should use it!" Xander said, gunning down the attacker in a red hoodie.

"We should use it!" Daanis called, digging through a satchel at her side.

"We should use it!" Lincoln muttered, otherwise still unconscious in the spot he'd been thrown.

"We should use it!" Ben grunted, engaged in hand-to-hand combat with the attacker in a brown hoodie.

"Wait, what?" One of the Johnsons replied, his team in a firefight against a heavily-armored assailant Stacey hadn't noticed before.

Stacey squinted through his pain to watch the fight unfold.

The CANSOFCOM team worked in tandem to draw the mosaic man away from the walls, exposing him on all sides to the Canadian operatives. Daanis retrieved a fat, silver tube from her bag and pressed a button on the side. Six metal spikes protruded from one end. For a moment she waited, poised, while Adam and Xander directed gunfire at the mosaic person's face to keep them off-balance. When she seemed sure, Daanis pounced at their enemy. The silver tube's spikes plunged into his crystalline back, adhering the device.

Stacey felt like he might vomit. He wasn't sure how much nausea stemmed from the confusing, messy situation rather than his headache. He honestly felt like it was one hundred percent for each of those reasons, which must be why he felt *two* hundred percent nauseous. Something filled his nostrils; after a moment, he realized it was the smell of burning ozone.

Something's wrong.

The device Daanis planted was unknown to Stacey's personal knowledge of conventional weaponry. It looked and felt almost alien, and as he watched, it behaved as such, too. It offered a low hum that grew louder and increased in pitch with every passing second, like the charging noise of a Polaroid camera. The recipient reached his thick, glassy arms behind his back, scrambling to remove the device.

Daanis stepped closer. "You can't fight forever," Daanis hummed in a low voice, her tone disturbingly gleeful.

"You can't fight forever," Ben growled, shoving his knife into the neck of the combatant in a brown hoodie.

"You can't fight forever," Lincoln murmured, pulling himself to his feet.

"You can't fight forever." Adam laughed as he threw the fighter in a green hoodie to their knees, shooting them in the back of the head with his sidearm, execution-style.

"You can't fight forever," Xander huffed, removing the weapons from the two unconscious DEVGRU operatives for no clear reason.

"Okay, what the fuck?" The same Johnson responded.

The device reached a peak, and it offered a slight, organic shudder, like an insect burying itself into the dirt. When it did, the mosaic man screamed in pain as he shattered into thousands of crystalline pieces. Both teams ducked to avoid the shower of sharp points and edges.

The Johnsons convened in the middle of the room, their armored attacker apparently incapacitated.

"Where's our target?" one said. "Where's Bin Laden?"

The pain in Stacey's head reached critical mass. He clutched the side of his face, digging his fingernails into his skin, begging for it to stop. Involuntary tears flowed from the corners of his eyes, dripping onto the floor.

"Over here," one of the other Johnsons called out.

In the far corner of the room, near where Stacey had first seen the occupants in the dark, was a man who looked very similar to the photographs of Osama bin Laden. He wore off-white pajamas, stained red from a cluster of bullet holes. His open eyes stared back at the operatives, sightless and empty.

"My God," Captain Johnson said. "We finally got him."

He turned to address the rest of the room. "Now can anyone tell me what in the hell we just saw?" His query yielded no response. "Have any of you, during any ops, come across . . . body modifications . . . like this?" More silence. "How would Al-Qaeda, or ISIL, or any related groups even afford this kind of technology?"

The other DEVGRU members looked uncomfortable. The CANSOFCOM team, on the other hand, stared at him, all five faces unblinking.

"Also, these aren't Pakistanis," continued the captain. "Hell, most of them aren't even from this continent! Who on earth did we just have a firefight with?"

The five Canadians smiled together, not one of them out of synch. Adam, Ben, Xander, Daanis and Lincoln spoke as one, harmonizing in the same playful, sing-song voice. "They're just insects, Captain. Insects trying to topple mountains."

With that, the CANSOFCOM team produced long, black sticks resembling cattle prods and jabbed them into the four standing DEVGRU operatives. The men seized up as electricity forced its way into their bodies. The Canadian team withdrew their prods, and the American team collapsed to the floor in spasms.

Stacey put a hand to his mouth, holding his breath; the adrenaline produced by his fear was almost as intense as the burning behind his eyes. Slowly, as quietly as he could, he crawled backward, away from the CANSOFCOM team.

What happened to the people I knew? Where was Xander's focus; his intensity? Why would Daanis sacrifice her drive for success by compromising a mission like this?

Ben had a wife and two children. Surely, he wouldn't risk losing them. Adam, though playful, had never demonstrated such irresponsibility. Lincoln? Okay, Stacey could believe Lincoln was a secret traitor or psychopath. Nonetheless, their synergy disturbed him. The dialogue and body language seemed fake, as if five mannequins had come to life and tried to emulate human behavior.

"Ah, yes," they turned in Stacey's direction, their words in synch. "The replacement."

Stacey used one shaking hand to unclasp the sidearm on his hip. His thumb chattered against the side of the weapon as he removed the safety. He curled up, knees to his chest; with both arms outstretched, the black pistol pointed forward.

"Hello, replacement. Mother is hungry."

Footsteps drew closer, and Stacey's finger rested on the trigger of his gun. Fear and pain caused such a quiver he couldn't get a clear shot on any approaching target. He held his breath, pointed the jittery pistol at the incomer's center mass, and pulled the trigger. The gun cracked and the muzzle flashed, revealing Lincoln standing there, an insane smile plastered on his face. Lincoln stumbled back, clutching his chest.

The flash from the muzzle sent Stacey's headache spiraling out of control. He dropped his gun and collapsed to the floor, shuddering as if feverish. Lincoln, who seemed far too composed after being shot, leaned over and picked Stacey up, throwing him over his shoulder. Stacey's head and arms drooped down Lincoln's back, sweat forming on his skin and evaporating into steam before it dripped to the floor.

Adam, Ben, Daanis, and Xander stood in a parabola. Through the tears and orange light, Stacey could see the six DEVGRU operatives lined up. They were only unconscious, as far as he could tell, though stripped of all weapons. When Ben saw Stacey on Lincoln's shoulder, he retrieved the cattle prod and held it out.

"The replacement makes seven for Mother," he said.

His cheeks stretched into an insidious smile that went well beyond a normal grin. It was as if he was waiting for someone to take their picture, but he didn't know when, so he was holding his happy face, just in case. The others shared the look, their eyes glimmering, glassy as doll's eyes. Stacey almost detected a deranged glee glinting behind their pupils.

"Time to go to sleep, replacement," they intonated at the same time, their different pitches and dialects merging into one amused, sinister voice.

Lincoln dropped Stacey to the floor. When he landed, a sharp pain went through his back, though it was nothing compared to the orange light stabbing his eyes. Stacey pressed his eyelids closed with all the force he could muster, willing the fire and the light and the agony to disappear.

Much to his amazement, it did.

Abbottabad, Pakistan
May 2, 2011-B

The orange light faded.

The force in his head receded.

The tremors throughout his body stilled.

An itching sensation replaced the pain in each of his eyes, focused into a small spot right in the front. The feeling made him uneasy, as if ants crawled across his pupils. Ben's cattle prod crackled close to Stacey's face, and he opened his eyes.

Everything was gone.

Instead of sand, walls, people, ceiling, and cattle prod, he saw stars. Billions and billions of orange stars. Though he found it hard-pressed to point out a difference between each orange speck of light, he could *feel* the difference.

A thick cloud of orange lights hovered in front of him, surrounding him. He saw the clouds everywhere, in any space described as empty. The lights constantly moved and expanded away, and he *felt* the motion. Tiny lights of carbon left his mouth as his exhaled; tiny lights of oxygen flowed into his body, entering his bloodstream.

An orange column of aluminum lights coalesced in front of him, working together with copper, carbon and hydrogen to produce small, excited specks of electrons. Thin, orange strands connected the molecules like threads in a spider's web. Surrounding the other end of the column was a mass of orange dots composed of hydrogen, nitrogen, oxygen, carbon, calcium, and phosphorus particles.

He squeezed and reopened his eyes. The orange starfield vanished, replaced with the scenery he already knew. The clouds of lights dispersed, and he returned to breathing invisible air. The column of orange dots and strands dissolved into the cattle prod; the mass around was Ben's hand. The device stopped crackling, and the electricity at the end vanished. Ben looked curious and amused. The rest of the team mirrored his look.

Stacey rose to his feet in the middle of the silent room, uneasy and hesitant. Daanis stepped forward, though when she opened her mouth, all five of them said, in unison, "One of the Refined. Mother will be so proud."

Ben reactivated his cattle prod and continued his advance.

Stacey pressed his eyelids together, willing the itchy, burning light to return. When he opened his eyes, the room once more became a mass of glowing orange particles. The four standing galaxies behind what he recognized as Ben reacted to him, as if they knew what he was seeing. Though his eyes moved to Ben's cattle prod, he could *feel* them as they drew their knives and guns. The simple wavelengths of visible light no longer limited his vision. He knew everything around him simultaneously, and by identifying the nature of the orange particles in their pockets and behind their barriers, he knew what they would do before they even acted.

Ben struck out with the weapon, but Stacey sidestepped him, stumbling. He held out an arm to steady himself, but his hand didn't connect with the wall or floor. Instead, his fingers clutched at millions of those tiny, orange strands holding together the gaseous particles in the air. To his amazement, they supported his weight, despite creating a pressure no more noticeable than a falling cobweb. Stacey pushed against the threads, and as they rebounded, he felt some of their warmth pass into the palm of his hand.

Instead of springing him back to his feet, the threads of the particles pushed that warmth through his body, like a shiver. As he left contact with them, his stomach dropped from the sensation of sudden g-force, as if he was dropping from an airplane. Stacey propelled across the room, knocking Ben and Daanis to the ground in the process. He reached out with both hands to call upon the orange threads all around him, clutching at individual ones with enough finesse to slow his propulsion without sending him flying back in the other direction. Still, he reached the far wall in less than a second, and his right shoulder stung as it struck the surface with a low *thunk*.

Stacey blinked to change his vision, surveying the three CANOFSCOM operatives still standing. Both of his hands were hot; of more concern, though, was the smoke rising from his fingertips.

He had apparently moved across the room at a speed they couldn't track, because those still on their feet were looking in the direction he had come from, rather than at him. Stacey decided to take advantage of the situation, placing his hand in the center of Lincoln's back.

I may not see them, but I know they're there. What happens when they break?

Stacey closed his eyes and willed his hands to touch the orange strands connecting the dots of carbon in the skin of Lincoln's back. He pressed forward, hard, both with his arm and with his mind, breaking apart the strands linking his starfield together and releasing the energy held there. The space in Lincoln's back under Stacey's hand glowed bright orange for a fraction of a second.

Then, it exploded.

A rapid-fire series of popping noises released so close to each other they couldn't be distinguished as a singular sound, like a sheet of bubble-wrap bursting all at once. Heat and smoke ejected from the middle of Lincoln's back, and the large man was hurled across the room like a ten-ton marionette. He slammed face-first into the wall where Stacey had just stood and collapsed to the floor, revealing a smoking crater in his back, as large and as deep as if he had been struck by a cannonball.

Ben and Daanis were already crawling to their feet to rejoin Adam and Xander, even as Lincoln flew over their heads. The four remaining CANSOFCOM operatives jerked to look at Stacey.

"Oh, this one will make Mother very happy," they said with glee.

Stacey's heart pounded in his chest. "Stay back!" He yelled, holding a hand up in an attempt to bluff them.

Adam and Xander raised their rifles, training the weapons on Stacey's chest. "No, we don't think so."

Ben and Daanis retrieved their machine guns as well, and all four took a menacing step in Stacey's direction.

Creaaaaaaaaaaaaaaaaak . . .

Everyone froze.

Stacey's arm tremored with fright. The four cocked their heads in a gesture of curiosity, all still in sync. Xander broke away from the other three toward an adjoining hallway from where the noise originated. The others remained very still. Waiting.

Silence.

"Wha—"

Xander flew, airborne, past the entrance of the hallway and out of sight. There was a spectacular crashing sound as he presumably struck another wall. Ben and Adam turned to aim their rifles at the hallway.

Silence again. "Oh my."

Adam was looking at Ben, suddenly suspended in an egg-shaped field of clear liquid. Ben scrambled in the fluid, trying to swim to the edge, but some force kept pulling him back to the center.

A high-pitched whining sound echoed down the dark hallway, its mechanical noise hypnotic in its unwavering consistency. A silhouette filled the doorway, outlined by arcs of crackling blue energy. It stepped forward, into the light.

A brown-skinned woman, with broad shoulders and a curvy, muscular build, wore some kind of padded, navy-blue armor along her body. A thick belt made of some kind of silver metal accented the suit, but it sported a disc where the buckle would be, encircled by a notched dial. The disc's diameter was similar to that of a base-ball, and something resembling fan blades spun in the center at a speed too high to see with clarity.

Reaching above and below the belt, embedded in the body armor, was a series of metallic, copper lines. They spread out from the woman's waist to create a sharp design all across her body, the pattern similar to the lines on a microchip. Some of those lines reached down the woman's arms and stopped at the copper-studded knuckles of her fingerless gloves. As Stacey watched, the fan on her belt produced arcs of electricity that raced along those copper circuits up to her arms, causing the knuckles to glow a bright blue.

The woman surveyed the scene, her expression daring them to make a move against her. She had a button nose and dark, frizzy hair. If it were lying flat, it would have been neck-length, but for her, it splayed up and out in every direction, creating a curly mess. Her eyes were hidden behind thick, circular goggles with mirrored lenses, reminiscent of those used for welding.

As Ben continued to struggle for air, Daanis and Adam opened fire on the woman. The bullets bounced away from her body, each one causing blue electrical sparks to shed away from her in the places they struck.

The woman seemed unfazed, even a little bored, and they redirected their gunfire toward her face. She simply raised a hand, as if shielding herself from the sun, placing her forearm between her eyes and their bullets.

The gunfire ceased, the two having emptied their weapons. They ejected their magazines, hurrying to retrieve new ones.

The woman, no worse for wear, said, "It was a nice try." Her voice was harsh and inhuman, as if she were speaking through some kind of voice-changing device. The tone, though, was distinctly American.

She dropped to one knee and lowered her head, planting both palms flat on the floor. Behind her, two people stood side-by-side: A tall figure in white and an amorphous phantom in black.

The figure in white already had its left arm raised in the direction of Ben's water-egg prison, as if to hold it in place. Daanis pulled her sidearm, and the figure gestured toward her with its free hand. A perfect sphere of clear liquid, the rough size of a bowling ball, shimmered into existence and wisped toward Daanis. It connected with her chest and splattered into droplets, though the force of the liquid projectile launched her through the open door of the house and back into the compound's courtyard.

Stacey backed against the nearest wall, trying to stay out of the way of this unconventional firefight.

The phantom in black raised its arms to produce something dark and glittering. Before Stacey fully registered the scene, machine-gun fire spat from the phantom's weapons toward Adam. The bullets pattered across Adam's torso, mostly absorbed by his body armor, before penetrating his neck and face in multiple areas. Blood burst from the back of his head, and he fell to the floor.

Stacey tried to run, to hide, but he couldn't make his legs move. The spectacles that had appeared before him held him captive.

Hot lead lit the hallway, coming from the direction where Xander had been catapulted. The phantom lifted its cape—or wing—or whatever it was that it wore. In any case, the bullets lost their momentum as they struck the makeshift shield. The figure in white held up its right arm, creating a flat, shimmering disc of water that spanned the hallway. Xander's gunfire couldn't penetrate it, either.

The woman in blue strode forward into the room, toward Ben, ignoring the new assault. She looked back at the other two newcomers. "Drop it," she said, her voice warbling electronically.

The egg of water holding Ben collapsed into a puddle, splashing across the floor. Ben fell with the water, but the woman caught him by the neck with one hand.

"Two things, and I'll be brief," she said, raising her voice above the gunfire in the background. "One, what exactly *is* the hotel?" Ben smiled, water leaking from his mouth. "Two, where is the center hub for the targeting facilities?"

Ben's voice went from playful to serious. "You are speaking with an officer of the Canadian military. Desist at once or you will be seen as hostile targets."

The woman let out a short laugh. "No. Ben Wilson died. You're just a disgusting imitation." She gripped tightly and jerked her wrist, snapping Ben's neck. Releasing him, and he crumpled to the floor.

Stacey turned to run from the murderer, but he stopped as he heard a thin sound, like a small piece of metal striking the ground. He looked at the doorway of the house and saw Daanis there, holding a grenade in each hand.

The woman in blue just stared at Daanis, and the figure in white stepped to her side. Stacey could now see a thin, tall man in jeans and a white hooded sweatshirt. The hood hid much of his face, but holes in his clothes revealed some kind of pearl-white armor lurking underneath. Behind him, the phantom in black stood next to Xander's body on the floor.

"How does it work?" asked the man in white, his tone surprisingly friendly. "Are you independent, like other mammals? Is there an insect-like connection? Can you communicate with the hotel, or with each other, remotely? I'd love to talk with you in more detail, if you want. You'd make a great study case."

Daanis offered another of those plastic smiles. "Mother says not to speak with strangers." She released the grenades handles.

The man in white sighed and made a hand gesture. Stacey's half of the room—and the part of the room with the newcomers—stayed completely dry, while water entirely submerged Daanis and the exit. The dividing wall seemed to hum.

Daanis still attempted to throw the grenades, but they didn't travel far; instead, they floated at an awkward diagonal angle, less than an arm's length away from her head. She dove to the floor, but it was too late. The explosives detonated with a deep roar, the sound muffled by the water. Though there was little flame, a heavy shock wave consumed Daanis, forcing a murky cloud of blood from her mouth as her lungs compressed. Seconds after the grenades detonated, the water splattered outward and collapsed, flooding the room at knee-height.

Daanis's face-down body floated with the current, finding itself stuck sideways in the door frame. Stacey turned to look at the three other people in the room while water rushed past his shins, pulling itself through the open door into the dry compound courtyard.

"Are you going to kill me, too?" he asked, his voice shaking.

The three ignored him, continuing their survey of the corpses surrounding them. He dropped his arms, watching them work. The phantom stepped into the light, revealing a small woman wrapped in black body armor and a thick cloak. Her face was stern and calculating, and she probably wasn't someone he'd want to upset.

The man in white crouched over the dead woman with the swords—the one who had tried to speak with Stacey. He looked up at the electric woman, his face scrunched up in sorrow.

"Battery, they got Butterfly," he said.

The woman in blue—Battery, Stacey supposed—turned to the man and sighed. She'd been checking on the small Inuit girl.

"Well, shit," she said. "I liked her."

The phantom held up a piece of the mosaic person's body, but she did not speak.

There was a pause, and the room was completely silent. Battery placed a hand to her ear, as if she was listening to something. Stacey shifted against the wall, still ankle-high in water and feeling more than a little uncomfortable.

"Wait, really?" Battery exclaimed after about thirty seconds, her voice more urgent than before. Her head snapped in Stacey's direction, her expression intense but unreadable. She gestured at the man in white. "Aquifer, make sure no one got missed on the second floor."

He nodded and flung his arms downward. The water still in the house swirled around his feet, bubbling, before launching him through the hole in the ceiling the mosaic man had made. Stacey heard his metal boots stomp around the floor above.

Battery pointed at Stacey. "Fields, right? Tell me about your eyes."

Stacey gulped. "What do you mean? I—"

She raised a hand to interrupt him. "I think we both know exactly what I'm referring to."

Stacey exhaled through his nose, apprehensive, his thoughts racing. *Should I comply? Should I fight? Either way might lead to my death.*

He opted to squeeze his eyelids together, willing the orange starfield to reappear. The dots and strands were all around him, some new and different, like the water on the floor. He looked at Battery and the other woman. The protons he'd seen at the end of Ben's cattle prod were everywhere around and inside Battery. He blinked, and his vision expanded. He realized the atoms pieced together to form proton-infused cells in her body. Her biology seemed almost symbiotic with electrical energy.

The other woman, however, was less interesting on an atomic level. She was just a normal human. Well, as normal as the others he had already seen through this new filter. There was plenty to look at *on* her, however. Stacey saw dozens of firearms, explosives, and bladed weapons. Not to mention the military-grade armor plating hefted along her slender stature. Stacey was impressed she could even stand in the gear, let alone engage in combat.

Who are these people?

Stacey blinked away the starfield. As his eyes readjusted, he saw his reflection in Battery's goggles, and he realized why everyone seemed to know what he was doing. For a brief moment, the centers of his eyes glowed a bright, burning orange, like two cigarette embers in a dark room. The light faded away as his normal vision returned.

The black-clad woman raised her hand to her chin, her expression studious. Battery had a wry smile on her face, and she raised her goggles, letting them rest on her forehead. Her root-beer-brown irises glimmered in the floodlights.

Aquifer clumped down the stairs behind Stacey. "No one's up there. Sorry, Battery."

Battery shook her head and motioned for him to come join the other two, in front of Stacey. "Silver lining, Aquifer. I think we found a new Refined."

"Oh, really?" He looked at Stacey. "What can you do?"

"I . . . I don't know," Stacey stammered. "I didn't know anything about this until right now." He examined his hands, which were still smoking a little. "I can see what everything is made of. I can make things explode." He looked up. "What is happening to me?"

In one deft motion, the cloaked woman reached behind her back and produced a black, sawed-off, pump-action shotgun.

"Whoa!" Stacey cried, holding his hands up in surrender.

"Cool it, Shadow," Battery added.

Shadow pumped the shotgun, and Stacey heard a bullet click into the chamber.

"Alright, easy," Aquifer said. "We need all the help we can get."

Shadow lowered her shotgun, making a series of hand gestures.

Stacey looked at Battery. "I'm sorry, I don't know—"

"Hush," Battery replied. "Don't interrupt while Shadow's talking."

Aquifer waited for Shadow to stop signing before he spoke. "She's right, Battery. We don't know much about Fields. But he *wasn't* at the hotel, and I'm going to go out on a limb and say we give him a chance."

Shadow shook her head and holstered her shotgun.

Battery reached for Stacey's arm, and he pulled away. Her eyebrows furrowed. "Let's go, Fields. You aren't safe here."

"Go?" Stacey replied. "Go where? We're in the damn desert."

She sighed. "You don't know us. You don't trust us. You *shouldn't* trust us. But you really want to stay here?"

She gestured at the bloody corpses scattered around them. The pile of DEVGRU operatives caught Stacey's eye.

"What about them?" he asked.

Aquifer gestured to the man resembling Osama bin Laden. "They got what they came for."

Battery made an angry face. "Even if they have no idea who he really was. What a waste."

Shadow made a quick, curt gesture toward Battery.

"Okay, okay, we're going," Battery said.

The three walked back into the hallway, toward what appeared to be a small bathroom, but Stacey didn't move.

"You coming?" Aquifer asked, turning back toward him and offering a reassuring smile.

"I don't even know where I'm going," Stacey responded.

"Only one way to find out." Battery's voice was distant and nonchalant.

Stacey looked around him at the sea of violence and confusion and betrayal. There was nothing waiting for him here in this Pakistani house. There was, however, a path to understanding the things happening inside of him, if he were to go with these people. For now, it seemed to be the best path.

As long as his path ultimately led back to Sam.

Stacey walked toward them, his boots squishing against the wet floor, his eyes watching for the corpses on the ground. He reached the hallway. Battery, Aquifer, and Shadow peered at him from within the bathroom. They stood in a triangle, their demeanor relaxed.

He inhaled, filling his lungs, and slowly blew his breath through his lips. "Okay, time to do this." He wasn't sure if the words were for them, or for himself.

Stacey stepped into the bathroom. As soon as he crossed the barrier, Shadow slammed the door shut and turned the lock. Aquifer adjusted the sleeve of his hoodie and said, "Proxy, we're all here. Bogeyman us."

Stacey waited, listening to the ambient noises: The wind through the sand outside, the water dripping from the second floor, the soft buzz of the floodlights in the main room.

Then, everything stopped.

He heard nothing beyond the slight inhales and exhales of his present company. The light seeping through the crack at the bottom of the door extinguished, the space becoming an inky black. Stacey looked around the bathroom, but there were no other windows or light sources to investigate.

His jaw reflexively clenched when the entire room rattled, as if the faintest of earthquakes were imminent. He looked around and saw the shower curtain and visible toiletries were reacting to what he was feeling, though no amount of vibration seemed to be moving the objects from their original placement. Stacey reached out and pushed his finger against a toothbrush that was lying on the sink; it moved forward a little before pulling into place, as if attached by a magnet.

Thin, straight cracks appeared along the floor, walls, and ceiling, forming perfect squares in the material. The grid lines rattled; to Stacey's amazement and horror, a random square cut from the outer wall of the bathroom sucked away, leaving only black emptiness.

More squares pulled away in all six directions, sometimes taking with them parts of the bathroom furniture. As more and more vanished, Stacey squinted, attempting to find anything present in the surrounding darkness. He saw, heard, and felt absolutely nothing.

In a strange, intelligent way, the squares beneath his feet were last, the walls and the ceiling having disappeared entirely. Stacey wondered what would happen when the ground finally gave way to the strange forces pulling at it.

He didn't have to wonder for long. Shadow, telegraphing her impatience, waved at the other three before allowing herself to fall backwards, away from her supernatural platform. She dropped beneath them and faded instantly out of sight. Within seconds, the squares flew away from Aquifer and Battery's feet, and they held up their hands in free-fall.

Stacey felt the grid lines underfoot wobble. He held his breath, anticipating what was to come. His muscles gave a hypnic jerk as his support gave way, dropping him into the abyss. His body knew it was falling, and he could feel the building momentum, but strangely, there was no whistle in his ears or wind in his face. It was as if he were in the vacuum of space, hurtling toward some new, alien planet.

He couldn't tell how long he fell, drifting with no sensation. The passage of time felt absent from this place, and the journey ended as suddenly as it had begun. Rather than an abrupt, violent landing or a forceful deceleration, Stacey was suddenly aware of pressure beneath his fingertips. The pressure spread to his toes, knees, legs and forearms; just like that, with the flick of a switch, he wasn't falling at all. Instead, he was stationary on his hands and knees, the blackness parting between his fingertips like smoke, revealing cold, grey metal. Stacey's brain couldn't reconcile the shift in motion. It reminded him of waking up from dreams where he'd fallen off a cliff and hit the bottom, suddenly realizing he'd never been falling in the first place.

Looking around, he found the ankles of his three new companions. Battery and Aquifer helped him to his feet, his legs trembling. Swiveling his head, he could tell they were all standing in a silver metal column. Its featurelessness made it difficult to determine the size of the chamber, but he guessed it was big enough to fit at least three times as many people.

In front of them, a hyperbaric door slid to the side, revealing dim fluorescent lights and grey concrete. Shadow strode out of their tube, not even looking back at the rest of the group. Aquifer followed, turning only to give Stacey a grin and a quick wink.

Battery put her hand on Stacey's shoulder. "You came this far. It's time to see what you were dropped into."

Stacey lifted his head and took a few steps, clearing the doorway. He found himself standing in the very center of a grey, concrete basement, though it was much larger than an average basement. It felt more like a small parking garage.

Around the outer walls were all types of stations: surgical tables surrounded by medical equipment; racks filled with rifles and pistols; workstations littered with electronic parts; and cartons of food and MREs.

Stacey took a moment to note a short, wooden staircase leading to a door in the far corner. *Maybe it's a way out, if it comes to that.*

He turned around to observe a space filled end-to-end with homemade computer towers and monitors, communications arrays, and even older equipment like ham radios. This wall was definitely the most fascinating part of this place. The screens were wall-mounted, some on top of each other, while the heavier equipment was situated on the floor or on the surface of one of the many different types of computer workstations set along the wall. Though almost every visible computer had lights indicating they were running or on standby, most of the monitors were dark. The lone exception was a small cluster of maybe eight or nine screens near the bottom-center of the wall's setup.

Sitting in a chair, facing these lit monitors, was a lean man with a goatee in a purple-collared shirt. He turned to Stacey as he stepped from the chamber and stood from the chair, walking forward.

"Private Fields, oui?" The man addressed him in English, though his dialect was mildly French.

Stacey nodded.

The man moved closer to him, extending his hand. Stacey took it and pumped it up and down in a sturdy handshake. "For now, you may call me Proxy," The man said, his tone amiable. "Welcome to The Faction, mon amie."

**Paris, France
September 1, 1997-A**

Quentin was inconsolable.

It wasn't because the princess was dead; Quentin wasn't one of *those* kinds of people.

It wasn't even because of her influence, though he couldn't deny its positive effects.

No, it was because of the *way* she'd died. Or, rather, that he was *lied* to about it.

He continued to mull on the exact nature and source of his distress in the darkness of his theatre room, the blue glow of the projector washing over him. It gave his face the palette of an ill man.

"Liars, Maddie," he spoke aloud in French. "All of them, liars. But never you, eh?"

Silence.

Quentin waited, his arms dangling from the sides of his chair, his faith in her response ironclad.

He received his reply in the form of a cold, wet sensation pressed against the back of his right hand. Peering down through the theatre's gloom, Quentin came face-to-face with a beautiful, brindle-patterned Dutch Shepherd.

Her pointed radar ears twitched under his gaze, and she presented him with a loving smile that, in Quentin's opinion, no other animal could replicate. The dog nuzzled his palm, asking for pets, and he was all too happy to oblige her.

While scratching beneath Maddie's ear, Quentin looked at the images passing across the screen. He had amassed quite a few contacts and favors during his years as an analyst at the Direction de la Protection et de la Sécurité de la Défense, giving him front-row access to MI6's records. Most of the images were from journalists, and they helped stitch together the last night of one of Europe's, if not the entire world's, most beloved political figures.

The night Diana Spencer, Princess of Wales, passed away.

"Maddie, something isn't right about this. Nothing here, nor anywhere in the driver's personal history, dictate a propensity for reckless substance abuse."

Quentin directed Maddie's attention toward the screen ahead.

"The photos, they . . . they don't show me a man prepared to die, by intent nor by irresponsibility. There's something else here, something . . . *nefarious*. Something planned. Something that's . . . hey, wait, where are you going?"

The dog had grown bored and wandered away from his monologue. She spun around, startled, as he hopped from his chair to catch up with her. When she realized the motion came from her human, her tongue flopped out of her grinning mouth while her tail, forever curled up into a question-mark, wagged back and forth. Maddie waited for him, and when he passed her, she followed him at his side. The pair left the theater room into the main hallway of his home.

Quentin sighed as he walked into the living room and plopped onto his couch, rubbing his temples. "Maddie, the DPSD is keeping us busy right now. I hear that other European agencies face similar, 'sudden' workloads. Even during this, some of the analysts are whispering of conspiracy, of intent. I'm hearing too many words like 'Shadow People' and whatever 'Lomaria' is supposed to be."

He looked beside him, where Maddie dutifully sat. Her right eye shone a bright brown in the sunlight, though her left iris displayed a sightless, milky-white cataract. It was a scar from her past, long before Quentin adopted her.

But we all have scars from our past, don't we?

"These theories," he said, "they don't lend much credence to themselves. But foreign powers, covering up a scandal by keeping their analysts from piecing together the clues before they disappear? That, that I will believe." Quentin stood up and wandered toward a glass door, sliding it open to step onto his patio. The cool, Parisian air filled his lungs as he took a deep breath. "Maddie . . . the Princess did not die for nothing. The truth *will* come out."

Paris, France
September 4, 1997-A

"How is your coffee, Q?"

"It is just fine, Moha—"

"No. No names. I am just 'M' to you. And you are just 'Q' to me. Anonymity will save our lives."

"Well, M," Quentin replied, "the coffee is unremarkably fine."

M, an older gentleman with wispy grey hairs and a furrowed expression, leaned forward, glancing around the small, outdoor café. "Your honesty is why I agreed to speak with you," he said. "It's clear you have some clout with MI6, but not the kind of relationship with them that makes you untrustworthy. Now . . ."

M retrieved a manila folder from within his green jacket. "You know where I work. You know the things I see, the things I hear. It's a popular hotel, and a good one, at that. The clients that come through here are respectable people."

Accepting the manila folder from M's outstretched arm, Quentin flipped it open, maintaining eye contact with the old gentleman.

"Then tell me what you heard, M," Quentin said.

M cleared his throat. "It's not what I *heard*. It's what I *know*. I *know* Paul, the driver. I know a great deal about the goings-on of royal families. Paul was not drunk that night. And Diana was not being honest with the public."

Quentin stared down at the documents on the table. They were black-and-white scans of medical records. Specifically, OBGYN records. "M, are you saying she was pregnant?"

The man pointed a wrinkled finger at the folder. "You tell me."

"But M," Quentin said hesitantly, "this is not in the Princess's name. This is a Jane Doe. It could be *anyone*. Even if it was her, am I supposed to believe that the pregnancy was worth her life?"

M shook his head. "It's not about *what*. It's about *who*. The things I've heard from my friends in Haiti and Dubai point toward a scandal—a relationship with someone in the Bush family."

Quentin chuckled, incredulous. "Really? Who?"

The old man shrugged. "No one knows. There's no evidence, of course. Some mention a phone conversation between the Princess and a private American contact, but there's been no way to verify it."

Quentin leaned back in his chair and sighed, his tone biting and irritated. "M, have I come here to waste my time? This is important to me; to the *people*."

M jumped from his seat and slammed his hands on the table, rattling the coffee cups. "I *KNOW* IT'S IMPORTANT! THEY CAME AND THEY TOOK MY SECURITY FOOTAGE! THEY FEIGNED NEGLIGENCE FROM A KIND AND RESPONSIBLE MAN! THEY DANCE AROUND THE EVIDENCE, IGNORING THE MISSING PAINT AND THE FLASH, LAUGHING AT US—"

Quentin raised a hand to stop him. "I'm sorry, what flash? I haven't heard of this."

M seemed to calm, looking around at the nearby guests who stared at him. One couple rose to leave the café, but M waved them back down into their seats, offering nonverbal reassurance of his composure.

"Q, I'm surprised you haven't," M said. "The moment her car entered the tunnel—right before it crashed—there was a bright flash of light. Some are saying it *caused* the crash, others say it was just a paparazzo or maintenance worker."

"Can you help me confirm this?" Quentin asked. "I have contacts in the DPSD whom I trust *very* much. I'd like for them to reach out to your collaborators to identify the whereabouts of any paid paparazzi working the night of the crash."

M began to speak, but something caught his eye. He looked over Quentin's shoulder, and his next words were difficult to understand through the quiver in his voice. "Can we walk?"

His eyes connected with Quentin's, betraying sudden terror. Quentin spun around in his chair, but the only people he saw were some of the outdoor café's patrons and the average passers-by on the sidewalk. He turned back to M.

"Of course," he said. "Let's walk."

The two continued their conversation in whispers as they moved down the bustling sidewalks and quiet back alleys. M agreed to help arrange connections between their contacts, isolating suspects who may have been the cause of the bright flash. Quentin further explained his rationale: If they can identify a responsible party, they can better explain and unravel the true nature of the Princess's death.

M also shared his theories about those involved. He felt MI6 had some stake in preventing the child from being born, due to the political issues raised if the Bush family was involved. M had also heard references to the word Quentin referenced by other sources, though M swore it was "Lemara," not "Lomaria." Dusk arrived before M said he needed to leave.

"Q, you should be careful," M said, offering one last piece of advice. "I've been able to distance myself from this for now, but my contacts are having strange, dangerous experiences. They're reporting being watched; being followed. They tell me of things in their home being moved around when they aren't looking, even if they're in the next room. Some have seen shadows of people, standing at the end of their bed or over their babies' cribs. None have been hurt yet. None that I know of."

M leaned closer. "I may have seen such a man today—at the café. If they know I'm involved, they'll be looking at you, too. If they're the same ones responsible for the Princess—just be careful, Q."

Quentin offered the man a handshake. "I will."

M turned away, waved goodbye, and traveled up the sidewalk. Quentin checked his watch and looked in the direction of his house. He was about half a kilometer from home, so a cab wouldn't be necessary.

It was a nice night.

He shoved his hands in the pockets of his lavender pea coat, mulling over the information M had shared with him. The idea of an unwanted pregnancy causing political discourse enticed him, but perhaps it enticed him *too* much. Conspiracy theorists loved to spin dramatic tales. All too often, the simplest explanation for a tragedy was the correct one, but the simplest reason was often too mundane, at least for the public's tastes.

In any circumstance, the "why," while important, was not at the top of Quentin's priority list. He needed evidence of foul play that, when forced into the public eye, created such a fuss that it dragged the "why" into the light with it.

The street and sidewalk ahead of Quentin was empty, the darkness of the night broken only by the stars and the occasional street lamp. He passed an empty telephone booth, deep in thought. The contraption was old and rusty, with a mounted telephone and white book highlighted by a glowing yellow light.

Quentin appreciated the lack of people on his walk home. It

wasn't that he hated people. After all, he didn't know *everything*, and people were a valuable resource when acquiring new information. But far too often, he found them bogged down by their emotions and their biases, unable to behave like rational animals. In those moments—in *most* moments—he would rather remain alone.

Well, Maddie could stay.

A flicker in the corner of his eye interrupted his thoughts. He turned around. The telephone booth was malfunctioning, losing its light and regaining it in quick succession. After a few seconds, it turned off altogether, plunging the booth into darkness.

He stopped watching the booth, opting instead to return to his journey home, but before he turned back toward the street, the light returned, dimmer than before. Quentin looked closer this time.

A black figure now stood inside.

Quentin stepped backward, startled by the person's appearance.

Did they come to make a phone call? If so, how did I miss their approach?

The figure stood still with the phone to its ear. *Completely* still. They didn't move a muscle, not even seeming to speak into the device. Quentin was relieved to see they weren't also raving, or brandishing a weapon, or approaching him. He tried to quell the goosebumps along his arms, reoriented himself toward his home, and quickened his pace.

Quentin's shoes clacked along the sidewalk, and he could painfully hear his breathing, more labored than before. He looked over his shoulder. The figure now stood in the middle of the street, staring right at him, its posture unmoving. Even under the lamplight, Quentin could only make out the black shape of a person. He could discern no features through the darkness.

Calmness could wait for another day.

Burst into a sprint, he made a hard-left turn into the series of alleyways he knew well. He passed by a dumpster and leapt over a puddle next to it, continuing to the end of the alley. As he reached it, he heard someone stomp into the puddle, splashing water into the air and against the dumpster. Quentin turned to the right, willing himself not to look back.

If it was the same person, they could only have reached the alley so soon by running, too.

He approached a chest-high wall and vaulted over the obstacle without slowing, using his hands to push his body up and over. Even while Quentin recovered from his landing, he heard shoes skidding to a stop on the other side. He had to continue.

Quentin entered a small park, and he diverted into a closely-knit nest of trees, making an effort not to disturb the foliage. When he felt he was out of sight, he crouched down, waiting to see who came around the corner of the alley.

He waited.

And waited.

And waited.

Nothing moved.

Quentin sighed, trying to release the tension from his muscles. His relief was short-lived, as rustling sounded to his right from a different area of the park. It grew louder, more fervent. A black hand appeared from the leaves, gripping a branch to steady itself.

He didn't wait to see the rest.

Quentin sprung from the trees, one of the twigs slicing a small cut on his forehead above his left eye. The sweat from his fear, combined with this physical excursion, rolled and burned into the new wound, but he barely noticed. Instead, he darted further down the street, slipping into the back alleys, only glimpsing the black figure pursuing him for a millisecond from the corner of his eye.

His heart pounded against his chest, and the blood from his cut tried to trickle down into his eye. He wiped his forehead every few seconds to keep his vision clear.

A door loomed ahead, held open by a brick. His only other option was to remain in the continuous maze of the alleyways, so Quentin chose the former, pulling open his salvation, kicking away the brick, and slamming the barrier closed. He turned to see a dark kitchen, where one member of the staff stared at him, a trash bag in each hand.

"Je t'aide?" she asked, as if unsure whether an offended or frightened tone was more appropriate.

Quentin just raised a finger to his lips, pointing back at the door.

Silence.

As they both waited, he grew nervous; she grew irritated. "Monsieur, nous sommes fermés—"

"SHHH."

More silence.

Quentin raised his hands in an exaggerated shrug. "I apologize; I have had a very strange night. If I may ask, do you have another way out of here?"

The employee looked him up-and-down, relaxing in response to his polite demeanor. "Yes, I can unlock the entrance for you," she replied. "Is everything okay? Should I call the Sûreté?"

Quentin looked back at the door. "No, I—I don't believe they can do much for me here."

Paris, France
September 6, 1997-A

Quentin sat in the center of his living room floor, facing his front door. He still wore the dirty and disheveled clothes from the chase two days earlier. Dark stubble covered his jawline, but the circles under his eyes were twice as dark. Maddie laid next to him, panting. She seemed stressed by his demeanor.

Gripped in his hands, pointed toward his front door, was a small pistol.

As soon as he'd returned home that night, Quentin rushed to the gun safe in his bedroom and retrieved the weapon. Though the DPSD provided formal training, his career as an analyst did little to prepare him for practical gun play. Nevertheless, its presence comforted him. He hoped it would be useful against the Shadow Person, should his investigation bring them together again.

Maddie's whimpering broke him from his thirty-six-hour trance.

"Maddie I'm—I'm so sorry," Quentin said. "You're right. I can't stay here forever."

Quentin climbed to his feet, his joints creaking. Staggered, he set the gun on the coffee table and walked into the kitchen. He poured food into Maddie's bowl, and set to work cleaning up the "accidents" she'd left on the floor due to his negligence. She finished eating in no time, so he took her for a walk to make sure she had the opportunity to use the restroom comfortably.

Once Maddie's needs were met, Quentin stripped his outfit and clambered into the shower. Cleaned and re-dressed in a new outfit, he tucked the pistol into his waistband against his back. He offered a quirky half-smile to his companion. "Let me make it up to you."

———————

The Dutch Shepherd trotted along the sidewalk, happy and carefree. Quentin held tight to her leash, keeping up with her eager pace. When they neared their destination, she sniffed the air, her question-mark tail wagging with renewed fury. Despite the stress of the last two nights, Quentin found himself tickled by her excitement. The pair stepped into the market.

Le Marché des Enfants Rouges.

The locale was an open market dating back three and a half centuries, holding an eclectic mix of fresh products from various nations. The market bustled with customers today, who cooed at Maddie, enthralled by her charm, and she ate up their attention. The patrons focused on Maddie; Quentin nabbed a fresh loaf of wheat bread and a bunch of bananas for Maddie. He also hunted down truffle pasta, a container of burrata, and some minced kefta.

He looked up from the Moroccan area of the market, feeling a chill rolling up his spine. Ahead, in the shuffle of the crowd, was a solitary, motionless figure.

The Shadow Person.

The black silhouette peered at Quentin, standing far enough away to avoid notice from the other patrons as they shopped. The figure stood in the threshold of a hallway that disappeared into a small warehouse, and as Quentin laid eyes on it, the figure turned down that hallway, out of sight.

"Come, Maddie," Quentin said, his voice an octave lower now.

He left his basket of groceries at the Moroccan stall and slipped the pistol from his pants into the pocket of his pea coat. Maddie stuck close to his legs as they weaved through the food displays and into the hallway.

"Sit, Maddie," he commanded. She planted herself a meter into the hallway, staying close to its entrance.

Quentin passed her and walked up to a door, pistol now drawn and steady. His shoulder pressed into it, and it swiveled open into darkness. He activated a penlight with his other hand and shined it around, but all it revealed were wooden crates of produce.

"Hey!" called a voice from the hallway. "Don't go back there!"

Quentin stuffed his pistol back into his pea coat pocket and exited to see an irritated market worker flagging him down. Maddie sat at the worker's feet, looking up at him with her mouth open and her tongue dangling to the side.

Quentin walked back to retrieve Maddie. "Sorry, sir," he muttered to the man.

He located their basket and paid for their food. As they left, Maddie stopped and whined, looking into the bustle of the market.

"I know it's your favorite place," Quentin said with a grin. "We'll come back soon, okay?"

Maddie's whining grew louder, but she turned to follow her guardian anyway, glancing back into the market one more time.

As they returned home and walked through the door, Quentin's house phone was ringing. He placed his bag on the floor, released Maddie's leash, and sprinted to its spot on the kitchen counter.

"Hello?" he answered.

"Q?" he heard through the line. "This is R."

"What is it?"

"We cross-referenced the paparazzi you requested with M's informants. Only one had unknown whereabouts on that night: a street photographer under ITV's employ. Particularly, one reporting to Nicholas Owen."

"So, Owen has the images?" Quentin queried, leaning against his kitchen counter.

"Not that we can tell," R replied. "All records, both physical and digital, indicate this photographer's been dark for the past week."

Quentin frowned. "Can you send me their information?"

"We'll meet in person, Q. The DPSD team has been under . . . some kind of surveillance. We're worried about interception."

"You're seeing the Shadow Person too, aren't you?"

"Enculer, Q, you can't just say this shit on an open line!" R exclaimed. "Yes, this specter has been trailing most of the analysts. To be more specific, the ones who have been helping you with this private Diana investigation. We're thinking it's MI6. Or the Russians."

"Of course, R. We'll talk about this more in person."

"Also . . ."

Quentin waited, but R remained silent. "Yes?"

"Well, we're worried about you, Q. You know you can have . . . obsessive tendencies. You've missed a week of work, and we don't

have many vacation days. Don't let this ruin your life."
Another pause.
"See you soon, R."

Canonbury, England
September 7, 1997-A

Quentin walked up the front steps of the apartment registered to "F," the ITV photographer. He had tried to set up a meeting with the man once he retrieved contact details from R, but to no avail. Left with no other choice, Quentin pressured R into keeping an eye on Maddie. He'd then caught a red-eye flight to England to confront the photographer in person.

Quentin's knuckles rapping on F's front door broke the still night. He heard no response until a lock pulled on the other side, and a doorknob twisted. A sliver of light shone through.

"Are you MI6?" said a young man's voice, in English.

Quentin smiled through the crack in the entrance. "No, mon amie," he said. "Officially I'm with French intelligence, at the DPSD. But I did not come here on their time. I came here to pursue a personal endeavor." The man kept the door partially open, but he didn't respond. "If the last week of your life was anything like mine," Quentin added, "I know you're wary of strangers. Have you been seeing the Shadow Person, too?"

That comment seemed to attract the attention of F, whose eyes widened. "Oh my God . . . it's not just me?"

"No." Quentin leaned against the door frame, crossing his arms. "I have seen it too, as have many of my colleagues. If it's not too much trouble, I'd like to ask you some questions that are better answered behind closed doors."

F hesitated, his eyes darting back and forth. "I have a friend who checks up on me every so often to make sure I'm still okay. If something happens, you won't get away with it."

"Don't worry." Quentin doubted the man's bluff, but he'd oblige his worries. "I just came to speak with you."

The door opened the rest of the way into a small, carpeted living room. To the left of the entrance was a coat closet, while the right side of the space was partitioned into a kitchen. Ahead of him was a short hallway with two doors, likely leading to a bedroom and a bathroom.

A young, pudgy man with a bushy beard closed the door behind him. He turned to face Quentin. "How do you know me, if you aren't with them?"

Quentin shrugged. "I have nosy friends."

F scrunched his nose at the reply.

"Look," continued Quentin, "I don't want to drag this out. You were in the tunnel the night the Princess died, oui?"

F nodded while opening the coat closet near his front door. Quentin hesitated to remove his pea coat; his pistol was still in the pocket. He had no desire to intimidate the photographer, though, so he passed it along to be draped over an available hanger.

The door closed behind F. "Yes. Yes I was, mister . . ."

Quentin put a finger to his lips, looking around the apartment. "I think it's safer if you know me as Q, and I know you as F. D'accord?"

F sighed. "Yes, that's fine."

Quentin held out a hand, gesturing for F to continue.

"I was in the tunnel, though that fact wasn't privy to most people," F said. "I also haven't shared them with ITV. I don't know the right step to take yet. I'm not sure if it's a government, or a private organization, or some grotesque combination . . ."

Quentin raised both arms, palms pointed in F's direction. "F, let me stop you. What is 'them?' What have you not shared with ITV?"

F blinked, taken aback. "The photographs. The reason I haven't left my home."

"I came here hoping you could share your testimony with me," Quentin said, shaking his head. "Do you feel you have damning evidence against the 'accident' theory captured on film?"

"Well . . . I can't say 'damning' to any particular organization per se, but they are quite disturbing."

"May I see them?" Quentin asked.

F held a finger up before disappearing into his bedroom area.

Behind Quentin, the doorknob to the coat closet began to rattle. Quentin turned to examine the door, but the rattling stopped. He shrugged and looked away.

The bedroom door reopened, and F appeared once more, holding a large envelope. "Let me start by saying I did not see any of this with my own eyes that night," he said. "The tunnel was far too dark, and I took a gamble in catching some close-up shots of the Princess by snapping my camera blind. This is what I was doing just before the crash happened."

F opened the envelope. "The first day after it happened, I worried my camera's flashes had startled the driver into wrecking the vehicle. I was so guilty I didn't contact Mr. Owen or anyone else at ITV. Then I chose to have my pictures developed, and I'm no longer sure it was *any* kind of accident." He produced four photographs in a stack and handed them to Quentin. "These were the last four pictures taken that night, Q."

Quentin flipped through them, steady-handed at first, but shakier as he paged through each image.

F had taken all four photographs at a diagonal angle between the front and left sides of Diana's car. From the view, it was easy to see the Princess; her blond hair, black Armani jacket, and bulbous earrings were visible through the passenger window. In the first photograph, she seemed to be smiling, as if someone had just said something funny.

Quentin flipped to the second photograph. The windows of the car were now a solid black—as if they'd been painted that color. He looked over at F.

"How much time is there between pictures?" he asked.

"About two seconds," replied F.

"Is the film damaged?"

F nodded his head at Quentin's hands. "Maybe you should just keep going."

Quentin slid the second photograph to the bottom of the stack. Here, the Princess's smile had faded. The rest of the car's passenger cabin made clear what distressed her.

She was sitting next to a dark silhouette of a person leaning toward her face.

The Shadow Person.

Quentin took a deep breath and pulled out F's final picture.

The Princess's face pressed against the window, her eyes wide in terror. The Shadow Person pushed against her from behind, one hand near her neck. They weren't watching her, though.

No, their head was turned toward the camera. Toward F.

Quentin stood to his feet. "What am I seeing here?"

"Creepy shit, right?" F said. "The man wasn't in the car, but then he was. Could he have used some kind of smoke to mask his appearance?"

"I don't think so, F. The windows were far too dark. And the car was still moving."

A whistle from the kitchen startled Quentin. "Were you expecting someone?"

"I'm sorry, Q. I was making tea when you arrived. Let me—"

"Ne t'en fais pas," Quentin interrupted. "I'm the one intruding. I'll pour you some. May I have a cup as well?"

"Of course."

Quentin went into the kitchen, the wall partition blocking his sight of the living room area.

In the kitchen, Quentin moved the kettle from the stove eye, and the whistling subsided. He rummaged around the cabinets to find proper teacups. After pouring two cups, he tasted a little of his own and choked a little. The tea offered the faint taste of berries, but it was far too bitter. A few more seconds of searching yielded sugar cubes. He plopped two of the cubes into his cup and tried again.

Much better this time.

"I forgot to ask, do you like sugar in your tea?" he called around the partition.

No answer.

Quentin shrugged and grasped both cups, carrying them back into the living room.

"I may have spoken too quietly. Do you like—"

F hunched over sideways on his couch, blood pouring from a gash in his neck. He seemed to have been fighting for air, but just as Quentin entered the room, rebellious light left his eyes. His body relaxed, sliding to the floor.

Behind him, the coat closet was halfway ajar.

Quentin set the cups on the coffee table near F's body and reached for the photographs.

They were missing, too.

A floorboard creaked behind Quentin, and without thinking, he dove to the side. Glass and ceramic shattered out of his field of view. He turned to see a living silhouette.

The Shadow Person had come for them.

Now that he was closer and in a well-lit room, some of the

Shadow Person's mystery stripped away. Quentin recognized the figure of a lean, muscular person wearing an all-black outfit, capped with a featureless black mask. The suit had probably been designed for anonymity rather than intimidation, though in a dimmer setting, it performed both roles rather well.

The Shadow Person picked themselves up from the floor, a black-painted knife in hand. They'd lunged for Quentin's back, and when he'd dodged, the specter had fallen into the coffee table, breaking it. They pointed their knife toward Quentin, their stance menacing.

Quentin had received some hand-to-hand combat training at the DPSD, but as with his firearms training, he hadn't put it to much use. He was in no condition to spar against a professional, especially an armed one.

Still, with his gun stashed in the closet, fighting was his best and only way to survive.

The Shadow Person lunged, bringing their knife down toward Quentin's neck. He grabbed a decorative pillow from the couch beside him and held it up, forcing the blade to plunge into the soft stuffing. Quentin twisted the pillow around his opponent's hand, freed the weapon from their grasp, and threw both items across the room.

The intruder swung a fist at Quentin's head. Quentin tried to block, but his reflexes weren't quick enough. The blow glanced off his arms and struck him in the forehead, still carrying enough force to knock him off-balance. He fell against the wall, while the Shadow Person reached into their boot to retrieve a small, triangle-shaped blade, fitting it snugly between their middle and ring fingers.

Quentin scrambled toward the coat closet. The silent assassin chased him in his peripherals, a dreaded nightmare manifested into reality. They both reached the closet door at the same time, and Quentin snatched his pea coat from the hanger before rolling to the floor. His choice allowed him to avoid a bladed punch from the Shadow Person, and splinters fractured from the wood of the door frame.

Quentin took advantage of the misdirection and lunged his entire body against the attacker's shins, flipping them over his shoulders and leaving them prone on the ground. He jumped over the destroyed coffee table and back into the kitchen area, fumbling in his coat pocket for the pistol.

Glass crunched behind him, and he turned to see the dark silhouette sprinting at him, already almost at the kitchen entrance. In a blind panic, Quentin dropped his coat, snatched the hot teakettle from the stove, and hurled it at their face. It struck them right where their nose should be, stopping them in their tracks, and some of the hot water spilled onto the front of their shirt. They pulled against their outfit to keep the steaming water away from their skin.

Quentin dropped to his knees and pulled the gun from his pea coat. Invigorated by the weapon, he racked the slide, aimed it at the Shadow Person's chest, and pulled the trigger.

The trigger didn't move.

He looked at the gun, excitement turning to panic, and pulled again, but the trigger still wouldn't budge.

The Shadow Person was back on their feet, and they took two steps forward before noticing the gun. They kicked the now-empty kettle in Quentin's direction and turned to flee.

Quentin dodged the kettle, groaning as he realized his mistake.

The safety!

His thumb flicked the switch, and he aimed around the partition at the fleeing silhouette. The recoil surprised him as he squeezed the trigger, and the bullet penetrated the plaster wall instead of the Shadow Person's body. They ignored the gunshot and ran into the coat closet, shutting the door behind them.

Quentin pursued the assassin, passing around the couch and gripping the doorknob. It rattled as if near an approaching train, refusing to turn. He kicked against the wooden door, but it was like striking cement. The barrier refused to move, break, or splinter. Raising his pistol, Quentin fired low at the door, trying to reach the legs of the person inside. The bullets ricocheted away from the wood and buried themselves into the carpet, not even scratching the paint on the door.

A few seconds passed before the rattling stopped, and Quentin tried the doorknob again, more cautious this time. It opened with no resistance, but inside he found an ordinary coat closet. A sparse number of coats and hangers lined the space, but it was otherwise empty.

Quentin reached for F's home phone and dialed the local police, leaving the receiver off the cradle as he prepared to leave the apartment. He considered searching the back panel of the closet, seeking some secret passage, but he knew it wasn't that simple. Whatever happened here was the same as what happened inside the phone booth—and inside Princess Diana's car.

This isn't just some clandestine group with an agenda, Quentin thought. No, this was something alien, far beyond the natural realm. Something the most unhinged conspiracy theorist would never consider. Something Quentin wasn't equipped to handle.

Something that wants me dead.

Paris, France
September 8, 1997-A

Quentin awoke to Maddie's light growling.

He had only just made it home, and he'd wanted a few hours of sleep before pursuing the new information gleaned from the disaster with F. Using his knowledge of digital forensics, he was able to strip his pistol's records from the international intelligence community's registered weapons database, preventing law enforcement from accusing him of murder. Afterward, he collapsed into bed, setting his gun on the nightstand.

That had been—he glanced at the clock. 4:37AM.

Two hours ago.

Quentin grumbled, looking at the foot of the bed where Maddie curled. Any other night, he would have attributed her noises to a dream. After the last week, however, Quentin could no longer afford to presume such things.

He flicked on the nightstand light, illuminating an undisturbed room. Maddie turned her head to see him, her tongue flopping from her grin. Then her radar ears perked up, and she turned to the bedroom door, growling again. Quentin reached for his gun.

It was gone.

Searching on and around the nightstand and bed, he failed to locate the weapon. He *knew* where he'd set it before falling asleep. If it had moved, someone else moved it.

Quentin tiptoed from the bedroom to the connected closet and bathroom, confirming they were also empty. As he stepped back into the bedroom, he heard the sounds of floorboards creaking elsewhere in the house. Footsteps trickled to Quentin's ears in muffled pieces.

He turned off the bedroom light and cracked open the door—just a little—surveying the living room and kitchen in his field of view. A person, dressed head-to-toe in black, furtively moved from room to room, searching for something. Quentin's gun was stuck in the waistband of their clothing.

Quentin left his door cracked and led Maddie into the closet, closing the door to keep her safe. He crept into the bathroom, which had a second door leading into one of the guest bedrooms. In *that* room was yet another entrance connecting to an open study and kitchen area. He followed this path, maintaining absolute silence.

Once he reached the kitchen, Quentin rose up to glance above the countertop. The Shadow Person walked toward his theatre, where Quentin had left the confiscated photographs from days prior.

Quentin slid a long kitchen knife from its wooden holster on the kitchen counter, holding it out in front of him. With his free hand, he activated his stove, opened a cabinet, and retrieved a package of stove top popcorn. He set the package on the warming stove top, hastened across the room, and positioned himself beside the theater entrance.

Ten seconds passed.

POP-POP-POP-POP-POP-POP . . .

The kitchen screamed, announcing the presence of freshly popped corn. Footsteps thudded from within the theatre room, and Quentin readied for the upcoming fight. As soon as the Shadow Person's leg crossed the threshold, the kitchen knife plunged down, passing through skin and muscle until it dug into bone. When he released the blade, only the handle protruded.

The Shadow Person cried out in a deep, guttural voice, collapsing to the floor from the pain. They tried to sit up, but Quentin punched them in the center of their masked face, knocking them back to the ground. He saw his pistol protruding from their waistband, and he snatched it, checking the safety switch this time.

He aimed at the Shadow Person and addressed them in English. "Start with that mask, eh? I want to see who I'm speaking with."

The Shadow Person raised their hands, their heavy, augmented voice reverberating throughout the living room. "No! Don't shoot! I'll talk."

They reached for the black mask and pulled it away. Long, blond hair fell past their shoulders, highlighting a pale-skinned woman with piercing blue eyes. She looked down at the knife handle jutting from her leg, then back up at Quentin.

"Bloody hell, you really fucked up my leg here." When she spoke without her mask, her voice lost its depth, revealing a feminine British accent. "Want to get this out of me, or what?"

**Paris, France
September 8, 1997-A**

Quentin placed a tourniquet around her leg to stop the bleeding, his gun trained on her while she told her story.

She claimed to be a former MI6 operative, and as far as she knew, the agency still employed her. She reported to them, and her directives came from the agency. The situation, however, was far stranger than a simple employee-employer relationship.

One night, about a month ago, someone had taken B (the name Quentin had given her) from her home in the middle of the night and anesthetized her. Once she awoke, people she couldn't see told her that her next missions would be exceedingly challenging, and MI6 required . . . reassurance. This reassurance came in the form of a surgically implanted device beneath her skull. The hidden people warned her the device would allow for control over her neural network, giving them access to her movements should she stray from her assigned tasks.

Unsure how to process her treatment at the hands of her government, B pressed forward. She tried to hide what happened from her husband, but he found the scars. When the darker version of MI6 ordered her to assassinate a Colombian senator, her husband tried to reach out to his own government contacts to learn more about what happened to her. They spent an uneventful day together.

That night, B seized up in bed, as if an electric shock traveled down her spine. Her body numbed, in a way very similar to the sensations reported by paraplegics and quadriplegics. It moved of its own accord, though she was still able to watch; in fact, her eyelids would not close, so she was *forced* to watch. B walked into the garage, where she retrieved a Philips-head screwdriver.

She then returned to the bedroom, forced the tool into her husband's ear, and held him down by his throat until he stopped struggling.

"Twenty-three seconds," B sobbed, still sitting on the floor of

Quentin's living room. "My husband suffered for twenty-three seconds before he died. I know that I didn't do it, but that doesn't free me from the guilt."

B tried to learn more about her captors—and how they operated—but her searches halted when she was forced to comply with the missions passed along to her. She'd considered simply giving up, just letting MI6 take control rather than cooperate, but she always remembered her husband.

"If I was going to be a spy and an assassin," she said, "I would do it on *my* terms, and reduce collateral damage. That is, until the day I find the assholes in charge."

Quentin stared at her, uncertain of her loyalties. "Okay, I get what you're telling me. Help me understand; how are you operating? Is MI6 surveilling you? And how are you moving around so quickly?"

B wiped her tears away, clutched the living room couch, and stood, her feet shaky. Quentin's pistol followed her movements.

"MI6 is keeping this off the radar," she replied. "The device in my head is supposed to keep me in line, though I'm not certain that it can even see or hear what I'm doing. It's more like . . . like the device receives a general command, and my brain is forced to carry it out."

"So, where are your operating from?" Quentin asked.

"The base is some kind of secret, underground facility. I think it's in India? My team is all Indian."

"And you get there . . . how?"

"I Bogeyman."

Quentin narrowed his eyes. "Excuse me?"

"It's Vivaan's nickname for it," B said. "I don't understand the science very well, but he says it's a joke. Something about Einstein and 'spooky actions.' Like I said, I don't get it, but it's very fitting nonetheless."

"How does it work?"

"Why the fuck are you asking me?" B exclaimed, waving her hands in frustration. "I'm just field ops; I go where I'm told. Vivaan and Dhruv are sent coordinates of targets, I get dropped into a big tube, and then shit gets weird. The tube goes black, I feel like I'm falling, then I 'land' somewhere else. When I'm done with my mission, I return to wherever I was dropped, and the same thing takes me back to India."

"What do you know about your coworkers, Vivaan and Dhruv?" Quentin asked.

B paused, thoughtful. "Well, they don't *seem* like bad people. And I don't think they have the same device that's in my head. I know they made the Bogeyman, and honestly, it's the only reason I believe they were chosen to work with me."

Quentin scratched his head, thinking. "Can we get them out?"

"Dhruv has commented that they're locked in some kind of facility, on the 'fifth floor.' There's a blast door sealing them inside. They get sent food and water by retrieving it from the Bogeyman using coordinates sent to them. If the Bogeyman is used for anything besides my missions or their supplies, they've been told the room will depressurize and suffocate them to death."

"So . . ." Quentin lowered his gun. "It's remote, right? The only thing stopping them is speed, resources, and a secure place to go."

He stood, offering his hand to B. "Let me show you something in the garage."

Karnataka, India
September 8, 1997-A

Quentin fell.

And fell.

And fell.

And then, just like that, he wasn't falling anymore.

Chamber doors opened, revealing an almost-empty pearl-white laboratory. The starkness of its coloring was only broken by a few items: Three dingy cots lined a wall; a small row of computers and monitors; and two short, stout men in white coats.

They faced the chamber as it rattled, announcing the recovery of their personnel. Quentin stepped forward, adjusting his Shadow Person mask. Appearing relieved, the scientists approached and addressed him in English.

"Was everything okay, Bella?"

Quentin sidled closer and pulled back a part of his outfit, revealing the handle of his pistol.

"I'm just calling her 'B' for now," he replied. "Vivaan and Dhruv, I presume?"

Frightened faces formed on the two men, and they stepped backward, away from the Shadow Person whom they no longer knew. One of them looked behind him, at an almost-imperceptible camera mounted in the corner of the ceiling. When he turned back to face Quentin, beads of sweat precipitated on his brow.

"Relax, guys," Quentin said. "I just want to talk. You have no reason to trust me any more than your captors, but guess what?"

The two captives glanced at each other, then back at the intruder. Quentin smiled beneath his mask. "Now you're on a deadline. You can trust that I want to help you escape, or you can refuse to assist, but it won't take long before they realize something is wrong. What would you prefer?"

One of the men, the one on the left, broke down first. "What are you trying to do?" he whispered.

Quentin pointed back at the Bogeyman chamber. "I need to know: Why small spaces? Why does the 'Bogeyman' always send people into small spaces?"

"This is . . . what do you call it . . . the 'Cliff Notes' version, yes?" stammered the man on the right. "The Bogeyman chamber casts a wide, but harmless, radiation field, wide enough to envelop the entire planet. When we want to choose locations, we have access to maps and video satellites to specify coordinates—"

"What you need to understand," interrupted the second man, "is that we're taking the atoms within the chamber and irradiating them with . . ."

He paused, as if to determine how much detail he should use with this stranger. "Let's just say 'quantum particle' radiation. We then coordinate for a cluster of quantum particles to form at the sister location. In a single moment, we *click* those two quantum clouds together like Lego bricks, sending along the connected plane whatever we chose to irradiate."

Quentin snapped his fingers to rush them along. "You seem very excited by your science project, but this is way too much detail."

The other scientist cleared his throat. "The particles to which my colleague refers don't fare well in open conditions. Think of them like a gas; they'll dissipate eventually, but if you contain them in a small space with solid barriers, they'll stay together longer. We only need a short window for the procedure, but those barriers ensure safe travel for whatever, or whoever, we irradiate."

Quentin shuffled toward the computers, keeping his mask-modified voice low. "Is there any way at all to overcome that limitation?" He sat at the computer and began to type. Footsteps approached him from behind, and one of the scientists entered his field of vision.

"Like we said, it's a safety issue," continued the scientist. "We can bombard a designated location with a massive number of particles to complete the transfer, but the effects are less consistent. We aren't sure how it will affect the travelers, and we don't know what lasting impacts the radiation spike will have on the sister location."

Quentin looked up from his typing. "Will you take that risk?"

Both scientists just stared back, eyes wide.

"But what about—"

"They have the data—"

"Bella's chip—"

"Where would we even—"

Quentin raised a black-gloved hand. "I'll take care of the details. I need your focus. I don't know enough about it to help." He returned to the computer and began feeding it floppy disks. "By the way, is this the only place your technology and its data exists?"

"As far as we know, yes."

"Good." Quentin exchanged floppy disks and fed new ones into the machine, watching its progress. "Then here's what I need from you two. We will be leaving in the Bogeyman. But! The Bogeyman will be coming with us. Can you do this?"

Vivaan and Dhruv put their heads together, whispering. As they consulted, Quentin continued to insert square storage drives into the computer. After a moment, he looked over his shoulder at them. One of them bobbed their head up and down.

"You understand what we're saying, right?" the Indian scientist said. "This will be *extremely* dangerous. It has never been tested or attempted in any way."

"I accept the risk. Do you?"

The two men nodded and began adjusting the Bogeyman, checking the controls beneath hidden panels and investigating the battery block connected to the device. Little time passed before they returned to Quentin's side.

"We're ready on this front," one of them announced. "It's time to enter the coordinates."

Quentin stood and allowed them to access the computer. "How specific can it be?"

"*Very*. Just provide them."

Quentin whispered the data into the scientist's ear, and the seated man typed on his keyboard. As they worked, the Bogeyman hummed behind them, quietly at first, but the noise increased in volume with each passing second. Quentin consolidated their new floppy disk collection and returned it to a small satchel tied to his hip.

The scientist at the computer stood to leave, but Quentin stopped him. "Wait. How long would it take to rebuild the data from these disks in a new PC?"

"No more than an hour or two," the other scientist said from behind him.

"Perfect. Then I just have one more thing."

Quentin navigated the PC and opened a newly installed file named "STALKER.EXE." He activated it and, within the menu of the program, set a timer for sixty seconds. "*Now* it's time to leave."

The three piled into the Bogeyman, and the chamber door sealed itself shut.

They were plunged into darkness as the humming increased. It raised in pitch, and unlike Quentin's prior travel, there was no sudden silence followed by an open expanse. Instead, they remained within the chamber as it rocked, sending them bouncing along the metal walls. If he didn't know better, he would have guessed someone had just pushed the Bogeyman from an airplane.

The rocking continued for several minutes, and one of the scientists yelled at the other two passengers. They crawled closer to hear him.

"This is taking too long!" he shouted. "Something's wrong!"

As the words left his mouth, the rocking stopped, and they slammed into the metal floor as if they were on a halting train. The chamber shifted, this time pulling upward like an elevator. Quentin could hear noises similar to a revving engine, despite the apparent slowness of the Bogeyman. Sparks flew around them, and acrid smoke hung in the air. The device was on the brink of falling apart.

But then, much to his relief, the doors opened.

The trio wandered in a daze from the Bogeyman chamber, stepping onto smooth flooring. Quentin watched as the scientists looked around at a long, bare, concrete room, designed like a small parking garage. A wide computer desk dominating a wall behind them broke the room's emptiness, and stacks of preserved food, medical supplies, and electronic equipment covered the wall to their left. Wooden steps led up to a door on the far side of the immense room.

"Where are we?" asked one of the scientists.

Quentin pulled back the Shadow Person mask. His hair was damp and matted from the humidity of the outfit, and he breathed a sigh of relief at the reprieve.

Before he could reply to the man, the door opened, and B poked around the corner, wearing some of Quentin's spare clothes. Her face lit up as she surveyed the room. "Dhruv! Vivaan!" Quentin cleared his throat, and she corrected herself. "Uh . . . D! V! You made it!"

She ran to the scientists and hugged them, identifying who was who in the process.

V looked to Quentin and repeated his question. "Where are we?"

Quentin sighed. "Quick tour, okay?"

Everyone nodded.

Quentin led everyone upstairs into his garage, though all he had parked was a Vespa scooter. They moved from there into the hallway that connected to his theatre room and one of the guest bedrooms. Maddie greeted them, and as the group scratched and cooed, she lavished in the attention.

Quentin continued the tour of the kitchen, study, bathrooms, and other areas. Maddie followed them around, her nails clacking on the hardwood flooring. After the showing, Quentin turned to V.

"As you know by the coordinates, we're in France," Quentin said. "But all I want you to see is this home, and the bunker beneath it. My parents passed away many years ago, and I inherited a large sum of money from them. Instead of investing in a gratuitous home, I chose something more modest, opting to invest in security features."

B cocked her head. "Security features?"

Quentin nodded. "The concrete structure beneath the house is a survival bunker. Both the bunker and the home are wired to maximize electronic surveillance, while also equipped with defensive measures."

He scratched behind Maddie's ears. "I fear these features will no longer be sufficient, considering our enemy's resources. That is why, D and V, I would like to establish stable transport for the entire home into a private warehouse, where the supplies can be repurposed into a safe place for us."

V shook his head. "That's insane! Why would you uproot yourself like this?"

Quentin removed more of the Shadow Person outfit, revealing a white undershirt. "I can no longer trust the heads of the DPSD, nor can I trust the leadership of MI6, the CIA, or India's IB. This subterfuge likely spreads further and wider than any of us can predict, and I only have faith in my ability to uncover the depth of this conspiracy from a secure place."

He looked at B. "Did you gather the supplies I asked for?"

She pointed to her feet. "They're already in the bunker."

"Good." Quentin turned to the scientists. "What can we do about radio communications? The warehouse is quite remote. Can we use the Bogeyman?"

"Actually, yes," D responded. "We've done it before with Bell—I mean, B. We can open a pinhole connection to any small space in the world and broadcast from there. The computer runs automatically, following the target. I like to think of it as a 'smart' phone."

"Set that up, too," Quentin said. "We've no time to waste."

Maddie whimpered.

The scientists repaired the Bogeyman while Quentin and B unpacked supplies. Maddie contributed in her own way, sniffing from person to person, overseeing their work. After nearly six hours of labor, D and V confirmed the Bogeyman was up and running again.

V approached Quentin. "Q, I want to show you something." He drew Quentin toward the computer array. "Just to start," the scientist said, "what did you do at our lab back in India?"

"I ran a worm on your server, and on all linked servers," Quentin replied. "I saw you using satellite coordinates, which meant you probably had an established connection to at least one intelligence agency. The worm connects to those servers and embeds itself, creating a false administrative access portal. From any internet-connected location, I can use that portal to remotely view any files or programs tied to those servers."

B looked up from her work. "Gesundheit."

Quentin smiled, and V turned to her, clarifying, "he used our lab to link us to almost every intelligence agency in the world."

Her eyes widened. "MI6?"

Quentin nodded.

"Good," she said. "Let's rain fire on these bellends once we get out of here."

V turned back to Quentin. "So, as I was setting up the Bogeyman system, I noticed the transfer process pulled some files that were *not* ours. You may have downloaded some of their files in the rush."

He pointed to the screen—at a digital folder.

DOSSIER CLASS FELDGRAU

Quentin leaned over and double-clicked the folder, revealing others. There were several in the list, but their data was corrupted by the transfer. Only three folders were intact.

BOGEYMAN TARGETS
FACTION HOSTILES
REFINEMENT CANDIDATES

His breath quickened, and he peered through the first folder. It was a collection of documents, each one labeled as a person's name. Most were appended with the labels [COMPLETE] or [PENDING]. He opened the first name in the list. The documents included the person's pictures, their identifying information, personal data, and even a brief psychological profile of the person. He closed the document and scrolled past the other names.

Abdelhak Benhamouda	[COMPLETE]
Diana Frances Mountbatten-Windsor	[COMPLETE]
Joachim Ruhuna	[COMPLETE]
Juan José Gerardi	[PENDING]
Mahele Lieko Bokungu	[COMPLETE]
Norbert Zongo	[PENDING]
Quentin Lefebvre	[PENDING]

The lights in the bunker turned red, and Quentin pulled away, spinning from the monitor station. He counted the faces in the room before looking toward the ground.

"WHERE'S MADDIE?" he hissed.

B, V, and D all shrugged.

"What's the light for?" B asked.

Quentin ignored her and ran to the door separating the bunker from the garage. He looked through the crack in it, trying to find his companion, but he couldn't see her in the hallway. Closing the door completely, Quentin sprinted back to the monitors. He flipped a switch, and the feeds cut to different perspectives of his house, both on the inside and on the outside. Everyone moved closer to watch.

Surrounding the home were at least a dozen men wearing black body armor and sporting sub-machine guns. Split into two groups, one worked its way through the front door and the other through the patio, their gentleness indicating an attempt at stealth. Neither group had bypassed Quentin's locks—yet.

Maddie, though, was nowhere on any of the cameras. Quentin flicked the monitor switch, and the computer displays returned.

"Absolute bare minimum time needed to create the Bogeyman jump is . . ." he asked, addressing D and V.

"At least five more minutes," said V.

"Get started. I'll plug in the coordinates when I get back."

"Get back from where?" B asked.

"Don't worry, B," Quentin said. "You're coming with me."

He grabbed D's attention and pointed at one of the speakers on his computer array. "This one can still hear audio upstairs. When I tell you to, press *this* switch." He pointed at a red switch mounted to the underside of the desk.

"Where are we going?" B pressed.

Quentin tossed his pistol to her. "We're getting Maddie."

**Paris, France
September 8, 1997-A**

The armed men opened the doors to Quentin's home, leaking inside like a heavy fog. The team from the patio fanned into the living room and kitchen area, while the team from the front door split their focus between the theatre and the garage. The garage team poked their heads into the space, noted no other entrances or exits, and joined the team in the theatre.

Inside the darkened room, Princess Diana's pictures slid across a fabric screen, illuminating the space. The six men divided into the aisles of seats, searching for anyone hiding. The last one to enter closed the door behind him.

And as it shut, B rose up from behind the closest seat and grabbed the soldier's mouth, stabbing him repeatedly in the stomach with a black knife. He flailed in panic and pain, but soon went limp. She disappeared beneath the seats with the corpse.

Holy hell, Quentin thought, peering at her through the spaces between seats in the top row of the theatre. *She's good.*

Across the room, the five men fanned out. When the man furthest from the theatre screen swiveled to return to the others, Quentin pounced on him from the shadows, driving a kitchen knife into his throat. The man's death was swift, but not silent; he released a gurgle as he passed, drawing the attention of the other four intruders. They turned in the direction of the noise.

"Seven . . . sound off. Seven?"

No reply.

"Light it up."

The four attackers took turns unloading bullets into the theatre seats, sending foam padding and hot metal passing right over Quentin's head. He squeezed himself into the floor, trying to avoid the onslaught.

Small-arms fire sounded further away, and the attack on Quentin ceased. He poked his head over the shredded seats to see B now engaged in a shootout with the four gunmen, using Quentin's gun to defend herself. One of the bullets found a home in an intruder's face, and they tumbled to the theatre floor.

Quentin remained low to the ground, waiting for his opportunity. It came soon, as the three armored men hunkered behind the seats to reload. The instant they released their magazines, Quentin leapt from the seats and into the middle of the group. He buried his kitchen knife into one of the attacker's eyes, then vaulted past the remaining two to put some seats between them. As he moved, he saw they were already reloading.

"B, Cover!" he yelled, diving to the floor.

She rose from the entrance of the theatre and squeezed off several rounds toward the two remaining attackers, preventing them from pursuing Quentin. Stuffing and gun smoke filled the air.

B stopped, quickly reloading.

"Last magazine," she called, and hurled the pistol toward Quentin.

He snatched the gun from the air, fumbling with it for a moment before securing his grip. The two other men tried to stand again, but he was a half-second faster. As their heads entered his line of sight, he pulled the trigger twice, sending a bullet into the skull of each of the attackers. They fell to the floor.

Footsteps sounded outside, and B poked her head outside the theatre. "Six more!"

Grrrrr . . .

Quentin froze at the noise. It sounded like it was coming from the kitchen area. He scrambled to the door connecting the theatre room to the hallway and the living room.

"Q, wait! Q! Fuck it, mate . . ." B pursued him.

Quentin rounded the corner to the living room and saw six men approaching, all scurrying like cockroaches from various parts of the house. He dove to the floor and blindly fired the gun, forcing them to take cover. One of the men fired a spray of bullets from around the door frame of Quentin's bedroom, likely hoping to get a lucky hit, but the shots were far above Quentin's flattened body.

Maddie suddenly pounced from the kitchen, biting into the leg of the closest intruder and latching onto him. The man raised his gun in her direction, about to fire.

"NO!"

Quentin raised the pistol from his prone position and began squeezing the trigger toward them, panic overtaking logic. He scrambled to his feet and ran toward Maddie and her opponent while he continued to expend his ammunition. Most of Quentin's shots went wild, but one struck the man's forearm and shifted his aim. The machine gun's bullets buried into the wood next to the Dutch Shepherd.

Two of the intruders were rushing toward Quentin from the living room to his right, but he barely registered them. He knew he only had a second—if that—to save his dog. He shouldered through the men, and B appeared at his side, engaging in hand-to-hand combat.

Quentin aimed his gun at Maddie's opponent and pulled the trigger, but only a hollow *click* of an empty chamber rewarded his efforts. Crying out, he threw the empty weapon at the man's head. The man stumbled, and Maddie released him.

Quentin swept Maddie into his arms and heard a commotion behind him. He turned to see one of B's combatants kicked onto the living room floor, while the other had a black knife buried into his neck. The three standing intruders fired their weapons from their cover, and she hefted the knifed combatant's armored body against her own, absorbing their bullets.

Quentin and Maddie crawled backwards into the kitchen, putting the counters between the attackers and themselves. Quentin's heart pounded in his chest, almost drowning out the endless chattering of machine-gun fire. He poked around the corner. B had advanced, closer to the kitchen entrance, still carrying her mangled and bloody makeshift shield. When she was close enough, she dropped the body and rolled into the kitchen.

"Where's your gun?" she asked.

"Empty," he wheezed.

"Fuck!"

"Just get behind the counter, B."

As the words left his mouth, the remaining intruders opened fire into the kitchen. The kitchen counters survived the bullets, but the foodstuffs and containers on top of them exploded around Quentin, Maddie, and B. The three hunkered down, and B made eye contact with Quentin.

"Don't move," he whispered.

Quentin looked away from her and up at the ceiling, yelling three short words.

"FLIP THE SWITCH!"

The gunfire continued for another five seconds before it died down. Quentin could hear a series of mechanical clicking noises behind the walls and inside the ceiling. Something shifted, thumping beneath their feet. Then, everything was quiet again.

"What was that, Two?" Quentin heard one of the soldiers say.

"Doesn't matter," replied another. "Let's finish this and move out."

Quentin saw a black-clad leg cross the threshold between the living room and the kitchen, and his eyes shifted to the small infrared sensor now activated in the same space. The moment the man's leg interrupted the sensor, a panel of the wall in front of him slid open, revealing a four-by-four grid of silver barrels. Before the man could react, the sixteen barrels fired in tandem, shredding his body and sending the remains flying backward, out of Quentin's line of sight.

"Two!" cried one of the remaining four intruders.

"Finish the mission, Five," commanded another.

Footsteps approached, this time coming from the guest bedroom and running parallel to the other side of the kitchen counter. Quentin took B's hand and held his breath.

THUNK.

"AH! FUCK! OH GOD OH GOD OH—"

CRUNCH.

Quentin closed his eyes as he heard something wet splatter across the living room.

That would be the hydraulic press in the floor, he thought. *Three left.*

Laced with panic, a voice said, "I'm radioing for backup. Outside."

Footsteps moved away from Quentin and B, and Quentin heard someone jiggle the handle of the patio door.

What did I put in the door, again?

A bright blue light flickered, and a buzzing noise filled the air, almost loud enough to cover the screaming. The smell of burning flesh filled the air, and something thumped to the floor.

Oh, right. Conductive handle. Two left. "Good luck surviving the night," Quentin called from behind the counter. "Tell me the names of the people who sent you and I'll let you out alive."

"Fuck you," one of the remaining men yelled from the direction of Quentin's bedroom. He heard something moving toward them.

Quentin turned his head. "I wouldn't walk through the—"

He was interrupted by a metallic sluicing sound, followed by a strained gurgle.

Quentin sighed, another heavy object thumping to the floor. "Spikes in the door frame. Basically just a glorified bear trap. Now, how would *you* like to die?"

"Stop! Stop and I'll surrender!" the final man called out. Something metal, likely the man's gun, clattered to the floor.

Quentin took a breath, looking over at B. She pointed at the glass door of the oven in front of them. The final man was visible in its reflection, knees on the floor and hands on his head. She nodded, and Quentin looked at the ceiling.

"KILL THE SWITCH!" he ordered, before returning his attention to the intruder. "Tell me who controls your team. Both agency and individual names."

"We don't—you don't understand, we weren't—"

The final man seized up, his body arcing as if electrified. He trembled, his fingers splayed. After a few seconds, he fell silent, slowly rising back to his feet.

B turned to Quentin. "This is what—"

With one impossible leap, the man crossed the distance between the living room and where they hid, his boots landing on the kitchen countertop. He peered over the counter at Quentin and B and reached for a holster on his hip.

Quentin rolled Maddie and himself to the right, while B rolled to the left. Bullets from the attacker's sidearm bit into the tile floor where they had hidden, shredding the surface. Maddie ran into the guest bedroom through the study, avoiding the gunfire. Quentin and B rose to their feet on opposite sides of the kitchen space.

Quentin wielded a skillet; B, a steak knife. The man chose to aim at Quentin, who ran at him, hunkering his face and right forearm behind the cast-iron utensil. The gunfire glanced away from the pan, though the force of it pounded against Quentin's bones and the echoes of lead striking metal left a ringing noise in his ears.

He collided with the man, shifting his grip to strike at the gun. The man's aim fell away, but he didn't release his grasp of the weapon. Quentin used the flat end of the skillet to sweep the attacker's feet, and the man fell backward, losing his balance on the countertop. B was there waiting for him, and as he fell back, the steak knife buried into his spine. He collapsed on top of her in the kitchen floor.

"B!" Quentin yelled, running to her side.

Before anyone could move, the house rumbled, carrying a similar vibration to what Quentin had experienced twice before in the Bogeyman. This time, it was different. It seemed deeper; less controlled.

"Hey, I'm fine." B said, rolling the body away from her. "Less so now, though, knowing that these men were probably just like me."

"The people in control of this are monsters, B. Let's get to safety and focus our efforts on bringing them down."

B nodded, her eyes stern.

"Come, Maddie," Quentin said.

Maddie returned to his side, and the three hurried into the living room, to the hallway. From the hallway, they sidled into the garage and opened a door-sized panel in the wall, revealing the wooden staircase to Quentin's bunker. Inside, D and V were hard at work, trying to maintain control of a smoking Bogeyman chamber.

"Priming a jump this big is a heavy strain on the machine," V called out, pointing to the message on the monitor behind him.

PLEASE ENTER COORDINATES.

"The sooner we complete it," he added, "The more likely we succeed without being harmed."

Quentin walked past him. "I got it."

He typed new lines of code into the computer, but he didn't get far before a sudden movement caught his eye—B leaned against a wall, seizing as if electrified. By the time he turned around, the seizure was dying down. He made eye contact with her, but her blue windows were devoid of emotion or thought.

She was now their enemy.

B reached behind her back and produced a sub-machine gun she must have stolen from the living room.

"GET DOWN!" Quentin screamed at the scientists. Too late.

A burst of bullets flew from the barrel of her gun, opening holes along V's chest and stomach. He shook as the gunfire rattled him, blood spurting from the wounds, before collapsing to the bunker floor. One of the stray bullets collided with some sort of fuse near the base of the Bogeyman, releasing a shower of sparks.

Quentin fell back to avoid being struck as well, his hand slamming against the keyboard. The text behind him flashed red.

PLEASE ENTER COORDINATES.

More bullets flew over Quentin's head toward the Bogeyman, behind which D hid. They bounced off the metal walls of the chamber, finding new homes in the surrounding concrete. One ricochet shattered one of Quentin's monitors. The chamber's hum reached a high, violent pitch, burrowing into Quentin's ears. The primary monitor emitted a separate beep, barely audible over the hum.

PLEASE ENTER COORDINATES.

D ran for the door to the garage as Quentin leapt at B, tackling her by the waist and arresting her aim. The remaining bullets in the weapon's magazine peppered the bunker's ceiling. Without missing a beat, B tossed the gun aside and withdrew her black combat knife.

The Bogeyman's pitch wavered from low to high, and everything tilted. D tumbled back into the bunker, while Quentin and B rolled away from each other. B rose, knife in hand, and approached Quentin, but she was attacked by Maddie, who collided with her legs. Maddie's teeth bit into her side, but B brought an elbow down onto the Dutch Shepherd's forehead. With a pitiful yelp, Quentin's companion released her, sliding back across the floor.

Quentin's eyes filled with involuntary tears, and he charged at B, unarmed. She met his advance with a strike to his left shoulder, dislocating it with a sharp jolt and a crisp snap. She followed through with the knife, and it dug between his rib cage, sticking firmly into tissue. Quentin cried out in pain, and she kicked him in the chest, sending him sprawling to the concrete floor. The chirping monitor reached a steady tone, the words now upside-down.

PLEASE ENTER COORDINATES.

Through blurred vision, Quentin saw D approach B from behind with a metal rod—probably a tool left over from the Bogeyman repairs. He raised the makeshift weapon and struck her in the back of the head. She was thrown forward, staggered, but she recovered before he could complete his second strike. As the bar whistled through the air, she caught his arm.

The Bogeyman wailed again, and the surfaces shifted, sending both parties collapsing to the ground. A box of medical supplies slid into Quentin's line of sight, stopping within reach. It gave him an idea, and he pulled himself up, reaching into the container.

B and D struggled on the ground while Maddie barked at them from a safe distance. Gravity shifted, lifting them into the air as if the bunker was falling from the sky. B used the disruption to lift D to his feet, pinning him against the wall. She grasped the metal rod and shoved it into his chest with the force of a railroad spike. He choked, blood leaking from an open mouth. His eyes drifted shut.

PLEASE ENTER COORDINATES.

B stood away from D's body, allowing it to fall. Over the noise of the Bogeyman, a second tone whined. Quentin saw her look over her shoulder at him, but he pounced before she could react. He pressed a flat object against her lower back, wrapping an arm around her to push a second flat object over her chest.

"Stay strong, B," Quentin whispered in her ear.

His foot struck a box on the floor, pressing against a button on the top panel. Two hundred volts of electricity traveled from the box into the defibrillator paddles adhered to B, using her body to complete their circuit. She seized once more, and Quentin saw her eyes fluttering in a rapid pattern, as if she were in REM sleep. He released the button and caught her body as she collapsed.

"B? B!"

She didn't wake up.

Quentin checked her pulse. He couldn't find anything. The defibrillator was supposed to disrupt the device in her head, but he was no medical professional. *Did I stop her heart in the process?*

PLEASE ENTER CO . . .

The lights turned off, as did the monitors to his computers. The Bogeyman wound down, its task seemingly complete, and an intense chill ran through Quentin's veins. Maddie whimpered behind him.

He paid little mind to the changes around him, pulling his penlight from his pocket. Everyone who could help was either dead or a security risk. At least B stood a chance of surviving. He couldn't let her die, too.

"Bella!" he screamed. "Come on, Bella." He didn't have any medical training—he'd have to improvise.

He laid her onto the floor and began chest compressions, pushing with all of his force. This went on for several minutes with no change in B's condition. He only stopped when he felt her bones bend against the pressure of his CPR attempt. He turned from her and reattached the defibrillator paddles, trying to jolt her awake with the device. Her body reacted to it, stiffening, but there was no other response.

Her lips were turning blue.

Quentin cried out and overturned his medical supplies box. Shuffling through the mess, he found a series of adrenaline-filled syringes. He slid one of the needles into her arm and injected the chemicals, whispering to himself.

"Just keep one alive," he said. "Just keep one alive."

He waited.

And waited.

And waited.

Her face darkened from lack of oxygen. Quentin had no other options available, and no idea where the Bogeyman had transported them. Even if he resuscitated her now, she'd probably have severe brain damage.

Despite his best efforts, B was gone, too. Quentin cried out, pounding his palms against the concrete floor until they stung. Maddie ran to him and pressed against his side, looking up at him with her mismatched eyes. Tears running down his cheeks, he pulled her into a hug, burying his face into her fur.

"It's just you and me now, Maddie," he said. "What are we going to do?"

The intensity of the silence around them registered in Quentin's ears. He had been privy to test a sensory deprivation tank while working on a DPSD project, and the total isolation from sound and light had terrified him. Now, despite being in his own home, the same sensation hung in the air.

Quentin pulled himself to his feet, penlight aimed ahead, while Maddie stuck close to him. The beam of light passed over the bodies of his brief co-conspirators, the fallen pile of medical supplies, the boxes of food and electronics, the portable generator, and the smoking Bogeyman. Everything *seemed* the same.

The two crept up the stairs into the garage. The air felt sterile, the slatted windows in the garage door dark. Wherever they had landed, it was probably nighttime. He continued into the living room.

Darkness permeated the space, and he was careful to avoid stepping on the fallen corpses of the intruders. He shined his flashlight at the glass patio door to see outside and gasped.

There was nothing.

The doors, the windows, *everything* beyond was solid darkness, like the darkness within the space of Bogeyman transport. Quentin pulled at the handle, but it vibrated, resisting his touch. He reached for one of the weapons discarded on the floor and fired it at the glass; the bullet bounced away as if made of rubber, but the door remained unscathed.

Quentin let the gun fall back to the ground. "Maddie . . . what are we going to do?" They returned to the bunker, where he connected his portable generator and activated it.

The space didn't seem to disrupt the resource, because his lights, computers, and other electronics came back to life. The Bogeyman hummed, announcing its viability. The primary monitor flickered on, displaying the folder that Quentin was browsing before the attack.

DOSSIER CLASS FELDGRAU

He turned back to his dead friends, his face scrunching. "I'm sorry we could not survive this together, mes amies. I appreciate all that you've done to combat injustice today. The people responsible will be exposed; I swear this to you."

He turned to the keyboard and opened the primary folder, his mouse hovering over a sub-folder.

FACTION HOSTILES

"If I am to keep my promise," he added, "I cannot do it alone. I must rely on the old adage . . . do you know this one, Maddie?"

The Dutch Shepherd grumbled and curled up on the floor, weary from today's battles. He offered her a thin, soulless smile before turning to the sub-folder and opening the list of names within.

"That's right. The enemy of my enemy is my friend."

Location & Date Redacted

Crazy shit, right?

I'm telling you, these individuals are more than just the sum of their parts. They're bold, they're powerful, and most of all, they're *dangerous*. Still, understanding them is only the beginning.

You might have noticed that I jumped around the timelines a little bit. 1989-A, 2001-B, 2006-B, 1999-A . . . You get the idea. I wanted to focus on the *people*, the perpetrators of our little endeavor.

Now, please allow me to act as a seamster, stitching their individual stories together into something a little more cohesive.

On with the show!

Folder 2: Conscription

<u>Folder 2.1, File 1</u>
<u>"The Rock"</u>
<u>Reported by Shadow</u>

Guatapé, Colombia
December 31, 1999-A

Catalina rested atop El Peñón de Guatapé, a two-kilometer-high rock jutting into the sky and overlooking a small town. Below her, bathed in moonlight, the townspeople gathered in celebration, with lights and dancing; singing and laughter. Catalina took a swig of the rum bottle next to her, surrounded by the isolation of the rock and the darkness of the night sky. The wind swirled her hair, muddying her vision. Beyond the breeze, she heard footsteps climbing the makeshift wooden staircase created to bring the townspeople to the top of the rock.

"It's funny seeing them celebrate down there, don't you think?" asked the new arrival.

Tilting the neck of the rum bottle into her mouth, Catalina turned her head, curious. A woman in a red jacket, sporting a pink-and-black pixie haircut, approached her through the shadows. Catalina frowned. She'd heard a masculine voice.

"Countries who deem themselves 'civilized,' dependent on their own technology, scramble in fear of the New Year," the mysterious voice continued, and Catalina squinted. The woman hadn't opened her mouth at all. Catalina's eyes drifted to something small and metal glinting off the lapel of the woman's jacket.

From the lapel came the man's voice. "They worry that their lack of foresight has led them down a path of destruction; that the computers their world relies on will fail at the turn of a new century."

The woman stopped, standing next to Catalina, remaining silent while her hidden compatriot continued his monologue.

"Yet here they are, a small town in South America, simply celebrating. Watching them brings me a tumultuous combination of inspiration and pity. I'm inspired, for they've found a way to make their corner of the world work in their favor. But I pity them. They are unaware of the dangers encircling their oblivious existence."

The voice paused. The distant shouts of the Guatapé townspeople below broke the silence, and the voice spoke over their celebration. "Though I don't suppose I have to tell you any of this, do I, Catalina?"

The moment he said her name, she swung her legs at the woman's ankles. She didn't connect with them, though. The pixie-haired stranger's body shimmered and pushed itself away from Catalina's attack in a gust of wind. Catalina reached for her boot and produced a snub-nosed revolver, thumbing the hammer.

The woman raised her hand. "We're not from any rival cartels," she said, speaking for the first time in a thick, Taiwanese accent.

Catalina just stared at her, gun raised.

"And I'm not working for your father," the man's voice added. "In case you were unaware, you father has passed away."

Catalina felt her nose twitch involuntarily at the news.

"So, you didn't know," he said. "I'm sorry for your loss, and that it had to come from a stranger."

Maintaining her grip on her revolver, she began to sign in LSC, then stopped herself. Before she could tug at the scarf around her neck, the woman lifted her hands and made a few gestures. [Do you know ASL?]

Catalina gestured back at her. [Of course I do. It's one of the first ones I learned.]

The man said, "Thank goodness. When I read your file, Butterfly and I had time to learn one form of sign language before we met you. I made an educated guess with the world's most popular one. I am not yet fluent, but some more practice will certainly help."

[That's very exciting,] signed Catalina. [Don't offer your condolences about my father unless you liked him. He was a remorseless killer, and he worked for the worst scum. The world is better place without him.]

"In all fairness, I didn't know him," the voice admitted. "I'll concede to your expertise."

The woman, presumably Butterfly, finally lowered her hands. "May I approach?"

Catalina nodded, saying, [How did he die? Was it the same group who almost killed me? Or was it pathetic and mundane, like a heart attack or car crash?]

"Actually, Catalina, the way he died is the reason we're here today," Butterfly replied.

The voice cleared his throat. "First, I want to introduce myself out here in public, but I will only do it once. My name is Quentin Lefebvre, and I am a former operative of France's intelligence bureau. As I mentioned, this is my colleague, Butterfly."

Butterfly waved.

"You must understand, nothing I'm about to tell you *has* existed, *does* exist, or ever *will* exist. It will not be found in public records. That was *my* doing. Anyone who can vouch for my authenticity or credibility is conveniently deceased; that was *their* doing. As such, my persona is distilled into a singular identifier: Proxy."

Catalina grimaced at the code names.

"Don't be like that," Butterfly chastised. "Our chosen names are for our anonymity, as well as the anonymity of those we help." She glanced over her shoulder before looking back at Catalina. "These enemies . . . they've killed my friends, my coworkers, and my contacts. They even hunted down my surviving relatives, people I barely even knew. They did the same to Proxy—and to your father."

[We don't share these enemies,] Catalina said, tucking away her revolver. [I've never met you in my life. The only enemies I have are the cartel, and you aren't with them. I'm nothing more than a freelancer.]

"You're selling yourself short, Catalina," Proxy said from Butterfly's lapel. "You are a 'freelancer' in the same way I am a 'traveler.' Call it what it is. You hunt monsters."

Catalina offered a slight shrug in response.

Butterfly looked over the rock on which they perched, and Catalina followed her gaze. The men, women and children in town were bringing out their Año Viejo dolls, life-sized figures in nice clothes wearing paper faces. The dolls were meant to harbor the negativity accumulated throughout the previous year. When the New Year began, they burned the effigies, giving the people of Colombia a symbolic fresh start.

If only we could all be so lucky, Catalina thought.

"Listen to me, Catalina," Butterfly said, still facing the town below. "These monsters you hunt aren't accidents. They aren't freak mutations or supernatural entities. These creatures are *designed*."

Catalina glanced at her, incredulous.

"Now, we don't know the intent behind the designs of the monsters you fight," Butterfly continued. "On the surface, they seem to be for nothing more than to spread pain and suffering. Based on Proxy's research, they may be something resembling revenge."

Proxy chuckled softly from the lapel.

"It doesn't matter why they were made," he said. "Not to me. The monsters are the least of my worries."

[What do you mean?] Catalina asked.

"The people who made them have their sights set on so many other goals. Terrorism, assassinations, natural disasters, human experimentation, and biological warfare, just to name a few."

Catalina shook her head. *This is insane. Who are these people?*

"These are only the things that *have* happened," Proxy said. "This is what has been done while we lived our own personal lives, oblivious for only a few decades. Can you imagine, as our world changes and our understanding of science improves, what is *being* planned?"

Catalina scowled and signed at him. [This is ridiculous, Proxy. You're raving like a madman.]

Loud, harmonious cheers erupted, and Catalina looked back at the town. The Año Viejo dolls burned, parading through the streets on sticks.

Midnight. The New Year. In this time zone, at least.

"I have the records, Catalina," Proxy said. "I have evidence of what I'm telling you. The U.S. Pentagon, Britain's MI6, India's RAW, and China's MSS are all under my observation. Did you know a KGB base was secretly built beneath the Kremlin, and is now co-opted by Russia's SVR intelligence? I didn't either, until I started watching these communities for patterns, for opportunities to identify the people in charge of this manufactured nightmare."

The flames around the Año Viejo dolls smoldered, leaving only blackened forms behind.

"Proxy isn't wrong," Butterfly said quietly, finally turning to face Catalina again. "I run a refugee camp in the Middle East for people like you. People with abilities. We've encountered things you'd never believe without seeing them for yourself."

"There's more of us out there," Proxy continued. "We have political allies in South America and a cluster of scientists in East Asia."

A gust of wind ruffled Butterfly's pixie hair, and Catalina's own hair whipped around her face.

"Collectively, we call ourselves The Faction," Butterfly said. The wind blew stronger, swishing Butterfly's jacket around her body. She shivered, pulling it closer.

[Okay,] Catalina said, [how do I meet the others?]

Butterfly frowned. "Most of our communication is done through instant messaging and public forums, to preserve security and anonymity. Sometimes we establish telephone or radio contact. In emergencies, The Faction cells may send messengers to meet. Anonymity keeps us alive. The day I compromise my camp's anonymity might be the day my people die."

[You didn't seem to have a problem sending someone else to meet me in person, Proxy. Why not come yourself? Why the smoke and mirrors?]

Proxy sighed. "There's no trickery here. I'm . . . for lack of better phrasing, I'm imprisoned. I have no way of physically reaching the outside world."

Butterfly extended her hand. "We came here because we have faith in you, Catalina. You've been fighting our fight for years without even knowing it. We just want to make it official."

Catalina stood still, but Butterfly didn't budge. Proxy broke the silence and said, "Listen, I need you. Butterfly has her own group to look after. She's only here as a courtesy. I'm starting from scratch, building my own group. I need people who can cut through the politics and the distractions of the other Faction cells and deal with threats in real time. Do you think you can handle the challenge?"

Oh, now he's goading me? Well . . . it's working. Catalina finally took Butterfly's hand, shaking it.

Proxy uttered a sigh of relief. "Now, you'll need your own alias. I knew someone much like you several years ago, and if I may be so bold as to offer a suggestion . . ."

His voice trailed away as a tone filled Catalina's ears. It was a distant, high-pitched whine, like the noise that old-fashioned television sets emit when they first power on. The sound wasn't loud enough to be bothersome, but it drowned out other noises enough to make itself noticeable. Butterfly looked at Catalina, and based on her expression, she heard the tone, too.

The tone arrived only a moment before—

ERROR

       ERROR

          ERROR

C

  O

    R

  D   R

    E   U

      T   P

       E   T

        C   I

        T   O

          E   N

          D

REBUILDING REPORT . . .

REBUILDING REPORT . . .

REBUILDING REPORT . . .

. . . REPORT RESTORED

Guatapé, Colombia
January 1, 2000-B

—the afterimages.

The two Faction members looked over the crest of El Peñón de Guatapé, at the town below them. Buildings, trees, and people shifted, translucent and separated into two doppelgängers. The original objects stayed in place, but their doppelgängers hung in the air, upside-down like a bat. Both versions of the world overlapped, much like the optical illusion present when one crosses their eyes while touching their fingertips together.

It wasn't just the town, though. Catalina saw afterimages of Butterfly and herself; she saw a phantom version of their rock floating above their heads like a mirage. Past the image and into the night sky, even the stars had duplicated, each pinpoint in the darkness finding a ghostly mate.

Then, just like that, the world returned to normal. The tone in her ears faded, and the afterimages collapsed into each other, reducing themselves back to a singular version of each object. Catalina didn't feel any lasting nausea, disorientation or any other physical symptoms that would have explained her experience as a medical one.

Butterfly rubbed her eyes and looked at Catalina. "So, that wasn't just me, right?"

Catalina shook her head.

The pixie-haired woman stood with the huntress at the edge of the rock, the wind toying with their bodies. Their shadowed forms were so close to a whole community of people, yet to Catalina, they were an entire world away. The pair swayed there, silent, the atmosphere peaceful. Catalina savored it, for she suspected another moment like this would not come for a long time.

A smile in her voice, Butterfly said, "I suppose it's just another sign of change."

**New York, United States
September 10, 2001-B**

Beep.

Beep.

Beep.

The steady tone of an EKG machine penetrated Zen's foggy consciousness. Following it were heavy footsteps scurrying, distant sirens wailing, and panicked people crying. Everyone was screaming. Despite the noises around her, her vision remained obscured; she was numb.

Am I paralyzed?

Am I drugged?

Did the winged man take me?

Boots clacked against tile near her left. She tried to turn her head, but she couldn't move. The footsteps stopped close to her arm, and someone's body heat radiated onto her exposed skin.

Who are you? She attempted to say, but she could neither move her lips nor form the words in the back of her throat.

The EKG, the frantic footsteps, the sirens and the crying continued at a steady pace, but that was all in the background of Zen's focus. In her immediate vicinity, silence had fallen.

More body heat, now near her face. The person wasn't touching her, but they were far too close for her comfort.

"Okay, you were right," a male voice said. It sounded distant and tiny, as if broadcasted over a radio.

Zen heard a rustling noise, then the sharp *thwick* of something telescopic extending.

More silence.

The same voice spoke again. "Go ahead, then."

A new sound emerged. This one was far more familiar.

It was the electric crackling of a stun device.

Energy poured into Zen's left hip. Her cells absorbed it, dispersing the power throughout her bones, her skin, her muscles, even her nervous system. As the electricity coursed through her, wounds she didn't even realize were there restructured into healthy forms.

Her spine creaked and snapped, the feeling moving from her waist and making its way up into her neck. As it passed along her upper body, she found feeling in her toes, then her legs, then her torso. The energy reached her head, exploding into her brain. Her eyes snapped open, the fog gone in an instant.

She sat up with a start, gripping the sides of her hospital bed with enough force to shatter the plastic into dozens of small shards. The electricity had closed the tiny holes created by a series of IVs in her arms, and needles ejected from her body, quivering in the walls.

Zen absorbed her surroundings. She laid in a simple white bed shoved in a small closet of some sort. Hospital staff scurried around her, carrying bleeding and dismembered people, either unconscious or screeching. The hospital was overpopulated with the dead and dying.

Before her stood a young Hispanic woman. She was petite with dark brown hair and bright green eyes. The eyes reminded Zen of David's, and the thought made her uncomfortable.

The woman wore a black leather jacket, black undershirt, darker jeans, and matching combat boots. On the flared lapels of her leather jacket were two opposing pins: A silver-mesh disc on the woman's right lapel, and a dark glossy orb on her left lapel. In her hand was a collapsible stun baton. While it was still extended, she had turned off its electric feature.

Zen found her voice. "Did you just rob a Hot Topic?"

The woman looked down at her clothes and back up at Zen, a wry smirk on her face. She laid the baton on the bed at Zen's feet and made a series of gestures in front of her body.

Zen shook her head. "I don't know—"

An electronic laugh interrupted her—the same male voice she'd heard before. Now that she was awake, she pinpointed its source: The silver-mesh disc on the woman's lapel. It was a speaker.

"Shadow says her outfit is still better than yours," the man's voice said, chuckling again.

Zen looked down at herself; she was dressed in nothing but a hospital gown. She snorted.

"Well, I can't argue with that." She looked around. "Where are my clothes?"

The woman in the leather jacket snatched up the baton and used it to point to a small table near Zen. On top of the table was a pile of burnt and shredded cloth ribbons.

"It seems, Zen, your body was the only part of you to survive your experience in the North Tower," the voice from her lapel said.

"How do you know my name?" Zen asked. "Actually, how did you know about . . ." She looked at her arms, which still housed errant blue sparks.

"I don't know you at all, Zen," the voice said.

"Bullshit."

"I don't, I swear. I possess a file documenting your personal and professional history, as well as detailed notes on the growth of your . . . 'Refinement,' as they call it. But I do not know who *you* are. It is that particular detail I wish to learn."

"Who are you?" she demanded. "Why the hell have you been watching me?"

"Oh, no no no," the voice replied, his tone apologetic. "These are not *my* files. These files belong to a very powerful enemy. An enemy whom I believe you and I may share."

"Do you mean the man with the wings?" Zen asked.

"Well, I do not know much about *that* particular Chimera, but I've studied some of his companions. For the most part, I've been trying to prevent the circumstances that he and his people orchestrate. Unfortunately, Shadow and I have not been very successful. If I'm being honest, I believe she was more efficient at this when she worked alone."

Shadow made a face Zen interpreted as agreement.

"Still, I have poured many resources into *knowing* our enemy. We have much to learn even now, but the documents I've gathered and the worms I've strategically planted have given me enough to *act*. I can't do that, though, until I have people who will be my proxies, representatives of a cause who can actually *survive* their encounters with the enemy."

Zen slid from the bed and stood to face Shadow. "So, what? You want me to be a soldier? A terrorist?"

"Zen, I want you to be the closest thing to a hero that the real world can afford to have. I want you to be a person capable of making the tough choices necessary to *protect* people. And I mean *really* protect them, not just pour salve on their wounds while they continue to fester under toxic leadership."

She considered his words. "If what you say is legitimate, then I should involve the police, the colleagues whom I've built a strong relationship with. Collectively, my precinct can offer the wisdom that I lack on my own."

Shadow shook her head, and the voice was silent for a moment. When he spoke again, his tone was softer, as if he were comforting a crying child.

"Zen. You told me you already encountered these people. You met a Chimera, right? The man with the wings?"

"Right."

"And did he escape?"

"Yes, I'm sure he did."

"Then Zen, you must understand. Your precinct is gone."

She bristled at the comment. "*Excuse* me?"

"I don't know if they'll be dead, or if they'll just be . . . *not* themselves. Maybe the only difference will be that they don't know who you are. You may walk into your precinct and find that everyone you know was replaced with new faces overnight, though people will swear that they've always been there. No matter how it happened, as soon as the winged man clashed with you, the people you know and care about were removed from your existence."

"You sound fucking insane, sir," Zen snapped. "I'll take you there, and we'll talk to my partner. He's the most honest man I know. Besides, we have a suspect with knowledge about this mess locked in a cell there. I can pull useful information from him; I *know* it."

The voice sighed, his breath blowing into the microphone. "Shadow, are you armed?"

Shadow wobbled her hand in a "so-so" gesture in front of the glossy pin on her left lapel, a device Zen inferred was some kind of button camera. She followed up with an "okay," creating a circle with her thumb and index finger.

"Well, if you're certain you'll be fine," the voice continued. "Could you please accompany Zen to her precinct?"

Shadow responded with a thumbs-up.

Zen said, "I'm going to need better—"

Before she could finish her sentence, Shadow tossed a bundle of clothing at her. Zen caught it, unraveling the wad to find a black-

and-white checkered flannel shirt and some blue jeans. She put them on and adjusted them until they were comfortable. They weren't perfect, but they fit quite well.

"Where did you find these?" she asked. "They aren't mine."

Shadow just stood there, stone-faced. The voice's response was sheepish.

"Actually . . . I'm pretty sure she *did* steal those."

———————

Zen and Shadow trotted down the New York City sidewalk, keeping an eye on the smoke and emergency vehicles in the distance. Thousands of people gathered around the rubble of the two fallen towers. Zen looked at her new acquaintance.

"So," Zen said, "It was the World Trade Center that they attacked?"

"Unfortunately, it was," the voice replied. "We were actually trying to establish a safe way to contact you when we learned of an impending large-scale event scheduled for the city. It was slated to occur on the eleventh, not the ninth, so we thought we still had time to act. I suppose their timetable was moved up by something."

"Do you know . . . do you understand *why* it happened?"

"I genuinely do not, Zen. Believe it or not, I'm still quite new at this. Other cells of my organization, The Faction, are not quick to trust one another or share intelligence. I've had to use my computing and data analysis expertise to map out a general understanding of the enemy's plans. But the *why?* The why still escapes me."

They reached the entrance of Zen's police precinct. Inside was an open space, filled at intervals with wooden desks for detectives and other staff. Six uniformed officers, three detectives, and one receptionist were visible in the lobby area. Zen could see officers posted at strategic vantage points, and they seemed more on-guard than usual. Detectives filled out papers on their desks, and the receptionist looked up from a book she was reading, greeting them.

"Detective Kipper!" the woman said. "We've been worried sick about you since the towers fell. Where have you been?"

"Hey, Janet. I, uh . . . I was working on a case and got caught up with a rough crowd. I needed to lay low until it was safe to check back in."

"Oh, my! I suppose you saw what happened, though?"

"Yes, I did. Such a terrible tragedy."

Janet shook her head. "Such a terrible tragedy."

Zen looked around the room. "Honestly, I'm shocked we have anyone in the precinct. I assumed most would be helping clear the rubble, and we'd be left with a skeleton crew."

Janet leaned in to whisper, her face conspiratorial. "That's what happened at first! But when the officers were assisting the survivors yesterday, somebody broke into our records office and stole a stack of files."

"What did they look like?" Zen asked. "Did they take anything important?"

"Zen, I'm just the receptionist; they don't tell me anything!"

Zen smiled and patted Janet's hand. "I'm happy you're okay, Janet."

"You too, Zen!"

Shadow had wandered away during the conversation, and Zen left the receptionist's desk to catch up.

"Janet seemed fine to me," Zen said smugly.

The voice chimed in, his tone worried now. "I suggest you hurry and get what you came here for. I don't like any of this."

Shadow nodded in agreement.

Zen pointed at a hallway leading further into the precinct. "I don't see Phil, but Trevor should be back there in holding. I'll pull him into interrogation and see what I can do to help you. Wait here."

———————————

Zen walked through the rows of desks and disappeared into the back of the building. Shadow put her hands on her hips and shook her head, surveying the other people in the room. As far as she could tell, they were not very interested in her or in Zen. She signed in front of the button camera.

"No, Shadow, I don't believe this is an exception to the rule. I believe this is a trap. Be ready and be safe."

She shrugged and walked to a small bar housing a pot of coffee and an area for cups, stirrers, creamers, and other supplies. Shadow poured some of the coffee into a Styrofoam cup and walked away from the bar, back into the center of the room. She sipped the coffee and winced. Not only did it taste terrible, it also burnt her tongue.

As she pulled the cup away from her face, a glimmering object caught the corner of her eye.

Zen walked down the hallway and into the holding cells. The only occupant was a ragged-looking man who reeked of alcohol sleeping on the bench.

Where's Trevor?

Turning around the corner, she approached four doors, each leading to interrogation rooms. She opened the first door—empty.

As she moved to the second door, Zen detected voices coming from the fourth, near the rear of the building. She released the second doorknob and crossed the distance to the active room in three strides. Pressing her ear to the door, Zen heard men talking. One of them sounded like Phil.

She opened the door and confirmed her suspicion: Phil was in the interrogation room, sitting across the metal table from Trevor.

"Well hey there, Kipper," Phil said in his gruff voice. "I was worried about you."

Shadow walked across the precinct floor toward a silver object on the ground. As she moved within line of sight, she realized that it was nothing more than a silver Maglite flashlight. It rolled beneath one of the empty desks, and she wouldn't have noticed it, except . . . it was whistling.

The high-pitched whine pierced her eardrums, causing her to stick her pinky finger in her ear in an attempt to clear it. Now that she could see it, she found that it shared a similarity with that night atop El Peñón de Guatapé.

The flashlight had an upside-down afterimage, some transparent doppelgänger that intersected with itself. Shadow had to rub her eyes to ensure it wasn't some trick of the light, something optical rather than physical.

It was still there, in the same state as before.

She reached for the flashlight; as soon as her fingers touched the handle, both the tone and the afterimage vanished, leaving behind a simple silver flashlight. Shadow lifted it from the floor and placed it on top of the empty desk.

After returning to a standing position, a new officer appeared in the doorway. The man didn't speak, but he nodded at some of the stationed officers, who nodded back. When he saw Shadow, he stopped, though only for the briefest of seconds. The look in his eyes in that moment, though, sent shivers down her spine.

Shadow was in the United States today, during a crisis, when federal and state personnel had their hands tied with damage control. Prior to this moment, she'd spent her life in South America, always hidden from the public eye due to her relationship with the cartels. Not once had she even come *close* to interacting with U.S. officials. She knew the man in front of her was a complete stranger. But the look in his eyes . . .

It was a look of recognition.

———————

"I was out dealing with the wreckage of the towers yesterday, but I've spent all morning grilling him," Phil said. "He swears he doesn't know anything beyond what he already told you."

Zen leaned, casting a shadow across Trevor's face.

"Did you know where you were sending me when you told me about your contact?" she asked the criminal. "Did you know who the man was, or what he could do?"

"What happened at the park, Zen?" Phil interjected, looking at her, his gruff voice softened with concern. "Did you meet his contact?"

Zen ignored Phil. "Tell me, Trevor. The big 'S' on the wall. Who is that? What does it stand for?"

Phil reached out and grabbed her wrist. "What are you talking about?"

At Phil's movement, Trevor bared his teeth at Zen in an aggressive grin.

"He didn't know before." Trevor's voice was low, almost subsonic, and his words hissed through his teeth.

Phil stood, his hand still around her wrist. *"But I know now."*

———————

Shadow's back was to the new officer, sipping her hot coffee, but she was vigilantly aware of his movements. She had opted to wander away from the entrance of the building, using the mirrored security cameras mounted along the corners of the room to track him. His behavior was casual, but she was certain that his ambling gait carried him closer to her.

The officer looked around at the other people in the room, and this time, almost everyone made eye contact with him. The only people who didn't react were one of the officers posted in the corner, one of the detectives working at his desk, and Janet, the receptionist.

Proxy was right.

Shadow inhaled, gathered her strength, and placed her free hand against her hip, close to the flat sheath strapped to her back.

In the reflection, the officer stood directly behind her now. He placed a hand on the grip of his pistol and reached for her, yelling at the top of his lungs.

"SHE'S GOT A G—"

Shadow swiveled and splashed searing coffee into his face. Steam rose from his skin, and his words morphed into screams of pain.

While he was still blinded, she followed with a punch to the gut, then another to the neck. Both attacks struck against an odd resistance, as if she were punching a bag of sand instead of a man. The officer seemed unfazed by the attempted assault and removed his hands from his face.

Some of his skin had melted away, revealing dark-green hues beneath the surface.

"Damn it," Proxy said. "Reptiles."

"Oh my Lord!" Janet screamed from the receptionist's desk. An officer close to the receptionist drew his pistol and put a bullet between her eyes. Blood sprayed the wall behind her, and she fell away from her desk, landing on the precinct floor.

"What is the—" one of the detectives began to demand, rising from his desk, but the other two detectives raised their weapons and gunned him down. The last unaffected final officer panicked, sprinting for the precinct's exit. Another officer grabbed him by the neck as he passed and twisted his head. The man's neck snapped, and he collapsed, his lifeless face pointing behind him.

Shadow's attention refocused on the officer in front of her when he clenched his muscles, straining against some kind of invisible force. His eyes watered, and tears leaked down his face. Scanning the precinct, Shadow could see the other seven people undergo a similar internal struggle.

Here we go again.

———————

Zen attempted to pull away from Phil as his grip tightened. His muscles bulged, keeping her close, but his eyes began to weep. Trevor's chair rattled and she glanced at him, noting a similar physical reaction.

Phil opened his mouth, and an eerie, inhuman creaking noise escaped from the back of his throat. His eyes rolled into the back of his head, showing their whites. They continued to pull against the sockets, and Zen heard an awful, unforgettable ripping sound. The tears turned red as blood leaked from his eyes, and the whites rolled back further, revealing a jaundiced yellow color. Punctuating these new yellow eyes were blackened vertical slits, the grotesque mimicry of some kind of lizard's eye.

Phil's lips curled back, baring his teeth at Zen. One by one, the stumpy bones bent inward, making room for something squirming within his gums. Blood leaked from the corners of his mouth, announcing a new set of teeth. These slid into place in fine points, as thin and as sharp as hypodermic needles. They bunched together in messy rows, resembling the wiry filaments whales use to catch krill.

Gunfire drew Zen's attention to the exit of the interrogation room. In that moment, the creatures that once were Phil and Trevor pounced.

———————

Shadow had only a moment to react. A pressure in her temple announced her expanding pupils, and time seemed to slow to a crawl as she observed her opponents.

There were eight armed Reptiles in the room, all with hideous, bleeding faces. They encircled her, providing her with only a few avenues of escape. She wasn't carrying any firearms, and the Reptiles were too strong to engage in hand-to-hand combat. The only items in her arsenal were the useless stun baton and . . .

Her knife.

She slid the wide blade from its sheath and slashed at the Reptile officer's throat. Blood leaked, rather than sprayed, but the wound instantly pressed together, stitching itself closed. The creature hissed at her and punched her collarbone as she sliced him; it felt as heavy as a sack of bricks, and the hit drove Shadow to one knee.

The metallic *click-clack* of small-arms weapons being racked echoed around her, and she drew in her surroundings, ready to react with the help of her Gaze.

Triggers pulled. Muzzles flashed. Bullets left their chambers.

To Shadow, the violence suspended in amber.

She rolled to the floor, bypassing six of the Reptiles' initial shots. She pressed the flat end of her blade against her forearm just in time to deflect a seventh bullet with the metal, and pivoted on the ground to put a desk between the shooters and herself. More projectiles struck the desk's surface, toppling the flashlight she had placed there only a moment ago.

Shadow rose to her feet and made a dash to the creature closest to her. Along the way, she darted around and over desks, creating an erratic moving target to disorient her attackers.

Her prey leveled its pistol at her as she approached.

Two hundred milliseconds to trigger pull.

She kicked the seat of the nearest chair, sending it up into the air. The Reptile officer fired, and the bullet left the barrel as the chair rose. One of the chair corners interrupted the path of the superheated lead, and the metal seat warped its direction, ricocheting it into the tiled floor.

Shadow leapt over the now-disfigured chair and slid the blade of her knife under the creature's chin, slicing beneath its jaw and into the roof of its mouth. She depressed a trigger on her weapon, and the canister of compressed air in the handle of the WASP diving knife released its contents, sending the pressure along a thin tube that threaded throughout the entire weapon. The exit was a tiny hole at the tip of the blade, and the air erupted, focusing one ton of force into the fine, narrow point. The back of the creature's head exploded, and the space left behind froze from the wind-chill.

The deceased monster dropped its pistol, and Shadow caught it with her other hand before returning to cover beneath the desks. The Reptiles approached, barraging her position with gunfire, and she checked the magazine of her new weapon.

Ten bullets.

She leaned from her cover and fired at one of the Reptiles' foreheads. The bullet left a bloody crater, but the officer recovered from the blow and continued its assault.

Nine bullets. Seven bulletproof assailants. Seems fair.

This time, Shadow rolled beneath her desk and hurled her WASP knife at another officer's face. The force of the throw embedded the metal blade into the creature's left eye and beyond, almost to the hilt, and it fell twitching to the floor.

Six bulletproof assailants. Let's close that gap a little more.

She raised her arm from behind her new position and fired twice, shattering the overhead lights and raining glass onto the Reptiles' heads. In their moment of distraction, she leapt to her feet and took aim.

Seven bullets. Six guns.

Her finger squeezed the trigger of her stolen pistol six times in succession, and six offending weapons exploded in the Reptiles' hands, freeing them of their ranged advantage. Shadow darted up to the closest Reptile, shoved her gun's barrel against its right eye, and fired her final bullet into the soft tissue. The creature dropped to the ground, and Shadow threw away her empty weapon, chest heaving from the adrenaline. The pressure in her temple grew worse.

Not out of the woods yet. There are still five to go.

Zen kicked lizard-Phil across the interrogation room while slamming against the wall behind her, trying to free herself from the lizard-Trevor on her back. The latter's grasp did not loosen, and it sunk its needle-like teeth into her neck. Zen grimaced in pain; she was still riding the high from Shadow's baton, but she wasn't charged enough to avoid immediate physical injury.

"I don't understand," she grunted. "Are you the real Phil? Did you replace him? What happened to him?"

The lizard-Phil hissed at her. *"I'm the only Phil that matters now, you interfering bitch."*

Zen responded by flipping lizard-Trevor over her shoulder onto the interrogation table. The force of her throw caused the table to implode, collapsing beneath the creature. The bite marks in her neck sparked blue energy, expelling some kind of vapor from the openings. After the mist cleared, the tiny holes closed.

She raised one leg above lizard-Trevor. "If you say so."

Her foot drove into lizard-Trevor's head, and it splattered beneath her heel.

Lizard-Phil drew its sidearm and unloaded the magazine into her chest. She took the brunt of the bullets, furrowing her brow as they pushed into her body, only to spiral right back out due to the residual electricity within her cells. When lizard-Phil moved to reload its gun, Zen acted.

She crouched, ripped a table leg from the decimated furniture, and charged at the creature that resembled her friend. It opened its mouth and hissed at her; she chose to make that space her target, driving the metal into the back of lizard-Phil's throat. It broke the creature's teeth into hundreds of pieces, passed into the soft tissue of its mouth, and exploded from the back of its skull, nailing its head to the wall of the interrogation room.

Zen backed away from the mess, her hands shaking.

"If that *was* you, Phil . . . I'm so sorry."

The gunfire elsewhere in the precinct ceased, but the grunts and crashes of a violent struggle continued. Zen growled, spitting out blood from a now-healed internal injury. She staggered across the room, pausing at the doorway. With a strained heave, she ripped the door from its hinges. Now armed with her unconventional weapon, Zen moved toward the sounds of violence.

Shadow slid across the floor toward the second victim of her WASP knife, retrieving the weapon. Swiveling the blade so that it pointed toward her incoming attackers, she steadied herself, ready to strike, absorbing her surroundings. Spent ammunition littered the ground, desks and chairs were overturned, and shattered glass covered every surface. In the chaos, that goddamn silver flashlight rolled in a lazy path around the precinct.

A commotion pulled her focus toward the hallway at the back of the precinct. Zen appeared there, the front of her flannel shirt covered in blood and bullet holes, and she was dragging an entire metal door behind her.

The woman's eyes met Shadow's. "Baton!"

Shadow took a step backward and slid the retracted baton into her hand. Spinning in a circle to avoid a punch from the nearest Reptile officer, she released the weapon from her fingers. It arced above the chaos of the precinct lobby, spiraling toward Zen.

As it approached, Zen planted a leg in front of her, the force of her footfall cracking the tile. Both of her hands gripped the same side of the door, hard enough to warp the metal.

"O'Malley!" she yelled.

One of the detectives spun in her direction, and she flung the door at the creature, the metal rectangle flying in a blur. Striking its midsection, the door lifted the creature from its feet and carried it across the lobby. When it reached the wall, still moving in a straight line, the metal door crunched through flesh, muscle, bone and concrete. Blood fountained from the point of impact; the lower half of O'Malley fell to the floor, while the upper half collapsed on the quivering door now stuck in the wall.

Damn, Shadow thought, raising her eyebrows.

"Damn," Proxy murmured from her lapel speaker.

Her hands now free, Zen snatched the thrown stun baton from the air. The moment her fingers clutched it, she brought her arm down, flicking it open. The tip crackled a bright blue; Zen raised the baton and pressed those electrified prongs under her chin. Still framed in the hallway, her skin glowed, highlighted by blue lines of electrical energy. Zen's eyes widened, breaking apart her calm demeanor and revealing something primal underneath.

Shadow shook her head, leaning away from another Reptile's melee attack. She felt as if she were watching the detective transform into a different person.

While Zen finished charging, Shadow turned to address the nearest Reptile officer, her WASP knife ready. What she was *not* prepared for, though, was the flashlight lying in the floor.

She attempted to take a step, but the silver tool was lying on the tile where her heel sought its footing. Her foot slipped on the silver flashlight, and she lost her balance, twisting out of control.

I swear that thing was halfway across the precinct two seconds ago, she thought.

Falling backward, she tried to catch herself, but the Reptile she had attempted to attack arrested her in the air, wrapping two sinewy arms around her torso. It leaned down, sinking sharp, ugly teeth into her shoulder.

Shadow blew air from her nose, pushing through the pain. It wasn't *too* terrible, but she didn't want any of those thin bones to break off inside her body and risk an infection. Rather than pulling away, she flipped her WASP knife upside-down, aiming for her attacker's stomach.

———

While Shadow struggled with the assailant, Zen completed her electrical charge.

"Simpson. Russell. Fumey. Don't look away from me." Her voice was deep and electronic, accentuating the command.

The three remaining lizard creatures faced her and sprang into action. Zen grabbed the closest one, lizard-Russell, and flung it into the ceiling. It crashed against the surface, falling face-first onto the tiled floor below.

Lizard-Fumey approached her, hissing as it sprinted. She backed up, close to an adjacent wall. As the creature drew close, she ducked beneath its haymaker and pushed it into the plaster. Zen then shoved the stun baton through its body, nailing it to the wall much like she did with lizard-Phil in the interrogation room. As the creature choked for air, she punched it in the face with enough force to cave in its skull, silencing it.

Lizard-Russell recovered on the precinct floor, but Zen was already engaged with the incoming lizard-Simpson. It grabbed for her, mouth open wide, but she caught it by the wrists. Planting a foot on its chest, Zen kicked lizard-Simpson across the room, ripping its arms from its sockets in the process. The creature flew away from her, trailing a shower of blood.

Lizard-Russell jumped to its feet, raising a canister of mace to Zen's face. It sprayed a burning stream into her eyes, and she felt its effects at once; everything she saw, smelled, and tasted was liquid fire. While the energy inside of her worked to alleviate the pain and clear her vision, she felt a series of heavy punches against her stomach. They carried enough force to knock the wind from her, but she remained firm. Too many thoughts rushed in at once, but one stood out the loudest.

You're indestructible. They can't hurt you. So hurt them. Hurt. Them.

———

Shadow swung her WASP knife, jabbing the blade into her offender. She depressed the trigger, and a hole the size of a basketball punched through its torso. It opened its jaws and released her, staggering backward. Much to her relief, she felt all of the teeth retract from her skin in one smooth motion. Shadow spun around and raised her knife at the Reptile, prepared to follow up her attack, but the creature fell to its knees and collapsed face-first onto the ground.

As she relaxed her stance, another Reptile struck the wall near her. She peeked around the desks and saw that it was still awake, despite the loss of its arms, and was already standing back up. Shadow vaulted over the desk and drove her knife into the top of its skull, burying the blade once more. The creature fell back against the wall, limp.

"Not to interrupt, but SWAT has been notified and is en route," Proxy chimed in. "I've primed the evidence room for Bogeyman transport. I suggest you two get there before they arrive."

Shadow turned at the sound of a deep, raw, electronic cry in time to see Zen raise the final Reptile above her head and bring it down against her knee with a sharp *crack*. The creature bent at a ninety-degree angle, and Zen let the body roll to the floor. Her eyes met with Shadows, those brown irises frantic and wild.

Shadow gestured to the detective and then at her lapel speaker; Proxy repeated his comments. Zen nodded and hurried Shadow down the hallway, toward the evidence room. Behind them, Shadow saw black vans pull up to the doors of the precinct, and men with rifles filed out.

"Holy shit," one of the SWAT officers exclaimed at the sight of the carnage.

"Stop! Stop or we will shoot!" another officer yelled, aiming his gun through the window.

Time to take advantage of my resources, Shadow thought, diving ahead of Zen.

Machine-gun fire chattered into the hallway, but the bullets that found Zen's back just bounced away, protecting Shadow.

"There," Zen pointed at a door to their left.

Shadow opened it and found herself in a small space filled with boxes of illegal contraband and drug paraphernalia. Zen continued moving, though, into the back of the precinct.

"Just a second," she called to Shadow.

"Shadow, stay in the room." Proxy sounded concerned. "She has ten seconds before I get you out of there."

[Chill out,] Shadow signed. [She'll make it.]

———

Zen arrived at the holding cells, where the raggedy drunk was pressed against the door, alarmed.

"Wha'ss happenin'?"

Zen punched a hole in the door of his cell and ripped the entrance open. The man stumbled back, startled.

"I'm letting you off with a warning, sir," Zen said, wrapping an arm around his waist.

She lifted him off the ground and sprinted around the cells—to the emergency exit. The kick she used to open the door sent the entire object flying from the frame. The alarm connected to the door sounded, ringing a loud bell throughout the building.

Zen tossed the man, restraining her strength; he only traveled a few feet before landing on his stomach on the ground. As she turned to leave, she addressed him one last time.

"Sober up. Be proud of yourself. And don't come back here again."

With that, she dashed back toward the evidence room.

SWAT members filled the hallway now. At her appearance, the front of the line opened fire on Zen. She raised her arms to protect her eyes and charged head-first into the group, bullets plinking away from her body as she moved. The detective connected with the first few officers, and the strength of her shove toppled the entire line backward several feet and onto the ground.

Zen opened the evidence room door and hopped inside, face-to-face with Shadow.

"I'm trusting you because you were right so far, but they know exactly where we are."

"It's not about where you *are*," the voice replied. "It's about where you *will* be."

As the words left the speaker, its sounds crackled and died. The footsteps outside the door vanished, dissipating into pure silence; the lights outside the evidence room went dark. *Too* dark. Even if SWAT had cut the power, Zen should still be able to see the daylight seeping in.

The room rattled, the boxes shuffling against the shelves around her. Zen put her hands against the door and tried to open it, but it wouldn't budge; even using her superhuman strength yielded no reaction.

"Is it another attack?" she whispered to Shadow.

As the question left her lips, Zen saw a thin grid of cracks forming around her, on the walls and the floor and the ceiling. Tiles made by these cracks sucked away, and Zen's eyes perceived only darkness beneath the surface.

Shadow gestured to the far wall of the evidence room, where enough of the tiles had flown away to leave a cavernous gap. Zen leaned over the edge of the space, but there was no wind, or light, or noise. The space beyond felt . . . *sterile*.

Zen looked over her shoulder at Shadow and saw the woman approaching, a mischievous smirk on her face. She tackled Zen, sending both parties careening into the void.

Zen fell.

And fell.

And fell.

And just like that, she wasn't falling anymore.

Her head swam from the disorienting effect as the darkness peeled away from her fingers, revealing a wide metal chamber. Shadow stood next to Zen and walked forward, sliding doors of the chamber opening to greet her. Zen followed, staying close, and peered around the wide concrete room outside the mysterious column.

"It's nice to see you in person," the voice said, traces of static gone.

Zen spun to see a thin man with slicked-back mahogany hair and a scruffy beard standing a few paces away. His green eyes glimmered with excitement, but they were undercut by the dark circles beneath them. The man offered his hand.

"Who are you?" Zen demanded.

"For the moment, my name is Proxy," he said. His voice sounded more tired in person.

Zen heard the clicking of nails against concrete, then felt something cold press into her hand.

"Oh, and that's Maddie," Proxy added.

She looked down to see a pretty, brindle-colored dog wagging a question-mark-shaped tail while peering back up at her. Maddie's tongue flopped out in a grin. Though one of her eyes seemed damaged, the other conveyed genuine excitement at the arrival of someone new.

Zen bent and pet the dog for a moment before straightening back up. She turned to Proxy and took his hand, shaking it. "Nice to meet you face-to-face."

Her eyes scanned around the room, noting the half-built racks of military-grade weapons.

"You know, I'm still not convinced about joining your group. This all seems pretty violent."

Shadow and Proxy exchanged glances.

"The violence is all around us, Zen," Proxy said. "The difference between you and me is that I've chosen to wade into it head-first. I'd rather get bloody wrestling with those who would collapse the World Trade Center and kill thousands of people, than stand to the side and let it happen, patting myself on the back about how clean my hands are."

He tilted his head at a sea of monitors mounted to the wall behind him.

"Come look. I can show you what I mean. But understand, Shadow and I have much work to do, and never enough time. So please hurry and make your decision."

Proxy turned to the monitors, but Zen stayed put.

"I'll see what you have to show me, Proxy. But if I stay, if I agree to help you with this, I need to know I'll have some agency in how you operate. We need to work together, as a team. No more failures, no more innocent deaths. If we do this, we do this right."

The smile that appeared on his face was a sad, weary one. "That's easier said than done, chérie."

Dunedin, New Zealand
December 26, 2004-B

Shadow and Battery walked down the pavement intersecting the pristine homes dotting ritzy suburbs. The hot sun beat down on them, staining their clothes with sweat. Battery wondered how Shadow could stand wearing black at all times. Even in her thin, cotton shirt and loose jeans, Battery felt ready to pass out.

Shadow was a few paces ahead of Battery, her back obscured by a hefty black backpack designed for camping. The pouches were all zipped and covered, preventing onlookers from identifying the contents within. Battery had offered to carry it for her, but she refused. In the three years she had gotten to know Shadow, Battery found the woman to have one consistent quality: stubbornness.

"Society," Proxy had said the first day they met. "The group that murdered your precinct? That's what they call themselves."

He had told her all about the scope of Society's actions, as well as The Faction's attempts to mitigate the damage caused by them. Battery had to admit, the work she was able to do as an NYPD detective paled in comparison to some of the successful operations pulled off by Faction cells—like the China-based Tai Sui or the Brazil-based Péndulo. For all intents and purposes, Battery had been promoted to a counter-terrorism unit.

These first three years had been a mixed bag for her, though. Battery and Shadow took apart some errant Society monstrosities let loose on small communities, stood in the way of attempted assassinations, and uncovered Society-controlled operatives stoking minor religious and political conflicts. For each victory, they were rewarded with the slaughter and consumption of friends and families, labeled with monikers like "terrorists" and "traitors" by the general public.

The whole ordeal was exhausting, even for Battery. She was tired of taking one step forward and two steps backward with every operation Proxy placed in front of them. It was time for her to decommission Society in a more permanent way. It was that determination which made her hopeful about the New Zealand mission.

"This is a needle in a haystack," Battery muttered.

"Be optimistic, Battery," Proxy responded in her earpiece. "We both know Shadow won't be."

A couple walking their dog approached from the opposite direction, giving Battery an idea. She reached into her pocket for the NYPD badge. Her role in society may have changed, but she afforded herself a few keepsakes from her former life.

"What do they call the police in New Zealand?" she asked Proxy.

Shadow stopped and turned back to look at her.

"It's . . . uh . . ." Keyboard typing ensued. "Apparently it's still 'the police.' The New Zealand Police."

Battery walked past Shadow and flashed her NYPD badge at the couple, flipping her wrist so they couldn't quite read the words on the shield.

"Excuse me, I'm with the New Zealand Police," she said, stopping the locals. "I'm investigating a series of small-time thefts in the area, and I had a few questions for you."

"No problem," the man responded. "How can we help, officer?"

"We're looking for unusual behavior, particularly by anyone you see regularly. I have it on good authority that they have a hideout near here to store valuables, and the comings and goings of these people could have seemed strange in the moment. Does any of this strike a chord with you?"

The man tapped a finger to his chin, deep in thought.

"No, officer, I can't say that it does. There's the occasional suspicious schoolkids, but that is nothing new. I didn't even know people's valuables were being stolen! Should we increase our home security?"

Battery made eye contact with the man and leaned in. "Always."

The woman put a hand on her partner's shoulder. "What about the beach?"

He furrowed his brow for a moment, trying to parse her words. "The beach . . . oh, yes!"

The man looked at Shadow and Battery.

"About two kilometers east is an isolated spot by the ocean called Tunnel Beach. It's a nice place to relax. Bring children and pets. My wife and I used to go every weekend, but as we grew busier, we settled for pleasant walks around the neighborhood."

He paused, and Battery gestured for him to continue.

"Over the last year or so, though, we've begun to notice people headed for the beach in abnormal clothes. Suits and suitcases, collared shirts and lab coats; once, I saw a man dressed like a security guard walk in that direction."

Battery grabbed Shadow's shoulder. "We'll look into it. Thank you for your time."

Before they could walk away, the man spoke again.

"Not from around here, are you, officer?"

Battery slowly turned to face him. "Excuse me?"

He smiled and tapped his lips. "The accent. Dead giveaway. You new here?"

"Not as new as you'd think," she replied.

———————————

The pair stood at the mouth of the dark tunnel leading to New Zealand's hidden beach, contemplating their next move.

Six hours ago, Butterfly's South-Asia-based Faction cell, Koshasth, sent some captured digital chatter to Proxy. The recorded conversation referenced some kind of large-scale event planned for South Asia. Details were vague; though ominous phrases like "disaster relief" and "population reduction" were used. One comment implied the "launch point" of the event would be near Dunedin. Deployment was imminent. Locating, securing and disabling the launch point was Battery and Shadow's goal. Battery could feel time ticking away as she stared into the tunnel.

Not one to wait, Shadow hefted the backpack from her shoulder, dropping it against the wall at the entrance to the tunnel. Battery lifted the ends of her shirt, exposing a belt made of thick, copper panels. Attached to the belt at her right hip was a black box with the dimensions of a deck of cards.

The Charge Belt was a makeshift device pieced together by Proxy and Shadow. The copper panels cinched against the skin of her hips and stomach, while the black box was an advanced battery capable of storing 200,000 volts. In a conflict or emergency, a simple flip of a switch flooded the belt, and then Battery, with more than enough electricity to prepare her for every occasion.

[Why do you want to stop here in the tunnel, instead of the beach itself?] Shadow signed.

"Just a feeling," Battery replied. "Back in New York, I found a facility that I think was used to prepare for the World Trade Center attacks. One of its entrances was a secret door in a stone wall under the Fort Tryon bridge. Look around."

Both Shadow and Battery searched the lip of the tunnel, their gazes trailing to the thick, sloping hills running off either side.

"See that? Plenty of room for a staircase, or even a small bunker, should there be another hidden door like the one in the park."

Shadow put a hand on the tunnel entrance and poked her head inside the cool, shaded space. After a few seconds, she pulled away, turning back to Battery.

[How do you suggest we look for it?]

"Well, last time I worked harder, rather than smarter. Now that I have your help, why don't we expedite the process, at the risk of losing our element of surprise?"

[I'm game. Let's prepare to breach.]

Shadow crouched, unzipping the camper's backpack. She retrieved pieces of curved black metal, connecting them together to form a bizarre-looking gun comprised of crescent-shaped humps near the barrel and handle. A flat black tray ran along the entire length of the top of the gun; Shadow retrieved a magazine matching its dimensions and slid it, face-down, into the tray.

Battery didn't know as much about firearms as Shadow, so she couldn't identify what she was using, but she trusted her judgement. She also admired her military precision. It was, surprisingly, a very attractive quality to the detective.

Battery's own process was much simpler. She activated the Charge Belt, and the hot crackle of electricity ran along the copper panels. Any other person would have perished like Topsy the elephant, but her body merely sucked in the blue energy, creating tingles of pleasure along her skin. She allowed herself a moment to enjoy the sensation before deactivating the belt. Small bolts of lightning crossed between her fingertips, the power buzzing in her ears.

Meanwhile, Shadow strapped a collapsible Kevlar vest to herself and added a utility belt ringed with closed pockets and magazine holsters. A black pistol attached to her right leg, tight against her black jeans. Reaching back into the bag, Shadow retrieved bundles of silver shapes, catching Battery's eye.

"What are those?"

Her partner just glanced at her before looking away. Shadow held the bundle in the air, unraveling it. The exposed bandolier held a row of stumpy, silver hatchets, each stainless steel, but with handles wrapped in a mesh made of thick red cables, not unlike paracord. Shadow draped the bandolier over her shoulder and fastened it. Satisfied, she turned and signed to Battery.

[You know what to do.]

The pair strode into the tunnel between suburbia and the ocean's edge.

It only took a moment to reach the center of the tunnel, and Battery held out a hand to stop Shadow. Cool air, far too cool to be the wind, blew in a thin stream against her forehead. She turned to the wall on her right.

Raising her fists, Battery brought them down into a hammer strike, colliding against the tunnel wall with enough force to rattle the entire structure. Rock shards flecked from the area she struck, and a door-shaped outline appeared, puffing out powdered debris before settling back into the wall. A hollow *thock* sounded as the vibrations returned to them, announcing an open, empty area behind the tunnel's stone surface.

Battery stood back. "That was easy."

Shadow walked in front of her, sliding some of the hatchets from her bandolier. Chopping at the tunnel wall, she wedged the blades into the rock, leaving them in the stone and forming an embedded archway. After firmly planting six of the bizarre tools, she walked several long strides away from the hidden door, preparing her curvy machine gun.

After a moment, Shadow raised a small remote into the air. She pointed at the wall, then at Battery, then at herself. Battery understood the message right away. She walked up to the side of the tunnel opposing the archway of hatchets and planted her feet, prepared to run.

Shadow pressed a button on the remote. The red cord around the hatchet handles sizzled and exploded with burning fury. The sound of it poured throughout the tunnel, rattling inside Battery's ears. Particles of earth and stone rose around them, creating a natural smokescreen.

Battery dashed forward into the unknown. As expected, she collided with a layer of the door Shadow's explosives hadn't destroyed. Her electricity prepared her, though. Her collision tore through rock and metal, catapulting her into empty space, still blind from the smoke. Her feet landed on a glass and plastic surface, crushing it into the ground.

She blinked away the soot from her eyes and absorbed her surroundings as quickly as possible. The entire area was one large, rectangular room. The outer surfaces were pearl white, and the only furniture in sight was a series of long tables lined with computers and monitors, much like the average design of a university computer lab. One of those tables, and its accompanying equipment, laid in shambles beneath her feet.

In terms of personnel, Battery swiveled her head and counted about ten men and women stationed at the computers, dressed in outfits ranging from casual clothes to formal business attire. These people all stood or looked around the sides of their monitors, staring at Battery with an uncomfortable smile on their faces.

In addition to the people working at computer stations, Battery noted several guards. Each corner of the room housed two people wearing black body armor and black masks—eight hostiles armed to the teeth, each hefting a large, imposing rifle.

"Ah, The Faction. Mother told us to expect you." Every person in the room uttered the greeting in unison, their voices cheery and melodic, almost as if singing their words.

The harmony of their words sent shivers down Battery's spine. These were no Reptiles. They definitely weren't Triggers, like the ones Proxy dealt with in France. No, this was something else entirely. Something The Faction had not yet encountered.

The dust settled; the armed men all raised their rifles, their movements in sync. She had just enough time to block her face with her forearms before they fired.

Hot, heavy bullets punched against her skin from every direction, but the energy she'd absorbed protected her. She ran in the direction of the rear-left corner, dropping her right arm to yank the nearest computer monitor from its table. Twisting back, Battery released the display, and it spun like a buzz-saw into the chest of a soldier, creating a loud *crunch* as it impacted his sternum. Her target flew, smacking the wall and sliding to the floor, no longer moving.

Battery steamed ahead, raising her right fist to form a punch. Her knuckles connected with the side of his head, no more forgiving than the metal tip of a launched rocket. The target's skull collapsed into itself, while his neck snapped at a ninety-degree angle. Even as her fist carried past the man, the residual momentum cartwheeled his rag-doll corpse into the air, landing him next to his partner.

"Two armed at nine, one and three," Battery murmured. "Ten unarmed at twelve."

The response to her comment was immediate. She heard the aluminum plinking of canisters rolling into the room, and instinctively covered her mouth. The canisters hissed out a fog of tear gas, and computer workers coughed and gasped for air, stumbling over the chairs and tables.

Even as the gas grenades entered the room, new gunfire sounded from the entrance, and Battery glanced over her shoulder. Shadow had engaged with the four armed men nearest her. The huntress weaved and dodged, expertly cutting into their weak points with concentrated bursts of bullets. One guard managed to hit her vest from behind, and she hurled one of the hatchets at him without looking. It connected with his chest, lodging there, and she used her remote to detonate it, incinerating the attacker.

Battery turned away from Shadow's machine-gun tête-à-tête and launched herself toward the two armed men at the rear of the room. They concentrated their rifle fire on her head and upper body during her charge, causing her to lose sight as she blocked the bullets. Her fists punched into nothing but pearl-white wall. They had dodged away during her moment of disorientation. An object rolled against her ankles, and she looked down to see two live grenades.

Battery had no time to avoid the blasts. The shrapnel pattered against her electricity-hardened skin, the shock wave lifting her into the air. Her vision whitened, a ringing in her ears drowned out all other noises. Blind and deaf, Battery crashed into the middle of the room. Shadow's tear gas cloud burned her eyes, nose and throat.

Coughing, Battery leapt to her feet, shaking away the effects of the explosives and the gas as her internal energy worked to alleviate any damage accrued. Through the fog, she saw a ring of humanoid shadows, the unarmed workers surrounding her. She readied herself, opting to be cautious rather than unpleasantly surprised. Throughout the room, a single word echoed in unison.

"Reinforcements."

She turned to see some of the Dunedin suburbanites she had spoken to earlier, including the couple who pointed them toward Tunnel Beach in the first place, rushing through the doorway. They were still in various casual wear, including one woman in a tennis outfit, but they all shared the same wide, plastered smile. Cradled in their hands were rifles, pistols, clubs, and machetes. Raising the weapons, they spoke. "Mother won't have you, and neither will we."

Battery rushed a small group of unarmed workers to her left. She opened her arms like a bird and picked the people up, carrying two with each arm. Halting her sprint, she allowed the momentum to carry them into the wall, seemingly knocking them unconscious. Battery couldn't allow them to make the fight any more dangerous than it already was, but *someone* had to survive this ordeal for interrogation.

Gunfire sounded to her right—Shadow had moved further into the room, trading bullets with the last two guards. One of them struck her submachine gun with a well-timed shot, and she seamlessly transitioned to her sidearm, hip-firing like an expert gunslinger.

Four suburbanites approached Battery. One had a rifle, two had pistols, and one had a machete. In her peripheral vision, she saw six unarmed computer workers preparing to pounce.

She turned and grabbed the end of the nearest table, swiping the flat end around in a complete circle, scattering the ten assailants across the room. A few of them flew right over Shadow's head before they struck the wall, forcing the huntress to duck a little. Shadow shot Battery a quick glare with her blackened cat-like eyes. Battery smiled sheepishly.

Whoops. Sorry.

The ten assailants were already on their feet again, no more than a little disoriented. The tear gas had almost cleared, and Shadow approached, the bottom half of the huntress's face covered by black cloth. The pair made eye contact, telegraphing their next move with little more than a short gaze. The hive-mind people swarmed in from all sides, weaving around the still-standing tables. Those with firearms stayed back, unloading their weapons at the two women. Battery moved between Shadow and their line of sight, letting the gunfire ricochet off her back and into the nearby furniture and incoming melee attackers.

Shadow ran at Battery and jumped into the air once she was within reach. Battery supported her foot with both hands and lifted her wrists, launching Shadow toward the ceiling. The huntress turned upside-down as she reached the apex of her flight, taking aim with her pistol during the momentary suspension.

Battery spun and struck the closest suburbanite in the chest, crushing it, as a series of rapid gunshots sounded overhead. Several of the attackers dropped around her like flies, bullet holes opening in their foreheads. The machete-wielding suburbanite ran at Battery, but Shadow landed on top of him, shooting him in the back of the head.

The four remaining hive-mind people scattered, and Shadow chased three of them, opening fire as they tried to run away. Battery turned to face an opponent bearing a wide smile and a cluster of grenades connected to fabric strips. It was only as he hurled the cluster in her direction that she realized he'd already pulled the pins.

"Are you serious?" she asked, grabbing a bullet-ridden monitor within reach.

The cluster traveled in an arc toward her, and she jumped to meet it, monitor raised. Emulating a tennis player, Battery smacked the cluster with the flat side of the monitor, sending it hurtling back to its caster. The would-be demolitionist had enough time to share an expression of surprise before the cluster struck him square in the chest, the force sending him backwards out of the secret room.

The detective turned away from the ball of fire and shock wave of energy erupting from the doorway. Shadow was on the other side of the room standing over the last three suburbanites, victorious. Battery made a tired thumbs-up, and her partner returned the sign.

Battery toward the entrance, concerned the explosion would create a cave-in, but if anything, their exit was wider than before. She sighed in relief and approached the four surviving workers, Shadow joining her side.

Three seemed unconscious, but one woman stirred. Battery picked her up by the shirt collar and dragged her to what must have been the last working computer station. The rough handling alerted the woman, and she struggled against Battery's grip. After dropping the woman into a chair, Shadow placed the barrel of her gun behind the captive's head.

"Three seconds," Battery said, her electronic voice amplifying her dour tone. "Explain the Society event being planned in the next three seconds, or Shadow sends you to meet your friends."

The woman coughed and reached for the keyboard. "Why, I'll just show you!"

Just then, Proxy sounded off in Battery and Shadow's ears. "Team, there's some kind of disruption in that room. It took me a moment to find a frequency to reach you."

The woman continued, unlocking the screen to a series of windows displaying topographical maps.

"The Faction is so silly. So stupid. The attack doesn't *happen* from here. This is merely a targeting facility. You're so, so far from anywhere you can be of any use."

Proxy spoke up again. "Battery, Shadow, it's already happening. We're too late."

As if she could hear his voice in their earpieces, the woman's smile grew wider. "Would you like to watch?"

On the monitor, a map of the world flashed. A red dot appeared in the Indian Ocean west of Sumatra, and concentric rings spread out from there to Sri Lanka, then India, then Bangladesh. Parts of each country began to turn red.

"An earthquake just struck the seabed. Faction-planted seismographs say it's one of the largest in recorded history," Proxy said. "There's a tsunami heading toward South Asia. I think . . . the casualty count will be high."

"What can we do?" Battery cried. "Bogeyman us there!"

"Battery, this is too big. There's nothing we can do to prevent it."

"AHHHH!" Battery brought down her hands on the table behind her, cracking it in half.

The woman snickered, as if told a joke she wasn't allowed to share. "Mother says . . . heh . . . Mother says she likes seeing you angry."

Shadow's eyes narrowed at the comment. She raised her arm and struck the woman across the face with the butt of her pistol. The woman leaned over from the blow, and Shadow grabbed a handful of her hair, pulling her up and slamming her nose into the edge of the table. Droplets of blood fell with the woman onto the pearl-white ground. When she rolled to sit up, Shadow pushed her again before putting a hand on her face, forcing the barrel of the gun into her mouth.

"How do the earthquakes happen?" Battery demanded. "Explosives? Some kind of underground machine? If they're being launched or broadcast from somewhere else, where is the broadcast location?"

"Battery, it's useless," Proxy whispered. "I don't know what these people are, but they aren't going to share Society secrets with us. Shadow, plug in the drive and run the worm."

With her free hand, Shadow retrieved a flash drive from her belt and inserted it into the computer. A folder appeared on-screen, and she used the mouse to open it and run Proxy's program. Data from the local servers began to download onto the drive.

"Mmmm-mm mrmphmm," the woman said, mumbling around the gun barrel in her mouth.

Battery and Shadow exchanged looks, and Shadow pulled the gun away. The woman cleared her throat and smiled again, looking behind them. They spun to see the other three surviving workers standing within arm's reach, motionless and staring, that terrible fake smile across their faces.

The woman spoke, and the other three joined her, sharing her words in a final quartet. What they said next, Battery knew, would give her nightmares for years to come.

"Mother, take us."

The moment they finished their request, the flesh melted from their bodies. It peeled back and liquefied, allowing all of the blood beneath the surface to pour out unabated. While the blood and skin poured around them, their exposed muscle fibers snapped apart like broken rubber bands, falling in small pieces from their skeletal frames. The bones and organs were just barely visible before they liquefied as well, pouring through their open rib cages in a crimson slurry. The bones frayed and crumbled into powder. When the horror ended, the four workers were nothing more than piles of clothes stained with melted meat.

Battery and Shadow looked around the room—the same process occurred with the others. Clothes and armor crumbled and flattened, and red goop poured from every available opening. Battery blew out a long breath from her mouth, overwhelmed and disgusted. Shadow just stared.

As the people finished melting, every active computer chimed. A red exclamation mark appeared across the screen Proxy's program was infiltrating. Hissing noises emanated from the ceiling.

Battery looked at Shadow. "Time to go."

Shadow nodded and withdrew the drive, interrupting the program's progress. The pair sprinted across the room while the hissing grew louder, sweating from a sudden rise in temperature. Nozzles dropped from the ceiling and flickered, revealing small spouts of flame. Incineration seemed imminent, but they were still ten paces away from the exit.

Battery placed her hand on the small of Shadow's back and pushed. Her partner launched through the doorway just as fire engulfed the room. The orange flame seared across Battery, white-hot against her flesh, and she cried out instinctively. The vacuum created by the heat collapsed her lungs, and she suffocated, falling to the ground. Her clothes turned into ash and fell away.

Finally, the torture ended.

Battery stumbled outside, still burning, but electricity swirled around her body, extinguishing the flames and restoring her lungs. She touched her head, surprised to find she wasn't bald.

Apparently even my hair is indestructible.

She stood, naked and smoking, with only the charred remains of her Charge Belt clinging to her frame. Coughing out black smoke, she used her arms to cover herself.

"I . . . uh . . . I think I'll need a new belt," she said, her voice weak.

Shadow smiled, the first genuine one in years, and embraced Battery. The detective leaned over and hugged her back, her grip much tighter than most would assume. After a moment, Battery looked down at Shadow and spoke, the strength returned to her voice. "Let's get back to Treehouse and sort out this disaster."

**Karnataka, India
April 15, 2006-B**

On the ground floor of the largest building within Gurur's Waste Water Treatment Plant, armed men in black scrambled. The workers were gone, the plant's normal processes halted. Two men waddled in full SCUBA gear up to a trap door in the corner of the plant. One opened it, revealing a space filled to the brim with water. The other cradled a football-sized purple capsule in their arms. Together, they dove into the murkiness below.

Shadow crouched in her cloak and hood, hidden in the rafters of the plant. Battery waited next to her in Navy-blue body armor and a new copper Charge Belt, watching their movements.

Sixteen months ago, they used Proxy's worm to retrieve data from a computer in a New Zealand "targeting facility." When they escaped, the drive had been pulled too soon, and the details it captured were incomplete. Nonetheless, they uncovered folders outlining a series of vaguely named projects, such as "Disaster Relief," "Bear Mascot," and the one that brought them here today: "Water Maintenance."

[Do you think the entire underground base is supposed to be flooded like this?] Battery signed to Shadow.

[Doubtful,] Shadow signed back. [I know what a revolution looks like; it seems that someone didn't take too kindly to what appears to be a Society invasion.]

[How do we get in there? Proxy's schematics say that it's several stories deep. We can't swim that far.]

Battery looked around at the men, who seemed confused. They were waiting for orders, which meant they didn't have an exact strategy either. Whoever flooded the facility likely *did*. If they had a way to survive, they also had a way to escape. Whether that was through this trapdoor or somewhere else, Battery was unsure.

Shadow finally responded, mirroring Battery's thoughts. [I vote we create a safe escape route, in case this is their only way out. Once this area is secure, we can decide how to handle any survivors and destroy the PAUS.]

Battery nodded. [You say when.]

Shadow raised her hands, but squawking chatter caught their attention. Below, two of the men were receiving directions on hand-held radios. Battery and Shadow leaned forward, and Battery tried to make out the words, which were, thankfully, in English.

"Potential breach . . . Contact at . . . Estab . . . perimeter . . ."

One of the men in black put the radio to his mouth and responded. "Confirm, Acharya's contact at Mysore Airport has been dispatched?"

"Yes, Asmach. The entire airport has been cleansed. Qegnaz-mach's teams and my own are setting the trap now."

"Good work, Grazmach," said the man—apparently named Asmach. "Stay in touch in case Acharya finds another way out and takes the bait at the airport."

The man turned and directed the others. "The chief engineer is a flight risk. Dejazmach, your team stays here to guard the primary exit. My team will make an aerial sweep of the area in case they get out some other way."

The men with radios stood at attention. "Yes, Asmach."

Battery heard the putter of helicopter blades overhead. Only then did Asmach and his team exit, leaving Dejazmach's team behind.

Shadow turned to Battery. [I suggest we divide as well. You wait for survivors at the airport. I'll continue my plan here.]

Battery nodded and climbed up, back into the air shaft. She closed the vent behind her, whispering, "Proxy, ping me. I need to be at the Mysore Airport."

Before the Bogeyman came for her, Shadow clipped a thick rope to the rafter at her feet, and then to herself. When Shadow bent her knees to jump, the rafter creaked a little, and some of the remaining men looked up in time to see a dark wraith descending upon them, its form billowed out like a winged nightmare. The falling specter spat a wave of bullets into their ranks as Battery's air shaft enveloped her in darkness.

"Shadow says her space is secure," Proxy announced. "The divers finally resurfaced, and we're interrogating them now, but they aren't saying anything."

Battery huffed, squinting from the rooftop of the Mysore Airport over the horizon.

As Proxy had dug deeper into the files retrieved from Dunedin, he learned more about the projects within. Apparently, "Water Maintenance" was a follow-up program to "Disaster Relief," the project responsible for the earthquakes which caused the tsunami last year. While "Disaster Relief" had been established for years, though, "Water Maintenance" was almost brand-new, slated to finalize within the upcoming weeks. The details of the new program were vague, but the recovered files outlined its location: the Gurur Waste Water Treatment Plan in Karnataka, India.

This time, we'll stop the disaster before it happens, Battery thought.

As she searched for movement in the fields, she responded to Proxy's update. "They clearly fear Society worse than they fear Shadow."

"A thought that makes me quite uncomfortable," Proxy said. "Any sight of the Karnataka scientists?"

"Nope. When I first arrived, the airport seemed abandoned. I haven't seen any movement by Society or by any civilians since I've been here. But I positioned myself on the roof, and I'm oriented toward the plant, so there's no reason for me to miss—"

Battery stopped speaking as three white-clad figures appeared above the hills and into her line of sight.

"What? What is it?" Proxy asked.

The figures drew closer, crossing onto the edge of runway. They were speaking to one another, their tone far too casual for their circumstances. They didn't even notice when the tall grass near them began to rustle.

Battery activated her Charge Belt and took a few steps away from the roof's edge. "Proxy, get Shadow over here. The survivors are in trouble."

Muffled gunfire, likely from rifles equipped with silencers, erupted. Battery dug the toe of her boot into the rooftop, her electricity-enhanced strength creating a thick divot. She bent into a running stance, exhaled, and sprinted forward. Her powered legs sent her traveling at a blur, and she cleared the rooftop, looking down as she flew above the chaos.

Two of the survivors were already dead, and the third was running into the airport lobby. The black-clad men approached the final survivor as they continued to shoot.

In their direction, Battery directed her fall. Still grouped together, they had little time to dodge her before she struck the tarmac with the force of a missile. The pavement crumbled into pebble-sized pieces, sending waves of shrapnel into the men, knocking them from their feet and sending them flying far away from her. Dirt and pulverized rock hung in the air like smoke.

The earth-cloud had little time to settle before gunfire erupted around her, bullets striking her from every direction. The few projectiles capable of piercing her new body armor simply bounced from her skin, leaving a growing pile of crumpled and deformed rifle rounds at her feet.

"One survivor, entering the airport," she yelled, but new gunfire poured from within the building. "Goddammit, another unit inside!" She launched from her spot, flying forward over the tarmac, and speared her fists into two of the men firing at her. Something inside their chests crumpled as they rocketed away.

"Battery, your area is too hot," Proxy responded. "Give me something more specific for Shadow."

Grenades skidded across the airport toward Battery, and she jumped high into the air, her feet no more than warmed by the resulting explosions. She came back to the earth, interlocking her fingers to create one large fist, and hammered her hands onto the closest attacker's head. The man exploded, splattering her armor with blood, and she looked away in disgust, wiping the fluids from her face and eyes.

"He's . . ." Battery looked at the airport, past the windows.

Some kind of humming noise tickled her inner ear, making itself known even over the gunshots. A watery mass appeared inside the airport and exploded, blowing the glass from the windows as it flooded the building. Water poured outside, sweeping the remaining men from their feet as it reached knee-level and spilled into the grass beyond the tarmac.

A torn metal rod floated past Battery, and she grimaced as she was struck with a macabre idea. Snatching the rod from the current, she used all of her strength to plant the rod into the ground beneath the impromptu river, leaving a jagged end pointed up.

You're going to regret this.

Battery slammed the palm of her hand against the metal spike, crying out in pain as she was impaled. The energy stored within her cells released to heal her from her injury, and arcs of electricity climbed up and down the conductive rod. When the electricity reached the waterline, it spread in an instant, causing the water to glow a faint blue. The seven remaining attackers stiffened, the electrical current creeping up their legs in bright blue tendrils. Smoke rose from the men, and two caught on fire.

Battery withdrew her hand from the rod, leaving the burned and bloody metal planted in the earth. Her palm crackled, energy sealing the hole shut in seconds.

Christ. That hurt.

Confirming her opponents had fallen, she investigated the airport once more. The scientist waded through the waters, entering a small office space on the left.

"He's inside, alone," Battery said. "Halfway into the building, a small office to the left of the entrance. I'll go retrieve—"

She stopped at the sound of chopping helicopter blades; the aircraft rushed down from the clouds, hovering above the airport.

"Proxy, I have more incoming. I don't know if I can get to him yet."

"Get out of there, Battery," he said. "Shadow's already on her way to pick up the scientist. Make sure you get back alive, too."

"Affirmative."

She turned and leapt away from the airport, flinging herself high into the sky.

The Bogeyman chamber opened, and the scientist in the strange vest stumbled out, dazed. Shadow drifted after him, as still and as silent as her adopted namesake. Battery and Proxy stood to greet the man.

"Hello," Proxy said. "I'm sorry to be so short, but there were many scientists working in the Karnataka facility. Were you a part of the project known as Water Maintenance?"

The man remained silent, peering around the room.

Metal against metal sounded, and the scientist's eyes widened as Shadow pressed the barrel of a pistol against the back of his head, her face stern. She made a gesture and pointed at the man's waist.

Battery followed her movement with her eyes, where he was reaching for something, then back up at the man. "Listen," she cautioned, "there's no need to be courageous. Not here."

As she addressed him, the man's face aged a decade; the hand fell still. Proxy took over the conversation.

"Maybe we've started on the wrong foot, yes? My name is Proxy. The colleague next to me is Battery. The woman behind you goes by 'Shadow.' These are, of course, not our real names; they are the names we have chosen. I would like to know *your* name, sir. As far as we know, you are the sole survivor of an attempt to eradicate your facility. Therefore, I imagine you have quite the story to tell."

The man stared at him before looking back at Shadow, whose gun hadn't yet wavered. He sighed and raised his hands in a submissive movement. When Shadow nodded, he reached to remove the glove. Once it was unfastened from his hand, he reached back and detached the pearl-white vest draped over his torso. He stepped over to a nearby desk and carefully placed both pieces of equipment on it.

Then he began to sob, sinking to the floor. Battery frowned.

What have they done to you?

All three Faction members let him stay there for a few minutes. Proxy stood still, his hands behind his back, while Shadow holstered her gun, shifting her stance every few seconds to indicate her discomfort. The man's crying began to desist, and the volume of tears falling to the concrete floor lessened. After he collected himself, he stood to his feet once more, wiping his eyes and his nose. His expression was serious, far more serious than it had been before.

"Where am I?" he asked, speaking in English.

"Treehouse," Proxy replied, his tone soft but curt.

"Is that a . . . code name, or something? How far underground are we?"

"We aren't underground."

The scientist made a confused face. "We fell for miles . . ." His voice trailed away as he pointed at the Bogeyman chamber. "What exactly is that device?"

Proxy walked to the man's side. "To oversimplify, it's a teleporter."

"You know, like *Star Trek*?" Battery added.

"But I was falling. I felt it." The man placed a finger to his chin, thoughtful. "Maybe it was some sort of psychological block. A way for my brain to process what was happening."

Proxy shrugged. "Maybe. I'm no scientist."

The newcomer looked him in the eye. "What exactly *are* you, Proxy? Do you represent my investors?"

"On the contrary, I am the enemy of your investors," Proxy replied, shaking his head. "Do you know what I'm saying when I say the name, Society?"

The man furrowed his brows. "No."

"Well, they have an investment in your facility, and they planned the assault on your laboratory. If I understand correctly, they wanted to weaponize a project there; something called 'PAUS.' It's . . . some kind of water machine? Do you know about the project?"

The scientist snorted and shook his head in disbelief, extending his hand to Proxy. "My name is Nadi Acharya. I'm the inventor of the PAUS. That device lying on the table over there? It is now the only working model of PAUS in existence."

Proxy took his hand and shook it, clapping his free hand on Nadi's shoulder. "It's a pleasure to meet you, Mister Acharya. I regret to inform you, though, that Society, the people who attacked you . . . they don't have to rely on PAUS to cause harm. We are aware of several devices within their possession capable of wide scale destruction. For reasons unknown, they have utilized these in the past, and we believe they will utilize them in the future as well."

Nadi placed his hands on his hips, as if attempting to absorb information.

Maybe this is too much at once, Battery thought, looking over at Proxy.

"I'm telling you this," said Proxy, "because we, The Faction, could use your expertise. You've worked in a facility designed to supplement Society with powerful, cutting-edge technology. The knowledge you possess of Society's technological scope and interests might prove valuable to locating where their weapons are, and how they may be disabled. I know that you've been through quite an ordeal, and it's understandable if you need time to think about it—"

Nadi raised his hand to stop Proxy. "I have nothing left. My friends and coworkers were murdered by these people. The project I spent half my life developing will never see the light of day, not without it becoming an instrument of death. My only real-world test of a machine meant for humanitarian purposes was to tear apart men trying to kill me. My home, and my family, was destroyed years ago by the Indian Ocean Tsunami . . ."

Proxy and Battery exchanged glances, and Nadi noticed the interaction. "What? What did I say?"

Shadow raised her hands and turned away, leaving Battery to reply. "Nadi, the tsunami . . . I'm so sorry. We tried to stop it, but we didn't have enough intelligence. We still don't."

Nadi shook his head. "Stop it? The tsunami was a natural disaster. How would you have . . ." His eyes widened. "No."

The scientist put his hands to his head, clutching fistfuls of hair.

Battery stepped closer. "Nadi, I know this is a lot to take in. We just want you to know what you're getting into."

"Shut—shut up. I said that I'm with you. And I already know a person who probably has deep roots in Society, as well as an involvement in the devices you're hunting. I've met him, several times, and I would bet everything I have he can give you valuable information. But if I'm to help you, I have an unwavering condition."

"Name it," Proxy said.

"I want to be present when you capture and interrogate him. I need to confront him, to understand what happened. Why he was driven to do this."

Battery looked at Proxy, who made an uncomfortable face.

"Are you combat-ready?" Proxy asked. "The last seven years have taught me that almost any attempt to reach out to Society or its operatives end in conflict and death."

Nadi frowned, looking at his feet. Battery saw his eyes drift to the PAUS vest lying on the table.

"Give me a few days with PAUS," he growled. "A week, at most. I'll give Society exactly what they wanted."

Berlin, Germany
April 22, 2006-B

Flashing, multicolored lights pulsated from a doorway, painting the sidewalks and screaming into the night sky with their fleeting hues. Deep, pounding bass reverberated through the confines of the building, infecting the air with a raw, sexual energy. An electronic remix of Bob Sinclair's "Love Generation" blared, the lyrics barely audible through the added bass and increased tempo.

Why must our children play in the streets?
Broken hearts and faded dreams . . .

Aquifer stopped at the entrance of the building, letting the lights and the music wash over him. Battery joined him at his side.

. . . peace and love to everyone that you meet.
Don't you know, it could be so sweet . . .

Aquifer pulled at his sleeve. It was far too tight against the cabling running from his white gloves to the modified PAUS device beneath his white button-down shirt. The black slacks and shoes indicated he wasn't a man accustomed to the scene before him.

. . . just look to the rainbow; you will see:
Sun will shine 'til eternity . . .

Aquifer glanced over at Battery, who adjusted the new silver Charge Belt he had made as a show of good faith. Formed from a smooth metal and fitted with a fan-like miniature electric turbine, it was quite unlike the boxy, limited battery packs she used previously. A thin battery lining the outer ring would contain the power necessary to "jump-start" the fan. Once it picked up speed, the electricity produced by the blades would keep them spinning, creating a perpetual energy source. The outer ring also included a dial, allowing Battery to run it for a continuous trickle of nourishment or to amplify her usual strength and resilience tenfold.

. . . I've got so much love in my heart.
No one can tear it apart.

A tall, muscular, bald-headed bouncer guarded the doorway to the club. He regarded them with a dismissive up-and-down glance, rolling his eyes before turning to the young, scantily clad women sauntering toward him. Battery huffed, activating her Charge Belt at its lowest setting. The fan blades whispered to life, sending nearly imperceptible blue sparks running through her skin, beneath her jeans and blue tank top.

Aquifer allowed his eyes to wander to the only identifying characteristic of the building: A pink neon sign, spelling the name of the nightclub in large block letters.

KARLSLUST.

"Sorry, we're all filled up tonight," The bouncer called in German as they approached.

"That's okay," Aquifer replied in the same language. "We won't be here long."

The bouncer reached for him, but Battery smacked him across the face. The strength of her strike bloodied his nose and sent him twirling to the concrete sidewalk, unconscious.

The two moved into the Karlslust, swimming into a sea of young, sweaty dancers. The bass, the lights, the lust, and Bob Sinclair's words swallowed them whole. It took every ounce of physical strength and willpower for Aquifer to continue his journey, but he continued to push in a straight line through the crowd.

Feel the love generation . . . yeah, yeah, yeah!

Feel the love generation . . . oh yeah-yeah!

They reached a closed door at the back of the dance floor, and two more muscular men stood on either side. The guards regarded Battery and Aquifer with indifference, but as the two drew closer, annoyance appeared on their faces.

"The restrooms are over there," one of the men yelled in German over the music, pointing to his left.

"What did he say?" Battery asked Aquifer.

"He thinks we're lost."

She regarded the men with amusement. "I'll have a word with them."

Battery strode ahead, reaching for the doorknob. The man who spoke before didn't even grab at her. Instead, he moved straight to swinging a right hook at her head. His fist slammed against her skull, showering sparks; instead of injuring Battery, the bones in his hand crunched. The guard howled, falling against the wall.

The uninjured man tried to put Battery in a hold, wrapping her into a headlock. She grasped his wrist and used it to twist his arm away from her, capitalizing on the martial arts techniques she'd been learning from Shadow. The man's arm pulled from its socket with a *snap*, and as he yelled, she open-palmed the back of his head, knocking him unconscious.

Hm, Aquifer thought. *Maybe I should take Shadow up on those lessons.*

Still whimpering, the guard with the broken hand backed up when Battery raised a fist toward him. She took a step closer, and he swore in German, pushing himself through the young dancers to flee, the patrons hardly noticing his panicked exodus.

Aquifer tried the door handle, but it was locked. He turned to the unconscious guard for a key, but as he knelt to the floor to search the man's pockets, Battery's foot whistled past his face, splintering the entire door from its hinges. Aquifer stood back up, embarrassed. He was still getting used to the idea of superhuman people—and their usefulness.

Battery strode into the dimly lit space beyond the doorway, Aquifer close behind. Even in the low visibility, they could see a red carpet, red-painted walls, and three booths covered in red leather. The left and center booths were empty; in the right one, however, were two figures. One was a young, blonde woman in a black cocktail dress, laughing at the man with her. The person charming her was older and pale, dressed in a black suit and tie.

"Kalt!" Aquifer barked.

At their abrupt entrance, the woman jumped and turned to them. The man just leaned forward, looking their way. When he saw the people addressing them, he raised a calm hand and snapped his fingers. Aquifer heard noises close to them, on both sides. He turned to see a well-dressed security guard to their left, pointing a large pistol at them, while another stood to their right, emulating his partner.

"Hope your thing works," Battery said, reaching for the dial on her belt.

"Me too," Aquifer muttered, clenching his right hand.

He raised his fist into an uppercut motion; the PAUS recognized his gesture and activated just as the guard to his right pulled his trigger. A quarter-meter-thick rectangle of water appeared between

Aquifer and the guard, shimmering from the pressurized force it contained. The bullet struck the wall and deflected away, sending water droplets showering behind it.

Behind him, Aquifer heard Battery's turbine raise in pitch, almost drowned out by a series of rapid gunshots. There was a dull *thud*, and the gunshots ceased.

The guard in front of Aquifer's wall continued firing, but the bullets ricocheted all across the room, forcing him to stop. When he lowered his gun, Aquifer dropped his right fist, collapsing the water wall, and made a circular gesture with his other hand. An orb of water the size of a bowling ball formed in front of it, and the scientist pinched his fingers together, rocketing the orb into the guard's torso. It splattered against the guard and knocked him off his feet into the nearest wall, where he drooped over, unconscious.

The blonde woman pulled away from the man now, standing to her feet.

"I think I should leave—"

Kalt stood behind her and grabbed her by her head, a hand to either side of her face. "Too late."

He twisted her head, snapping it with enough force to spin it around, her dead eyes facing backward. His hands released her face, and her body crumpled to the ground, the cocktail dress bunched up around her hips.

The man turned to the two Faction members. "Acharya." His once-German accent was gone, replaced with a lifeless, monotone voice.

Aquifer raised a gloved hand. "Zugführer Kalt. You wanted to see PAUS become a weapon. You sold your soul to Society to kill political and religious extremists. Was it worth it?"

Kalt laughed, the sound deep and throaty.

"Acharya, there is so much you don't understand. Did I want PAUS as a weapon? Sure. That's *my* responsibility to Society. But it was far too much of a hassle to wrestle it from you."

He chuckled again, but the expression devolved into a hoarse coughing fit.

Aquifer scowled. "PAUS was appropriated as a follow-up to Society's Disaster Relief project, which killed hundreds of thousands of people. Do you not understand this? Even if you got your weapon, Society would use it for their own reasons. Maybe people *you* love will die in the process."

Kalt sighed. "You disrespect me, Acharya. You have no idea what Society is. Who we are."

He leaned in and smiled an evil smile. "Disaster Relief is out of my purview altogether. The person you should be upset with is the one you know as Zala. Don't get me wrong, we all benefit from each other's successes, but I didn't kill your colleagues."

Aquifer paused at the answer. "We? Are you saying everyone, every investor, is a part of Society?"

The smile grew wider. "Even your precious Noam."

Kalt stood up straight, clenching his fists. The Zugführer seemed to be taller than before, and the skin of his face stretched thin, as if resisting his growth.

"No," Acharya whispered, pushing aside the sinking feeling in his stomach. "You're lying."

I've known Noam for years. There's no way . . .

"Maybe you should stop trusting your friends," Kalt responded, rotating his shoulders and stretching his neck. "They're likely to get you into more trouble than you can handle."

Past the doorway, the music silenced.

Aquifer leaned back, poking his head around the doorway and looking out onto the dance floor. The main room grew dark as the flashing lights died, and the mass of dancers stood still, their forms hunched over. One by one, the young people turned toward them, revealing yellow, lizard-like eyes glowing softly in the dark.

"Did you think we wouldn't be prepared?" Kalt asked, stepping over the dead woman's body to walk toward them.

The Reptile dancers hissed, the noises echoing through the quiet dance floor. They crept through the darkness, illuminated by their yellow gaze, swarming toward Battery and Aquifer.

"No." Aquifer said, his voice calm. *I'm not dealing with this shit right now.*

He walked up to the door frame, communicating with PAUS via a series of subtle finger twitches from his right hand. The heavy, mechanical device beneath his shirt emitted several soft clicking noises, similar to that of a chirping cricket. Though he couldn't see them, sonic waves bombarded the dance floor, each returning to his PAUS, using sonar to build a map of the room's dimensions.

We don't have time for distractions.

Aquifer raised his right arm, extending a gloved hand. The Reptiles closed, about to reach the doorway, bloody teardrops on their cheeks and displaying dripping, needle-like fangs—just as Battery had described. His hand swished back and forth, as if he were tightly conducting an orchestra.

In a heartbeat, the entire dance hall filled with water.

The Reptiles swirled around the poorly lit fluid, attempting to re-orient to the sudden shift in their environment. Hundreds of yellow eyes fixated on Aquifer's still-raised hand, and they swam toward him, teeth bared. He responded by lifting his left hand, holding it close to his body as his fingers twitched. The dancers reached the doorway, where the water field ended. The first to arrive reached through the space, clutching for the scientist.

Aquifer rotated his left wrist, fingers still extended, as if he were turning a dial. The water in the dance hall shimmered, pressurizing in gradients from the outside in. As a result, a pressure vacuum formed in the middle of his water field, and the mass of lizard-people surged backward, trapped in the center of his whirlpool. They uselessly struggled, unable to swim through the currents to reach the scientist.

"Pest," Kalt spat, striding in Aquifer's direction.

Battery blocked the Zugführer's path. "You know, he isn't the only one looking for answers."

Kalt looked at the detective, rolled his eyes, and moved to push past her. Battery swung her open hand toward his chest, but he caught her arm, stopping it mid-swing. The grip around her wrist tightened, and Battery looked at Aquifer in surprise. His eyes moved up to Kalt's face. Something about him seemed wrong. He seemed *distorted*, as if he were too large for his own skin.

Without warning, Kalt's free hand rose to clock her in the temple, the bones of his knuckles crashing into her face like a falling cinder block, and she fell to the floor. Warm blood dripped down her face from an already-healing wound.

"Battery!" Aquifer said, moving to help her.

"Did you not expect that?" Kalt taunted. "We did not form Society because we were weak. We formed Society because we are *strong*."

He emphasized that last word with a kick to Battery's stomach. Aquifer was unable to keep up with the sudden momentum as she was propelled upward by the kick. She crashed through the ceiling, leaving a hole revealing the starry night sky, and flew out of sight, into Berlin.

"I think he's a Chimera," Proxy chimed into Aquifer's ear. "Aquifer, run. NOW."

The scientist looked at the weakened-but-struggling prey in his water trap, then at the approaching Zugführer. "No, Proxy. I can handle hi—*shit!*"

Kalt swiped an arm at him, and Aquifer ducked, pulling his right thumb into his palm to "lock" the water trap in the dance hall. With PAUS updated, he could roll away and release his arms without worrying about the horde of Reptile dancers. He stood to deal with Kalt, creating a pair of water spheres in the air, one for each hand.

"Be reasonable, Zugführer Kalt. What do you gain from all of this death?"

The man, taller and more distorted than before, snorted. "You haven't aligned yourself with the right people to take a moral high ground, Acharya. Do you know what you're fighting for, or what you're fighting against? Do you understand why we make the choices we've made? Because *I* do. I see the bigger picture; the irresponsible choices your kind has made. Society does what it does to make you *better*. Fighting us only leads to more death on both sides."

Kalt gestured his head toward the dance hall, where the sea of lizard-dancers had fallen limp, floating without direction. "I had them here to detain you and your device, Acharya. Society didn't plan for them to die. You *chose* to kill them. Just as you chose to kill your friends when you refused to give over PAUS at full functionality, and when you drowned the scientists during Zala's attack."

Kalt leaned forward. "You're no better than us. The least you can do is kill for a good cause, a cause that you understand."

Aquifer maintained his spheres, keeping his hands aimed at Kalt as he responded. "Help me understand, then. Tell me about Zala's end-game with her 'Disaster Relief machine. Spell out why her program took away my family, and why her militia took away my friends."

His opponent raised a finger to his lips, like a car salesman feigning secrecy about a "once in a lifetime" deal. "Acharya, I didn't come here to spout our organization's secrets to our enemies. I came here, waiting for you, so I could explain ourselves. I want you to help us grow. You don't like the way we've been doing things? Use your ideas to make it better." Kalt took another step toward Aquifer. "Like I said, you don't know the first thing about what either side stands for. Society wants a better world. Don't you want that, too?"

Above their heads, a whistle grew louder with every passing second. Kalt looked up, and Aquifer pinched his fingers, sending two orbs rocketing into the man. One splashed against his chest, and the other against his face; together, they caused him to stumble a few steps, but they had no other noticeable effect. The water fell to the ground, and Aquifer saw a series of thin vertical lines forming in Kalt's exposed face and arms, as if his skin was tearing.

"I'll pass on working alongside mass murders," Aquifer growled.

The whistling was ever-present, but Kalt spoke over the noise. "You already are."

The whistling descended upon them, culminating in an exploding ceiling between Kalt and Aquifer, rattling his bones. Rubble and plaster flew everywhere as the cloud of wreckage cleared, revealing Battery in the center. Electricity arced around her body, etching black burn marks into the floor near her feet. She rose to face Kalt, revealing her Charge Belt turned nearly to its maximum voltage.

"So, you're Chimera, huh?" she queried, her voice robotic and booming. "I met one of you before. Still have a score to settle with him."

Kalt shrugged. "Can't help you with that. I keep to my own business."

"Well, I'll just take it out on you, then. Stand and look pretty for me."

Proxy sounded in Aquifer's ear, his voice flustered. "I don't know why we still give her communicators if she's just going to fry them all. Aquifer, tell her to be careful. We still want him alive. Maybe we or another cell can extract useful intelligence from him, even if he doesn't know where to find what we're hunting."

Aquifer turned to Battery. "Proxy says not to kill him."

She looked back. "No promises."

In response, Kalt's mouth widened into an amused grin, the corners pulling back as if attached to strings. The lines in his skin lengthened, becoming jagged and uneven as they tore apart. His frame filled the room, and his head touched the ceiling. The skin tore open, and white hair poked out from below in tufts.

Battery shook her head. "Now we meet the *real* Zugführer Kalt."

A tear formed at Kalt's hairline, spreading down the middle of his face. His eyes remained a piercing blue, but they darkened around the edges as his face pulled away from his head. A black nose poked out, and more white hair appeared. Aquifer noted its thickness; it wasn't human hair at all.

It was *fur*.

Kalt shook his head violently, and his skin flew away from his head, sliding down from the rest of his body. There was no blood or gore, nor was there any indication he experienced pain. A piece of Kalt's face landed at Aquifer's feet; it had a rubbery quality, like Latex.

The Zugführer had a human suit, and now Aquifer could see why.

Standing before them was a gigantic . . . polar bear. His face had those circular white ears and a stubby snout with a black nose at the end, and white fur covered the rest of his body. Extending from his hands were short, black claws; before their eyes, the claws extended, tripling in length. The bear-man was so tall his head pressed against the ceiling, causing a slouch.

Kalt didn't share all of a polar bear's physical attributes, though. Rather than four legs extending outward, his silhouette was humanoid, with two distinct legs and two distinct arms. Instead of paws, his arms had longer, more pronounced appendages, clearly meant to emulate fingers. White skin visible beneath his fur reflected the light, more like marble than flesh. Rather than darkened animal eyes, Kalt retained human-like irises and pupils that denoted an intelligence far greater than an average bear's.

And probably far greater than a human's, too.

The Zugführer bear crouched and roared, the noise deafening. "Surrender yourselves!" The words echoed around them, the voice of a much larger creature. "Relinquish the PAUS to Zala. Lightning woman, I will place you at the forefront of our armed forces. Acharya, I will guarantee you freedom to pursue your other projects. I'll even do my best to convince Zala to use PAUS for its intended purpose, in addition to her own needs."

Aquifer shook his head.

"Counter-offer," Proxy said through a speaker on Aquifer's lapel. "Provide us with intelligence about Society. Help us understand what you are, and to what end these heinous acts are committed. Let us dismantle any equipment capable of wide-scale destruction. Tell us about the people you've chosen to replace or control, and why they're so important to you."

Battery looked down at the electricity swirling around her body. "And give us insight into Refinement. What we were made to *do*."

She raised her head to meet Kalt's blue gaze, and Proxy continued. "You and the rest of Society have spent a great deal of time and resources just to accomplish what we *know* about. Without context, it seems disgusting and terrible, a violation of humanity itself. If we understand you, maybe we can work *together* to achieve your goals without destroying countless lives."

Kalt shook his gigantic, angular head, the furry ears twitching a little. "Without context, what *The Faction* does seems disgusting and terrible, at least in the public opinion. After all, it's *your* people who are seen as terrorists, not mine."

Battery's shoulders tensed, her radiating energy flickering in anger. "That's Society's shadow-government psy-ops bullshit, and you *know* it!" she yelled. "Any Faction attempt to warn people about Society meets a cruel fate at your hands. The people you placed in the media spin it against us."

The bear-man shrugged. "A snowman isn't built with the awareness of his eventual death. If you wanted to tear down that snowman and rebuild him before he melts, would you waste your time explaining yourself and waiting for his consent?"

She gritted her teeth. "A snowman isn't a conscious, intelligent animal."

"It's all about perspective," he snarled, revealing long, pointed fangs. "Your kind seems quite ignorant to me."

Punctuating the critique, Zugführer Kalt smashed a hand-paw down upon Battery's head, crushing her into the ground. Concrete flaked away from the impact zone, and she remained pinned inside the new crater.

Aquifer raised a hand to assist, but the bear-man had greater reach in his natural form. He swiped at the scientist with his other arm, launching him through the doorway of the nightclub and into his own water trap. The pressure sucked him in immediately, and he struggled, kicking against the current. In his panic, air bubbles escaped his mouth, and he began to feel lightheaded from lack of oxygen.

After a few seconds, Aquifer calmed, closed his eyes, and let the current take him. He raised his arms, and, with a few gestures, he reeled in an air bubble from Kalt's room, bringing it to a stop around his head. He gasped, sucking in the limited oxygen.

Looking around, he found himself pressed against a bundle of bodies, driven by the currents he had made. He altered the PSI around himself with a series of subtle finger movements, but he halted as yellow light appeared to his left, heralding two strong arms wrapped around his torso. Aquifer turned and came face-to-face with yellow, bleeding lizard eyes and rows of thin, sharp teeth protruding from what was once a young, pretty woman.

He cried in terror, the action involuntary. Something about the murky darkness enveloping him made the monstrous face much more disturbing, as if he were being attacked by an angler fish at the bottom of an oceanic trench. She took advantage of his fright by biting down on his shoulder, trying to take a chunk of his flesh. Instead, the sturdy metal of his PAUS vest deflected the attack. Many of the needle-like teeth shattered, shards scattering through the water. She screamed, the air from her lungs erupting in malleable bubbles toward the ceiling of the nightclub.

Opting not to continue his more complex command, Aquifer pulled all five of her fingers into his palm, tapping his thumb twice against the surface of his hand. This gesture dismantled the field keeping the water together; the moment he completed it, gallons upon gallons of liquid crashed out of Karlslust's front doors, flooding the streets of Berlin. As the deluge drained from the nightclub, bodies swirled around in a jumbled mess, separating Aquifer from the lizard-woman.

He found his footing with ease, guiding himself to the floor with a series of ultrasound pulses. The moment his feet touched solid ground, he steadied himself, forming another bowling-ball-sphere. Standing on the darkened dance floor, the scientist waited, his breaths measured and slow.

Screeching from the darkness, the yellow-eyed woman leapt toward him. She drew close, scurrying through the ankle-high water, and Aquifer steadied the arm directing his water sphere. When she was within two meters, his fingers pinched together. The sphere zipped into her face, pressure and force ripping her head from her shoulders. The decapitated body staggered, fell, and spurted streams of blood into the pools of water around it.

Aquifer stood in the darkness, daring not to move, waiting for any other lizard survivors. None arose or made themselves known. The only sound was the pitter-patter of moisture falling from the ceiling onto the dance floor. Satisfied, he turned to the back room, but the two occupants had vacated it. Creating a hydrophobic ultrasound pulse to dry himself, he spoke into his earpiece. "Proxy . . . where did they go?"

"Shadow says to follow the sounds of property damage," the analyst responded.

Aquifer turned and sprinted toward the Karlslust's entrance, beholding the spectacle outside.

Car alarms blared around them as Battery and the bear-man traded punches, each block shattering windows with a shock wave, each throw opening a new hole in a wall or crater in a road. Both dueled with precision and finesse. Each showed signs of fatigue, but neither was prepared to give up their fisticuffs tête-à-tête.

Kalt roared and punched Battery, but she side-stepped the thrust to grab his arm, flipping his massive form over her shoulder. Even as the Zugführer landed on the ground, shattering the pavement around him, he was already rolling away, ready to strike again.

Aquifer took a deep breath and sat down on the wet concrete, chest heaving. *I'm just gonna rest for a second. She's got this.*

Kalt clutched a nearby Vespa and threw it at her like a horseshoe; rather than meeting his strength with her own, Battery dove beneath the attack, allowing the vehicle to shatter against the brick wall of the building behind her. She met his throw with a running leap, careening into his abdomen and launching him backward.

The bear-man stood as she reached his form, raising furry arms to block her punch. Her electricity-infused fist rocketed into him, and he struggled to avoid being propelled further away. As the blow struck, the parked vehicles around them rattled, their windows shattering and car alarms screaming. They continued their sparring match, ducking and diving between super-powered jabs and swings.

Aquifer returned to his feet and prepared his PAUS. The movement attracting Battery's attention, and Kalt took advantage of her momentary lapse in focus. The bear-man slapped her across the skull, dropping her to her knees with enough force to splash water high into the air. The moisture fell back to the earth around them in a temporary rainfall, obscuring their bodies. Battery stayed on the ground, watching her opponent. Kalt looked to Aquifer. He'd stopped moving and was staring at the bear, expectant.

"You keep bragging about how much smarter you are than us," Battery said, her electronic voice carrying her words through the shower. "Still . . . we managed to build a better bear trap."

The bear-man's eyes widened in surprise, and he began to turn away, but it was a futile effort. Something small and fast tore through the water droplets over Battery's head and struck his right shoulder with a wet *slap*. Blood sprayed from the point of contact, and his entire right arm launched away from his body, splashing onto the wet pavement.

Kalt roared in pain and anger, diving low enough to avoid a second high-velocity projectile. He ran toward the nightclub with his head down, barreling straight for Aquifer. The bear-man was no more than a few strides from the entrance of the building when another fast shape found its target, shearing away his other arm. He spun to the ground in a spray of blood, landing face-up near Aquifer's feet.

The scientist bent down on one knee and spoke in a low, calm voice. "See . . . coming here, we thought you might be more than human, something tough to kill and impossible to capture. So, Battery went a few rounds with you to test your limits."

Battery walked up to them to finish the commentary. "Once we guessed what kind of trauma you could survive, it was only necessary to draw you outside, into Shadow's sights."

The two trappers waved into the darkness. Up from the fourth-story window of a nearby building, a small light flickered. Shadow crouched on the ground with her elephant gun protruding from the window's edge, the light illuminating her full cloak and armor.

Battery squatted to Kalt's level. "You'll be much easier to contain and interrogate without your stick arms, snowman."

The bear-man laughed, wincing in pain from the missing

appendages. The blood had stopped leaking, the wounds somehow already closed, though no new arms grew in their place.

Growling through his teeth, he leaned forward. "You two understand nothing of Society, and you never will. We may be strong, but we are also proud. Nuclear deterrence? That was *our* idea. No life of ours is taken without mutually-assured destruction."

He bit down onto one of his own teeth, which crumbled; a red, glowing foam filled his mouth, spreading down his neck and into his stomach. Battery and Aquifer began to back away as the foam grew brighter, and Aquifer gestured frantically with his PAUS.

"Your arrogance is your downfall, Faction. When the Spring arrives, you *will* melt. And Spring is arriving soon."

With that final comment, the paraplegic polar bear exploded into a ball of fire.

As the explosion occurred, Aquifer completed his final gesture, forming a barrier of water. At first, he considered submerging himself in a ball full of water, but he reconsidered when he remembered the increased potency of sound waves in liquid. It could put him in *more* danger.

Instead, a hollow bubble of air, surrounded by a two-meter-thick wall of water, formed a sphere around his body. The explosion threw him backward inside the bubble, and the fluid around him rippled from the force. Aquifer intensified his ultrasound field, increasing the water pressure enough to make the fluid act more like a solid mass.

The bubble crashed through a nearby building, traveling through walls, floors, and ceilings before continuing its ascent. The series of impacts jarred his body within the field, causing whiplash while also distorting the water beyond the field's capabilities to manage. With a splash, the field collapsed, drenching the scientist as he soared through the night sky.

Aquifer made patterns with his hands, wincing as each motion spread the sharp pain across his neck and spine. A rooftop approached at a high speed, and he had to plot out his next movement if he was going to survive. Finishing his gestures, he aimed at the rooftop. A giant cube of water, running along the edges of the building and stretching two stories high, appeared in an instant.

The scientist curled his body into a ball as he traveled toward the cube, uncertain which way he would land in the turbulent conditions. As luck would have it, his knees entered first, shielding him from additional injury to his neck. He coasted into the water, slowing to a stop. With a few hand motions, the water line began to lower, maintaining its square form while trickling excess liquid over the sides of the roof. Within a minute, he floated to the ground, his feet touching dry land.

"Owww . . ."

The Bogeyman chamber opened, and Battery stepped out. Her clothes were in charred tatters, and the blue energy dissipated around her as the turbine in the Charge Belt wound down. She rubbed her hands through thick hair, shaking away white plaster dust, while Aquifer watched.

"You look like hell," he said, wincing and reaching for his neck.

Shadow, back in her black civilian clothes, sat at Proxy's computer chair, silent as ever.

"Nice shooting," Battery commented, her voice returning to its normal tone.

[It's a shame we weren't able to interrogate Kalt, though,] her partner replied.

"Yes, it was. But . . ." Battery held up her fingers, ticking them down with each item she listed. "We killed a Chimera. Aquifer took out at least a hundred of those lizard creatures; assuming there isn't an infinite amount, that's fantastic. Kalt still gave us general information about how Society thinks and behaves, which is invaluable. He also mentioned something about Aquifer's former investors all being Society, or even Chimera themselves. They could all be high-profile like Kalt, so if we get their names, we might have better luck with one of them."

Shadow shrugged.

"I'm happy we are on the same page, mon amie." Aquifer turned to see Proxy standing there with Maddie on a leash, panting a little. "Sorry to dip out at the end of your operation, but I trusted Shadow to run the show. Maddie had an accident in the living room." He frowned. "It's very unlike her."

He unclipped her leash, and she trotted away, her blind eye causing her to veer a little too close toward the nearest wall.

"In truth," he continued, "this is no time to lament what could have been. This is a time to celebrate!"

Another sharp pain shot through Aquifer's neck. "What are we celebrating?" he grumbled.

"Our victory," the analyst replied, flashing a smile. "What we gleaned from Kalt today is a major turning point for The Faction. We knew what Society *does*, but now . . . now we can begin to understand how they *think*, what motivates them. Understanding why they're driven to point a gun helps us know who they'll shoot next." Proxy leaned over to pet Maddie, and Battery joined him as he continued his thoughts. "We need to disperse this information amongst the other cells. I hope their analysts and profilers will be able to help build a pattern for us to follow."

Aquifer nodded, then sat down, knees shaking.

"Hey, are you okay?" Battery asked him, stepping forward.

"I was kind of . . . launched through a building," he said. "I may need a neck brace."

"You got it. Great work, by the way. You'll make a fantastic member of The Faction."

Aquifer formed a thin, grim smile. "I appreciate that. And I look forward to getting to know all of you better as we dismantle this . . . this . . . this Lovecraftian regime." He laid down on the floor and groaned. "Until this heals, I won't be able to be active in the field. Is there anything I can work on for you? I'm a bit of a restless tinkerer when I'm bored, so if there's a way I can improve our tech here at home or out in the field . . . just let me know."

Battery, Shadow and Proxy traded glances with one another, smiling. Proxy pulled out a list from his pocket, and Battery snatched it from him, found a pen, and jotted something down at the bottom of the paper. She then handed it over to Aquifer, her eyes gleaming as if she were presenting a letter to Santa Claus himself. "We were hoping you'd offer."

Treehouse
December 21, 2007-B

"Wait, wait . . . You said it was a *circus*?"

The four Faction members gathered around the dining room table, laughing over wine and Mont-Blanc aux marrons, one of Quentin's specialty desserts. Maddie laid in the floor nearby, enjoying a treat of frozen bananas.

The laughter died down, and Quentin continued his story in spite of Nadi's incredulous outburst. "Now bear in mind, this was at the beginning of my time with The Faction . . . I still had no idea what I was doing. I found out I was trapped in this . . . *place*"—He gestured at the glass patio door, and its black nothingness—"and I had not yet begun to form my own cell. The Obelisk cell was kind enough to bring me along on a mission via portable camera to take advantage of my expertise. You may not remember this, but the U.S. embassies in Tanzania and Kenya experienced failed terrorist attacks back then. Authorities found suspicious-looking trucks parked outside the two buildings, and when they engaged with the drivers, there was a firefight. An officer was wounded and the drivers were killed. They were found with the detonators pressed in their hands."

Catalina took a sip of wine, and Zen leaned forward. "Wow, Quentin, what a *fun* story so far!"

The table laughed, but Quentin held up his hand. "About eighteen hours before this happened, we learned of a planned attack and I was asked to try to find out where the equipment would be stored. It wasn't hard to pin down the 'coincidence' of a traveling carnival tent being set up near each proposed location. So, they fly into Kenya and HALO jump to avoid Society detection. I'm pretty terrible with heights, so I was nearly pissing myself during the fall, even though I wasn't even there!"

Nadi and Zen burst into giggles, while Catalina shook her head in disbelief.

"I swear on my life, Catalina," Quentin insisted. "You overestimate my competence far too often!" He returned to his story, animating his actions with his arms. "We HALO jump into Kenya and almost land on the damn tent. The caged animals are losing their minds, and my poor camera holder is dancing around like a man in a spider web trying to disconnect my parachute. Then, out of nowhere, the tent's lights turn on, and the *goddamn carnival music starts playing.*"

"*What?*" Nadi and Zen blurted out together.

"It's the creepiest thing I've ever heard in my entire life. We're hiding among the boxes of supplies, expecting some kind of military-grade Society presence to appear at any moment. Then we see one shadow . . . and it's a clown."

"Fuuuck that," Zen whispered.

"This clown wanders around outside the tent, fully-dressed with the makeup and the wig, sniffing the air. It gets closer to us, and in the moonlight, we can see its face: Yellow lizard eyes, big red nose, sharp, needle-teeth . . ." Quentin visibly shivered, and Nadi felt goosebumps form on his own arms. "It was the first time I saw these things; hell, first time I'd even *heard* of them. The thing stands there, sniffing around, but I guess the smell of the animals was strong enough to mask our scent. It lurches back into the tent like it's auditioning for *Dawn of the Dead.*"

Nadi put down his fork, rapt with attention.

"To make a long story short, we sneak into the tent and find a big metal truck, which is out of place from everything else. Opening it up, we find tons of explosives, already wired and ready to go. Then we have ourselves a small debate."

Quentin took a bite of his dessert, chewed, and swallowed. "The easy answer was to steal the explosives, or detonate the truck, taking away their firepower. But the problem with this strategy is that no one *knows* about it. Society just gathers more resources and does the exact same thing in a slightly different way. So, I proposed a *different* strategy."

"What kind of strategy?" Nadi asked.

"The suggestion I made was to disarm the explosives; clip the wires or unplug the fuses in a way that is effective, but subtle."

Nadi interrupted him again. "But what if they noticed before the attack? Wouldn't it put people in danger?"

"Was it a risky move? Did I make a gamble? Yes, and yes. But I saw the alternative as nothing more than a delay of the inevitable, while my plan had long-term benefits."

"How so?" Nadi queried, sitting back in his chair.

"Just look at the news articles about the attacks! The day it happened, they failed to detonate their explosives. Obelisk called in an anonymous tip that morning to watch out for extremist terrorists in the area, so the guards responded before the drivers figured out what had happened. Then, not only were lives saved *that* day, but the fear of having almost been attacked prompted the embassies to tighten security against future offenses." Quentin raised his wine glass. "To my knowledge, neither embassy has had a direct attack, nor anything resembling one. Sometimes, our plans work out the way we want them to. À votre santé."

The others raised their glasses and repeated his words. "À votre santé."

They drank and returned their cups to the table. Quentin turned to Nadi, who raised his hands in a defensive pose.

What do you expect me to talk about? Nadi thought. *I've been stuck in a lab my whole life.*

"I'm sure there's something you can contribute," Quentin teased. "Maybe an old romantic conquest? I mean, we're not trying to nap, so *please* don't talk about your science projects."

"Ha-ha, Quentin."

"Don't ask Nadi about his old work," Zen said in a defensive tone, a smile creeping into her voice. "You have to start with the Fisher Price See-'N-Say wheel, and then work your knowledge base up from there. Tell me, do you even *know* what a turkey says?"

"Ouch," Quentin gasped, clutching his chest. "Maybe you and Catalina should spend less time together."

"Not a chance," Zen replied, and Nadi noticed the two women subtly touching hands. He smiled.

Catalina followed her gesture of comradery with a motion to catch everyone's attention.

[Okay, I've got one.]

"Oooh," Quentin rubbed his hands together. Zen propped her head onto the table with her elbow, staring at Catalina, while Nadi relaxed and sipped more wine.

[This was back when I was still hunting monsters, way before

Quentin found me. A young farmhand in a rural Peruvian town learned about me and sent me a letter. According to him, some kind of creature was roaming the town at night, eating the livestock.]

"Like a Chupacabra?" Nadi interjected.

[Something like that. But beyond that, the creature was breaking into houses and eating the family pets. Not the families, not the food, but the live pets. It wasn't going through an open window or digging a hole into the basement, either. The families would wake up and find the only damage to the door was scratches around the locks . . . because it was picking them with its claws.]

"No way," Nadi said.

"Did no one ever *see* the creature?" Zen asked.

[Apparently not. It was intelligent enough to avoid detection for . . . well, I think it was about three weeks by the time I arrived. The only exception was the farmhand who wrote to me. He told me his theories on the creature, too, based on his experiences.]

"What were his thoughts?" Quentin queried.

[He was convinced the thing was a "nagual," which in Peruvian culture is like . . . a shape-shifter, or a werewolf. Naguals aren't limited to wolf form, though; stories reflect naguals who transform into large jungle cats, or even birds and horses. When I pressed him on his reasoning, he explained that he was tracking its movements.] She stood up, poured herself more wine, and sat back down, basking in the tension of the room. [The farmhand lived on the edge of town, not far from where the wealthy family in charge of the town had a house on a hill. Though the farmers made a living in agriculture and livestock, the wealthy family was fortunate enough to have ancestors who mined out a large vein of gold in the area many years ago. The class divide did not go unnoticed, and many despised the family. Not the boy, though.]

Catalina sighed and shook her head. [The family had a young woman about the farmhand's age, and I'm certain he had feelings for her. This fascination with the family is why he began to notice the shadow of a hulking beast, scaling the hill to the house every morning. He suspected that someone in the family was a nagual, and he feared it might accidentally hurt the girl. There was also worry that she might be the nagual herself, and the town would eventually catch and kill her.]

[So, I decided to approach the family and confront them on this.

They were taken aback and quite rude, but I put together a list: The mother, the father, the uncle, the daughter, and two housemaids. Each were interrogated, but none gave indication that they knew of being a nagual.]

[This was not much of surprise, of course; with the idea of a were-creature comes the possibility you have no memory of what you've done. The creature had not hurt any humans, either, so I felt I could afford some leniency in my . . . methods. I went to work, stalking the streets of the town at night, checking back in on the house to see who was missing or behaving strangely. After two nights, I learned the farmhand was right.]

The room was silent for a moment, the others holding their breath in suspense.

Quentin finally spoke up. "Well, who was it? The parents, or the child?"

"Were the maids cared for properly?" Zen asked, adding her thoughts. "Maybe one of them was the nagual, and eating the livestock and pets was some kind of subconscious drive for care and nourishment."

Nadi rubbed his head. "In these things, it's usually the butler, and there's no butler here, so . . ." He shrugged.

Catalina looked around the room at each of them and signed again. [It was the farmhand.]

Cries of protest erupted around the table.

"What!"

"No!"

"How?"

She raised a hand to quiet them. [The farmhand wanted nothing more than to be with the girl. In animal form, he must have been in a dream state, and he projected his desires into his memories of seeing the creature go to her home. The reality was that he *was* the creature. The boy was too kind of a soul to hurt others, but his animal instincts craved prey, so somehow his urges were reduced to just livestock and pets.]

"How did you find out?" Zen asked.

[It appeared that, by investigating and instigating the family, I became an unwanted presence quite quickly. The girl, especially, spoke out against my hunt, claiming she felt "threatened" by me. This must have leaked into the farmhand's subconscious, because the night following her comment, I was attacked by a gigantic jaguar. The creature on four legs was as tall as I am on two, and instead of black spots, it was covered in spikes made of bone. Its tail was long and prehensile, like a monkey's, and it ended in another bone-spike; I think that was how it picked the locks.]

Catalina hung her head in sorrow.

[My life was in danger, and I had no gauge for how to rehabilitate such a creature in the moment. We exchanged lethal blows at length, but our fight ended with a bullet in its brain. The jaguar reverted to the shape of the farmhand, dead in the streets. Whether he knew it or not, he invited me to his town to kill him.]

Nadi's eyes welled up as he remembered the day his lab was attacked. *I had no choice but to flood it*, he reminded himself. *No choice.* Still, he wasn't convinced.

[I tell myself that it was still a good thing,] Shadow continued. [I had no resources to control his abilities, and in his suggestible state, it was only a matter of time before others in the town were killed. I'm . . . I'm still waiting to be convinced of my own justification.]

The room was silent once more; suspense had melted to sobriety. She looked at Zen.

[We should consider ourselves fortunate, Kipper. Not every Refined evolves into something as manageable as what we have. Some have abilities which only cause harm, others have mutations which make them unable to enjoy the outside world . . . and then there are those like the farmhand. Those who have something they can't even understand or control, something that gets them killed before we can help them.]

Zen bowed her head, twirling her thumbs together. "Yeah. I know."

The silence continued, more tense and uncomfortable than before. After a moment, Zen looked up at her comrades. "I have a good story."

The energy in the room picked up a little, and the other three glanced her way.

"Oh yeah?" Quentin asked. "Pre-Faction or post-Faction?"

"Post. You two will remember this. My story is more for Nadi, a lesson I wish I didn't have to learn the hard way."

"Hm?" Nadi responded, his curiosity piqued.

She turned to the scientist. "In South America, the various countries present have had governments of . . . fluctuating stability. We believe this chaos opened up opportunities for Society to burrow into those nations' political spheres and gain tighter control than they seem to have in more stable countries. This means they have stronger political power, more positive public sentiment, and more flexibility to run dangerous experiments and establish questionable facilities without impediment from Society."

Catalina nodded, seconding Zen's comments. The detective continued. "Brazil's Faction cell, Péndulo, saw this weakness as an opportunity. While our operations are simpler and shorter, they've run a 'long con,' embedding their own agents within the governments controlling Colombia, Argentina, Chile, Venezuela, Peru, Bolivia, and, of course, Brazil. They've been working to produce change by feigning compromise with Society-based policies and using The Faction's forces to curb Society's attempts to establish power outside the law. It's a controversial approach, but respectable, in my opinion."

She took a breath. "About five years ago, not long after I joined The Faction, Péndulo asked us to assist with a rescue mission. One of their political agents was kidnapped, along with ten other hostages. His name was Guillermo, though I believe his Faction alias was Cyclamen."

"Cyclamen . . . like the flower?" Nadi asked.

Battery shrugged. "I guess. I don't know. But Cyclamen the *person* was the state governor of Antioquia, in Colombia. Some of the 'People's Army,' who we believed to be operating under Society control, abducted him and several other people. They hid out in the mountains, where Péndulo feared he was being tortured for information on The Faction."

Abduction and torture, Nadi bitterly thought. *How unoriginal.*

"It took Péndulo operatives over a *year* to find where he had been taken," Battery continued. "Shadow, some Péndulo agents, and I broke into the bunker where the hostages were hidden. We dispatched the fake People's Army guerilla fighters without any innocent casualties. The hostages were untied, and we led them out into the mountains to get them home. Once we were back in the trees, the hostages ran away, leaving the rescue party alone in the middle of nowhere. We split up to catch them, thinking they're scared, and that's when we learned what Society had done to them."

Nadi bent over in his chair, entranced. "What were they doing?"

Zen lowered her voice. "Remember the Triggers Quentin ran into back when he was chasing the Shadow Person? They were experimenting with a new version of mind control; specifically, a version adaptable enough to control Refined."

Nadi's eye's widened. "Oh . . ."

Quentin added his two cents. "Honestly, it was a matter of time before this happened. We weren't ever really sure the technology didn't *already* exist. This served as a confirmation, more than a surprise."

"The problem is what Society chose to do," lamented Zen. "Cyclamen was Péndulo's plant, but the other hostages? They were all Society plants, people intentionally brought to the abduction site under false pretenses. They were also all Refined." She paused for effect. "The kidnapping was arranged as an excuse to experiment on Refined, but it also doubled as a trap for Péndulo. As soon as they cleared the bunker, their chips activated, and they scattered to draw the team apart. It worked, and they were able to tear apart several Péndulo operatives before the situation was contained. In the end, we killed every hostage in self-defense, including Cyclamen."

Catalina and Quentin were shaking their heads.

"We'll never know if Society retrieved any Faction intelligence," Zen said, "but their primary goal was clear when we re-explored the bunker: Ambush the rescue party, implant the survivors with chips, and return them with Cyclamen back to Péndulo, touting it as a victory. Hell, they could stay dormant for years, even decades, springing to action when Society calls for them. It's a nightmarish Trojan horse scenario."

"Damn," Nadi sighed.

"What I'm trying to tell you, Nadi, is to be careful. Control is a primary way Society operates. If you see anyone, *anyone* acting out of character, or you start finding gaps in your *own* memory, let us know immediately so we can try to help. We don't want anyone else to end up like Cyclamen."

Nadi sat back in his chair, trying to absorb the information. There was a silent lull in the room. "Whew," he said. "These are some heavy stories. I appreciate them, sure, but they're heavy. There's a lot to digest, for sure. But you know what would help?

Some ground rules for new recruits, the ones who come after me."

He pointed at Catalina. "Limit who you trust."

His finger moved to Quentin. "Always be prepared."

Finally, he turned to Zen. "Maintain your identity."

Quentin smiled and nodded. "Huh. Strangely, I like it."

[I'll drink to that,] Catalina signed.

They raised their glasses and repeated Nadi's new mantra. "Limit who you trust. Always be prepared. Maintain your identity."

Arizona, United States
January 8, 2009-B

Nadi walked through the busy parking lot, his eyes on his target: The Casas Adobes Safeway supermarket. Its black-lettered sign hovered over him, the red-and-white stylistic "S" symbol refracting the hot desert sun. Waiting inside the supermarket was a fresh treat. Rather than hunting monsters, today he was on the hunt for something delicious.

He and his Faction cell opted to rotate shopping locations around the world with as much frequency as they could manage. This was true for groceries, as well as supplies to supplement Nadi's technology, munitions runs for Shadow, and other miscellaneous essentials to make living in Treehouse bearable. As their shopping excursions rotated back toward the Western U.S., Nadi volunteered to run, eager to pick out some local fruits for himself.

As he approached the divide between the black pavement of the parking lot and the white concrete signaling the walkway into the supermarket, Nadi saw a small white table clustered with people. He drew close enough to see a few well-dressed men and women sitting beneath a banner that said "UNITED STATES CONGRESS." Glancing down, he noticed a smaller tent sign announcing "CONGRESS ON YOUR CORNER."

Shoppers and passers-by were wandering near the table, their chatter amicable as they discussed local politics. The seated men and women seemed to take the commentary in stride, answering with smiles and kind voices. Nadi grinned at the interaction and walked past the sliding doors, allowing the air conditioning to wash the dry heat away. Inside, shoppers were scarce enough to clear a passage for Nadi to move with impunity. He plucked items from the shelves and dropped them into a handbasket. Once he reached the produce section, he scouted around until he found what he desired most: Grapefruits. His mouth curled into another self-satisfied smile, and he loaded every healthy-looking grapefruit into the basket, weighing it down.

Nadi glanced back at the list. He had moved through most of the store, but some of the items were stilling missing from the basket. He circled near the entrance, where a line of windows offered him visual access to the local politicians outside. They were still happy and smiling, deep in conversation with an elderly couple. He bent down to pick up a bag of pretzels for Zen, and when he stood back up, something outside caught his eye.

Walking with urgency toward the table was a young, balding man with sunken eyes and tattered, shabby clothes. He probably wasn't homeless, but his torn jeans and grubby white t-shirt indicated a level of recent self-neglect. The man walked down the sidewalk, his eyes focused on the table, his right hand gripping something near the waistband of his jeans. Something about the man made Nadi uncomfortable, with his mismatched gait and intensity, indicating he wasn't thinking with a clear head.

"Limit who you trust," Nadi whispered, and he knocked on the window as the man passed.

The sharp raps against the glass distracted the man, who glanced through the pane at Nadi's face, as well as the Congress table, who seemed surprised by the noise.

"Everything okay?" one of the women at the table asked.

Her voice drew the man away from Nadi. He furiously muttered something that sounded like "Gabrielle," turned, and hastened toward the table, hand still beneath his shirt. The man was only a few feet away from the table, mouth open as if he were about to say something to the politicians.

Then he stopped.

He stiffened.

And he tremored, as if electrified.

Nadi recognized the symptoms of a Trigger from Proxy's and Battery's stories, and it was no surprise when the man glanced toward the window to look at the scientist, a sudden recognition in his eyes. Nadi dropped his basket of grapefruit, preparing himself. Silent and emotionless, the man walked into the store's entrance, pulled a pistol from the waistband of his jeans, and fired his weapon.

But Nadi was one step ahead, rolling behind the nearest supermarket aisle. The shelves wouldn't guarantee protection from the gunfire, but they could at least obscure the shooter's aim. Bullets tore through the barrier between the two men, rupturing bags of potato chips and scattering their contents across the floor.

The once-aimless residents of the store screamed at the gunfire and abandoned their carts. Customers and employees alike ran outside, yelling for the people at the Congress table to scatter as well. If it were not for the shooter and the scientist, the store would be empty.

"Always be prepared," Nadi said to himself, retrieving a weapon of his own.

His original mobile PAUS model was effective, but quite heavy and bulky. In addition to its cumbersomeness, the gloves necessary to use gesture control were thick and hot. It worked well for combat, but it was impossible to carry around in other occasions.

Rather than alter his current PAUS, Nadi opted for a simplified alternative.

In his hands was a classic squirt gun. It housed a white, plastic-like frame with a yellow, capsule-shaped water tank sitting on top. To the casual observer, it was no more than a toy, particularly when considering its jovial color scheme. Nadi even added a feature that allowed water to enter the tank and spray in a thin stream from the barrel, cementing its legitimacy. The feature could be turned on or off with a small switch near the trigger.

Nadi turned it off.

The gunfire stopped, but footsteps were jogging down the aisle perpendicular to Nadi. He scrambled to his feet and backed away, distancing himself from the shooter. As he backed out of the aisle, he kept his head on a swivel, but the man had still not appeared from the other end. Nadi kept his water pistol raised, his heart pounding in his chest; he felt naked and weak without the complete PAUS.

Movement entered the corner of eye, and he turned to face the shooter; the man must have doubled back to sneak up on Nadi. Both lifted their weapons and fired.

The Trigger was ahead by a half-second; the bullet smashed into

Nadi's left collarbone, sending shards of pain through the connected arm. His body twisted in reaction to the gunshot, and the water gun swung to the left as he pulled the trigger. In an instant, a baseball-size ball of water formed in front the barrel and launched forward with the speed of a bullet. The water splashed against the shooter's right arm, the force sending him twirling to the ground—though he retained his grip on his pistol.

Nadi took advantage of the moment to plug a small radio into his ear and call Treehouse. "Proxy! Shadow! Battery! I need an immediate retrieval from the supermarket!"

He ducked behind a waist-high bin of toys as the shooter rose back to his feet, unfazed by the attack. Nadi clutched an innocuous white ring surrounding the water tank of his gun, twisting it like a dial. Aiming from behind the bin, he pulled the trigger again; this time, the launched sphere was the size of a basketball.

Caught unaware, the attack struck the shooter in the chest, splashing into him hard enough to carry him backwards through the supermarket windows. He landed outside on the pavement, shards of broken glass slicing deep into his flesh. Without missing a beat, he sat up and began his trek to the entrance of the store, ignoring the now-empty "CONGRESS ON YOUR CORNER" table.

"Aquifer, the men's restroom is almost primed for transport," Proxy replied in Nadi's ear.

"On my way—"

Bullets whistled over his head as the man's pistol cracked several times in succession. Nadi rolled away from the gunfire, placing more aisles between them while bee lining toward the restroom.

Shoes stomped close to him, and he shifted to see the shooter speed-walking close behind. The man's white shirt was stained red, and pointed pieces of glass covered his torso and his vacant face. The man's right arm was limp, but he had little trouble firing with his left. The gun barrel pointed at Nadi's chest, and the finger creaked on the trigger.

Nadi fell backward to the floor, screaming from the pain in his left arm. Bullets flew over him as he raised his water pistol and fired a third time. The shooter was getting wise to his machine, though; the sphere formed, but he was already diving away. Produce exploded in a shower of water as the attack ruptured a vegetable bin.

Both men scurried to their feet, vying to be the first one to land a lethal shot. Rather than taking proper aim, Nadi opted to shoot a new water sphere near the man's legs. It didn't quite strike the shooter himself, but the force of the splash was enough to sweep his feet back out from under him.

"Aquifer," Proxy announced in his ear, "Thirty more seconds until it's done, and then you're good to go."

Nadi clutched at his injured arm, wincing. "I don't think I have thirty seconds!"

He leaned closer to the prone man, twisting the dial to make his sphere the size of a beach ball. Before he could fire, though, the shooter kicked a puddle of water into Nadi's face, clouding his vision and causing him to hesitate. A single gunshot greeted the second of weakness, and the scientist felt a sharp, prickling warmth in his right hand.

Staggered, Nadi stepped back to see the water pistol decimated, torn apart by the gunman's bullet. Shards of plastic alloy embedded in his palm like a rash, preventing him from closing his hand completely. Blood dripped from the various punctures, and a dull pain was growing in intensity with every passing second.

I'm going to die, Nadi thought.

The shooter stepped forward, gun raised, crunching the pieces of Nadi's weapon into the wet floor. Pulling the trigger of his pistol, he was met with the *click* of an empty magazine. Still, Nadi went cold. His hands trembled, and his head lightened. As he had no way to defend himself, there was only one option left: Run.

The scientist spun, barely missing the gunman's swinging fist. He splashed down the back hallway of the supermarket, pulling the bathroom door open and diving inside. The shooter was close behind, and he managed to get a foot in the door before Nadi could close and lock it.

"Aquifer, Bogeyman is primed, but you need to close the space to activate it."

"I'm . . . working . . . on . . . it." Nadi growled through his teeth, kicking at the shooter's leg.

The man was strong, made even stronger still by the device controlling him. Nadi, on the contrary, was no fighter, not built for such direct confrontations. PAUS had been a reliable form of defense and offense during Faction missions in these last few years, and he regretted being so unprepared for a day like today.

After a moment, a hard shove against the other side of the door knocked Nadi to the ground, sending waves of stabbing pain coursing through his injured arms. The bathroom door swung open, revealing the blood-soaked man, his face as still and expressionless as a statue's. He walked inside and closed the door behind him, locking it. Nadi crawled backward, using a urinal to pull himself up.

The shooter walked to the sink and began punching the mirror, over and over, seemingly with no regard to his own well-being. After a few strikes, the mirror fractured. He reached for a sharp piece, but a low rattling against the wall shook the shards from their place. They fell into the sink, and the man fished around until he found a makeshift dagger.

Nadi sprinted for the door, fumbling for the lock, but his injured, blood-slicked hands couldn't properly grip it. The gunman reacted by kicking him in the hip, knocking him back down. The pain was unbearable, and his consciousness slipped.

Sirens sounded in the distance, growing louder by the second. Closer, an opening door squeaked in the distance. The shooter ignored the sound, standing above him with his sunken cheeks and raised makeshift dagger. Too weak to move, Nadi closed his eyes, resigned to fate.

A sharp knock against the bathroom door interrupted the inevitable, followed by an attempt to open it. Responding to the ratcheting sound, Nadi opened his eyes. With the volume of a thunderclap, a grapefruit-sized hole blasted through the bolted lock. The door flew open, knocking the Trigger back.

Darkness crept around Nadi's vision, but Catalina stood in the doorway, a sawed-off shotgun in hand. She strode through, wearing a grey tank top and grey sweatpants, tiptoeing her bare feet around wood and glass and metal. Nadi's attacker rushed at her with the mirror shard, and she leveled another shotgun blast at his face, disintegrating his head from his body.

She turned to Nadi and motioned for him to stand, even as the decapitated corpse was falling over. When he didn't respond, she shook her head and squatted, lifting him over her shoulder. Together, they left the bloody mess in the men's restroom and walked next door to the women's restroom. Once they were inside, the door closed, Catalina lowered Nadi and retrieved a short radio, sending signals through it in Morse code.

After a moment, the door rattled, and the world fell silent. Nadi and his rescuer fell through the void, seeing only what Bogeyman convinced their minds to see.

Treehouse
January 9, 2009-B

Nadi awoke to Zen, her face twisted with worry. When she saw his eyes open, her face lit with excitement.

"Hey! He's up!"

Quentin and Catalina appeared around Nadi's bed, where he lay covered in bandages and IV tubes. The three inspected him, talking over one another.

"How are you—"

"Are you feel—"

[Does anything hurt —]

"Guys, guys, I'm fine," Nadi interrupted. "There's no reason to dote on me."

Their responding smiles were sheepish, even Catalina's.

"I . . . I wasn't prepared enough," he continued.

Quentin frowned. "But you made—"

"It wasn't *enough*, Quentin."

Nadi looked around the room, addressing all of them. "You warned me about this, about how Society is everywhere. These codenames are supposed to protect us, to be used as a mental division between a safe zone like Treehouse and the rest of the world. Nothing can be trusted, and half-measures may as well be no measures at all."

Zen spoke up. "Nadi, you didn't—"

He held up a hand to stop her, wincing at the pain it caused. "I'm not stupid. I don't know if I have the aptitude to excel at physical combat like you or Catalina. But I have my knowledge, and I have my work. My PAUS should be able to follow me everywhere." Nadi looked down his injured self, then back at his team, glowering. *"Everywhere."*

California, United States
April 28, 2011-B

"He's bringing them *here*?" Battery asked, disgusted. "What the hell?"

Rain poured around her, muffling her microphone and forcing Proxy to lean closer to hear her words. She brushed the moisture from her button camera, allowing him to see her compatriots: Aquifer in a white hoodie and jeans, and Shadow in her black leather jacket ensemble. Proxy could see through their other cameras that Battery herself was in a blue button-down shirt and white-washed pants, and around her neck dangled a pair of circular goggles customized by Aquifer.

The three turned their attention to the structure before them, giving Proxy a good look at the gigantic red sign plastered above their heads.

HOTEL
CECIL
LOW
DAILY
WEEKLY
RATES
700 ROOMS

The advertisement was decrepit and faded, embedded into the tall beige building presumably known as "Hotel Cecil." Also in poor condition, the hotel stood ten stories tall and consisted of three buildings pressed side-by-side, forming alleyways between each one. As it was nighttime, the alleys were nearly pitch black, and the only sources of light were streetlamps lining down the sidewalk and the headlights of passing cars.

"Proxy," Aquifer said into his transmitter, "I know Mr. Singh has been tracked here, but maybe there's some kind of underground base? Surely he wouldn't invite Canadian Special Forces into a rat-trap like this?"

"I can't speak to their final destination," Proxy replied, opening a file on one of his monitors. "But my records show Mr. Singh *did* in fact sign off on sending six CANSOFCOM members to meet him in the Cecil Hotel. We can't ignore this as coincidence, not while we're receiving chatter about U.S. Special Forces preparing to invade the area where Butterfly's Koshasth cell is hiding."

"Her cell has been our biggest ally in locating and disabling the earthquake targeting facilities," Battery added. "I don't believe it's a coincidence Society would peg them as terrorists and rally innocent troops to attack them in an unstable area. There would be no public repercussions; knowing my home country, there might even be praise."

"So, what, my former investor from Mumbai is going to convince a bunch of soldiers from Canada to fight in Pakistan for him?" Aquifer asked, incredulous.

[Your former investor is Society, and probably a Chimera, too,] Shadow signed. [I'm sure he can handle both political and military roles.]

"Wait—I see them!" Battery exclaimed, her hand extending in front of the camera to show Proxy which direction she was pointing.

Five men and one woman walked down the street in civilian clothes, laughing and staggering in a way reserved for the very intoxicated. Each person trailed a young, beautiful woman dressed in a skimpy outfit. Mr. Singh was nowhere to be seen.

"I don't think they're here for a formal visit," Battery muttered.

"Where's Singh?" Aquifer demanded.

[They're headed to the hotel,] signed Shadow. [If he's inside, I don't think they intend to speak with him any time soon. Still, they were brought all the way here for a reason. We need to follow them, and possibly stop this hookup from happening.]

"Shadow's right," agreed Proxy. *Though I doubt they'll appreciate it.*

"Okay." Battery turned to Shadow. "You follow them at the ground floor and stick close to the group. If they start to go into any of the hotel rooms where you can't see them, find a reason to be there or keep them out." She pointed at Aquifer. "You've met Singh, so I need you to stay outside the hotel and watch the perimeter for any signs of him, or any of your other investors. I don't know what's waiting for us in there, so eyes outside for suspicious changes will be invaluable."

He nodded.

Battery added, "I'll approach from the roof and work my way down. If I'm lucky, I'll find some incriminating supplies or information through the other guests."

They broke their huddle. Shadow sprinted for the Canadian team entering the hotel, Battery climbed the fire escape on the side of the building, and Aquifer primed his upgraded PAUS implants, all while Proxy watched through their respective surveillance equipment.

———————

Shadow's next few minutes were dull. She watched the men and woman flirt with their "dates" in a sloppy, drunken mess. They each asked for hotel keys, and by some miracle, the front desk had six consecutively numbered rooms available. Continuing toward the elevator, they stopped and laughed about how their entire group couldn't fit, breaking off four of the couples to catch the first ride, while the other two couples waited. She moved closer, blending in.

When she reached the elevator and joined the small crowd, they reacted strangely. The large, burly drunken man and the thin, athletic drunken man did not notice her, but both of their "dates" did. The women looked at her, smiled in unison, and spoke as one. "Having a fun night?"

The synergy of their voices chilled Shadow, but their faces and tones were warm and friendly, so she offered a tight smile and a nod. The exchange complete, both women returned to doting on the drunk, vacationing Special Operatives.

Shadow looked around the room, noting a man behind the desk, a middle-aged couple on the lobby bench, and a mother with two playful children trying to find her room key. When she first glanced their way, everyone, including the children, seemed to be staring at her, but when her eyes fully focused, they were simply two people, carrying on with their lives. Shadow shook her head at the disparity between the moments, writing it off as a trick of the mind.

———————

Battery wrenched open the entrance to the roof and climbed down the stairs, moving with swift purpose past halls and doors, scanning for clues. The top floor was deserted, and the hotel rooms were all locked. She pushed her way into the stairwell and hopped over the railing, dropping to the concrete landing of the floor below.

Backing into the new corridor, she saw more of the same. Dim lights, the echoes of isolation . . . and a faint, pulsating noise. She furrowed her brow and moved ahead, following the sound. It led her to a thin door placed at the intersection of two hallways.

Battery opened the door, revealing a small, janitorial space. The pulsation was louder here, rhythmic like a heartbeat. Cautious, she moved into the closet, searching for a source. She found herself drawn to the far wall, where a series of thick metal pipes ran from the floor to the ceiling.

Testing the temperature of the pipes, she found them warm, but not hot. Battery pressed her ear to one of them, hunting for clarity. She met firm pressure from each pulsation, as if her face rested against a flexing muscle. The sensation felt organic, but it made Battery nauseous at the same time.

Something isn't right about this.

"How are your updated implants? Still itchy?" Proxy asked Aquifer. The rain had stopped, but Aquifer's clothes were soaked.

The scientist scratched his arm, irritating the already red skin. "Yeah. But worth it."

"If I'm being honest, I wasn't sure about your decision at first. Over the last year or so, though, they've become one of our most valuable assets. It's a shame what you had to go through, and if they ever turn into a burden for you, I would understand."

Aquifer laughed. "You're too kind. No, I'm not going anywhere. And I would never trust anyone else to operate PAUS. Assuming they even *could*, with the language I made to control it."

"I understand. Just . . . be kind to yourself, too."

"Okay, thanks, *Pita*."

The traffic between Aquifer and the Cecil Hotel was rapidly thinning, the headlights fading away. He looked around, but he saw no reason for impeded traffic.

"Strange," Aquifer muttered.

"What is it?"

"The traffic. It's . . . it's gone. There are no more cars on the street around the hotel."

"In Los Angeles?"

"That's what I was thinking."

"Hold on." Proxy was silent for a few seconds. "Wait . . . what the hell?"

"Problem?"

"Yes. I pulled the public blueprints of the Cecil Hotel to prime some escape areas in the building, just in case."

"And?"

"Bogeyman isn't responsive to the space. It's as if . . . there isn't a building there."

Aquifer looked up at the hotel. "There sure is, though."

"Aquifer . . ." The analyst sounded worried now. "This is unfamiliar territory. I don't like this."

Just then, the streetlamps up and down the sidewalk near Aquifer and the hotel flickered off, one-by-one. The darkness spread out around him, until there wasn't a lit lamp in sight.

"Me neither, Proxy. Me neither."

Shadow arrived on the sixth floor with her two targets and their dates. The doors opened, and they entered the hallway. The tall, burly man's room was close to the doors, and they ducked into the room before Shadow could react. The thinner man's door must have been further down the hall, because they kept moving forward.

Before he could get away like the rest of the group, Shadow grabbed the soldier by his shoulder and spun him around to face her. He staggered, surprised, and his date shot her a look of annoyance.

"Wha's this?" The man mumbled. "I din' 'member bringin' two ladies with me . . ."

"I think she's just lost," his date said in a soothing voice, staring at Shadow. "Let's go inside."

"Wait . . . wait . . . lost? I gotta help. Iss' my duty to help." The man tried to stand taller and puff his chest, offering his hand to Shadow.

The woman pulled. "Let's go. Mother will be angry if we . . ."

Mother?

It registered. The synergy between the women. The way people looked at her in the lobby. Those wide smiles. These were more of the hive-mind people, like the ones they fought in New Zealand.

Shadow signed a message into the button camera, warning Proxy.

A moment later, the screaming started.

———————————

"Battery. Aquifer. Shadow says the hotel is filled with those people from Dunedin."

Battery backed away from the pipes as Aquifer responded in her ear. "I remember you telling me about them," he said. "They were, like, in-synch or something? And they melted when they were captured, right?"

"Yes," Battery replied into her radio. "I'm headed to Shadow now."

She turned to leave, and the closet door shut in her face. Turning the knob, it wouldn't budge; pushing against the wood, it remained firm.

"The hell . . ."

Battery activated her Charge Belt, and the fan blades whirred to life. Energy flowed beneath her cells, freeing her of physical limitations. She planted a solid kick in the door, but it only bent, refusing to splinter, instead behaving like a soft plastic.

Behind her, the pulsating pipes grew louder.

———————————

Shadow turned toward the sounds of pain and terror. Rather than one source, she found five behind the closed doors of the hotel room. Wet, hungry noises accompanied the cries, making her skin crawl.

"Mother is waiting for you," the woman next to her said to the Canadian soldier.

"What . . ." he responded, stepping away from her.

His date's face grew into a wide, haunting grin, her eyes stretched far beyond anything natural. She directed her face toward Shadow and took a menacing step in her direction. "Mother is waiting for him."

This is getting out of hand.

Shadow reached behind her back, beneath her jacket, and unholstered her Polish machine pistol, the Reczny Automat Komandosow. She aimed the odd gun's long, squared barrel at the woman, signaling for her to stop. The man stepped forward, trying to get between them, but his date pushed him away. He caught himself from falling by propping one hand against the wall, seeming somewhat indignant.

"Hey, that's not . . ."

OHHHMMMMMMMMMMMM . . .

A deafening noise, deep and guttural like a Tibetan horn or didgeridoo, rumbled through the hallway around them. Whatever the noise was, it rattled Shadow's bones, shaking her to the core in a way she had never experienced before. She and the drunk soldier looked around, seeking out its source, while the young woman stared at Shadow with her insane smile.

Then, the gates to hell opened.

Battery increased the voltage of her belt and stepped back, preparing herself for a running start in the small space. Electricity crackled, creating pockets of hot ozone in the air, but she focused on one thing: The door. She ran forward and plowed into it, crashing forward and outside the closet. Her victory, however, turned to disgust.

Something wet and sticky soaked through Battery's clothes; she looked down at what appeared to be blood. Turning, she surveyed the door she had damaged. Wood shards poked down around all four edges, pointed toward the point of impact. Within that empty space, red liquid dribbled down to the floor.

The door was . . . *bleeding?*

As if in response, the corridor began to shake, emitting a thundering, guttural tone.

OHHHMMMMMMMMMMMM . . .

In the corner of her eye, Battery saw the wall crack and split apart in a vertical line. She turned to face the opening, steeling herself for an attack, but what appeared instead caused the hairs on the nape of her neck to rise. Dialing the belt to an even-higher voltage, Battery stepped back and spoke into her insulated radio.

"Shadow, we need to leave. Now."

As tall as her entire body, jutting from the wall in front of her, quivered an unblinking eyeball.

––––––––––––––––

OHHHMMMMMMMMMMM . . .

Where the soldier had placed his hand, the wall split apart in a vertical line from floor-to-ceiling, sending plaster dust raining to the carpeted floor. It stretched enough to reveal a ring of endless rows of flat, yellowed teeth, not unlike those of a hippopotamus. He lost his balance and fell sideways, his left hand and forearm slipping into the tooth-filled hole.

The grotesque, sideways mouth closed around the soldier's hand, crunching into the flesh and bone, drooling blood down the wall. He screamed in terror, struggling to pull away, but something inside the giant mouth held him down, pulling him further inside. It closed again, crunching into his forearm.

"Shadow, we need to leave. Now." Battery said in her earpiece.

Shadow rushed to his side and tried to help pull him away, but she wasn't strong enough. As she considered whether her combat knife could saw through his arm in time to save him, the man's "date" pounced on her, knocking her back.

"LEAVE HIM ALONE."

Without a second thought, Shadow raised her Reczny pistol and squeezed the trigger. A burst of bullets sprayed into the woman's neck and face, splattering viscera into the carpet. The "date" crumpled to the floor, freeing Shadow up to assist the Canadian soldier, who still wailed at the top of his lungs.

She unsheathed her knife with her free hand, considering her options. The man was already buried into the wall up to his left shoulder, sprinkled with his own blood, and reeking of sweat and urine. Across from him, in the other wall, an identical opening had appeared. Rather than being filled with teeth, however, the interior of the spreading crack was filled with pink, fleshy folds which contracted at regular intervals.

Protruding from the new opening was the soldier's left hand and forearm, fingers wriggling as if they had lost their circulation.

The mouth holding the soldier tight bit down once more, consuming his left shoulder and pulling his left leg into the orifice. On the opposing wall, the fleshy canal pushed out more of the soldier's consumed body. Another bite, and the screams muffled as the maw consumed him. The other wall birthed out the man's face, though it smiled, rather than screamed.

"Mon Dieu," Proxy whispered, presumably watching through Shadow's button camera.

Shadow made a few short gestures in front of her button camera before pointing at the end of the hall, where a window perched. Following the motion, she lifted her machine pistol and fired a burst down the corridor, shattering the glass. She sheathed her knife and was in the process of holstering her weapon when the newborn spoke, still frozen in a wide-eyed smile.

"Praise to Mother."

"Heads up, Aquifer," Proxy said in his ear. "Shadow needs you to catch her from the Southeast side of the middle hotel building."

"When?" he replied.

"*Now.*"

Aquifer sprinted across the dark, empty street, pulling back the sleeves of his hoodie. Rows of flat, pearl-white discs ran flush with the skin of his forearms, four alloy circles lined up along each appendage. He lifted his arms and flapped them down to his side; a pool of water appeared beneath his legs and erupted upward, propelling him through the air parallel to the Cecil Hotel.

Droplets followed him as wind rushed past, ruffling his dark hair. The ultrasound caused the discs in his arms to twitch, as if ants crawled on the implants. He began to fall, so he pressed the flats of his hands together to form a cross. When he broke them apart, a bus-sized cube of water appeared on the ground where his arms pointed. Water filled his nose and ears as he entered the cube, but it also slowed his descent to a safe speed, and he coasted to the ground.

Once he touched solid earth, still in the middle of suspended water, he lifted his right hand and snapped his fingers twice. Instead of collapsing into a flood, the water around him vibrated, shimmering in the ambient light. Within a few seconds, the mass of liquid evaporated into steam, floating away from Aquifer and drifting down the streets and hotel alleyways. With the water now airborne, an ultrasound pulse stripped him of moisture, instantly drying his hair and clothes.

Above, gunfire sounded, and a window shattered on the sixth floor, raining glass to the concrete below—and Aquifer. He lifted his right arm in an uppercut motion, angling it so his outer forearm faced the sky. A concave rectangle of water formed, deflecting the glass. Once the shards finished falling, he whipped his raised arm down to his side, snapping his fingers one time. The water-umbrella evaporated into a fine mist and dispersed in the slight Los Angeles breeze.

"In position," Aquifer said, creating circular motions with his hands.

OHHHMMMMMMMMMMM . . .

Battery backed away from the giant eye in the wall of the hotel, its green iris watching her movements with an intense interest. Around her, more cracks peeled away from the walls and ceiling, exposing dozens of eyes in varying sizes and colors, all staring at her.

The floor began to open beneath her feet into a large, wet hole filled with flat, yellowed teeth. She stepped around the opening, moving toward the stairwell door, but something grabbed her foot. Looking down, she found her ankle wrapped in thick black hair-like strands. They led right back to the inside of the open mouth.

More strands whipped out of the opening, writhing like an octopus's tentacles and wrapping themselves around Battery's neck. The clusters of hair pulled her to the ground, her hands on either side of the mouth's opening while her face hovered above the waiting orifice. Inside, she could see the teeth replicated in rows, circling down into wet darkness along with the hair strands.

The eyes surrounding her stared, their gaze hungry.

With her hands planted on the floor, she leveraged her electric strength to free herself. The strands around her neck and foot were thin and sturdy. Were she not charged, they would have cut into her flesh like a garrote. She pressed against the floor, straining to pull away from the hair-tentacles holding her hostage. After a moment, she heard a series of snapping sounds, followed by the jolt of sudden release. Clumps of black hair fell around her feet.

More mouths opened around her in a pattern as random as the eyes, and Battery sprinted down the hall to the stairwell door as more strands appeared. She lowered her body and decimated the barrier, sending pieces of its wood and streams of blood scattering across the stair landing. The ominous cry echoed, rattling the concrete and metal beneath Battery's feet.

OHHHMMMMMMMMMMM . . .

Tendrils of black hair flowed toward her, reaching to pull her back into the hotel hallway. She crouched and jumped, grabbing the railing of the stairs to the floor above. With ease, Battery hoisted herself over the railing and kicked in the door. Ahead of her was a dark hallway, ending in a small staircase for the door back to the room.

"Almost out," Battery muttered, watching the walls before her tear apart into angry eyes and hungry mouths.

OHHHMMMMMMMMMMMMM . . .

The remaining bits of the original Canadian soldier had fallen still, dangling in place as it was slurped into the mouth in the wall. On the other side, the new Canadian soldier was working himself free from his fleshy womb. Unlike the original man, this one was naked; whatever the hotel produced, it must not include clothes or equipment.

Shadow turned to sprint down the hall, where she had just broken the window with a spray of gunfire.

"In position," Aquifer said in her earpiece.

Other areas of the walls, floor and ceiling were cracking open in jagged lines, revealing not just new mouths, but various sizes and colors of giant, unblinking eyes. The mouths moistened in anticipation, the eyes fixating on Shadow.

I'm out of time.

She took a step forward, but the smiling naked clone-thing finished freeing himself from the wall, tackling her to the ground.

"Mother wants you, too," he giggled, eyes wide. The carpet began pulling apart beneath her, hot breath ruffling hair.

Nope. Not doing this.

Shadow raised the pistol, placed the barrel to the man's temple, and pulled the trigger, scattering his brains across the hallway.

Gripping his waist, she rolled over just as the mouth was wide enough to take a bite and shoved the hotel's own child down its throat.

Continuing her roll, Shadow pivoted to her feet into a mad dash. New mouths opened around her, spewing strings of living black hair to ensnare her, but she relied on her Gaze to duck and weave around them.

As she settled a step on the carpet, a wide mouth formed another step away, too large to hurdle. She shot the wall, where a blue eye watched her, bursting the organ in a spew of clear fluid. The hotel's cries grew louder, and the eyelid closed. She jumped toward the new space and planted a boot there, taking a few strides along the wall, parkour-style. When gravity pulled her back down, she kicked away from the wall, rolling onto the carpet past the large mouth's reach.

She was only a few strides from the open window, but it was too dark outside to see anything. Holstering her gun and tucking her knees into her chest, she hurled her body into the night air, free from Cecil Hotel's reach.

Aquifer, I'm trusting you.

Wind blew through her hair and leather jacket as she dropped into the night, hearing the hotel's cries fade the further she fell. But her descent was brief. Before she even reached the story below her exit, clear and glistening safety rose from the ground and surrounded her. Bubbles crawled from her nose and mouth, and she righted herself in this underwater space.

Looking down, she could make out Aquifer's white hoodie, the arms gesturing to control his PAUS implants. The bubbles cleared away. She was inside a fifty-foot column of water, large enough in diameter to fit at least ten more people. She relaxed her body, floating to the surface of the column to suck in fresh air.

She descended, slower this time, and swam to the edge of the column. Aquifer was dissipating the column's base, a little at a time, shrinking it down to nothingness. It took no more than a minute for her boots to touch the pavement outside the hotel, and the water column faded into a low-lying cloud. Aquifer flicked his fingers toward her, and a tickling sensation washed across her skin; with it, the water soaked into her hair, clothes and equipment evaporated away, leaving her bone-dry.

[Did you see Singh?] she signed to Aquifer.

"No. Did you?" he replied.

[No.]

"What happened to the Special Forces people?"

[Nothing good. But we may have just discovered a major Society point of interest. We can come back here later, better-equipped, and—] The already-still night grew even quieter, the temperature dropping at an unnatural rate. Cold air prickled her skin, and as she exhaled again, her breath appeared as a plume of fog. The mist created by Aquifer's evaporated column condensed into pea-sized particles of ice and fell to the ground, increasing visibility.

"*Bhains ki aulad!* What now?" Aquifer cried.

As if to answer, the sound of metal scraping against pavement alerted Shadow to the other end of the hotel, where a side street separated the building from the business next door. The fog there was thicker, but it fell away in waves, while a thin sheen of ice formed on the road. Emerging from this temperature anomaly was the silhouette of a tall figure, dragging something on the ground behind it.

"Battery, there's someone out here with us," Aquifer said, raising his arms.

Shadow reloaded her gun.

OHHHMMMMMMMMMMMM . . .

"Working on it," Battery said into her earpiece. "I'm trying to not get eaten, then I'll deal with what's outside."

Exasperated, she ripped more black tendrils from her form, continuing her push down the top-floor hallway. The mouths were relentless, and it took all the strength she had to continue moving. She had taken to punching the eyes or kicking the teeth whenever possible. Each hit seemed to affect the hotel, slowing its assault.

Tear them. Destroy them.

Battery pushed down those dark thoughts.

It's just the adrenaline. The electricity. You're in control.

Despite her self-assurance, she felt her teeth gritting, her arms ripping faster, her legs kicking harder. After what seemed like an eternity, she grasped the final door and yanked it from its hinges, sending streams of blood sliding down the frame. Ignoring the phenomenon, Battery shoved her way to the rooftop, gulping the clear night air. Behind her, the hotel's moans faded in the hallway, seeming to admit defeat. A cool wind struck her face, and she felt herself begin to calm.

"Okay, now where—"

Something fluttered above her head, drawing her attention; whatever it was, it was big. Did Los Angeles have birds large enough to be that loud?

No, this sound was . . . familiar.

Battery scanned the night sky, searching for the source of the flapping wings, but nothing was visible. She stepped further onto the rooftop, looking around. The space was empty, with the exception of a cluster of four water towers next to the door that she had just vacated.

The detective raised her transmitter. "Where are they?"

"See the three hotel segments?" Proxy replied. "They're on the side-street in front of the middle one, due Southeast."

A new noise caused her to swivel. The water towers rattled as if filled with fighting snakes. All at once, the towers' lids opened, launching more of the hotel's black tendrils with the force of missiles leaving their silo.

"Come on!" she yelled, kicking away from the water towers in a super-powered sprint.

Her escape attempt came too late. Thick coils of black hair showered her, wriggling around her body and encircling her legs, arms and head. With no leverage to deploy her strength, she was helpless as the tendrils lifted her into the air, pulling her back toward the towers. Despite her disadvantage, she squirmed and pulled, trying to tear herself free.

It took mere seconds to reach the towers. Some of the strands pulled away from her body, retreating into three of the receptacles. Rather than pulling a metal door closed, the water towers shut themselves in a fleshy, organic way, like a sphincter. This left one tower open. Below her, past the black hair, the clear water bubbled, darkening to a green tint.

The tendrils lowered into the mysterious chemical, dragging her along. The reduction of strands had not improved her chance of escape, and the metal walls of the water tower soon surrounded her, blocking out all other noises other than the bubbling liquid. She felt herself sweating, droplets falling past the blue energy surrounding her.

Is the water boiling?

She drew closer, into the fumes of the chemical.

Oh God, no . . . it's acidic. You're being digested, Zen.

———————

Shadow finished reloading her Reczny, this time flipping out the collapsible grip for steadier aim against the machine gun's recoil. She held it with both hands at eye-level, keeping her iron sights centered on the incoming figure.

"Hello?" Aquifer asked, swirling his fingers to create a water-cannonball in front of him.

The figure did not respond, but as it drew closer, Shadow heard the distinct hiss and gasp of assisted breathing, reminiscent of an emergency oxygen mask.

"Are you . . . okay?" Aquifer said.

The mist cleared, revealing the person approaching them. He wore a thick, yellow-orange suit, consisting of loose-fitting jacket and pants. Yellow horizontal stripes wrapped around the torso and ankles of the suit, marking it as a firefighter's uniform. He was fitted with heavy gloves and boots, covering up the ends of the uniform. A green gas mask, complete with mirrored lenses and a dangling oxygen canister, wrapped around his face, and a red firefighter's helmet covered the top of his head. One gloved hand loosely gripped the wooden handle of a firefighter's axe, its red-painted blade scraping the pavement.

When the Fireman was twenty feet away, he stopped, staring at Shadow and Aquifer, his breathing ragged and his axe dangling from his hand. He did not speak or move, as if he were studying them, waiting for a response.

"What . . . what do you want?" Aquifer called out. Shadow stood next to him, gun raised.

The Fireman's free hand rose, the motion slow and limp. He formed a loose fist and unfurled his index finger in Aquifer's direction.

"You want *me*?"

The Fireman nodded once.

"Uh . . . no, thank you."

Aquifer's denial seemed to incense the man, and he continued forward, axe raised in a threatening gesture. Shadow stepped between the two men and shook her head.

I'm out of patience.

Aiming at the Fireman's chest, she squeezed the trigger of her Reczny.

Her machine pistol chattered, releasing a horde of bullets at the newcomer. They struck him . . . but caused no harm; instead, the ammunition stopped as they touched his clothes, releasing a tiny puff of fog and dropping to the street. A pile of misty, undamaged rounds piled at his feet.

Shadow lowered her weapon, furrowing her brow at the results of her attack. Aquifer walked to her side and launched his water sphere, sending it barreling toward the Fireman. His hand rose as the sphere approached, the gesture almost casual. As his fingertips touched the outer edge of the incoming liquid, the entire orb halted in midair; within seconds, it became hazy, freezing into solid ice. He examined it for a moment before pushing it aside. Gravity returned, and like glass, it shattered against pavement.

Aquifer and Shadow looked at one another, then back at the Fireman, who was still approaching in his menacing stance. Shadow ran forward, keeping the trigger of her Reczny depressed, spraying the man's face and body with bullets. Everywhere they touched, they froze and fell.

Nonetheless, Shadow persisted, distracting her combatant with the bullet storm. Three more water-cannonballs whizzed past her head. Still shrugging away Shadow's bullets, the stranger sidestepped the first sphere, allowing it to splash in the distance behind him. He backhanded the second sphere, which froze into ice and dropped next to him, shattering again.

While he blocked the second orb and watched the third one approach, his grip on his axe tightened. The axe head burst into flames, though they were not the orange hue of conventional fire. Instead, the flames were a deep crimson, as vibrant as the light of dawn. He swung his axe like a baseball bat at the third water sphere, and when the two collided, the clear liquid glowed crimson for a moment before exploding into thousands of droplets and bursting the sphere as silently as the popping of a soap bubble.

Moving in tandem with her partner, Shadow retrieved three metal pellets from her jacket pocket and hurled them at the Fireman. When they were close to his face, Aquifer formed an egg-shaped prison of water around him, slowing the pellets' progress so they floated in front of the man. Shadow looked away as her flare-pellets detonated, creating a series of flashes that would have easily blinded her.

I hope Aquifer looked away, too. I don't need him sidelined right now.

She glanced over, a little concerned, but Aquifer was already flattening the water-egg, keeping the Fireman suspended while opening him up for outside access. Shadow drew her combat knife and jumped at the man, swinging her arm down so the tip of the blade would embed itself into the top of his skull. Before her attack completed, the water around him glowed crimson again, exploding into droplets with enough force to push Shadow onto her back.

The Fireman regained his footing and raised his axe in the air above Shadow, ready to bring it down onto her head. She lifted her arm in response and extended her palm; two silver tubes protruded from the sleeve of her jacket, beneath her wrist. A flat pedal flipped into her hand, and she curled her fingers to squeeze it once, spray-ing shotgun pellets point-blank into the Fireman's face with an unflattering, hollow *crack.*

As with her machine pistol bullets, the pellets halted their progress as they touched the man's gas mask, each releasing a hazy fog before dropping to the earth. The axe completed its swing, and she rolled out of the way. During her roll, she snatched a compact .22 pistol from her ankle holster and emptied its magazine into his face, attempting to serve as a distraction rather than an assault as she moved away.

The axe head burst once more into crimson flames, and the Fire-man drove the blade into the pavement, only inches from where Shadow had been standing. A wide chunk of the street fragmented and exploded into the air, spreading away from the point of impact like a wave. The blast caught Shadow and flung her a dozen feet, landing her hard on the ground near Aquifer. Her vision blurred, and she was reminded of her battle with the spider-like creature in La Encarnación.

Above her head, Aquifer raised his hands to form a thick wall of water between the Fireman and The Faction fighters. Within sec-onds the wall solidified into ice, revealing the Fireman's silhouette, before shattering into tiny pieces, pelting Shadow and Aquifer with ice pellets. The Fireman crossed the distance between them, and he was moving fast.

"Shadow, get up," her partner begged her, pulling her away from their attacker.

Shadow shook her head, trying to reorient herself.

Proxy crackled into her earpiece. "Team, listen closely. Just west of you is a parking garage. It's at the intersection of South Spring and Seventh. A supply closet at ground level is being primed for Bogeyman transport as we speak. Try to shake this person and get there as soon as possible."

Battery spoke up as well, her voice out of breath. "First . . . things . . . first."

The Fireman closed in as Shadow pulled herself to her feet and Aquifer prepared more water defenses. A whistling noise grew in pitch above their heads, faint at first but louder by the second. Shadow looked up to see a silhouette falling from sky, encircled by arcs of blue electricity.

———

The acid bubbled inches from Battery's face, splashing too close to her eyes for comfort. She reached out and dug her fingers into the flimsy metal walls of the water tower, producing an awful screech as she used it to halt her descent. The hair strands squeezed tighter, trying to wriggle her free, but she held firm.

In the distance, the sounds of machine-gun fire alerted her to her teammates' confrontation. She gritted her teeth and whipped her feet beneath her, swinging like a gymnast. Once they were planted on the other side of the water tower wall, the hair strands loosened in an attempt to better grip her. In the moment of lapsed capture, Battery twirled her belt's dial to the highest setting and did the unthinkable.

She plunged her bare hand into the acid below.

Even with the increased energy protection, the burning liquid was able to sear off the first few layers of her skin. At the same time, thick bolts of electricity poured from the injury into the acid, the hair-tentacles, and the surrounding conductive water tower. Raw power snaked through the strands holding her captive, and somewhere below the roof, the hotel faintly cried. The tendrils loosened more. If she hadn't already gained a footing inside her metal prison, she would have fallen right into the acid.

With her free hand, Battery ripped apart the remaining bonds, slapping her burned, electrified hand against the tower wall to keep the hungry creature at bay. She pulled herself over the edge of her prison, squinting to see past the blinding blue light of her belt's higher voltage. Once she vaulted over the side of the tower and steadied herself on the hotel roof, she slipped her goggles from around her neck and stretched them across her eyes.

Darkness enveloped her vision as the headgear filtered away the electric blue light. An ambient light sensor in the goggle frames activated, adjusting the tint of the lenses to account for the darkness of the night. Her eyesight cleared; not only was the electrical glare gone, but her night-vision had sharpened, allowing her to see beyond her natural capabilities.

Behind her, the other three water towers reopened, prepared to spew more hair-tentacles at Battery. Rather than giving them the opportunity, she bounded away, listening to Proxy's message about the parking garage.

"... get there as soon as possible."

At the edge of the roof, her chest heaved. She'd almost been digested. *Digested.* But she had no time to dwell on the thought further, for the tendrils snaked out of one of the other towers to continue their relentless attack. Without a second thought, she jumped over the side of the building, falling toward her teammates and their attacker.

"First ... things ... first."

Battery raised her arms, fists crackling with energy, and gathered her strength. Plummeting over a hundred feet to the pavement below, her body aimed at the newcomer with the axe. Aquifer and Shadow looked up at her, as did the Fireman. Her allies backed away, aware of the destruction her impact would cause, but this new foe held his ground. He raised his free hand and unfurled his index finger, pointing up at Battery.

Between the heightened voltage burning through her muscles and her increasing momentum, her collision with the man would leave a scorched crater in the earth, her fallen form a literal lightning strike. She worried about the effect on the surrounding businesses, but her companions came first, and she didn't have time to underestimate the new, eerie enemy. Still, if Aquifer and Shadow were not far enough away, they'd get caught in—

Her body touched the tip of his extended finger, and she halted in the air, her momentum drained.

Electricity still swarmed around her, strength swirling inside her muscles. Still, the force she collected during her descent was just . . . gone. Now she hovered above the Fireman, her body cold and weightless, somehow supported only by the end of a single, gloved finger. She tried to fight it, to pull away, but each muscle she accessed shifted only a little before a soft, chilling force halted her efforts. Frost spread across her skin in patches as her heartbeat slowed, but the muscle in her chest continued to pump with the help of the electricity pouring from her cells.

After a moment, the Fireman pulled his finger away; warmth flooded Battery's body, and the pull of gravity reappeared, dropping her to the pavement. Shivering, she rubbed her arms as she crawled to her feet, trying to regain her strength. The Fireman stood above her, open hand raised. As she watched, the glove burst into deep crimson flames, which danced along his palm and fingers without burning anything. Breathing muffled, ragged breaths, he brought his arm downward, smacking her across the face.

The instant his hand connected, the flames disappeared with a sharp whisper. Her body blurred for a fraction of a second, and then she was gone, her body drilling into the concrete where she'd stood and continuing into the earth beyond. When Battery regained her senses and looked around, she was in an impossibly deep hole, covered in mud and grime. The starry sky was a mere pinpoint of light above her, at least a quarter-mile away.

She sighed, stretched her stiff neck, pulled herself to her feet, and scrambled up the side of the tunnel to rejoin her team.

———————————

Shadow stared at the smoking hole in the ground where Battery had just been standing, mouth agape. The Fireman looked up at them and began walking around the mouth of the chasm he created.

Shadow turned and signed to Aquifer. [Go. Get to the retrieval point. I'll keep him distracted, but he's after you, not me.]

The scientist began to protest but stopped, clearly considering the logic of her words as the Fireman drew nearer. He nodded, flapped his arms, and jettisoned down the alley in a spray of water, away from his attempted abductor. The Fireman moved to pursue him, but Shadow ran into his path, throwing three more pellets into the air near his mask.

The flare-pellets ignited in the small, dark space between the buildings, staggering them both. Shadow tried to look away, but some of the light had still made it through her eyelids and seared her retinas. She blinked away the spots of light in her vision, and the Fireman shook his head, perhaps trying to do the same. The momentary respite allowed Shadow to reload her Reczny, and by the time he recovered, she was opening fire.

Bullets froze around him, though they were almost all concentrated around his gas mask this time. As each one stopped and hovered, the frozen mass on his face grew until he could no longer see past them. He began to swat them away in advance, using his arms to free his line of sight.

Shadow kept her trigger depressed, backing away as he pushed past the wave of bullets to continue his slow approach. The head of his axe burst into crimson flames, and he raised it in preparation to strike her. Aquifer was gone, but she needed an escape route, too.

Then her opening arrived.

"Hey!" A voice called at the Fireman's back. "We aren't done yet!"

Battery stood at the lip of the hole, her clothes tattered and her body covered in mud and dirt. Her hair, normally splayed around her like a lion's mane, was flattened, weighed down by gunk. Every flash of blue light from the electrical arcs near her head highlighted dirty streaks. Her eyes were hidden behind her goggles, but she was under some kind of trance. Baring her teeth, she hunched over with her arms raised, challenging the Fireman.

When the Fireman turned to face Battery, Shadow signaled she was leaving. Battery barely registered the message as she stomped toward her opponent, and Shadow slipped away into the darkness.

"I don't care if you're targeting someone specific in The Faction," Battery growled, addressing the axe-wielding man before her. She was within his reach now, and his hand burned crimson as she spoke. "If you try to hurt any of my friends, you'll have to go through—"

He flicked her in the chest.

The crimson fire extinguished with another sharp whisper, and Battery found herself unable to breathe. The world around her turned into a nauseating blur, and she barely registered the metal, glass, and concrete smashing around her body like ocean waves. Her ears screamed from wind resistance, and she tried to stop whatever was happening, but it was no use. Locked in, she was a child riding the loop of a roller coaster.

With a final crash, Battery's momentum slowed enough for her to register her flight backward through the air. Her back struck a thick wall, creating a crater. Electricity swarmed, rebuilding her pulverized bones. Her difficulty breathing came from her own skeleton; it had caved inward where the Fireman had flicked her, despite the level of protection her charged form provided.

Battery pulled herself from the crater, ducking her head as pieces of brick and concrete rained from above. Rock and glass coated her body, adhered by the mud, and the electricity arcing around her baked all of it into a dried grime. Twisted and flexing, Battery broke away the outer shell of muck from her clothes and skin.

A series of Battery-sized holes stretched before her, drilling through at least a dozen buildings across at least five blocks. At the end of the line of destruction, Battery could make out the street between the Cecil Hotel and the neighboring building. The Fireman was gone, leaving behind shattered earth and evaporating frost.

"Battery? Battery! It's Aquifer. Shadow and I made it back. Are you okay?"

She tried to speak, but devolved into a coughing fit, not yet used to her regrown lungs. Once the hacking ceased, she stood up straight, spitting dirt and blood from her mouth. Another cool breeze blew, and with her body drained of its energy, she felt more clear-headed than before. "Yeah. He's gone. And I've never needed a shower more in my entire life."

Treehouse
May 3, 2011-B

"We don't have time for this," Proxy insisted.

"I'm sorry, Proxy, but I'm not comfortable jeopardizing our position right now."

Proxy slammed his hands down on the surface of his computer desk. *"This isn't speculation!"*

On the monitor, Butterfly grimaced at his outburst.

He took a breath and spoke in a calmer tone. "I've already sent Aquifer to collect some protectorates from Obelisk. Koshasth has worked with them before, right? You may still not know my own team very well, but you'd trust Obelisk if they agreed to help, wouldn't you?"

"That's not the issue, Proxy, and you know it." The pixie-haired woman leaned closer to her webcam, whispering. "Obelisk is based in North America, so you'd need coordinates and blueprints to Bogeyman them to the Koshasth compound."

"Yes. What's your point?"

"There's too many risks," she explained. "You and I have stayed in contact about what your team has encountered so far, and I'm seeing faster Society response times to your operations than any of Koshasth's missions. If you trust your team with your life, then the only other explanation is that Society can track whatever radiation Bogeyman creates when you teleport. Sending help would just mark us on the map."

Proxy rolled his eyes. "You're already marked, Butterfly! We've been tracking the fake Spec Ops team since they left Los Angeles, and they are *definitely* en route to meet up with the U.S. team who has been talking about storming a Pakistan base. *Your* base."

"That doesn't guarantee they know our exact location. This could be a ruse."

"A ruse?" scoffed Proxy. "To what end?"

"Listen, my—"

Footsteps sounded from the speakers on Proxy's desk, and Butterfly turned away, speaking to someone off-camera.

"Yes. Yes, of course. No, it's okay. Tell them I said goodnight. We have a busy day ahead of us."

She returned to the camera. "My team isn't the only one hunting for Society's earthquake targeting facilities."

"Right, we've been helping—"

"No, you don't understand." She had raised her voice. "Someone *else*, who isn't reporting to Obelisk or Tai Sui or anyone else from The Faction that I know, has been uncovering and dismantling targeting facilities. Most of them were incinerated, leaving behind little evidence, as was the case for your team in New Zealand. But my partner Ctenizidae pulled some of the intact hard drives."

"And?"

"This third party is retrieving bits of data about both Society *and* The Faction. In fact, they must have some connection to one group or the other, because they only seem to be hitting locations that Koshasth has found."

"Isn't tearing these places apart a good thing?" asked Proxy.

Butterfly was silent for a moment, rubbing her forehead. "Proxy, I know Treehouse is still very new, comparatively, but you need to separate your ideals from this situation. No one knows the culprit, which means we don't know their motives. Those motives may interfere with what The Faction is trying to achieve . . ."

Proxy completed her sentence, finally understanding. "And if they have access to our communications, sending your coordinates to anyone may cause them to fall into Society's hands."

Butterfly nodded. "Exactly. They may be bluffing, with the expectation that Koshasth will *expose* themselves in an attempt to *defend* themselves."

Proxy shook his head. "I don't know about this, Butterfly. You're gambling the lives of the Refined civilians you've collected. They aren't trained in combat like you and Ctenizidae, no matter the extent of their abilities."

"Well . . . It's a gamble either way. I'm using my best judgement." She reached for her webcam. "Good night, Proxy. Or whatever time of day it is in that place."

He offered her a short, nervous chuckle. "It's always night here, Butterfly. It's always night. Stay safe."

Proxy ended the call.

"So, what's the plan?" a voice asked.

He turned to see Battery and Shadow in civilian clothes, leaning against the concrete wall of the basement.

"I'm going to use *my* best judgement," he responded. "Suit up and be ready."

"Proxy, you there?" Aquifer said over the radio.

The analyst rushed to his desk to respond. "I'm here. Did you make it to the Obelisk base okay?"

"Yeah. You didn't mention their . . . creative entrance."

"I sent you for a reason, Aquifer. What did Obelisk say?"

"They agreed to send reinforcements. I'm at our rendezvous location with Prism and the Spectrum Triplets."

"Stand by." Proxy looked at his monitor. "Butterfly hasn't given a green light yet, but I fear she will soon."

"Actually, Prism has something to tell you," Aquifer commented. "Hold on."

There was a muffled, rustling sound from the radio, and then a low, grinding voice spoke.

"Proxy, we've been keeping an eye on the DEVGRU soldiers in the U.S. They are *not*, I repeat, *not* compromised. In fact, in our attempts to reach out to them, we've learned many of their companions are, and it seems they're starting to notice."

"That's good, Prism, but—"

"Wait. They're being misled. Whoever they trust for intelligence has planted the idea that the source of their suspicions and distrust are associated with Osama Bin Laden."

"Which is bogus." Proxy's face flushed with annoyance. "He's just someone in the Koshasth cell Society chose to make a public enemy after the September 9th attacks."

"We have a problem with this," Prism rumbled. "They may be misled in their target, but if they're flying to Pakistan, that means they *do* have a target. The hive-mind people who replaced the Canadians might bluff and set a trap, but Obelisk *knows* DEVGRU; they're headed to kick down someone's door."

"Damn it."

"Look, Proxy, I respect Butterfly's wishes, but I think we should be there. I know their coordinates, so I'll give you the name of a nearby building that we can use to walk to the Koshasth compound. Everyone wins; she stays private, we get to help her, and you have the peace of mind that this wasn't for nothing."

"Okay." Proxy sighed. "Tell me where to send you."

———

Proxy sat in his chair, twirling his thumbs and anxiously waiting for any communication from Koshasth or Obelisk. Behind him stood Battery, Shadow, and the recently returned Aquifer, all in full combat gear.

"Is it not comfortable?" Aquifer asked Battery, who was squirming in her new navy and copper body armor.

"It's just that I haven't broken it in yet," she replied, patting him on the shoulder. "What about you?"

"What you do mean?"

Battery gestured to the pearl-white metal armor that was partially visible beneath his jeans and hoodie. "Isn't your PAUS a part of you now? Why wear more? I imagine it would make fighting more cumbersome."

He smiled at her. "Well for starters, I'm kind of allergic to bullets. Remember that whole 'getting shot' thing? Not the best time of my life."

"Okay, okay, no need for the sarcasm."

"On a serious note, this armor actually connects to my PAUS implants. While the implants use weak antennas powered by solar and biochemical energies, each layer I add includes a stronger battery, more range, and a wider scope to what I can affect and control. Think of the implants as my voice. The armor is my megaphone."

"Very cool. But why the clothes, when you already have armor?"

Aquifer rolled back his sleeve and gave her a closer look at one of his gauntlets. The pearl-white metal was broken up by a series of seams, beneath which a black mesh was visible. Once she had a change to examine it, he pulled the sleeve down again. "I misspoke earlier by calling this armor. It's *armored*, sure, but it's also a cluster of panels housing computers, microphones, and projectors meant for irradiation. I would be a fool not to cover it all up, when leaving it exposed may turn it into a target in combat."

The sound of hands clapping caused the two to turn around, where Shadow was applauding in Aquifer's direction. [It's been five years, but you've finally started thinking like a hunter.]

Aquifer raised an eyebrow. "Thanks, Shadow . . . I think?"

Just then, a video chat window popped into Proxy's monitor. Butterfly appeared on the screen, Prism stood in the background with his glassy, mosaic body.

"Look at who I found wandering through the fucking desert," she said, glaring at Proxy.

Prism lifted his hand and waved, sheepish.

Her eyes narrowed. "I explicitly told you not to send anyone."

Proxy began to speak, but Butterfly raised a hand to stop him.

"Still . . . Prism explained the situation with the U.S. troops headed this way. You said you were tracking them?"

"We were tracking the Canadian imposters, not the Americans. They picked up some new person from Alberta, Stacey Fields, who flew out of the country about a day ago. I think he was meant to replace the hive-mind clone that Shadow killed in Los Angeles. As far as I can tell, *he's* clean, but he's a sheep among wolves. The whole CANSOFCOM group went dark a few hours ago, and as I'm searching it appears to be the same situation for DEVGRU. Attack may be imminent."

Butterfly shook her head. "We have too few combatants here, and everyone but the Obelisk team and I are asleep. Our odds concern me."

"You still have Treehouse, Butterfly." She regarded him warily through the webcam, but he persisted. "You know we can help. We're a small cell, but we're powerful."

The camera on Butterfly's side of the call shook, and Proxy heard distant explosions through his desk speakers. An albino man, Ctenizidae, crossed in front of the screen as he spoke to her.

"I'll prepare them," he commented in a wispy voice. Then he disappeared into thin air.

Moments later, gunfire began to chatter, muffled only by a layer of wood and plaster. Butterfly stood from her chair and strapped a sheath to herself, swinging it behind her back beneath a thin, flowing robe. "I have to help Koshasth."

"Wait!" Proxy's cry was too late; in a blurred movement, she was gone. He looked to Prism, who was about to leave. "Let us help."

The mosaic man considered for a moment, then hurried to the computer and began typing. Coordinates appeared in their chat window. "Hurry, Proxy."

With that, he beckoned for the hoodie-covered Spectrum Triplets to join him, and together they smashed a hole in the ground, falling out of sight to the floor below.

"Get in," Proxy said, pointing at the Bogeyman chamber, his forehead sweating.

Battery, Aquifer and Shadow rushed to the teleporter, and the doors closed behind them. Proxy pulled the data Prism had sent him and opened up an outline of the Koshasth compound, hurrying to find an enclosed spot small enough to send his team. Each passing second burned a hole in his brain, reminding him of the urgency. The still-open video chat allowed him to see gunfire and explosions through the hole in the floor created by Prism, and in some instances, he heard voices yelling, either to communicate or to express their pain.

"Live one out!" An unfamiliar voice yelled, followed by a muffled explosion and a colorful burst of light.

First-floor bathroom. Proxy found his entry point.

"Sending you now," he informed his team.

As he spoke, multiple voices repeated the same words in unison, heard through Butterfly's webcam.

"We should use it!"

Proxy hit ENTER to activate Bogeyman, but he was met with an error message. The door to the bathroom was cracked open, keeping it exposed to the outer area. Bogeyman couldn't form a connection with it.

"God damn it," he whispered, searching for another area to send them.

The voices appeared again, their synergy familiar to what Proxy saw and heard in New Zealand and again in California.

"You can't fight forever."

Their words were following by screams of pain, a high-pitched whining, and an explosion that sounded like glass shattering.

"Wait, was that Prism's voice?" Aquifer yelled from the Bogeyman chamber.

Proxy neglected to answer, still intent in his search for an entry point. None appeared, other than the exposed bathroom. As he hunted, the gunfire ceased, and a conversation reverberated through the webcam.

The voices were not from the members of Koshasth or Obelisk.

"Where's our target? Where's Bin Laden?"

"Over here."

A brief pause.

"My God. We finally got him."

Another pause.

"Now can anyone tell me what in the hell we just saw? Have any of you, during any ops, come across . . . body modifications . . . like this? How would al-Qaeda, or ISIL, or any related groups even afford this kind of technology?" Boots scraped against the floor as people shifted their positions, but no one answered the person. "Also, these aren't Pakistanis. Hell, most of them aren't even from this continent! Who on earth did we just have a firefight with?"

The synchronized voices appeared, likely the replaced Canadians from the Cecil Hotel.

"They're just insects, Captain. Insects toppling mountains."

Electricity crackled, and a series of heavy object seemed to fall to the floor.

The Bogeyman alerted Proxy that the bathroom he had first chosen was now primed for transport. The movements in the house must have swung the door just closed enough to seal off the space.

"Hang on, team," he said, pressing ENTER again.

This time, Bogeyman rattled and hummed, indicating a successful link between two different locations in space. Though he couldn't see it, three people were crossing the threshold, materializing in a bathroom in Pakistan.

He activated Shadow's button cameras on her body armor.

"Ah, yes. The replacement."

The hive-mind was speaking to itself.

"Hello, replacement. Mother is hungry."

Gentle footsteps sounded.

"The replacement makes seven for Mother."

A single gunshot sounded, followed by footsteps and the dropping of a heavy object.

Battery whispered into the radio. "We're here."

The voices spoke again, echoing through both Butterfly's webcam and Shadow's button cameras.

"Time to go to sleep, replacement."

Through Shadow's cloak cameras, his team eased open the bathroom door, staying as quiet as possible. In the distance, electricity crackled.

"One of the Refined. Mother will be so proud."

More electricity.

Proxy's team was in the hall, and he saw a flash of orange light from the doorway at the end, followed by the sound of something hitting a wall. A popping sound, like a twisting sheet of bubble wrap, preceded yet another heavy *thunk*.

"Oh, this one will make Mother very, very happy."

A new voice, squeaking in terror, yelled at the hive-mind.

"Stay back!"

The team reached the end of the hall, and Shadow leaned around the corner.

The room was dark, but still lit well enough to make out the silhouettes of dozens of sleeping people, spread across the floor of the open room. Near the doorway, snug in his sleeping bag, was a young Inuit boy. Standing in the middle of the room, surveying the slumbering Koshasth cell, was Butterfly. She turned, swishing her ornate robe, and smiled warmly right at Shadow's camera, as if she could see Proxy through the monitor.

The scene only lasted for a second. Butterfly and her sleeping people flickered, transparent. Their bodies floated in the air, turning upside-down, and faded into the sky. The darkness vanished, and the room filled with bright spotlights, bloody corpses, and five standing people, two of whom pointed rifles at a young man. Proxy scanned the area, and tears filled his eyes. Butterfly's robe was around her body, surrounded with blood.

He wiped his eyes, already forgetting the phantom scene.

"No, we don't think so."

The four soldiers he'd tracked shared this response in unison, staring at the young man. For a brief moment, the man's eyes burned orange like lit cigarette embers, but they faded to a normal color as the hive-mind spoke. Neither Battery nor Aquifer reacted; they may not have noticed.

Aquifer leaned around the corner as well, and his hand began to gesture commands before he leaned out of Shadow's camera frame.

With his shift in movement, the floorboards creaked, and Shadow pulled back as well.

Footsteps approached them. Shadow drew a weapon as Battery stepped in front of her. One of the hive-mind soldiers, backlit by the spotlights, entered the enclosed space. He looked at the three intruders, and recognition filled his eyes.

"Wha—"

Battery punched him in the chest. He flew across the hallway and struck the wall at the end, collapsing to the floor.

Aquifer's arms swung back into the camera frame, completing some sort of PAUS command. In the main room, another hive-mind soldier spoke.

"Oh my."

Battery was in front of the other two in the hallway, and she reached down to activate the turbine in her Charge Belt.

Electricity flowed in smooth paths along the copper lines Aquifer had embedded in her suit, casting a blue glow in the dark hallway. She motioned for the other two to follow her and stepped into the doorway between the hall and the main room. Shadow stepped behind her, but Proxy couldn't tell where Aquifer was.

Gunfire erupted, hidden from Proxy by Battery's silhouette. Sparks flew as bullets ricocheted from her, and she raised a hand to protect her face, holding her ground as they continued to fire. After a moment, the shooting ceased. Proxy suspected that her goal was to waste their ammunition and ambush them during a reload.

"It was a nice try," the detective said in her energy-altered voice.

She dropped to one knee, exposing Proxy to a view of three people. One man was struggling in an egg-shaped prison of floating water, while another man and a woman attempted to reload their rifles. Shadow raised her arm and unleashed a volley of bullets with a machine pistol, gunning down the man as he reloaded. A sphere of water flew past her camera from the right, colliding with the woman and sending her flying out of the building through an open door.

The young man who was being threatened backed against the wall, trembling, watching Proxy's team engage the hive-mind people.

Machine-gun fire lit up the hallway to the left of Shadow, so she ducked and lifted her cloak as a shield; Proxy winced, aware that her body armor would not necessarily protect her from being bruised by the force of the bullets. Her cameras vibrated under the assault, but they steadied again as Aquifer generated a barrier between them and their attacker. During this exchange, Battery walked into the room, toward the imprisoned hive-mind.

"Drop it."

Shadow turned away from the room at this point, engaging in a gun battle around the edges of Aquifer's barrier. Both she and her opponent were skilled at evading one another, and most of the bullets missed their target or struck Kevlar plating. In the periphery, Proxy heard splashing water, then Battery's voice.

"Two things, and I'll be brief. One, what exactly *is* the hotel? Two, where is the center hub for the targeting facilities?"

"You are speaking with an officer of the Canadian military. Desist at once or you will be seen as hostile targets."

Electronic laughter. "No, Ben Wilson died. You're just a disgusting imitation." Bones cracked.

Shadow scored a round in her opponent's temple, dropping him to the ground in a pool of blood. She turned at the noise of metal pins landing on the grounding, displaying to Proxy the remaining hive-mind soldier with grenades in her hands.

Aquifer said, "How does it work? Are you independent, like other mammals? Is there an insect-like connection? Can you communicate with it, or with each other, remotely? I'd love to talk about yourself in more detail, if you want. You'd make a great study case."

The woman stretched her mouth into a hideous grin. "Mother says not to speak with strangers."

As she moved to throw the grenades, Aquifer used his PAUS to fill her side of the room with water; the grenades hovered near her, she swam to the floor, and the entire ensemble collapsed when they detonated. The room flooded, and her destroyed body floated away. Shadow, Battery and Aquifer spread out, examining the fallen Koshasth cell.

"Are you going to kill me, too?" The young man asked off-screen.

As Shadow examined chunks of mosaic glass, Aquifer and Battery spoke in the background.

"Battery, they got Butterfly."

"Well, shit," Battery replied. "I liked her."

Proxy added Shadow's observations. "The Obelisk volunteers, too. Society found a way to kill Prism." Shadow lifted a piece of Prism's body as evidence, and Proxy continued. "This is a fucking nightmare. Of all the cells, why Koshasth? I know they were helping us find targeting facilities, but this was a haven for Refined refugees and non-combatants. Society was cowardly for choosing them." He sighed and rubbed his eyes. "Also, that gentleman with you appears to be the replacement they didn't have a chance to convert with Cecil. In case you didn't catch it, he's also Refined."

"Wait, really?" Battery asked, looking at the man.

"The hive-mind called him as much before you joined in. I also caught some sort of orange light in Shadow's feed, which I think was from him. His eyes were glowing orange when you first walked in."

Battery gestured to Aquifer. "Aquifer, make sure no one got missed on the second floor."

The scientist nodded and launched himself through the hole in the ceiling created by Prism and the Spectrum Triplets. Battery pointed at the soldier.

"Fields, right? Tell me about your eyes."

"What do you mean? I—"

"I think we both know exactly what I'm referring to."

The terrified man squeezed his eyes and reopened them, revealing irises and pupils replaced by orange light. He blinked, and the light vanished.

Battery lifted her goggles, but Proxy couldn't make out her expression from Shadow's camera angle.

Aquifer rejoined them. "No one's up there. Sorry, Battery."

"Silver lining, Aquifer. We found a new Refined."

"Oh, really?" he asked. "What can you do?"

"I . . . I don't know," replied Fields. "I didn't know anything about this until right now." He paused. "I can see what everything is made of. I can make things explode. What is happening to me?"

Proxy spoke up in their earpieces. "We just took a heavy blow tonight, people. The best thing we can do to honor their memory is to rebuild, and to use our resources to finish what Koshasth began. I vote we indoctrinate Private Fields, since he's already been exposed to Society."

Shadow pulled out her shotgun and pointed it at Fields, clearly telegraphing her disagreement.

"Whoa!" Fields cried, holding his hands up.

"Cool it, Shadow," Battery added.

"Shadow, don't be like this," sighed Proxy, leaning into the microphone. "We glean more from Fields alive than dead."

Though he couldn't see it through the camera angle, he heard her pump the shotgun.

"Damn it, Shadow!" Proxy yelled.

Aquifer chimed in. "Alright, easy. We need all the help we can get."

Shadow holstered her gun and raised her empty hands. [We don't know this guy at all. He could be Mister Rogers or he could be Hannibal Lecter. I—]

Fields interrupted her. "I'm sorry, I don't know—"

"Hush," Battery replied. "Don't interrupt while Shadow's talking."

[Thank you, Battery. I just don't trust him. We aren't playing it smart by bringing him into Treehouse.]

"She's right, Battery," Aquifer admitted. "We don't know much about Fields. But he *wasn't* at the hotel, and I'm going to go out on a limb and say we give him a chance."

Proxy cleared his throat, addressing the team. "Ultimately, I'm running ops here. I appreciate everyone's input, but this is *my* decision and *I* take full responsibility for it."

Battery reached for Stacey's armed, but he jerked away.

"Let's go, Fields," she said. "You aren't safe here."

"Go?" Stacey replied. "Go where? We're in the damn desert . . ."

Battery, Aquifer, Shadow and Private Fields continued to converse, but Proxy wasn't listening. He pulled up public records about the soldier and his husband, Sam Fields. *Maybe he can be saved. Society wasn't expecting us. His husband can be rescued before he's killed or replaced.* A hospital. Sam works as a computer technician in a hospital in Alberta. Proxy dug deeper, retrieving information from the man's personal schedule and Outlook calendar. *He's scheduled to work today, right now. Fields's husband is in a public space. Maybe they have time.*

Aquifer radioed in. "Proxy, we're all here. Bogeyman us."

The analyst primed the bathroom for retrieval, activating Bogeyman. As the transfer occurred, he went back to his search, finding a cloud service for storing security footage. Working backward from there, he made his way into the hospital cameras, flipping through for signs of a man resembling Sam's picture.

The Bogeyman chamber opened, and he heard voices close by. Just then, a figure on the monitor caught his eye—Sam, exiting a server room on the fifth floor. *We aren't too late.*

His team exited the Bogeyman, first Shadow, then Aquifer, and finally Battery, with Private Fields in tow. The young man examined Proxy's basement, his face both nervous and curious.

Proxy turned in his chair and addressed him. "Private Fields, oui?"

The man nodded.

Proxy stood and approached him, extended his hand. Fields shook it. Proxy was pleased to meet him, but he could feel the clock toward Sam's demise ticking away. Still, he remained cordial.

"For now, you may call me Proxy. Welcome to The Faction, mon amie."

Location & Date Redacted

Okay, we're all caught up. The team has officially banded together.

We're far from over, though.

The next few reports are a bit scattered, so I consolidated them into something a little more linear. These are mostly mission files, documented after the fact, but I trust their accuracy.

Why don't we start right where we left off, then?

Treehouse
May 3, 2011-B

"I hate to be rude, Private Fields," Proxy said. "I know you just arrived, but I must ask you to leave."

Stacey frowned. "You can call me Stacey . . . Proxy. What kind of name is that?"

"One that protects me." Proxy offered a thin smile.

"Well, why am I leaving?"

"Because"—Proxy made eye contact with Stacey—"Your husband is in danger."

Stacey's stomach twisted into a knot. "Excuse me?"

Proxy sighed, but before he could speak, Battery chimed, "Here's the cliff notes version—we'll talk more later. Society is the bad guys, and The Faction is the good guys. Society really likes to fuck over potential Faction recruits by hunting down anyone they care about and killing them . . . or worse."

"But that doesn't have to happen to Sam," Proxy added. "Little time has passed, and I just saw a live feed of him at the hospital where he works."

Stacey shook his head, trying to process the information. "I won't let him get hurt, not for *any* group, including your own."

Proxy grabbed his shoulders with vice-like hands. "Then shut up and go convince him to come with us."

Releasing Stacey, Proxy looked at Aquifer. "Go with him, please. I don't know what Society will do, but Stacey is not prepared to fight them alone. He doesn't even understand his own Refinement."

My what?

Aquifer nodded, pulling Stacey back into the chamber. Stacey entered the strange, hollow device, and the doors began to close. At the last moment, he heard Proxy yell at the metal column.

"Sam was on the fifth floor, near a server room. Hurry!"

Blackness surrounded them, and he was falling again.

Alberta, Canada
May 3, 2011-B

Aquifer and Stacey burst from a janitor's closet, surrounded by bustling medical staff and the faint smell of ammonia. Stacey looked around, noting a sign placing them on the fourth floor. The two men rushed to the stairwell, climbing to the floor above. Stacey ran down the new corridor, Aquifer close behind.

They reached a receptionist's desk, where Stacey stopped. "Hey, Melody," he said, addressing the white-haired, older lady sitting behind the counter.

"Oh, hey Stacey! This is a surprise. You looking for Sam?"

"Yes. Do you know where he is?"

She turned and pointed a finger down an intersecting hallway. "He just ran to his office. Would you like me to page him?"

So we're not too late, Stacey thought. He left her question unanswered as he sprinted toward his husband's office.

It took about a minute to get to the small room Melody had directed them to; without waiting for a knock, Stacey shouldered his way into the room.

There was no Sam.

Much to Stacey's concern, though, were the things he *did* see. An open window with curtains fluttering in the breeze. A desk whose ornaments were scattered across the room. A solitary chair, only comforted by a jacket.

Not just any jacket. Stacey's heart skipped a beat. *Sam's jacket.*

Aquifer waited at the doorway, speaking into his radio. "Proxy, Sam's gone. Does he show up on the cameras?"

While the man waited for a reply, Stacey walked into the room, picked up the orange bomber jacket, and draped it over his arm. "I'll give your ugly jacket back to you when I see you," he whispered, a terrible sensation welling up inside his chest.

"Stacey? Hello?" Aquifer called to him, breaking him from his trance.

"Yes?"

"Where else could he be right now?"

Stacey pondered for a moment. "Well, our apartment would be the next place I'd look."

"Then that's where we'll go. Did you hear that, Proxy?"

Another pause, and Aquifer looked around the room. "Yeah, it's small enough."

The scientist walked into the office with Stacey and closed the door. It began to rattle, all noise and light fading from the room, and Stacey prepared himself for another trip down the dark tunnel.

———

Please don't let this end like Karnataka, Aquifer prayed.

The coat closet near the entrance to Stacey's apartment vibrated then swung open. He and Stacey emerged, separating to search the place. Stacey looked in the living room while Aquifer moved toward the bedroom. As the scientist opened the door, the scene he witnessed sickened him.

The walls and ceiling were coated in warm, red blood, obscuring their former colors. Stacey and Sam's bed was piled high with a wet mass of skin and organs; Aquifer thought he saw kidneys, lungs, and even a heart. Above the headboard, a flayed skeleton had been bolted to the wall, the moist bones dangling from the neck-down. The only area left untouched was a man's face and head.

Sam's face and head.

Stacey's former husband had been skinned before having his organs removed, and the contorted pain on his face was all Aquifer needed to know he'd been alive for the procedure. Pain and terror were in his dead eyes, and his killer had turned the man's head to face four words carved into the nearby wall.

WELCOME TO THE FACTION.

The doorbell to Stacey's apartment rang, and Aquifer heard the soldier yell out. "I'll get it! It might be Sam."

Aquifer turned to say something, but he saw a silhouette move outside the bedroom window. The figure looked like a man, but large shadows jutted out from behind him, like wings. Aquifer rushed to the window and looked outside, but the figure was gone, assuming it was ever there in the first place.

He stepped away from the bedroom window and walked outside the blood-soaked space, back into the hallway leading to other areas of Stacey's apartment. The doorbell rang again. Turning, he watched Stacey reach for the doorknob. As he did, Aquifer felt the temperature around him begin to drop; his next breath became a plume of mist. "Stacey! Don't open the—"

The front door exploded into thousands of pieces, the shock wave throwing Stacey across the hallway. In the frame, surrounded by spreading patches of frost, was the Fireman, hefting his axe. The intruder took one slow, deliberate step into the apartment, his gas-mask-goggle-eyes fixated on Aquifer.

Stacey rolled to his feet near Aquifer. "Is this a Society thing? Did he come for Sam?"

Aquifer shook his head. "No . . . I think this one is for me."

"Then where's Sam?"

Aquifer looked into Stacey's eyes, shaking his head again. "He's gone, Stacey. I found him in the bedroom."

Stacey's eyes widened, and he started toward the room. Aquifer put a hand on his chest to stop him. "You don't want to see him like this."

The soldier knocked Aquifer's arm away and shoved him, tears beginning to form in his eyes. The Fireman's footsteps neared.

"Back off." Tears welled in Stacey's eyes. "You don't know a goddamn thing about me. Who the hell are you?"

Aquifer tried to stop him again, but the Fireman's axe swung into their space, separating them. The scientist backed away as Stacey sprinted for the bedroom. As he primed the PAUS, the Fireman turn toward him. Heavy breathing from the behind the gas mask were the only noises Aquifer could hear.

Addressing the intruder, he said, "I've actually been thinking a lot about you, trying to figure it all out. You want to know what I believe?" The Fireman reached out to grab Aquifer's hoodie, but he ducked away, stepping backward. "Somehow, through some crime to the laws of physics, you're stealing away kinetic energy and keeping it stored as potential energy."

Frost formed around them, emanating from the Fireman. When Aquifer tried to point at the ice, his opponent jabbed out with the blunt end of his axe, almost hitting him.

In response, Aquifer formed a cube of water around the Fireman's legs from the knee down. Before the silent attacker could react, Aquifer increased the water pressure enough to keep his shins trapped inside, then swished his arm upward. The cube turned upside-down and flew to the ceiling, overturning the Fireman in the process. Aquifer released the cube, and the Fireman fell onto his head, his crumpled body showered in water.

From the bedroom, Stacey screamed at the top of his lungs.

The water around the Fireman's body crystallized into ice, and the shell cracked and fell away as he pulled himself back to his feet.

Aquifer raised his arms. "That's why the temperature is dropping. The speed at which atoms vibrate give objects their heat. If you steal away their kinetic energy, you stop that vibration, and the object freezes."

Stacey was still sobbing behind the closed door of the bedroom, and Aquifer felt a pang in his chest for the man, thinking of Ananya.

The Fireman was back on his feet, though, the head of his axe burning in crimson flame. Aquifer repeated the same motion as before, overturning his opponent and showering him with water.

"And that fire you make . . . that's the kinetic energy you stole, right? In Los Angeles, you took it away from Shadow's bullets, and from Battery's attack, and used the pure force against us. Am I getting warmer?"

Frost formed on the metal surface of his PAUS, and he was beginning to feel sluggish.

"Or colder?"

Once more the Fireman stood, and once more, he was captured by Aquifer's water cube.

"The problem is, you're taking and giving kinetic energy . . . but you aren't using it for *yourself*."

The cube flipped, sending the Fireman sprawling.

"How do you stop the movement when the object moving is you?"

The Fireman was on his feet for the fourth time; Aquifer tried to gesture with his arms, but it felt as if he were pushing through molasses to do so. The axe-wielding man was now approaching faster than the scientist could form commands. Within seconds, a gas-masked-face was right in front of his own. He attempted a nervous swallow, but he was paralyzed, cold seeping into his bones.

The bedroom door burst open, and Stacey stood in the frame with glowing orange irises. Tears staining his face evaporated into steam, and blood caked his clothes. He looked behind him again, at what was left of his husband. "DID YOU DO THIS TO SAM?"

The Fireman backed away and stared at Stacey. Aquifer felt

some of the warmth return to his body, and he gasped for air, collapsing to his knees.

"ANSWER ME!"

Raising his axe, the Fireman ignited the head with crimson flame and strode at Stacey. Aquifer made another gesture, and water materialized around the attacker's legs once more. The Fireman stopped, looking back at Aquifer's outstretched hand. This time, before Aquifer could complete the gesture, the water glowed crimson and exploded into droplets, freeing the Fireman. He turned the axe toward Aquifer and planted it in the ground.

The floor of the apartment rippled and fragmented out in a wave, the kinetic force shredding everything in its path. Aquifer had no time to protect himself as the wave approached, and it caught him, flinging him back into the air. The wave reached the outer wall of the apartment and disintegrated it, exposing the room to the city skyline. Aquifer went with it, barreling over the edge of the hole and rushing toward the streets below.

Aquifer fell out of sight, but Stacey's anger and pain brought his attention back to the Fireman. He didn't see a man with an axe and mask, though.

No, he saw so much more.

The orange starfield revealed a power radiated from the Fireman. Whatever it was, it caused the orange dots and strings around the man to flicker and fade to a duller color. Looking at his hands, he understood, by some instinct, he wouldn't be able to get close to the Fireman without losing access to the energy he'd used in Pakistan.

Nevertheless, this "Society" bastard was going to pay.

The Fireman charged, swinging his axe, and Stacey bounced against the strands in the air around him, jettisoning away from the attack and landing across the room. As he did, he noticed the color returning to the particles in the space the Fireman vacated. The orange dots chained themselves back together, one strand at a time, linking each atom.

Every dot . . . linked together.

The Fireman launched at Stacey a second time. Stacey lined up three points with his vision, connecting them with a series of bounces around the room. This allowed him to make a wide berth around the attacker's vampiric aura at super-speed. The axe buried into the kitchen countertop, and the Fireman struggled to pull it free.

Linked together.

Back in Pakistan, he had touched Lincoln and snapped apart the bonds in his body, creating some kind of explosive reaction. He'd done it while touching his target. Could he create the same effect on an object out of reach?

Stacey turned to the Fireman, focusing on his axe. He reached out with his hands, trying to will the atoms to pull apart, but the only reaction was an orange glow around his own hand, the air around it heating. He couldn't extend his influence very far, after all.

Still, everything linked together. *Everything.*

The Fireman retrieved his axe from the countertop and walked toward Stacey. The soldier raised his hand again, fingers splayed, palm facing the incomer. He used his new sight, his Atomic Vision, to draw together particles in the air, forming a constellation within a starfield only he could see.

The cluster of atomic bonds was too thin for his whole hand to interact with, though, so he modified his gesture. A pinpoint of light hovered in front him in his Atomic Vision, the beginning of a chain reaction, the first domino orchestrated to fall. The light drew closer to him as he extended his clenched fist. When his index and middle fingers unfurled, it nestled in the empty space between them.

With his right arm outstretched, Stacey used his index and middle fingers to aim a "finger gun" gesture at the Fireman. Visible only to him was a narrow tunnel of realigned particles stacking together from the domino particle, forming a straight line in the direction of the Fireman's chest. The orange dot of light attached to him had bonded so that one of its magnetic poles connected to his index finger, and the other to his middle finger. To tear it apart, releasing its energy, all Stacey had to do was separate those two fingers just a little.

That's exactly what he did.

The bond he touched broke, emitting a single *pop* like a bursting popcorn kernel. The released energy spread, seeking direction. It found guidance in the aligned chain of particles as a train finds guidance on its metal tracks. The visible spectrum presented it as an orange beam of light, no thicker than a whiteboard marker, erupting from the air in front of Stacey's fingers, burning everything it touched as it raced ahead.

The orange laser streaked at the Fireman's heart, but he dove away from what would have likely been a lethal blow. Nevertheless, the beam pierced his left shoulder, searing a hole through skin and muscle before destabilizing and bursting into a flash of orange heat behind his body. The cauterized hole was hot enough to ignite his fireproof jacket, though it took little time for the flames to sizzle and smolder out.

Clutching at his shoulder, the Fireman stumbled into the wall, his pain obvious despite his continued silence. The axe dropped to the floor as he examined the deep burn and the unexpected wound.

Stacey looked at his fingers, the ends of which warmed and smoked. Pointing them at the recovering assailant, his irises returned to their glowing orange state, and he prepared to repeat his attack. The particles in the air once again carved an empty groove of space through which the released energy could travel.

As the Fireman stood and retrieved his axe, the breathing labored behind his gas mask, a voice interrupted their combat.

"You, bloodhound! You came for me, not him." It was Aquifer, calling from Stacey's right, where a new hole introduced the apartment to Alberta's cityscape.

Stacey peered past the crater to see the scientist standing on a column of water stretching fifteen stories up from the ground, reaching their level. The water beneath his pearl-white metal boots created small bubbles like Alka-Seltzer. Whatever the chemical reaction, it allowed the man to stand on the liquid construct as if it were a solid mass.

Aquifer smiled. "What is the English phrase when playing with dogs again?"

He made a hand movement, forming a water cube around the Fireman's legs. The cube twisted ninety degrees, slamming the man onto his back before he could use any stolen kinetic energy against the attack.

"Ah, yes. Go fetch."

The scientist swept his arms out into the open air, and the cube launched as if it were an ignited firework. The Fireman was dragged with it, and together, they hurled across the street, crashing against the wall of a building. Water splashed at the impact, and the Fireman tumbled in a free-fall to the pavement far below.

Aquifer made a motion, and the column of water shifted diagonally like a leaning stack of quarters, allowed him to step back into Stacey's apartment. He looked at the man, the expression sad and frustrated, yet empathetic. Stacey felt the residual heat from his own ability cool.

"Stacey, I am so sorry we were too late," Aquifer said. "What Society did was cruel and terrible, and that's exactly what we want to prevent for others, too. You aren't obligated to be a part of The Faction, but we would at least like to keep you secured at Treehouse for a little while, until we can work out a safe way of moving forward."

Stacey clenched his fists, new tears leaking from his eyes. "There is no forward for me. Not without Sam."

Aquifer faced the ground, and his next words were low and unsteady. "I understand. Trust me, I do. But this isn't a safe place to be right now, not even to mourn. Please get whatever you need and come with me."

Stacey looked around through blurred vision and sniffed. Many of the household items he'd want were destroyed in the fight—or covered in his late husband's blood—except . . .

Sam's favorite jacket. The tacky, orange-and-green jacket.

Somehow, it remained unscathed on the kitchen counter where he laid it, centimeters away from the thick notch where the Fireman's blade had struck. Stacey picked it up, feeling its heft and texture. One arm slipped through a sleeve, and then another; before he knew it, Stacey was wearing Sam's warm, comfortable bomber jacket. It still smelled like him.

Maybe Stacey had been too harsh on the jacket before.

He turned to face Aquifer, now donned in orange and green, pulling the fabric close to his body. A new tear ran down his cheek, and he wiped it away. "Sam should be wearing this, but he can't. Until every person responsible for that has paid, I will care for it at all times. Do not touch our bomber jacket. Am I clear?"

Aquifer nodded. "Crystal clear, Private Fields." The scientist pointed behind him, through the hole in the wall. "Let's go. It won't take the Fireman long to recover, and I'm sure he's pissed now."

Treehouse
May 5, 2011-B

Stacey received a knock on his bedroom door.

He stood to open it, and Aquifer was there, dressed as casual as possible in a plain white t-shirt, ragged jeans, and blue socks. He looked at Stacey's grey sweatpants, white tank-top and bomber jacket.

"You're dressed enough," said Aquifer. "It's time."

"Time for what?" Stacey asked.

"Time for you to learn about why you're here, and why we want you to stay."

Aquifer led Stacey through the house, down into the garage, and past the secret doorway to Proxy's basement. There, the other three people—Shadow, Battery, and Proxy, if he remembered correctly—sat in an arc, with two empty chairs facing them. Stacey took one of the chairs, while Aquifer sat in the other.

Proxy fidgeted a little, but he was smiling and peering at Stacey with kind eyes. Maddie was sitting up next to him, her question-mark-shaped tail brushing the floor as it wagged.

Battery and Shadow were whispering to one another with wide grins on their faces, leaning over so their noses almost touched. Stacey thought he heard one of them giggle, and he smiled as they turned to look at him. Just like that, their tittering stopped, and they returned to their seats.

"You're an intelligent man, Private," Proxy said, breaking the silence. "Rather than lecture you, we'd prefer you ask your own questions and explore this alien world on your own terms. Do you find that fair?"

Stacey cleared his throat. "Yes . . . yes, I do."

"Well?" Proxy asked, extending his hand.

Stacey looked at each of them one more time before he spoke. "Who are the people that killed my husband? Who is Society?"

Proxy and Battery traded glances. "What we know about Society could barely fill an index card," Battery responded.

She extended a hand, and Proxy plopped a small laptop into it. Turning on the screen, Battery flipped it around to show Stacey a collage of supporting documents and images. "The oldest known records of Society activity that we can confirm were from the Dachau concentration camp in Germany," she continued. "This was in 1942, a few years after the second World War began. The documents you see here were redacted, but what we've pieced together alludes to genetic experimentation on prisoners. Considering the Nazi involvement in the camp, I'm sure they were highly unethical."

Aquifer leaned in, turning to look at Stacey. "We, as well as other cells of The Faction, have a few theories. One is that prisoners were turned into something more . . . or less . . . than human, and were then released into the world, either by intent or via escape."

Shadow sat up and signed, Proxy translating her words. [On the other side, it's possible that high-ranking Nazi officials or high-paying clients engineered themselves into more powerful entities. This theory is given credence by the apparent political power Society possesses today.]

Proxy shook his head. "The third theory, which I personally subscribe to, is that this document tells us nothing at all. What are the chances that the oldest document we could find is also the one that implies an origin for our enemy?"

Stacey nodded, understanding where Proxy was going. "Not high. It *would* be useful information to leak if you wanted to mislead your opponents, though."

"*Exactement*." Proxy lifted his arms.

Both Battery and Shadow rolled their eyes and sat back. "We've encountered many conspiracies in our time together," Battery said, turning to Proxy, "But that doesn't mean *every single one* is a conspiracy. Sometimes the simplest answer is the right one."

Proxy shrugged. "We may never know."

Shadow sunk her shoulders in a silent sigh. [No matter where they came from, we know Society exists. We've uncovered their connections to world governments, private manufacturers, health industries, illegal experimentation, drug trafficking, terrorist attacks, assassination plots, and natural disasters. Proxy and other Faction cells have wormed into the communication crossroads for most of these institutions to build a network of intelligence, and they've uncovered Society ties to the Suez Crisis, the Vietnam War, and the Falklands War.]

"Not to mention the September 9th attacks on the Twin Towers," Battery said in a low, quiet voice. "I was there for that one. I still remember the ungodly eyes of the man who detonated explosives against the foundations of the South Tower."

"And the Indian Ocean tsunami in 2004," Aquifer added. "Battery and Shadow watched a Society-manufactured earthquake create a flood strong enough to wipe out my family's hometown."

"Bogeyman, the machine over there," Proxy pointed, "was only obtained because I was investigating the possibility of Princess Diana's assassination. As it turns out, she *was* murdered, and that machine was used to do it."

Stacey rubbed his temples with his fingers. "I . . . I don't understand. Why do this? Any of it?"

Battery leaned forward. "Now we're in even-muddier waters; the why."

Shadow nodded. [The pattern we come across over and over again is that wars with Society attachment are created in areas where Faction cells are located or are rumored to be. Even the war in Afghanistan that you were influenced by in your own career seemed to be an elaborate attempt to stomp out Koshasth, whose primary focuses were gathering Refined refugees and exposing the facilities used to manufacture natural disasters.]

Proxy sighed. "Thank goodness some members weren't there for the attack. We're still trying to establish contact on that front."

Stacey glanced at the man's face and noted the dark circles under his tired eyes. *What kind of hell have these people been through?*

"Don't worry, though," Aquifer chuckled, addressing Stacey. "We aren't that egotistical. Yes, we've worked hard to be a foil in Society machinations, but there's no doubt that each of these conflicts and disasters also have ulterior motives designed to further Society's agenda . . . whatever that may be."

"Well," Stacey said, "Where *does* The Faction fit into all of this?"

Proxy offered him a thin smile. "The Faction originally formed in 1963 after the assassination of John F. Kennedy. Circumstances of the murder attracted a collection of foreign intelligence officers from China, Japan, and the Koreas. They were spurned by their employers and governments, so they began a secret investigation into the assassination, eventually linking it to other political phenomena of the time."

Aquifer continued Proxy's explanation. "With the advent of public technology and communication, more people were becoming wise to Society activity. Some formed wild conspiracies, shunned by their peers, while others slipped through the cracks to find a growing underground resistance. The Faction became so big that pockets of fighters formed in the areas of the world that housed Society's most troubling activities."

"Little time passed before Society became aware of The Faction," added Battery. "Then, The Faction was subjected to Society's biggest strength: Subterfuge."

"Are you referring to what happened to my team in Pakistan?" Stacey asked.

She nodded. "Just like that. It took many, many, Faction deaths before each cell sealed themselves off, staying in groups small enough to recognize signs of infiltration or replacement. Each cell created its own ecosystem and environment, its own way for dealing with Society, and we work hard to keep interaction between cells minimal. Our cell is named Treehouse. Around the world are cells like Péndulo, Obelisk, and Tai Sui; a few nights ago, you and the U.S. DEVGRU team were manipulated into dismantling most of Koshasth."

"And that's the other side of Society's subterfuge," Proxy interrupted. "Not only can they physically control people in various ways, but they also manipulate public sentiment so that The Faction is the 'bad guy,' continually wounding our attempts to ally with political or military groups not yet associated with Society. Hell, innocent men and women gladly serve as soldiers against The Faction, provided Society presents the right narrative."

He pointed at the monitors. "I imagine if you look at the television or the internet in the next few days, you'll see that a brave Faction fighter was gunned down at Society's orders as a scapegoat for a mass-murder Society *themselves* created. And do you know what will happen? The public will cheer at the accomplishment, as if some great evil was ended."

Stacey sat silent for a moment before replying. "Still . . . is The Faction even helping? You're telling me you fight and kill, infiltrate and destroy . . . so, you *are* terrorists, aren't you?"

The entire group laughed, but it was a soft, sad sound. Proxy was the one who answered. "Of course we're terrorists, mon amie. When those in power would cause their citizens harm, the ones who fight for peace are considered the public enemy."

Everyone took a thirty-minute break from the dialogue, replenishing themselves with food and water and relaxing their bodies by stretching and lounging. While they loitered in the living room, Stacey pointed out the blackened patio doors and windows. "I'm sure the exact location is need-to-know, but where *are* we? Is this some underground base? It certainly doesn't look like it."

"We aren't underground," Aquifer called from the kitchen. "We aren't anywhere at all."

Stacey laughed. "Well, if you didn't want to tell me—"

"No, he's being literal," Proxy interrupted.

"What?"

"The Bogeyman downstairs, the teleporter. Its ability to transport people and objects is hindered by the need for a small, enclosed space. I'm not sure what the exact dimensions are; the people who made it died a long time ago, so Aquifer and I have done our best to learn how to control it."

"Still, what we can do is limited," Aquifer added.

"Right. For now, any building or natural structure I can pull up using a map or satellite feed is fair game to target with Bogeyman, provided it's a small enough area. Otherwise, the signal is rejected, and I have to keep searching nearby until I find something the device allows."

"That's interesting," Stacey said, "but what does it have to do with my question?"

"When I first obtained the Bogeyman, the limitations were fewer. The scientists involved could locate a wider range of targets, place someone in a moving vehicle, or even disregard its need for an enclosed space." Proxy sighed. "That last part was what led us here. We were under attack in my home, *this* home, and the scientists warned me about the strain that a large transport to an unsecure location could have on Bogeyman. Still, I pushed them to teleport the entire building to a safehouse, an open warehouse of sorts. Trying to move such a large object, including its own form, to such an open area was too much. We teleported away from Paris, but we never reached our destination. Instead, we drifted . . . in-between."

He gestured around at nothing in particular. "Neither here nor there, the outer layer of the building frozen, the air and the water and the electricity in some sort of impossible, perpetual loop. Temperatures never change, and the food that was already in my pantry never grows old, yet it can never be eaten. It's the most grotesque form of sterility imaginable. And . . ." Proxy shuddered. "It's also my prison."

"What do you mean?" Stacey asked.

Proxy gestured to his own body with his hands. "Private Fields, how old do you think I am?"

Stacey examined him for a moment. "I don't know, late twenties?"

"How flattering," Proxy smiled. "I'm forty-five. Maddie is twenty-one in human years."

"Wait, don't dogs only live to be, like, ten?"

Proxy swept an arm around the house. "When we reached this in-between place, we became part of Treehouse. Part of Bogeyman. We can't leave; the machine won't take us anywhere. We don't age; at least, not that I can tell. But . . ."

He went to the kitchen and picked up a knife, pricking his finger with the sharp point. A small droplet of blood formed. "Apparently," he continued, "we aren't immortal. We still get hurt, and I presume we can still be killed. Shakespeare said it best." Proxy lifted his bleeding finger. "If you prick us, do we not bleed? if you tickle us, do we not laugh? If you poison us, do we not die? And if you wrong us, shall we not revenge?"

His hand fell to his side.

"We're all subject to strange sciences, Private Fields, but at the end of the day, we're all still human."

Rested and energized, Stacey returned to the basement, now eyeing Bogeyman with a new degree of wariness. Once everyone seated, Battery attracted his attention. "As you're already aware by now," she said, "There's more to Society than public influence and strange science. If you are going to fight with us, you need to understand the scope of what we've dealt with so far."

Stacey nodded, pulling Sam's jacket tighter. "Okay."

"At the bottom rung of the operation are the normal people who are altered or replaced in a way that makes them loyal to Society. Your former friends from Pakistan were among those. These people are spies, saboteurs, scapegoats and foot soldiers. They're used to disrupt from within, or to attack without warning."

She glanced around the room at the rest of her team, and they signaled for her to continue. "These people vary in types, their strengths and weaknesses wholly dependent on what they are. We've classified these types with different names."

Shadow retrieved the laptop and opened it to a still image from a police precinct, as seen from a security camera. In this captured moment, several of the officers' faces were visible, including slit lizard eyes and rows of hypodermic needle teeth. Stacey furrowed his brow and leaned forward at the sight of them.

Battery pressed on with her monologue. "First type: Code-named 'Reptiles.' They look normal, but can transform into . . . *this.* Glowing eyes with night vision, sharp teeth that hurt like hell, and a thick, scaly hide lying right below the epidermis. Tougher and stronger than a normal human, but not invincible. If you use enough force, or if you manage to penetrate them in areas that also hurt humans, they can be killed."

Shadow added her thoughts, Battery stopping to translate. [We know the least about Reptiles, and that makes them dangerous. It's uncertain how they're made, how they think, or what happens to the people they replace. Are they the original human, abducted and genetically altered in some way? Are they a foreign species created by Society, dressed up to pretend to be the person they replaced? Also, how do they communicate; is it subsonic, or body language, or something else altogether?]

She stopped, so Battery picked up the figurative baton. "An important note is that these creatures, or people, are *always* operating under Society control, no matter how they look. As far as we can tell, their transformation primarily occurs to enhance their combat abilities."

Stacey blew out a puff of air. "Christ."

"No kidding. Shadow?"

Shadow flipped to a new image: a photograph taken of the outside of a hotel.

Battery said, "Second type, one we just discovered and classified: Bellhops. *These* were your friends from Pakistan. About a week ago, our cell learned quite a bit about them, and the experience was . . . uncomfortable. Our discovery of the origin of Bellhops was how we found you, Stacey. Whether you like it or not, your friends' deaths are the only reason you're alive right now. Or at least, the version of 'alive' you're accustomed to."

Aquifer held up a hand. "Battery, he's had a tough time already. Maybe we should—"

"No, Aquifer. He gets the full truth here, including all of its ugly details. If he can't handle *talking* about this, I don't want him watching my back in combat."

"I'm fine." Stacey waved his hand. "Please, continue."

"Thank you, Stacey." Battery offered a grateful nod. "This hotel is located in Los Angeles, and it was built in the early twentieth century. So far, Proxy hasn't found any records of the place that would make it a target of suspicion. Nonetheless, the entire building is . . . well, it's alive."

A laugh escaped Stacey's mouth before he could stop it.

Shadow scowled, but Battery seemed to ignore his reaction. "It seems ridiculous," Battery said, "but it's true. The hotel almost ate Shadow and myself when we explored it. The halls and the rooms can grow eyes, mouths, tentacles, and probably a bunch of other nasty shit. Eating people is how it produces new ones . . . the like-minded clones."

Shadow switched to a GIF cut from security footage in some kind of cafeteria. It looped around the same thirty seconds, in which a dozen or so men moved in tandem, placing their utensils in their mouths, taking swigs from their drinks, and even sneezing at the same time.

Battery gestured at the GIF. "Bellhops share some kind of connection, unaffected by distance or location. They speak, feel, and experience the same things, but are also capable of operating individually when needed. The Bellhops state their directives are received by 'Mother,' who we assume is the Cecil Hotel itself. How Society controls this phenomenon to achieve their own goals is one thing we *don't* understand."

[Luckily, their hive minds are the limit of their additional abilities, to our knowledge,] Shadow added. [They are just as weak and fragile as a normal human; even more so, in my opinion, because their uniformity makes them predictable in combat.]

"So . . . my friends were . . . eaten?" Stacey asked.

"Well . . . yes." Battery replied.

Stacey hung his head.

"Are we good to move forward?" she pressed.

He sat back up, rubbing his hands together and stretching his neck. "Bring it on."

Shadow's computer switched to a still image again: The interior of a supermarket, where a bald man with sunken eyes aimed a gun down an aisle. The man's face was expressionless, devoid of any emotion. At the other end of the aisle was Aquifer, huddled on the ground with what appeared to be a toy water gun in his lap.

When the image was revealed, the scientist sitting next to Stacey shifted in his seat, his discomfort apparent.

"Third type: Triggers," she said, continuing her presentation without noticing Aquifer's discomfort. "These differ from Reptiles and Bellhops in many ways. For example, there isn't a biological component. The people are physically abducted, and then a microchip is implanted inside their brain. When the chip is active, they receive a command, and they are then compelled to carry out the command to completion."

"That's another element of Triggers which makes them different," Proxy added. "Most of the time, they are still the same person as before. Other than surgical scars, there's no sign that they are any different. Even *they* may not know what has happened to them."

"That's not the case very often, however," interrupted Battery. "Generally, the people are made aware of the implants, and are then instructed to carry out tasks of their own free will. If they refuse, the chip activates, often forcing them to hurt themselves or their loved ones before completing the refused task anyway."

She looked Stacey in the eyes. "I want to be straightforward with you. These people are the closest to a normal, healthy person you'll find under Society control. You may be confronted with people you learn to recognize as Triggers, but make no mistake: We do not know a safe way to remove or disable these chips at this time. This means those people are the enemy, and if you have no other choice, it is imperative that you disable them by any means necessary to ensure the safety of your comrades and of the mission."

Stacey nodded.

Lifting her hands, Shadow took over. [Triggers are regular humans, but when they are under control of the chip, they cease to feel pain or to pay any attention to their bodily limitations. They will be stronger and more durable in this state, fighting until they literally can fight no more.]

Stacey slumped into his seat.

"You okay?" Proxy asked, but his voice seemed far away.

Am I okay? No, I'm not okay. My husband was tortured and murdered. My team was replaced with evil clones. The world is full of lizard people and sleeper agents and fucking monsters. And I'm just an insignificant speck in all of this while the world descends further and further into hell. "I'm fine," Stacey replied, straightening his back.

Proxy frowned. "Let us know if you need a break again."

"I said I'm fine. Let's keep moving."

"Very well. Aquifer?"

The scientist turned to Stacey. "Moving up from these people, we have Cryptids. Literal monsters. Genetic aberrations that are scattered around the world. Sometimes they roam general areas, turning into legends and superstitions, feeding off small towns who no one will pay attention to. Other times they guard places of interest to Society, acting as modern-day Sphinxes. Every once in a while, Society weaponizes them."

[Before I was with The Faction,] Shadow said, [I hunted these Cryptids, thinking they were some kind of natural or supernatural anomaly. In that time, I saw giant spiders pretend to be men so they could lure children from their homes. I fought an alligator the size of an elephant who could camouflage like a chameleon. I heard stories about whispering phantoms who plague the outer ring of Chernobyl and the forests of Aokigahara, devouring many of those who enter.]

"You truly never know what you'll encounter when you raid a Society point of interest," Proxy said. "It may just be men with guns, or it may be a beast plucked straight from a Lovecraft novel."

"Why the diversity?" Stacey asked. "And what's the point of just letting these creatures run loose after they're made?"

"You'll find yourself asking those kinds of questions often around here," Aquifer muttered.

Stacey looked at him, waiting for him to continue.

"Oh no, we have no idea what the point is," Aquifer added. "And quite frankly, they're far further down the totem pole of concerns than other problems caused by Society."

Battery cleared her throat. "That's because we're always dealing with the things running the operations: Chimeras."

"Chimeras?" Stacey repeated.

"Yes. In mythology, chimeras were creatures who consisted of the fusion of many animals. Similarly, the few Chimeras we've encountered have human-like intelligence, but bodies which resemble . . . something else."

"Like what?"

"In Berlin, we encountered a creature that was essentially a giant bear wearing a human suit. In New York, I confronted a man with wings and talons who was as strong as me."

Stacey pondered for a moment. "So, they weren't like the Cryptids you described before?"

"No," Proxy answered. "The Cryptids are odd, and they act on instinct, often staying in one area. The Chimera are intelligent and ruthless, masquerading as humans in positions of political, scientific or military power. When we locate one, it's only because they've had a heavy involvement in some atrocity."

"Stacey, the Chimera are *dangerous*," warned Battery. "No one person can survive an encounter with them. It took every resource available to Treehouse to contain the one in Germany, and we had maybe ten seconds before he blew himself up, taking out a city block in the process. This Chimera told us others like him would do the same. Rather than admitting defeat, they will ensure mutual destruction of those who fought them. Please, do *not* engage with a Chimera alone."

"I won't," Stacey responded, "but you have to admit, this is overwhelming."

"True. Society has clones and cyborgs, phantoms and monsters, political figures with super-powers and hidden agendas. Still . . . The Faction has a group of people with a genuine desire to do whatever it takes to keep humanity safe from death, destruction and manipulation. Also, we have the Refined."

"You've mentioned that a few times, now. What are 'the Refined'?"

Battery looked at Aquifer, who turned to address Stacey. "You, Private Fields. *You're* Refined. So is Battery. So is Shadow."

Proxy retrieved the computer from Shadow and began typing while Aquifer continued. "Refinement is a Society project whose goal is to trigger mutations in eligible humans, producing new ways to defy physics, biology, the conservation of energy, et cetera. The result is an eclectic mix of individuals with inhuman abilities seeded amongst most major populations."

"How did this happen? I never agreed to be part of any project or experiment."

Proxy spun his computer around, revealing a list of digital files. One folder stood out from the others.

REFINEMENT CANDIDATES

Proxy opened the folder and clicked the first item in the list. Documents filled the screen, highlighting notes from a team of scientists discussing the process of Refinement and hypothesizing about its results.

"You never had a choice, Private," Proxy explained, addressing the images. "Refinement started decades ago, back when several major countries agreed to mandate fluoridation for public water supplies. The chemicals the public understands to be fluoride in their tap water is, in fact, a mutagenic compound that initiates the Refinement process. It makes its way from there into 'purified' water and sodas, and it became entangled with our bloodstream over time, even passing along the mutagen from mother to child via breastmilk."

"This is only half of the process, however," Aquifer added. "Consuming the mutagens simply stores them in your cells; it's the process of sculpting wet clay into a pot. In order to 'bake' that clay, to trigger the reaction that eventually leads to a transformation, the population is administered a series of enzymes during their developmental stage."

Stacey put a hand to his mouth. "You don't mean—"

"Yes. The conspiracy against childhood vaccinations has a foothold in reality, though not for the reason most people believe. Are the vaccines necessary to stave off real diseases? Almost certainly. But are they also used as a front for Society experimentation?

Definitely."

The soldier looked down at his hands. "Why aren't there more people like me?"

Aquifer shrugged. "We think the Refinement process is a very delicate one. Most people exposed to it never show signs of abnormal behaviors or abilities. The argument could be made that record-breaking athletes, budding pioneers in STEM fields, or even the increasing destabilization of mental health are side-effects of inactive or subtle Refinement cases, but that's impossible to prove and a slippery slope to suggest."

"This isn't accounting for the people who *do* become Refined, but their bodies reject the transformation process," Proxy said. "You may be too young to remember, but there was a public incident about fifteen years ago in Riverside, California. A young woman's Refinement activated, generating some sort of bio-toxin in her bloodstream. After one drop of it was exposed to the air, an entire hospital floor lost consciousness, and one of the doctors working close to her had permanent neurological damage. The woman herself passed away that night, unable to tolerate her own ability, and Society covered up the incident, blaming *mass hysteria*."

Stacey nodded. "The Toxic Woman of Riverside. I read about her."

Battery jumped back into the conversation. "Many attempts at Refinement fall flat, while others end in disaster. Still, those who successfully uncover and understand their abilities are rare. The specifics of Refinement aren't *designed*, so the effects are random and can be dangerous from person to person. You said you struggled with migraines and light sensitivity for most of your adult life before your ability triggered, and we still don't know exactly why it happened in Pakistan. My ability is completely dependent on being electrified, so if that had not happened during a childhood accident, I may have never known. Everyone is different."

She locked eyes with Stacey. "With that difference comes danger, Private. We may be able to repurpose Refined civilians to help us fight Society and their monsters, but they were first Refined by Society for a reason. Is it to create a stronger army? Is it to dissect them and use what they learn to build more technology like Bogeyman and PAUS? We aren't sure. It means, though, that not all Refined are on our side, even if they want to be. On more than one occasion, we may find ourselves fighting against people like us."

[And that means you need to learn how to master your Refinement,] Shadow signed. [To better understand how it works and how you can use it in combat. You also must learn your limits and decide how you'll supplement them when necessary.]

Stacey frowned at the two women. "Doesn't that seem . . . ill-advised? I've trained with firearms in the military for years, and I've only developed my Refinement in the last three days. Shouldn't I play to my strengths?"

Proxy leaned forward in his chair, his voice soft and quiet. "Stacey, if you were to rate your own proficiency in firearms, where would you fall in a scale of one to ten?"

"I don't know, maybe a seven or eight?"

Proxy looked at the woman next to him. "Shadow?"

She stood and produced a compact pistol, turning it so the handle faced Stacey.

"Take it," pressed Battery.

"Why?"

"Just take the damn gun."

This is insane.

Stacey retrieved the weapon from Shadow. In response, she drew a long, flat Bowie knife.

"Okay," Battery said. "Prove your proficiency. Shoot her."

"What?"

Battery furrowed her brow and looked at the rest of the team. "Do I have a stuttering problem today?"

"Wait, wait," Stacey lifted his hands in a submissive pose. "I'm not going to hurt anyone."

"You won't." Battery smiled, the grin dark and mischievous. "I know my girl Shadow. If you don't hit her, she's going to stab you with that knife."

Shadow took a step forward, raising her blade.

I can't do this. Stacey stood still, and the room grew quiet.

Then Shadow retrieved a smaller throwing knife from her boot, lifted it, and propelled it into Stacey's thigh, pinching into his muscle.

"AHH!" Stacey grabbed his leg, appalled. "You people are out of your fucking minds!"

Shadow took another step forward and made a series of gestures simple enough for Stacey to understand.

[Shoot. Me.]

"Fine." Stacey raised the gun, aiming to wing her in the shoulder, and squeezed the trigger.

Shadow twitched, twisted, and the bullet slapped against the back wall of the bunker. Stacey frowned and fired again, trying to avoid a lethal shot, but the woman glided around it, incorporeal. A third shot, a third miss.

She was now halfway to Stacey, none the worse for wear. He panicked, his training kicking in, and he aimed at center mass. This time, her knife hand blurred, and there was a high-pitched *ping* as the bullet deflected against the flat of the blade, ricocheting into the ceiling.

He stopped. "I'm so sorry, I didn't mean—"

She crossed the distance between them and stabbed him in the shoulder, sending fiery pain down his arm and into his neck.

"GOD DAMN IT!"

For a moment, Shadow stood there, her black, cat-like eyes staring into Stacey's soul. Then she turned and sat back down, leaving the knife stuck in his shoulder. Gasping, Stacey dropped the pistol, grabbed the knife handle, and pulled the blade free. Blood leaked from the wound, staining his shirt.

Aquifer opened a nearby box of medical supplies. As Stacey clutched at his injury, the scientist produced iodine and a bandage, sterilizing and taping up the wound. When he was done, Stacey backed away.

"I'm done. I'm out of here. I'll take my chances with Society."

"Stacey, wait," Battery said. "Ask yourself this: How useful was your proficiency in firearms?"

He paused. "Well . . ."

"Exactly."

"But this?" He looked around the bunker, touching the stab wound. "This isn't normal."

Aquifer firmly gripped Stacey's uninjured shoulder as he spoke. "*None* of us are! And that's our point. Standardization will get you killed. Conventional methods will get you killed. Thinking outside of the box"—he held up his arm, showing the PAUS implants—"or taking advantage of your unique abilities"—he gestured at Battery—"Or even finding unconventional ways to adapt conventional methods"—he looked at Shadow, who was returning her gun to its hidden holster—"*that's* how you deal with monsters, and mutants, and horrific technologies. You just need to find out how to make your . . . what did you call it before, your Atomic Vision? You need to find out how to make that work for you."

Stacey hung his head. "I don't know where to start."

"I think I do," Aquifer said. "Your headaches. I believe those came from a part of your brain, some developing section that doesn't belong there. Much in the way bats have an area in their brain that lets them translate sound waves into visual cues, I think you have a new area in yours that emits . . . well, not sonar. Something else."

"Like what?"

"It's hard to say," Aquifer admitted. "Some kind of magnetic field? Maybe even something as elusive to define as 'telekinesis.' In any case, I think you have the ability to send out 'waves' from your body, and for whatever reason, your brain translates everything around you into its core components, the atoms that make up the world. You mentioned that you were a chemistry major, didn't you?"

"Yeah."

"Well, it obviously took a while for your Refinement to mature and to blossom. While it developed, your studies and your propensity for the subject may have influenced its direction."

"Hm . . . wow." Stacey scoffed dryly, but the movement created a pang in his shoulder. "Thank goodness I didn't choose musical theater."

The group laughed, and it was infectious enough to bring a smile to Stacey's face. He looked down at the bloody spot on his shirt.

I get it. This is military training 101 all over again. I'll never understand what hell I'm going to go through unless the hell starts here, in a controlled environment.

"It's with that connection that you can reach out and affect the atoms around you," Aquifer continued, now that the room had quieted down. "Not big things, of course. You're probably not going to pick up a car with your mind. But the little things, the specks that make up matter? That's fair game." He pointed as Stacey's hands. "Based on what you've told me, it seems that you use your body as a medium. You release the atomic bonds in other objects, even air, using the resulting force to propel yourself and to link two points together with heat and plasma."

Aquifer chuckled. "You're like an action figure from the eighties, Stacey. Especially with a self-determined naming convention like Atomic Vision. You want to blow something up? You have an Atomic Punch. You want to get somewhere quickly? You have an Atomic Dash. You want to shoot a laser out of your freakin' fingertips? You have an Atomic Gun."

"All joking aside," Battery said, "your ability has the potential to expand as we explore it, and there's no way to know for sure what the scope of it might be. Classifying the things you *can* do helps us understand them, and it helps *you*, the user, learn from them."

Stacey shook his head in disbelief, but he couldn't argue with their logic.

"Who knows," Aquifer said. "Today, you're pulling particles apart to harvest the energy holding them together. Tomorrow, you could be splitting the very atoms themselves."

Treehouse
March 8, 2012-B

Battery watched Proxy scramble from the dining room table, where the other four were gathered, and sprinted toward the garage. Maddie, excited by the sudden movement, chased him, her tongue flopping behind her as she ran. The man and his dog burst through the garage and into the basement, disappearing from Battery's sight. She stood to pursue them, a distant voice from the radio in the bunker repeating itself.

"Zeta Alpha Gamma, one-eight-three-nine-six-eight-two-zero. Color of the day is burgundy. Does anyone copy? I repeat, color of the day is burgundy. Proxy, are you there?"

As Battery entered the garage, the analyst reached the microphone and opened the channel while Maddie barked in the background, running off to wrestle with a toy.

"Millipede?" Proxy yelled. "Is that you? Holy shit, we've been trying to reach Koshasth survivors for almost a year! Where have you been?"

"I'm so glad to hear your voice, Proxy," responded Millipede over the radio. "I've had to stay under the radar; Society is coming after us hard. I managed to gather most of the remaining Koshasth members and refugees, but some were killed while in hiding, while others have chosen to no longer be involved with us."

"That decision won't make them any safer," Proxy said, grimacing.

"Trust me, I tried to convince them, but they wouldn't listen. Despite the setbacks, we're still debating on whether we want to set up camp and continue Koshasth in Southeast Asia, or if we'd rather try to assimilate into Obelisk or Péndulo."

Proxy sighed. "We tried to stop them, Millipede. I swear, we did. It was just too late."

"I don't blame you, Proxy. No one is to blame for what happened in Pakistan other than Society."

By now, the rest of Treehouse were gathering around Proxy and Battery in the basement, listening with bated breath. Maddie returned to Proxy's feet, her favorite stuffed rabbit held in her mouth.

"That means a great deal to me," Proxy replied, wiping his eyes.

"As much as I'd like to continue catching up with Treehouse, that's not why I'm breaking radio silence today," said Millipede. "A contact of mine, one of the few who wasn't scared off after the Pakistan attack, has reached out to me with some new intelligence regarding the Disaster Relief program you and I know so well. They've planned another earthquake, and Koshasth no longer has the strength to stop it."

"Who's the target?" Battery asked.

"Oh, hey, Battery! Details are scarce, but if I understand correctly, Society intends to sink Fiji into the ocean."

She frowned. "The entire archipelago? Why?"

"Why do they do anything?"

"Well, what else do you know?" Aquifer asked.

"So," Millipede replied, "Koshasth was able to use the information you retrieved from New Zealand to dig into the specifics of Disaster Relief. Apparently, the device responsible for the earthquakes is, in fact, a machine of some sort, buried somewhere underground. They use a series of strategically placed buildings we already know as 'targeting facilities' around the world to ricochet the machine's seismic vibrations beneath the earth's crust and point them toward a selected location."

"Well, say what you will about their goals," commented Aquifer, "but you can't fault their ingenuity."

Battery shot him a glaring look. Millipede seemed not to hear the scientist, or he simply didn't feel like the comment warranted a response, because he continued unabated.

"The problem is, we still don't know the location of the machine, and we don't even have specifics about the targeting facilities used to direct it. The most my contact could tell me was that they were preparing a targeting facility 'along the coastal U.S.' It couldn't be any more ambiguous."

Proxy pulled up the incomplete map retrieved from New Zealand. He zoomed into an outline of the United States, and a series of red dots began to appear. Once the map rendered, he overlaid it with a home-brewed map he was using to track known Society bases and points of interest.

"Maybe that's enough," he said, pointing to each side of the map. "See these two Society locations, Treehouse? They are the only bases we know about who fit the location parameters with the resources necessary to direct a seismic wave powerful enough to sink an archipelago. I don't know for certain if they are the targeting facilities we're looking for, or if they're even targeting facilities at all, but . . ."

But it's all we have to act on, thought Battery.

"It's more than we can do, Treehouse," Millipede said. "Thank you for working on our behalf."

"We'll try our best," Proxy replied. "How much time do we have?"

"My source says seventy-two hours, maybe a little longer before the attack begins."

"Christ, Millipede, that's not much time. We'll let you get back to your team. Go make Butterfly proud."

Millipede's voice choked up. "I try every day."

The transmission ended, and Proxy swiveled to face his team.

"So, what do we need to do?" Stacey asked.

The analyst stood and addressed the map. "To stop the attack on Fiji, we have a series of goals. First, we locate the targeting facility that is being prepared to communicate with the earthquake machine. Second, we must prevent the security system from incinerating the interior before we can back-trace the incoming signal to its source. Third, once we find the origin point, we shut the machine down. Permanently."

He sighed. "And we need to do this in three days."

Typing on the keyboard in front of him, the dots he had addressed earlier highlighted, filling the screen to show a radius.

"There's no time to tackle these locations as a full team. Even if there was, assaulting one base first may close our window of opportunity for attacking the other one. Taking this into consideration, I'm separating you into pairs. Aquifer and Shadow, you're going *here.*" He pointed at the radius on the left. "Gold Hill, Oregon. The facility location isn't exact, but it appears to be along the rural outskirts of the town. Rather than wasting time stumbling around the woods, I'm dropping you in the middle of town to ask about strange activity. I'm willing to bet a defunct mining town like Gold Hill will have developed a superstition or two about Society operations."

Aquifer reached for his armor, and Proxy cleared his throat to stop him. "This is urgent, but you'll scare off the townspeople if you come armed to the teeth. Your equipment will have to be scarce."

Shadow frowned at that, but Proxy ignored her, turning to the other two people in the room. "Stacey, you've spent the last nine months learning about your abilities and training with us to test them, but you've never been a part of a mission of such magnitude."

"No time like the present," Stacey muttered.

"Damn right. I'm sending you with Battery *here*." Proxy pointed at the radius on the right. "Centralia, Pennsylvania. Another small mining town, though it's mostly abandoned now. A coal fire began in the mines beneath the town decades ago, and it continues to burn today. There are cracks and sinkholes everywhere, flames burst from the ground at unexpected times, and smoke leaks into the air throughout the day."

"Sounds lovely," Battery said in a sarcastic tone.

"Je suis d'accord. A few of the original families still live in the place, but I don't know what kind of mindset allows for such a decision, so you may not receive much help from them. No, you will more likely have to search on foot. That's where Stacey's Atomic Vision comes into play."

Battery looked at Stacey, who nodded.

"Right, I've been working on the range of my Vision. If the facility is behind a wall or near the surface underground, I should be able to see an abrupt change from one arrangement of atoms to another. I just need to be close enough to see it well."

"Again, we don't have an exact location," continued Proxy, "but our best guess places an entrance near the Centralia Municipal Building. I'll drop you there."

With that, the team broke apart and shuffled through the room, preparing themselves while Proxy typed on the computer. As Stacey fastened a flexible bulletproof vest over his t-shirt, Battery walked over to him, trying to gauge his mood.

"Well, Fields," she asked, smiling, "are you ready for the Big Leagues?"

"We'll see," Stacey replied, slipping his arms through Sam's jacket and straightening the sleeves. Once he seemed comfortable, he stopped and rubbed the fabric of the outerwear, and Battery thought tears were forming. He wiped his face with the back of his hand and made eye contact with Battery, the spirit of anger and determination swirling behind his pupils.

"But call me Bomber."

Oregon, United States
March 8, 2012-B

Aquifer stood next to Shadow at the crossroads of Fourth Avenue and Dardanelles Street, looking to the left, then to the right. In one direction, City Hall waited for them with its elected officials and public records. In the other direction were the millers and machinists, blue-collar townspeople, gathered at their final bastion of sanity, the Longbranch Saloon. Both Faction members traded glances.

"Want to check out City Hall?" Aquifer asked.

Shadow signed only two words, [Loose lips,] before walking in the opposite direction he had suggested.

He huffed and followed her toward the saloon, catching up to walk next to the woman in her black clothes and leather jacket. She sported an addition to her attire today: A tall black messenger bag, draped in a diagonal line across her body and bumping against her hip. Aquifer himself was in blue jeans and a white, button-down shirt with the cuffs unbuttoned and the sleeves rolled down to hide his pearl-white implants.

They walked through the doors of a bustling saloon, filled with workers just relieved from their shifts. Many were already drunk, laughing and shouting and crying, releasing their daily cares into the open air. One man stumbled in front of Shadow and Aquifer in a mad dash to the restroom. Shadow reached the bartender first, pointing at a bottle of whiskey on the shelves and holding up two fingers. She sat down at a stool in front of the bar top, and Aquifer sat next to her, feeling uneasy.

"I can't imagine this is the best use of our time," he said.

She ignored him and looked around the saloon, stopping to stare at some of the other patrons.

She's going to start a fight if she doesn't stop staring, worried Aquifer.

As they waited, two glasses of whiskey arrived in front of them.

"Opening a tab?" The bartender asked.

Shadow shook her head and held up a roll of cash, more than enough to cover the drinks and a tip.

"Well . . . thank you, dear," the woman said, surprise in her voice; someone else called out to her, and she hurried off to serve them.

"Shadow, are you sure—"

The huntress held up a hand to silence Aquifer. [We're limited on time. I shouldn't always have to explain everything I do when we're in the field. Just trust me.]

"Okay." He took a sip of his whiskey but nearly choked on it, covering his mouth to hide it from Shadow.

A few minutes passed before Shadow stood up and grabbed Aquifer's hand, pulling him to his feet. She gestured to two men in flannel shirts—one red, one green—sequestered away in the corner of the saloon. [Them. Come translate for me.]

They walked up to the tables, where Red Shirt was speaking to Green Shirt.

". . . and I kept telling him, he and his buddies are gonna get shot out there some day. The government's got things to hide, and they won't hesitate . . ."

He stopped speaking when Shadow reached the table and plopped down in a chair across from them. Sheepish, Aquifer pulled out another one and sat.

"Can I help you two strangers?" Red Shirt asked.

Shadow began to sign, drawing attention from both men. Aquifer spoke her words. [Hey there. We were passing through, thinking about settling down in the area, but we couldn't help but to overhear what you said about your son. Would we be intruding if we asked more about what happened? It's such a lovely town, but we don't want to raise our own kids in a place that's dangerous.]

"Hell, we'd love to see some new faces in Gold Hill," Green Shirt said, looking at Red Shirt. "You shouldn't be worried. Jim was just talking about his son and his friends being nosy—"

"I can tell my own story, Craig," Jim snapped. He turned to the newcomers. "He's right though, there's no reason to worry. My kid's a teenager now, you know how they can be."

Aquifer nodded and faked an understanding smile.

"My kid thinks he's already old enough to steal a little of his dad's liquor, so he takes a bottle and rides up with a bunch of his buddies to The Vortex a couple nights ago. I mean, I get it, kids will be kids; I was just like him with I was his age. Still, a man has to—"

Aquifer raised a hand to stop him. "I'm sorry . . . The Vortex?"

"You don't know? That's about the only thing out-of-towners know about us anymore. It's a damn tourist trap."

"What is it?" Aquifer asked.

"It's just some dumb attraction, sitting on the side of the high-way about five miles north of here. Its gimmick is that the area around it has 'weird gravity.' Balls roll uphill, chandeliers hang at an angle, stuff like that. Not worth the ticket price to see, if you ask me."

"I'm sure it isn't." Aquifer smiled. "But it sounds like your son went there?"

"Yeah, they went up the middle of the night, probably already a little drunk, but of course the building is closed. So, they decide to just go *behind* The Vortex and hang out in the woods. When I think back to how cold it gets out there, and about all the wolves and coyotes that wander around, it's a miracle I didn't beat his ass when he finally came home."

"It sounds like you love your son very much," added Aquifer.

"Damn right I do! But they didn't see any wolves that night. Nah, my son said that a bunch of men in uniforms with guns came outta nowhere and started yelling in his face, blinding him with their flashlights. The kids got spooked and ran back to the truck, and I guess the scare sobered 'em up enough to get them back home safely. The Lord works in mysterious ways."

Aquifer glanced at Shadow. "He certainly does, Jim."

"That's what I was telling Craig, though," Jim continued. "The government is always hiding things. Always keeping secrets. There shouldn't be anything back there that interests them! It's just like Area 51. I bet they have something they caught in the woods that they don't want anybody to see."

"Maybe they do, Jim. Maybe they do. Could you excuse us? My wife isn't feeling too well."

The men turned their attention from Aquifer to Shadow, who had both hands on her stomach, bending over the table.

"Oh no!" exclaimed Craig. "Miss, you alright?"

Aquifer helped her up. "I think she just needs a little fresh air."

Together they moved through the saloon, and Jim and Craig were too busy taking another drink of their beers to notice Shadow straightening back up to a comfortable position as they walked toward the exit. Putting his glass on the table and burping a little, Jim lowered his voice and leaned over to Craig, but Aquifer could still make out the man's parting comment.

"You know, those were the nicest two Mexicans I've ever met in Gold Hill."

Pennsylvania, United States
March 8, 2012-B

The rattling of the supply closet stopped, and Battery walked out into the unlit linoleum hallways of the Centralia Municipal Building, Bomber in tow. Hunting around, she located a small white switch on the wall and flipped it. A loud buzzing alerted her to the incoming light, contained by flickering fluorescent tubes in the ceiling, and gave her a reprieve from the darkness.

Battery adjusted the copper-studded fingerless gloves of her body armor, which barely fit beneath her white tank top and blue nylon jacket, the mirrored goggles around her neck swaying. "What do you see?" she asked.

In response, Bomber's eyes glowed orange, and he looked around. "Nothing right away."

The two moved through the halls of the municipal building, Bomber scanning along the way, but nothing stood out to either of them. Along the outer wall, they checked for signs or clues, but that, too, proved fruitless. At one point, when passing a glass exit door, Battery thought she sensed movement outside. When she turned her head, though, she saw nothing but overgrown grass and trees.

"God, this place is creepy," she muttered.

"Well, this is what happens when the government doesn't take enough care of its people," Bomber said with a smug tone.

"Hey, don't start that shit with me, Canadian," she responded. "For all we know, the public healthcare and education you tout around is just another opportunity for Society experimentation."

He stopped, standing still for a moment. "Okay, fair point. Sorry."

When they finished sweeping the area and Battery concluded

there was nothing indicative of a targeting facility inside the building, they agreed to leave and form a circle around it, widening with each pass. Moving toward one of the glass doors, the two pushed their way outside. The air smelled strange to Battery, but green flora covered everything, obscuring much of her view of Centralia. The town felt abandoned, almost post-apocalyptic.

Battery heard twigs break behind her, and she swirled around. An older woman in a light-pink dress was aiming a double-barreled shotgun at them.

"Who the hell are you people?" the woman demanded. "Just 'cause that building isn't being used right now doesn't mean you can go loot it whenever you want."

Battery raised her hands and edged her way in front of Bomber. "Ma'am, I'm sorry if we scared you. We're with the police . . ."

She reached for her jacket pocket, and the older woman moved her finger to rest on the trigger.

"Easy, ma'am," Battery said, stopping. "I'm just showing you my badge."

Continuing her motion, the detective slipped her old badge from her pocket and held it up for the woman to see.

Lowering her shotgun a little, the woman leaned forward, squinting at it. "NYPD? You don't have jurisdiction here. More government employees, sneaking around Centralia and trying to find ways to make the rest of us leave. I've seen it too many times, and I'm not falling for it again. I don't give a damn how much you people want those mines, this is my *home* and I'm not going anywhere."

Battery pulled her badge back and placed it in her pocket, still standing between Bomber and the woman's gun. "That's not what this is about, ma'am. We have a convicted"—she leaned forward to whisper—"*a convicted pedophile* who escaped from jail a few nights ago. When he crossed state lines, it turned into an FBI thing, but if you ask me? They're just a bunch of bumbling idiots."

The woman grumbled and lowered her shotgun. "Seems like you've got a little sense."

Battery smiled and continued. "So, yes, I *shouldn't* be here. But this guy was my case, which means he's my responsibility. I don't want those Federal monkeys in suits making things worse. Sometimes you gotta play a little outside the law to catch the bad guy, isn't that right?"

"What has the law ever done for Centralia?" The lady in the pink dress chuckled. "A whole bunch of nothing, that's what. Well, I didn't catch your names, detectives."

Battery considered using fake names, but the woman had already seen her badge. "Detective Kipper, ma'am."

Bomber poked his head out and rejoined Battery at her side. "Detective Fields, ma'am."

The woman walked up to them. "You can call me Esther. I'll help you find the bastard, and I'll string him up myself if I have to. Unless you two already know a lot about Centralia?"

Battery shrugged, glancing at Bomber. "Sure, why not?"

Oregon, United States
March 8, 2012-B

The door to the small restroom inside the Oregon Vortex attraction building vibrated for only a moment. Creaking it open, Aquifer looked around, then tip-toed with Shadow into the lobby.

"Where in the holy hell did you come from?"

Aquifer jumped, but Shadow casually turned toward the source of the exclamation. A middle-aged, frumpy woman stood behind a counter near the entrance, staring at them with her mouth agape. The huntress nudged Aquifer, and they both moved to the counter.

"Did you not see us come in a few minutes ago? How strange," he said, smiling and offering his hand. The woman did not shake it.

Shadow began to sign, drawing attention from the woman, and once again, Aquifer spoke, translating her words. [My colleague and I are amateur filmmakers, and we came here wanting to learn more about The Vortex. But along the way, we learned about some strange activity out in the woods near here, and we decided that it would make a *much* better story. You've probably seen some of it yourself; would you mind if we asked you a few questions before we bring in our film equipment?]

The woman crossed her arms. "Military activity? I haven't seen anything like that out here. It's just me and the tourists."

Aquifer stared at her. "We didn't say what kind of activity it was, though."

"Doesn't matter, I didn't see or hear anything."

Shadow narrowed her eyes and walked up until she was leaning against the counter. The attendant wiped sweat from her brow, avoiding eye contact with her. In a flash, Shadow grabbed the front of the attendant's shirt and pulled her against the counter, using her free hand to retrieve a pistol from a shoulder holster beneath her leather jacket. The barrel of the gun was now inches away from the screaming woman's forehead.

"Fucking hell, Shadow," Aquifer said. He turned to the attendant. "Excuse my colleague, but we are so low on time. An extended charade would only put millions of lives at risk. So, we'll be straightforward. We aren't filmmakers; we are a group of people trying to prevent those military guys out in the woods from doing a very, very bad thing."

"What are you, radical environmentalists?" the attendant asked.

"No. But we *are* the impatient kind of people. I've been honest with you, and we know you aren't being honest with me. What do you know about the people in the woods?"

Shadow released the woman's shirt and stepped back, though she kept the gun trained on her.

"I'm not supposed to say," the attendant mumbled. "I promised I wouldn't."

Shadow flicked the safety of her pistol and fired a shot above the woman's head, planting a fat hole in the wall behind her. The attendant screamed and grabbed her ears.

"We really, *really* cannot waste time right now," Aquifer insisted. "If you're in danger, we can help you, but right now it is imperative that we know what is out there." He looked outside the window at the setting sun. They were running out of daylight.

The attendant sighed. "It wasn't long before the attraction of The Vortex became too niche and out-of-the-way to succeed, as far as money goes. Even the business I got after that TV show was filmed here only helped a little. Our finances were in the red. So, when Uncle Sam came in and offered me a steady check to let them perform military exercises out in the woods near here, I jumped at the chance."

Shadow and Aquifer looked at each other.

"Then there *is* a place out in the woods?" Aquifer asked.

"I haven't ever been out there before or anything, but later at night you can hear 'em talking and shooting and stuff. Every once in a while you'll hear some weird animal sounds, but those don't usually happen more than once. If I could make a guess, based on what I've heard and seen . . ."

She grabbed a paper and pen, drawing some crude images. "This square is us. The dots behind it are all the trees in the woods. You go out back, and you start walking two-o'-clock from here, what you're looking for shouldn't be more than a mile away." The attendant circled a space diagonally to the right of The Vortex attraction.

"Thank you," Aquifer said, while Shadow holstered her gun. "And I apologize for the violence."

Pennsylvania, United States
March 8, 2012-B

With so many trees and so much greenery, Battery expected to hear chirping from bird, crickets, or *any* living thing. Instead, her sole source of sound was the light crunching of their footsteps over rock and dirt. The place didn't seem *too* different, other than the occasional smoking cracks in the pavement, but the environment must have changed drastically to scare away the wildlife.

"No, we don't really get many visitors," Esther was telling them. "Just the occasional vandal, and sometimes the government or large corporations will send someone to buy us out."

"You mean the remaining people of Centralia?" Battery asked.

Bomber turned his head turned the ground and activated his Atomic Vision, the orange light furiously bright even in the daylight. Battery noticed and leaned forward to keep Esther's attention. *Damn it, Bomber, learn to be more subtle.*

"Yeah," Esther replied. "We grew up here, and we don't mind the fires or the smoke. It's easy to get used to, a hell of a lot easier than it is to move off to somewhere new, spending our last few decades dying around strangers."

"I imagine it's still tough, though, to have so many people trying to push you from your home," Bomber said. "Speaking of which, have any come by recently?"

"No. It's been a while since it's happened, thank God. We haven't seen anyone before you in . . . at least six months."

Bomber turned to Battery. "Is this a dead end?"

"We'll rule that out once we find the facility," she responded.

He activated his Vision again and looked down, his face contorting into one of surprise.

"Tunnel," he said. His Vision faded, and he pointed ahead. "That way."

"What's in that direction?" Battery asked Esther.

"Oh, nothing much, just the church and cemetery."

"Is it still used?"

"Not anymore; not really. It's fallen into disrepair, I'm sorry to say."

Battery looked to Bomber. "I believe our 'pedophile' may have plenty of places to hide, then."

He nodded, and they pressed on.

After a few minutes, the trees parted, and they stood on a broken road, staring up at the concrete staircase leading to the entrance of a white chapel. The building had three towers, each topped with a gold symbol consisting of a vertical rod supporting three uneven, horizontal ones. The trees around here were leafless and dead, starved by the heat and the smoke that was present as they climbed the stairs.

As they reached the entrance to the church, a beat-up truck drove down the road and stopped behind them. Two older men carrying hunting rifles hopped out and approached.

"Who the hell are you?" one yelled.

"It's fine, they're here trying to catch a pedophile who's hiding in town," Esther called back.

The man spat. "Bullshit. There isn't anyone new here, not without us knowing. No one but them."

He aimed his rifle at Battery and Bomber, and his cohort followed suit.

"Don't be an asshole, Hank," Esther chastised, raising her shotgun at the two men. "And what would your wife say, John?"

Battery tapped Bomber on the shoulder and nudged her head toward the door. While the locals bickered, they inched over to it and slipped inside the church.

The interior was an open space, complete with dusty pews, a dirty chandelier, and a dulled back wall covered in portraits of saints. Bomber used his Atomic Vision to scan the building.

"Metal ley lines underground," he said. "Some kind of tunnel. They lead"—he pointed toward a large, white pulpit near the end of the church—"there."

They hurried around to face it from the other side, positioned like priests delivering a sermon to ghosts. Bomber gestured at the lines of copper atoms he said he could see running throughout the pulpit, leading to a spot hidden beneath the white cloth. He fiddled with the area until his fingers found a raised section. Looking at Battery, he pressed it.

A hydraulic hiss washed over them, and dust flew into the air in plumes. Their feet shook, and a rectangular chunk of the floor behind the pulpit sank, moving down and forward like a platform on an escalator. Bomber straightened his jacket, while Battery turned the dial of her Charge Belt to a medium setting. The turbine blades whirred to life as they descended into the earth.

Oregon, United States
March 8, 2012-B

Dusk was upon Aquifer and his huntress companion as they prowled the woods. Some areas had higher growth than others, and he squinted to spot irregularities. He was on edge, and Shadow seemed to be as well. As he primed his implants for an attack, Shadow fiddled with something inside her messenger bag. They passed a thick growth of trees on the right, but something about it caused Aquifer to double take.

"Shadow, wait," he said, and she stopped, looking at him.

Aquifer approached the growth, rubbing his eyes as he attempted to spot the irregularity. Drawing closer, a ringing filled his ears, the high-pitched whine similar to the noise from an older television set. He put a finger in his ear, trying to dull the noise, but the sound persisted at the same volume.

Once he was face-to-face with the plants, he realized the issue. The leaves were upside-down, growing as if the trunk of the tree was planted in the sky, each one split into a duplicate, translucent doppelgänger. As he studied them, the upside-down leaves floated like phantoms in the air, rustling the entire time.

"Are you seeing this?" he asked, looking over his shoulder.

Shadow nodded her head, her eyes studious, and she moved closer to him. Together, they reached out to the phantom leaves, but the moment they touched the space the leaves occupied, the entire image disappeared, an out-of-place mirage. As it vanished, so did the ringing in their ears.

Before them was an opening through the dense growth, hacked into existence by some kind of blade. Torn greenery and branches littered the grassy floor around them. The carved-out opening was dense enough to block out the setting sun, barely revealing a clearing littered with fallen wood and . . . apparent black marks in the dirt and on the foliage.

The two passed into the clearing, Aquifer identifying the marks as the telltale signs of scorching. Peering around the clearing, he saw other signs of a struggle. Large-caliber bullet holes pocked the nearby tree trunks, timber and chunks of earth lay askew, and a single tire track—perhaps from a motorcycle of some kind—led Shadow and Aquifer forward, toward a large hole in the ground.

At the sight of the wreckage, Shadow drew her pistol, scanning the clearing and the approaching hole, but there was no indication to Aquifer of immediate danger. Still, he primed his PAUS, readying himself for a surprise attack. The two wary Faction fighters reached the lip of the hole.

It had a rectangular shape, and it once had a grassy lid covering the surface to camouflage it from intruders. Someone had burned or blown away the lid, revealing a flight of metal stairs. They descended, their movements slow and cautious. Shadow was ahead of Aquifer, her gun still raised, but as they reached the bottom, the high-pitched ringing returned.

The two gazed into a room designed much like the one Shadow and Battery had encountered in New Zealand. It was an open area, though the rows of desks in this one aligned along the walls so larger, more sophisticated monitors and computers could be mounted there. When he first entered, ears still ringing, he saw people in various types of clothes working away at most of the computers, while clusters of armed guards waited at each corner of the room. Crossing the threshold, every single worker and guard turned to stare at them with emotionless expressions.

Then, just like that, they were gone, shifting upside-down and floating as ghosts into the ceiling.

In the place of the workers were piles of bloodied, bullet-ridden bodies. Red covered the floor and the walls, and most of the computers and monitors were obliterated. Bullet casings, hundreds and hundreds of them, lay on the floor, the tables, the bodies; whoever did this came with more than enough firepower. The ceiling overhead was covered in thick, white foam that blackened in some areas. Aquifer presumed it was fire-suppressant.

He looked at Shadow. "Do you know who did this?"

She shook her head. [Maybe it's the third party Butterfly warned us about.]

In the distance, far past the bunker and the trees, police sirens blared. For the moment, though, Aquifer ignored them, drawn toward a lone, active monitor. On the screen was an open file: TARGETING FACILITIES. Within the file was a long list of metadata about the facilities, including locations, purposes, and whether they were active or inactive.

Shadow plugged a flash drive into the computer and activated Proxy's program while Aquifer looked more closely at the information. He scrolled back through the file path, hunted for immediate information, and found what he had hoped to find: DISASTER RELIEF TARGETS. Fiji was the only current target. He opened it to view the projected path, watching the three-dimensional map ricochet a red line from an origin point against several targeting facilities, ending beneath the archipelago.

Zooming into the origin point, Aquifer pulled the coordinates, layering them across a topographical map. The image and identifying data clarified, and he was left staring at their goal.

"Mount Hayachine," he said. "The machine is inside Mount Hayachine, in rural Japan."

Shadow looked at him, then held her hand up, palm facing him. Her face remained stoic, but her hand did not fall or waver. After a moment, he tentatively reached out and high-fived her. One corner of her lip twitched into the tiniest of smiles.

"Who's out there?" a voice called from the woods outside the underground facility. "Show yourselves!"

"Finish the file transfer," Aquifer whispered to Shadow. "I'll see what's going on."

He walked up the stairs, positioning his hands so he could summon an offense or defense without hesitation. When his head cleared ground level, he saw darkness filling the woods; it was almost night. On the other side of the clearing, two uniformed police officers pointed guns and flashlights at him. The attendant must have called after Shadow and Aquifer left.

"Hello, officers," he said, finishing his climb back onto the grass. "How can I help you?"

"You can start by telling us what your business is out here at this time of night," one of the men replied, moving into the center of the clearing with his colleague.

"Oh, I'm just exploring the area," Aquifer replied, flashing a smile. "I'm a tourist, see, and I always like to—"

"Cut the crap, boy," the first officer interrupted. "We know you and that other one shot up The Vortex store. Where is she?"

"Whoa, what the hell is this?" The second officer said, peering down into the dark hole behind Aquifer.

"Officers, if I could just take a moment . . ."

The scientist trailed off at the sound of loud, flapping wings, bringing forth immediate memories of what he had heard last year in Bomber's apartment. The trees above rocked from steady gusts of wind, and dirt flew into his eyes. He looked upward to identify a source.

Branches stopped rustling and started crackling, broken by a falling, heavy object. A figure burst through the tree line between the two officers and collided with the earth, creating a crater that showered the area with dirt and pebbles. The flapping wings and gusts of wind were now fading into the distance above them. In front of them, though, the figure stood. As it did, Aquifer saw something in its hand that was distinguishable even in the darkness.

"Ah, fuck," The scientist said, chilled vapor escaping his mouth in a puff.

"Where did you come from?" The first officer exclaimed, raising his flashlight and pistol at the Fireman.

Ignoring him, the newcomer strode toward Aquifer with a purpose, his ragged breathing behind the mask now audible. The first office grabbed his arm to stop him.

"Don't make me repeat myself—"

The Fireman's hand burst into crimson flame and thumped the policeman's chest with a lazy, casual motion. There was a sharp whisper as the flame extinguished, like the popping of a soap bubble, and the officer's body blurred with kinetic energy. He shot backward into the nearest tree with a speed and force Aquifer couldn't track, exploding into blood and limbs with wet, ripping noises. Arms and legs flew into the woods, but his torso and head were merely red mush.

"OH MY GOD! OH MY GOD!" cried the second officer as the Fireman turned to address him.

Aquifer lifted his arms to stop his nemesis, but his target was prepared. In the Fireman's other gloved hand was a melon-sized rock he must have picked up when he landed. At the sight of Aquifer's gestures, that hand turned crimson, and the rock launched sideways toward the scientist with another sharp whisper.

It blurred into a menacing projectile and exploded into shards as it collided with Aquifer's chest; the blow would surely have been lethal had he not been wearing a refined, slimmed-down PAUS breastplate beneath his shirt. Instead, the breastplate bent into a concave shape against Aquifer's sternum, pressing against his ribs and his lungs. The force of the contact with the rock lifted him into the air and flung him across the clearing, entangling him with the vegetation.

Consumed by shock and struggling for oxygen, Aquifer lost consciousness.

Pennsylvania, United States
March 8, 2012-B

The conveyor from the pulpit reached an end after a few minutes, much to Bomber's relief. A cobblestone tunnel emitting a heatless glow curved before them. The only noises he heard were the whining of Battery's belt and their labored, adrenaline-fueled breathing. Nevertheless, he pressed on with Battery, seeking their quarry.

Just a few meters ahead, the tunnel stopped, its path blocked by a thick, steel door. Battery reached out and tried to yank it open, but it wouldn't budge. She looked to him. "How thick is this?"

He scanned the door, measuring its contents. "Almost a meter and a half."

Battery gave him a sideways glance.

He smiled. "Like, four or five feet."

She nodded, stepped back, and gestured to him. "You wanted to try it. No time like the present."

He took a deep breath and approached the door, eyes still aglow. When he reached it, he crouched so he was facing the bottom right corner of the thick steel. Pressing his index and middle fingers against the corner where metal met stone, he focused on the atoms composing the door—on the energy filling the empty space between them.

While he created explosive energy by forcing those bonds to break, he now employed patience, teasing apart chained particles, reaching from one side of the door to the other. Moving his fingers upward and to the left, a soft orange line separated the metal, and he continued to employ the bond-breaking process, working to create an arc in the metal large enough for two adults to pass through.

Battery stood to the side to watch Bomber operate, arms crossed. "What is it like? Does this feel different than the Dash, or the Gun?"

His laughter was brusque, and his hand shook a little. Sweat dripped down his brow. "Yeah. Did you ever play with one of those puzzles, maybe at the doctor's office, with a glass maze with a metal ball inside? You know, the one where you have to use a magnet to guide the ball up and down the curves of the maze without moving too fast or pulling away?"

"Oh, I definitely remember those. I could never beat them. I'd always drop the ball and get impatient."

"Well this is like that game, but much more difficult and with the potential of blowing us up. So . . . no pressure, right?"

Battery laughed. "Right. No pressure."

Despite his jab at the process, their conversation had eased his tension as he moved along the door. He finished, ending the arc at the bottom-left corner of the metal structure.

Battery walked past him, clapping him on the shoulder with a gloved hand. "Congratulations. Your Atomic Scissors work well."

With that, she jabbed an electricity-covered heel into the center of the barrier, pushing it out of the severed lines in one clean motion. It skidded into the new room and creaked onto its back, landing with a weighted *thud* that shook the rock beneath them. Black smoke rushed from the uncovered space, and the two explorers devolved into a coughing fit.

"Rule two: Always be prepared," Battery choked out.

She retrieved a pair of bandanas: One orange, one blue. She handed the orange one to Bomber, and they both tied their respective cloths around their mouth and nose to filter out some of the smoke. Furthering her protection, she snapped her goggles over her eyes. Bomber's own eyes stayed glowing, allowing him visibility into the room through a different spectrum, but he cupped his hands around them to avoid the smoke. Together, they ventured ahead.

Crossing the threshold, they wandered into a curving hallway filled with smoke, heat, and an orange light burning along the right wall. They moved closer to see through the smog—it wasn't a wall at all, rather, a row of reinforced windows. The panes overlooked a wide room two stories below whose dimensions resembled a football stadium. Flames and smoke licked the floor of the room, almost obscuring what it contained.

Almost.

"Are those . . ." Battery asked.

"Yup." Bomber stood still, analyzing the makeup of the figures below.

The floor beyond the transparent wall housed at least a hundred metal golems, standing twice as tall as an average human. Their bodies were stocky and smooth, without many visible characteristics adorning the tarnished silver frames. The golems' heads were nothing more than silver domes with rectangular slits for two eyes and one mouth. Smoke poured from both around and within them.

Bomber tore themselves away from the scene, continuing forward with Battery along the overlook until they reached a circular platform. The platform contained a foreign-looking computer station; the panels and keys looped and curled around each other in a strange, alien way. Still, most of the characters resembled an English keyboard, so Battery began to type, searching for the information they needed.

The monitor lit up to the screen that was last viewed, a window containing project notes dated February 2nd, 1958.

"This place is . . . it hasn't been a targeting facility for long time, if it ever *was* one." Battery scrolled through the information, trying to understand what she was seeing. "What I'm reading here discusses harnessing the power of coal, altering its properties to power new technologies."

"To power those things, then?" Bomber asked, looking beyond the window of the platform.

"I don't know. These must have been their last project, but . . . I guess the experiments with the coal vein in Centralia went too far, and this lab had to be shut down."

"Will we find what we need here?"

"I don't know. I'll keep look—"

"Don't worry about it," Proxy radioed in. "Shadow just made contact. They found the machine's location, as well as some other data we'll discuss later. I believe they're tied up in Oregon, though. Could you go help?"

"Sure. Let's go," Battery said to Bomber.

He turned to leave, but a blinking red light on the computer station caught his eyes. He frowned, looking around for any other lights or signs of security, but nothing else moved. Shrugging, he followed Battery.

The two hurried along the smog-filled hallway, rushing to reach the ramp back to the surface. Bomber thought he saw movement in the smoke below, but he was too focused on their exodus to investigate further.

They reached the platform cut from the floor of the church and activated it, retreating up to the pulpit far above their heads. Metal creaked and scraped from the direction they had left, but the sound of the escalator quickly drowned it out.

When Battery and Bomber returned to the surface, their faces still covered in goggles and bandanas, the three citizens of Centralia they met earlier were waiting for them. Hank and John had rifles raised, while Esther stood between them, her face marred by shock and betrayal.

"You weren't looking for anyone, were you?" she demanded. "You're just stealing our coal to give to the government!"

"See, I told you, Esther," Hank said, shaking his head. "No good."

Battery and Bomber pulled away their rags.

"People, this isn't what you think," Battery said in a calm, authoritative tone, raising her goggles from her eyes. "We aren't here to steal anything. We came here retrieve something that will save people's lives."

"Bullshit!" Esther spat. "I trusted you once. Not again."

Battery's voice became sharper, sterner, as Bomber grasped at the atoms around him, preparing to perform an Atomic Dash.

"I'm telling you the truth," she said. "Our mission is time-sensitive, though. Let us leave in peace or we will resort to violence."

John laughed. "You two aren't the ones with guns, you know. What do you . . ."

His voice trailed off, the earth rumbling beneath their feet. The pews and pulpit rattled, and the five occupants staggered to keep their balance. Cracks formed along the floor, revealing flickering flames and smoke. Bomber looked at Battery's worried face, wary of what might happen next.

As if to acknowledge his concern, a large metal hand broke through the floor, grasping at John's leg. He screamed and struggled, but the hand pulled, folding and breaking him until he was small enough to fit through the offending hole. His mutilated corpse vanished into black smoke.

Behind Battery and Bomber, the torso of one of the Coal Golems emerged, its rectangular eyes and mouth spewing smoke. It swiped at Bomber as it pulled itself from the hole, but he Dashed a short distance from its reach in an orange blur. Loud and methodical, the Golem creaked toward Battery instead, who increased the voltage of her Charge Belt.

The Golem raised its arms to crush her, but gunfire interrupted its attack. Bullets sparked and ricocheted away from its tarnished silver skin, leaving no damage, but the Golem ambled toward its attackers nonetheless. Battery grabbed a metal leg and pulled, sending it crashing to the church floor. Bomber struggled to his feet as he watched it all unfold, trying to maintain his balance atop the quaking earth.

"Get out of here!" Battery yelled at a horrified Esther and Hank.

Before they were able to move, more Coal Golems burst from the ground, both from within the church and beyond, if the crashing sounds outside were any indication. An army of automatons was amassing in the span of seconds, and the present Faction team was woefully under-prepared to deal with them.

Still, they forged on.

"Bomber! Get them to safety!" Battery barked.

His cigarette-ember-eyes lit into twin trails of orange light as he Dashed again, the world around him becoming a blur, swooping the locals up in the process. He was just in time, too, as the metal fists of a nearby Coal Golem smashed into the empty space where their heads have been. With Esther and Hank whisked away at super-speed, those metal hands did no more than crush a crater into the floor of the church.

"Proxy! I think *we* need backup, actually," Bomber heard Battery say into her radio.

"Well I'll let them know, but it may take a moment," Proxy replied in Bomber's earpiece.

"It's just a robot army; no rush," she snapped, flinging her body into the closest Golem.

The metal man was launched backward by her attack, smashing into the back wall of the church, rattling the portraits. Despite the dent in its torso, the Golem seemed unfazed, and it was on its feet in no time, swinging back at her. She dodged the punch, grabbed the offending arm, and yanked the entire appendage from its body. Smoke poured from the hole in its shoulder, but it continued its assault.

Bomber turned away from Battery and hurried the civilians

toward the entrance of the church, but as he opened the doors, he saw the hell wrought upon Centralia. Coal Golems burst from the concrete and earth, bringing pits of smoke and fire with them. In movements both slow and methodical, the automatons faced Bomber and the church. Hank scowled at Bomber.

"I knew we shouldn't let outsiders—"

He was interrupted as a Golem's hand reached out from behind them and palmed his head. His surprised screams were silenced in an instant by the closure of the metal fingers, crushing his face and skull into a red jelly, hot blood squishing between each digit. Some of the blood splattered Esther, who shrieked, dropped her shotgun, and ran outside.

"Wait!" Bomber cried after her. "Goddammit."

It was too late to chase her, though. The Golems swarmed the church, and Bomber needed to join Battery in the fight.

Oregon, United States
March 8, 2012-B

I'm getting too old for this.

Shadow sprinted up the stairs of the targeting facility as Aquifer was knocked across the clearing, her messenger bag bouncing against her hip, her Beretta M9 pistol in her hand. Beneath the moon and stars, the Fireman stood over a cowering police officer, crimson flames licking his raised axe. Without missing a beat, she raised her pistol, unleashing its contents.

Mimicking her strategy in California, the bullets clustered around the attacker's mask area; as each reached their target and were robbed of their momentum, they hovered for a second, obscuring his vision. She maintained this tactic until she was within reach of him. The police officer had rolled away and sprinted out of the clearing, allowing her the freedom to attack by any means available.

Shadow's time hunting monsters both before and after The Faction was beginning to take its toll her. When she left her father and began her journey, she had been a young, spritely teenager. Now she was thirty-four, having spent the last two decades constantly fighting—without the benefits of Treehouse which Proxy and Maddie gleaned. Her joints ached, her hearing dulled, and even with her Gaze, her reaction time were slowing.

Still, she had one thing on her side: Experience. *Every enemy is predictable if you spend enough time fighting them.*

The Beretta empty, she hurled the gun at the Fireman's face, buying herself another second or two. Reaching into her messenger bag, she retrieved an explosive hatchet, much like the ones used to breach the targeting facility in New Zealand. Rather than striking the Fireman with it, she planted it in the grass between his legs while he was still blinded. Sprinting behind him, she triggered the detonation cord wrapped around the hatchet.

A fiery shock wave erupted from the earth beneath her opponent, but he seemed unimpressed. His body swallowed the force of the blast as if it were a gentle breeze, the frost around him extinguishing the fire in seconds. Still, Shadow reached into messenger bag and squeezed something mechanical, and the front end of the bag was torn apart by machine-gun fire. A barrel poked through the ragged hole in the fabric, sending dozens of armor-piercing bullets to collide against the back of the Fireman's head and shoulders.

"Oregon team," Proxy said in her ear. "There's something major going on in Pennsylvania. Let me know when you're able to help."

Shadow glanced toward Aquifer, who seemed to be struggling to remove his dented PAUS breastplate. She looked back at the Fireman, who turned to face Shadow's barrage, unaffected by the higher-caliber bullets.

Sorry, Proxy, we'll reply when we can.

The Fireman took a step, then another, building to a run with his axe raised. In response, Shadow pulled her weapon from the messenger bag and took careful aim.

In her hands was the AKS-74U, a fusion of both rifle and submachine gun. It resembled a shrunken-down version of its more famous counterpart, the AK-47. Beneath the barrel of her brown-and-black weapon was a tubular attachment which possessed its own grip and trigger. Maintaining steady hands on the chattering machine gun, Shadow wrapped her other hand around this second grip.

With the Fireman charging at her, she had a clear shot at his face, so she allowed the bullets to gather there. When he was about to swing, she side-stepped and twirled behind him, emulating a matador. While he recovered from the miss, Shadow aimed near his feet and pulled the trigger of the AKS-74U's tubular attachment.

A canister launched from the tube with a *thunk*, striking the grass a few steps away from the Fireman and bouncing up into the air. It was almost within the Fireman's reach, gliding up to chest-height, when it detonated. The white phosphorous within the canister ignited as soon as it contacted the open air, producing a dizzying amount of smoke and flames. The phosphorous splashed across the Fireman's outfit, setting it ablaze.

In this brief moment of respite, Shadow reloaded both the gun's magazine and its grenade launcher. Not waiting to see what might happen next, she unleashed a new storm of bullets into the smoke and flames encompassing the Fireman. They vanished within the vapors.

The flames around the Fireman dying down, he localized his ability to extinguish the white phosphorous, though his yellow-orange suit had darkened to soot-black. The lenses of his goggle glimmered through the smoke, and Shadow met them with a second white phosphorous grenade. The Fireman was ablaze once more.

Shadow loaded a third and final grenade into her launcher, noting her other resources. Inside the messenger bag were a few more magazines of AKS-74U ammunition and three more explosive hatchets. Sighing, she retrieved a hatchet and waited, cradling the machine gun against her hip with her other hand.

The Fireman was apparently losing his patience with the white phosphorous. The flames vanished, and a crimson explosion leveled a tree near him, rocketing his axe-wielding form toward Shadow. She had just enough time to roll away before he landed, planting his weapon in the earth with a sharp whisper. The ground split and tore, and a shock wave rippled from the point on contact, sending Shadow sprawling into the center of the clearing.

She recovered right away, hurling her hatchet at him. The man caught it with his free hand, and she pressed the button on her remote, but it was too late. Frost wrapped around the explosive, and the Fireman's power sucked out its ability to ignite. He flipped it so the blade was facing Shadow, encircled his hand with crimson flame, and sent it back to its owner.

Shadow's pupils twitched, and time slowed.

Her Gaze was the only thing keeping her alive. Even with it, she just barely registered the returning hatchet's velocity and angle. It cut the air, ripping through the sound barrier, and she swiveled to the side to avoid it. Her Gaze allowed her to watch the hatchet pass her face, her reflection visible in the metal as the blade almost removed her nose. To her relief, it passed by without causing her harm, instead plowing through a nearby tree trunk hard enough to punch a hole from one end to the other before continuing into the woods beyond.

The Fireman charged toward her even as she recovered from the near-miss, and she pushed herself to act. This time, she lifted her gun and fired her final grenade at a nearby tree trunk, then rolled to dodge the Fireman's strike. As they both moved, the grenade ricocheted from the trunk, bounced against a neighboring tree branch, and landed in the same space as the Fireman's feet. White phosphorous covered him once more. Shadow dropped her gun and retrieved her last two hatchets, holding one with each hand.

I'm running out of options.

A blackened, frosty figure strode from the smoke and flames, wiping at the lenses of its gas mask. Shadow tensed, ready to make a final dash with her hatchets.

Then, someone whistled.

Both fighters stopped, turning to survey the clearing. Aquifer limped toward them, shirtless, clutching at a gash in his chest surrounded by an enormous purple bruise. Circular PAUS implant discs were spaced along his torso, embedded into his skin. He stepped into the center of the clearing, not far from the other two people.

"That was a cheap shot," he wheezed at the Fireman. "But then again, so is this."

Without further explanation, he twirled both arms out in a concentric, circular motion, then punched his right fist into the sky at a diagonal angle.

A sphere of water encased the Fireman and blasted him into the air like a rocket, following the angle of Aquifer's arm. Their assailant became a speck against the horizon before he curved back downward, passed the foliage, and landed at least two miles away, far enough that Shadow could not hear the collision.

She shot a stern look at Aquifer. [Maybe lead with that next time?]

"Eh, you had it under control."

[Are you okay?]

"It's nothing major. I'll heal. Hurts like hell, though. How about you?"

[He never even touched me.]

"Show-off. Let's go help the others."

"It's a war zone over there," Proxy's voice sounded in Shadow's ears. "I suggest you come prepare yourselves at Treehouse first."

Pennsylvania, United States
March 8, 2012-B

Orange afterimages filled the church as Bomber Atomic-Dashed from Golem to Golem, avoiding their strikes. He raised both hands, formed his finger guns, and fired beams of energy into the two closest automatons. Their metal exteriors glowed red for a moment, but they faded back to silver, seemingly unaffected.

"My Atomic Gun won't work," he announced. *Maybe their time in the mines conditioned them to resist extreme temperatures?*

Battery only grunted as she dismembered a Coal Golem into just a smoking torso and head, wriggling and helpless on the ground.

"Battery?" Bomber asked, concerned.

She roared, the voice terrifying in its electronic distortion, diving into a new cluster of Golems.

What's wrong with her?

Bomber held his breath and Dashed straight onto one of the Golems trying to attack Battery, planting himself on its wide shoulders. Leaning down, he slapped his palm on its dome head and ripped apart the bonds along the metal. With a popping sound, the head turned orange and exploded into silver shards. Still, the Golem persisted, swiping at Bomber to knock him away. He Dashed to a safe distance and reconsidered.

Okay, so I can still destroy the bonds in the metal itself from close range. But their computer isn't in their head. There has to be a central computer somewhere. Or, at least, a power source.

The orange starfield appeared before him, highlighting his mechanical prey. He examined the Coal Golem, though it took little time to find what he was seeking. Returning his vision to normal, he Dashed up to the automaton and placed his hand on the center of its chest. More atomic bonds broke, and a new explosion ensued, blowing open a hole where Bomber had touched it.

Smoke and flames poured from the opening, and the Golem staggered back, its movements sluggish now. Within seconds, the heat and haze dissipated, and its form dropped into a slumped, standing position, as motionless as a statue.

"Battery!" Bomber yelled, Dashing at another Golem. "They're powered by hot, compressed air. There's a coal engine in the chest; if you can breach the engine walls, you'll vent the heat, and they won't have the energy to move anymore. Think of it as poking a hole in a hot air balloon."

He heard no response over the creaking Golems.

"Battery?"

She suddenly appeared and cried out, plunging a fist into the chest of the nearest Golem. Smoke and flame rushed out, slowing the death-machine first to a crawl, then to a stop.

Bomber Dashed next to her, using Atomic Punches to keep the Golems at bay. "Battery, what's going on?"

She turned to him, blue electricity running beneath her skin, her eyes hidden by her goggles. Reaching out and ripping them from her face, he revealed wild, animalistic eyes. She responded to his sudden motion by shoving him to the floor, lifting a Golem behind him into the air, and ripping the automaton in half.

"GIVE ME THE GOGGLES."

Hands shaking, Bomber tossed them to her, opting to turn his attention back to the assault.

Tarnished silver bodies piled up on the floor of the church, restricting Battery and Bomber's movements as they attacked the Golems, but more and more automatons poured inside to surround them. One punched at Battery, who grasped and twisted the offending arm until it pulled her close enough to rip open its chest with her hands, disabling it. Another grabbed her from behind and squeezed, but she swung her legs back and kicked it repeatedly until she exposed its weak point, forcing it to release her.

Bomber Dashed around the church, leaving behind twin trails of light which formed mesmerizing geometric shapes. He stopped to assault a Golem, feeling his eyes burning as two fiery dots. Dashing upward, he kicked it in the chest, using the connection to his foot to detonate the metal. The explosion sent him further into the air, turning him upside-down, Sam's bomber jacket fluttering behind him.

Body and eyes glowed orange, and he Atomic-Dashed in midair, colliding both knees into another Golem to destroy its power source.

He had no more than returned to the earth when two Coal Golems struck out in an attempt to flatten him with metal stomps. An orange aura surrounded his body, and he Dashed backward, then to the right, then forward, using his propulsion to scale one of the Golems and disable it with an explosive strike. Rolling away from its falling form, he reached out and traced a glowing orange line across the chest of the second attacker with his index and middle fingers. The moment his skin left the metal, the line detonated, venting smoke. Bomber backed away from his victories, panting.

Then, he looked down at his body, from which smoke also rose.

"Oh, right," he muttered.

While training, he had discovered his Refinement wasn't like Battery's; while she embraced her driving force, consuming electricity into her herself, he could only affect the environment *around* him. He could touch and tear and rearrange properties, releasing and directing energies, but he was not immune to the effects he produced. Too many unnatural interactions with the atoms around him in a short span of time could cause his body to overheat, or worse. He was still learning to pace himself.

Bomber looked back at Battery, who fought her way out of the crowd of Coal Golems, tearing them apart in the process.

I don't think I'm the only one with Refinement side effects.

A new cluster of metal attackers piled on top of her, burying her beneath smoke and metal. Bomber rushed to assist, but another Golem swiped at him with his arm, sending a sharp pain through his shoulder as he tumbled across the room. Heavy footsteps surrounded him, and he prepared another Atomic Dash.

Before he could move, the Coal Golems circling him were smothered by standing columns of water. The liquid bubbled and boiled, rushing between their joints and stealing their heat. The automatons fought to escape the columns, but the rippling pressure within held them there against their will. Soon, the bubbling slowed, and the Golems stopped moving. Bomber heard fingers snap, and the water columns evaporated away, toppling the inactive machines. Behind them stood Aquifer.

The scientist had foregone his usual outer layer of clothing, opting to cover himself with sectioned pearl-white armor from neck-to-toe. The shaping and color of the armor reminded Bomber of a solder from an Eighties space fantasy, sans helmet, and he chuckled a little.

"Did you forget to do your laundry? I thought you wanted to wait until Comic-Con for your cosplay."

"Would you rather I take my sweet time getting dressed while you get the worst shiatsu massage of your life?" Aquifer retorted.

"Honestly, seeing you now . . . fifty-fifty."

The Golems surrounded them, and they stood back-to-back, fending them off.

"Where's Battery?" Aquifer asked.

"Over there, under the pile. Where's Shadow?"

"Outside, waiting for us. Let's not keep her much longer, maana?"

The armored man grabbed Bomber around the waist and launched them both across the room in a spray of water. They landed atop the pile of Golems, and Aquifer's PAUS breastplate began to generate clicking noises.

"Oh, this won't do," Aquifer said, clucking his tongue. "This won't do at all. Bomber, stay very still."

Bomber froze in place, keeping an eye on the advancing army.

Aquifer made a series of swift gestures, and the room flooded with water, suspended within the confines of the church. Pockets of air remained around Bomber and Aquifer's heads in the form of bubbles, allowing them to breathe in the space. Around and below them, the water began to heat up, draining the Golems of their essence.

Raising his arms, Aquifer used his PAUS armor to create pressurized separations of water in strategic places along the pile of Coal Golems atop Battery. He then pried them apart, sending the automatons floating away. The water's temperature was uncomfortable now, and Bomber felt sweat forming along his brow.

The moment Battery was visible, Aquifer retrieved an air pocket from beyond the church boundaries and placed it around her head. He then used a shifting pressure field to glide Bomber and himself down to her level, near the back wall of the church. When there were no more Golems between The Faction fighters and the wall, Aquifer raised both arms, twisted his wrists, then brought them down, pointing toward the front of the church.

The entire body of water launched forward, maintaining its shape as it destroyed the entire front wall and entrance. The wave swept the Coal Golems outside with it, but an ultrasound field surrounded the three humans, keeping them in place. Centralia's waterlogged church was filled with smoking craters and missing a wall, but Bomber and his comrades were safe for the moment.

They took a moment to recover before rushing beyond the church, toward the sounds of gunfire. Dead trees lined the area around them, but a pavement road ran right past the church. From both areas remained dozens of Coal Golems, emerged from flaming pits and sinkholes along the property. Some of the monstrosities caught in Aquifer's underwater prison ceased to move, but others remained operational in spite of the flood.

A loud *ping* sounded, and sparks flew from an approaching Golem. A small hole appeared, releasing a concentrated ventilation of smoke and fire. The Golem wound down as the expulsion slowed, like a teakettle removed from its stove eye. As it came a halt, Bomber turned toward the source of the shot. In the distance, far from the Golems' reach, was Shadow, bent on one knee on the pavement road and shouldering a long, black rifle with a hockey-puck muzzle. The rifle rested upon a large tripod, supporting much of its weight, while a second gun and a box of ammunition lay next to her.

Two more Golems moved to attack Battery, Aquifer and Bomber, only to receive two armor-piercing rounds. A moment later, the distant echoes of gunfire caught up with the bullets, washing past Bomber's ears. The two Golems, leaking pressurized smoke, creaked to a halt. Seeing this, some of the other Golems broke away from the pack, approaching Shadow.

"We shouldn't make her waste too many bullets," Battery said, cracking her knuckles. The metal studs on her gloves pulsated with the excess electrical energy around her body, but she seemed to have calmed a little after her dunk in Aquifer's impromptu swimming pool.

Bomber nodded and ran toward the automatons. Next to him, Battery spun low and used her legs to sweep a Golem to the ground. Bomber took the opportunity to vault over its fallen form, planting a hand on its chest to detonate the metal surface. As he landed, another Golem swung a fist at his face, but a wall of water deflected it. To his amazement, a platform of water appeared over his head, and Battery leapt onto it, using it as a launching pad it to propel her fist into the offending Golem's coal engine.

Around them, more Coal Golems dropped like flies, whittled down by Shadow's rifle. She'd downed most of the automatons who'd approached her, but more filled their place, gathering in her direction. Bomber acted, Dashing in her direction. To his left, Battery leapt with her powered legs, and to his right, Aquifer launched with his water propulsion. All three soared to Shadow, landing together between her and the Golems.

A wave of metal attackers approached, but Battery's punches, Aquifer's water prisons, and Bomber's explosions slowed them down. Bullets whizzed past Bomber's head, burrowing into the Golems' chests, releasing heat and smoke.

"Shadow says she's joining the front line," Proxy informed the others.

Shadow rushed forward, past Bomber and his two other compatriots, blasting into the Golems with some kind of shotgun. She signed to Battery, and Battery gestured upward at Aquifer. The scientist next to Bomber created a water platform above their heads, beyond the Golems' reach, and Shadow released a shotgun blast before Battery tossed her onto the platform. As she landed, she retrieved shotgun shells from a satchel hung around her, reloading the weapon.

Bomber Atomic-Dashed with renewed intensity, bouncing around the battlefield like a glowing orange pinball. Obelisks of water scattered the plain in a regular pattern. After ricocheting between five different Golems, disabling each one with a well-placed hand or foot, Bomber Dashed into one of the obelisks, allowing the water to cool his body down for a brief moment before continuing his rampage.

Beneath Bomber's onslaught, he saw Battery and Shadow wading through the Golems, tearing and blowing them apart. Aquifer stood beyond the battlefield, creating shapes of water to assist the other three fighters.

The Coal Golem army was rapidly thinning; at this point, there were fewer than twenty of the machines remaining. Realizing this, they seemed intent on taking at least one of The Faction fighters with them, so they rushed Battery, piling onto her in an attempt to smother or crush her. Bomber came to her aid, joining Shadow atop the pile, the pair dismantling the Golems in a flurry of gunshots and Atomic Punches. Pulses of water flew past Bomber, shearing layers of automatons from the heap.

With much effort, the trio thinned away the herd until they found a final layer of already-dismantled Golems with fist-sized holes scattered along their forms. Battery emerged from the wreckage, gasping for air. After helping her to her feet, Bomber searched the area, but no more Coal Golems crawled from the earth or lumbered over the horizon. There was a shared sigh of relief.

"How is everyone?" Battery asked, removing her goggles and dialing down her Charge Belt.

[I'm fine,] Shadow signed.

"Me too," Aquifer said, then winced and clutched at the armor covering his chest.

"You sure?" Battery asked, and Shadow nudged her to get her attention.

[He's not fine, but he isn't dying. I think meeting somewhere in the middle is the best we can do.]

"True, that," Bomber commented, warily regarding Battery. She seemed unaware of what had transpired between them in the church.

"Shadow, did I hear right earlier?" Battery asked. "You ran into the Fireman again?"

[Yeah. He literally dropped from the sky. We weren't in Gold Hill for more than forty minutes.]

Battery looked at everyone. "Maybe Butterfly was right. Maybe Society has a way of tracking Bogeyman."

"But we used it, too," Bomber interjected. "How did they know which location Aquifer was in?"

"Lucky guess?" Aquifer said. "Or maybe these Coal Golems were activated for me, too, and they covered their bases in both places."

Shadow attracted their attention. [The reality is that Society has eyes everywhere, so it's impossible to know for sure. Still, we should all keep our own eyes open to suspicious activity, both inside the Treehouse and out in the rest of the world. We don't want to be caught unawares by more surprise attacks, if we can help it.]

Battery burst into cynical laughter. "Good luck with that."

Treehouse
March 8, 2012-B

Ragged and tired, Bomber stepped through the Bogeyman doors with the rest of his team and was greeted with the beaming faces of Maddie and Proxy. The Dutch Shepherd ran up them, sniffed their clothes, sneezed, and wandered away.

The analyst held up the flash drive given to him by Shadow and Aquifer. "What you've collected today is a treasure trove of intelligence on Society's operations. You should all be very proud of yourselves. We have access to every targeting facility, every laboratory, every point of interest . . . this doesn't contain much detail about the exact nature of the projects in each location, but we now have their coordinates, which is a major step in the right direction. This third party who is working their way through the targeting facilities seems to have our best interest in mind."

Aquifer winced and removed his PAUS breastplate, exposing the bandaged gash in his chest. "So, when's the party?"

Shadow punched his shoulder.

"Ow!" the scientist exclaimed, rubbing his arm.

Proxy cleared his throat.

"I know you've had a long day, and I'm more or less speaking to myself right now. Get some rest, and we'll look over this data once our mission is complete. Our top priority is the Tôhoku mountain base, where the earthquake machine is located. You have six hours to sleep. Then, go get the gear you need and prepare to leave. Your journey will take half a day by foot, and we don't want to waste any time."

Bomber plopped onto the floor, shooing away Maddie's attempts to lick his warm face.

"Half a day?" he asked. "Where are we going, again?"

Proxy flashed him a smile. "Japan. You're going to Japan."

**Treehouse
March 8, 2012-B**

Fire and blood filled Catalina's vision, hazed by heat and smoke. Cries of the people, those in revolt, rang in her ears. She felt shadows encroach upon her, and her father's voice growled from the darkness. Catalina reached for a weapon, for *something* to defend herself, but she was naked. Naked and alone.

He was coming for her. *It* was coming for her.

And then she was awake, drenched in sweat, trembling. A voice whispered something in her ears. A name.

But what name?

It was only then she noticed a shadow standing above her, at the edge of her bed. In one swift motion, Catalina snatched her Ruger pistol from beneath her pillow and leapt from where she lay, her blankets trailing her like a shroud. She kicked the shadow to the ground and pressed her Ruger against its forehead as the blankets settled on top of them both, enveloping them in darkness.

"Whoa! Whoa! Wait! It's just me," the shadow said in a muffled voice. "It's Stacey."

Frowning, she removed the blankets and stood, helping him to his feet. [What the hell are you doing, standing over my bed like a psychopath?]

"I'm so sorry," Stacey said sheepishly. "I just . . . I just need your help."

[What's up?]

"It's Zen. We need to talk about her. *To* her."

Catalina sighed. [Yeah. I know. I'll take care of it.] She sat down on her bed, cross-legged, fluffing her pillow. Looking up, she noticed that Stacey was still standing there. [Good night, Fields.]

"Oh . . . right. Sweet dreams!" Stacey shuffled out of the room.

Catalina put the Ruger back under her pillow and sighed again. *If only.*

Madison, Tennessee
March 8, 2012-B

"What in the world are we doing out here?" Zen yawned, looking around the dark, empty high school football field. "We only have, like, two more hours to sleep."

Catalina ignored her, opting instead to examine the gun in her hand. It was a Taurus Judge revolver, loaded with .410 bore shot. Essentially, a miniature shotgun. It may not be the most powerful pistol in the world, but it definitely packed a punch.

"Hello? Cat?"

Catalina grinned at the nickname, the only "cute" thing she allowed Zen to say about her.

[We're here for a brief sparring match,] Catalina signed. [I need to show you something before we travel to Japan.]

She gestured at the Charge Belt she had instructed Zen to bring along. [Drop that for now.]

"Okay." Zen placed the belt in the grass at her feet and assumed a fighting stance.

Catalina did the same, placing her Judge on the ground, and their sparring match began. Zen rushed her, taking a swing at her head, and Catalina moved to the side, as lithe as a jungle cat. Wind whipped past her face, and Catalina smiled.

Well done, Zen. You know not to hold back with me.

Catalina ducked low and drove her palm into Zen's solar plexus, knocking the wind out of the detective. Zen backed up, gasping, and Catalina took a step forward to follow up with a right hook. At the last moment, Zen spun into a back kick, catching Catalina in the rib cage with the heel of her foot. Sharp pain ran through Catalina's midsection, and she stumbled back, annoyed with herself.

I'm getting too soft. At least, I am with her.

Zen planted both feet in the grass and raised her forearms to shield her face. Catalina ran at her, then feigned to the left at the last second, striking Zen in the thigh with a shin kick. Her opponent cried out, lowering her hands a little, and Catalina took advantage of the opportunity. As Zen's hands fell, Catalina clapped her palms across the detective's ears.

Disoriented and dizzy, Zen swung an uppercut toward

Catalina's jaw, but Catalina moved to the side, catching it by the wrist. In one smooth, sharp motion, she twisted the arm, breaking it.

"AHH!" Zen cried, backing away. "Damn, Cat, you really *don't* hold back."

Catalina smiled and pointed at the Charge Belt. [Go ahead.]

Zen nodded and retrieved her tool, securing it around her waist and activating it. The turbine spun to life, and blue energy ran beneath her skin toward her broken arm, audibly snapping it back into place. Zen stretched her neck and emitted a sigh of relief.

[Better?] Catalina asked.

"Yeah."

[Why don't you turn it up some more? Maybe halfway?]

"Well," Zen frowned, "I don't want to hurt you if we spar again."

[Don't worry. You won't.]

With a wary expression, Zen turned the dial on her belt, covering her body in thin blue sparks. As they rushed along her body, her eyes widened a little, her expression almost manic.

[How do you feel?] signed Catalina.

"Whole." Zen giggled. "Amazing."

[Good.]

Catalina retrieved her Judge, crossed the distance between Zen and herself, and shot her partner in the face.

The huntress knew the pellets from the shotgun shell wouldn't penetrate Zen's skin, but the force of the blast knocked the woman into a seated position on the freshly cut grass.

Catalina raised her Judge. [Fight me again.]

"What the hell, Cat?" Zen yelled, crawling to her feet. "That was a bitch move."

[Then move my way and fight, bitch.]

Zen growled and charged at her, electricity encircling her hands.

Catalina's pupils twitched, and time slowed.

Zen's Refinement made her strong, empowering her muscles beyond the limits of any normal human. With that strength came enhanced speed, making the woman a formidable opponent. As fast as she was, though, Catalina was just a *little* faster.

Zen unleashed a flurry of punches, the attack no more than a series of blue flashing lights, but Catalina was one step ahead, backing away while dodging the blows. When she saw an opening, she raised her Judge and fired a second time, causing Zen to stagger a little. Zen narrowed her eyes and dialed her belt to the highest setting, the high-pitched whine of the turbine filling the football field.

That's right. Give in to it.

The detective leapt at least a dozen feet into the air, careening toward Catalina. Catalina rolled away, and Zen crashed in the space she had been, creating a crater in the earth. As she spun toward Catalina with wild, animalistic eyes, the huntress raised a hand to caution her.

[Look at that. You almost killed me. Is that what you wanted?]

Zen opened her mouth, frozen for a moment, then looked at her hands. "Why did I do that?"

[That's the problem,] signed Catalina. [You're used to fighting targets with impunity. With that lack of responsibility, you've failed to realize a fatal flaw in your Refinement.]

Zen reached down to turn off her Charge Belt, but Catalina raised her hand again. [Leave it on.]

"What's wrong with me?" Zen asked, her voice quivering.

[It's the electricity, Zen. It's giving you strength, and power, and invulnerability. It turns you into an apex predator. And your brain seems to recognize that, stripping you of your humanity with every crank of that belt.]

Zen looked down at the belt. "What do I do?"

[You learn to control it better. Zen, you need something to guide you. Something psychological to overpower that animalistic instinct.] Catalina shook her head, averting her eyes for a moment. [Zen . . . You need to be honest with yourself. Every time you charge, your body stands still in time. It repairs itself, but it's more than that. The residual electricity regenerates your cells, refreshing your body at its base level.]

"What are you saying?"

[I'm saying that you need to look in the mirror more. You look the same today that you did when I met you eleven years ago. I'm saying you're going to outlive me. You're going to outlive Nadi and Stacey. Hell, if it weren't for Bogeyman, you'd outlive Quentin and Maddie, too. I'm saying one day, you're going to be the only original member of Treehouse left. And you need to be your best self when that day comes.]

Catalina gestured to Zen in a "come here" motion. [Punch me.]

"I . . . I can't." Tears formed in Zen's eyes. "I don't want to hurt you. And I don't want to outlive you."

A thin smile formed across Catalina's face. [You don't really have a choice. Now, hit me.]

Zen took a shaky step forward and jutted her fist toward Catalina, stopping it an inch from her face. Catalina's smile widened.

[There it is.]

Zen pulled her arm back. "I don't understand."

[It's me, Zen. When you want to hit someone, think of this moment. Think of me. See, I'll always be your shadow, even after I'm gone. I'll always be standing beside you, moving with you every step of the way. In those moments that your Refinement wants to take control, think of the way you regained your independence to protect me. Can you do that?]

"Yeah," Zen wiped the tears from her eyes. "I can do that."

Catalina walked over to her and wrapped her arms around the woman, who hugged her back. Zen was awfully strong for her size, but Catalina liked it. It was comforting.

"You know I love you, right?" Zen asked.

[Duh. It goes both ways, you big lightning rod.]

After a moment, they pulled away.

[Well, let's get back to Treehouse,] signed Shadow. [Tomorrow's Stacey's first supply run, and I can't wait to see how it goes.]

Manchester, England
March 9, 2012-B

Four flashlight beams swept across the dark, empty sports supply warehouse, illuminating clothes and equipment. Bomber stepped out of the shadows wearing a black outfit, hunting his inanimate quarry, and his three cohorts joined him. When the beam cut away the blinding darkness to reveal ice-climbing supplies, they disabled their lights, moving forward, but Bomber stood still.

"Bomber! Get over here!" Battery whispered.

This is ridiculous.

Shaking his head, he approached the shelves and picked apart the gear, looking for the proper equipment for his size. In the corner of his eye, he saw that Shadow had already found everything she needed, and she wandered nearby, examining other sections of the warehouse. The slender woman walked up to an archery kit. She smiled, adding it to her collection.

"Who's there?" cried a woman's voice from across the warehouse, and the group froze.

A new flashlight activated.

"I know someone's over here," she said, walking closer.

The woman rounded the corner, revealing herself to be a security guard for the company. When she saw Battery, Aquifer and Bomber, she froze.

"Oy! Stay where you—"

Shadow sprung at her from behind, wrapping around the guard's body and securing her in a firm choke hold. The woman sputtered and tried to pull the huntress away, but Shadow's lithe form dodged her defensive moves. After a moment, the woman lost consciousness. Shadow released her, taking the time to ensure her fall to the floor was a gentle one.

"What was that?" Bomber exclaimed.

Aquifer side-eyed him. "Did you want to take a stab at explaining yourself to her?"

"No, it's just . . . why are we doing this?"

"We don't already have this equipment, but we need it now," Battery replied with a confused tone.

"I know that," Bomber scoffed. "What I'm saying is . . . why are we robbing stores and attacking innocent people? Didn't Proxy start Treehouse with a pretty large balance in his account?"

[That money was exhausted long ago,] Shadow signed. [When we need money now, we usually just rob from large banks whose customers won't be affected. But since we just take supplies, rather than buying them, money isn't an issue very often anymore.]

"So . . . you're bank-robbers, too? I don't know. Between the violence, the theft, the disregard for others . . . Society is bad, but I don't know if we're much better."

Battery strode over to Bomber, stopping centimeters from his face, an intense, angry look in her root-beer-brown eyes. "Stacey, I want to be very clear. This is still new to you, and I get it. But we don't live in the same world you grew up in. We live in a world where people are manipulated and murdered by an intelligent design. That intelligent design *creates* the laws that we break. It *deems* us terrorists. When a crisis arises and we do our best to address it, shortcuts to our goal are sometimes necessary to save lives. I can go work at a fast-food restaurant for two months to earn the money, then find the right legal arms dealer or survival equipment supplier within the country I'm authorized to live in. By then, though, it's too late, and disaster has struck. What we do isn't perfect, and we won't help everyone, but we have to believe in the results we produce, the lives that we save or change for the better."

"I know it isn't fair," Aquifer added. "To be the 'good guy,' it seems as if you have to follow the rules, to do the 'right thing.' But the lives we live are an endless string of compromises, idealistic choices which are whittled down to their bare bones, forcing you to pick and choose what pieces of your goals you're still willing to keep and which pieces you're willing to discard."

The scientist sighed and leaned against the nearest shelf. "Do you know why I invented PAUS?"

Bomber shook his head.

"It was a humanitarian project. I wanted to bring reprieve to populated areas suffering from drought, as well as protection to areas exposed to natural disasters. Through what I *believed* to be legitimate dealings with key leaders of affected countries, I offered a tax-free way to save lives, to build better countries. But Society only saw it as a weapon."

Aquifer chuckled, but it was a low, angry sound that made Bomber's skin crawl. "They came for it, and my first response was to prove them right—to turn my mechanism of peace into an instrument of death. Despite that, I couldn't save the people I cared about. So, I escaped alone, but those contacts? Those connections? They're gone. No one will ever allow PAUS to see the light of day for its intended purpose, and I doubt anyone outside of The Faction or Society will ever know it existed."

Aquifer pulled back his sleeves, displaying his pearl-white disc implants. "Well, I kept proving Society right. I made PAUS into a better and more-refined weapon, turning it into the one thing I never wanted it to be for the sake of preventing something more terrible from happening to others. What's worse, I've made *myself* the weapon now, because without my creation, I have no hope of surviving this life I've chosen to live."

Shadow stepped forward, close enough for Bomber to see her

hands. [I grew up in a cartel, raised by a father who saw me as a tool, so much so that he killed my mother to prevent her from freeing me from a life of crime and violence. They beat me, shot me, stabbed me. One even managed to slice open my throat, stealing my voice . . .]

She pulled down her shirt's collar, revealing the knotted scar along her neck. [Then I learned about the existence of Society's monsters, about how they plagued the people who couldn't fend for themselves. So, I escaped during the chaos of the Bolivarian Revolution, beginning a new life as something more than a thief or a brute. If my skills were steeped in killing, then I chose targets worthy of my attention. Still, not one monster I managed to kill was simplistic. The spell the creatures wove with each small town they preyed upon created a sort of bond, a bond that often left the town heartbroken or in ruins by the time I left. Despite my attempts to do the right thing, I felt the presence of my father each time I pulled the trigger.]

Her voice soft, Battery said, "I'm not sure what your childhood was like, Stacey, but I didn't grow up in the right time or place to be a multiracial woman. I was bullied for my differences, and the only people who stood up for me were my parents and a young man whom I cared for very much."

Her eyes watered a little, and she wiped them with the back of her hand. "Did you know a side-effect of my abilities is a natural affinity for open electrical currents? Whatever bond I have with the energy, it seeks me out whenever it can. I'm a walking lightning rod, and that makes me very dangerous to the people I care about. As a result, the blossoming of my powers led to the loss of one of the few people in my childhood who didn't make me feel like an outcast."

She sniffled, then coughed to speak in a steadier tone. "The sentiment never changed as I grew up, went through the Academy, and became a detective. I wasn't black enough for the black community, but I was *too* black for the white community. Officers and civilians alike decided the kind of person they expected me to be at the first sight of my face. Still, I pushed through it, becoming a protector, shielding them from danger because I knew that *I* could take it when they couldn't. Friendships weren't important, relationships weren't important; it was my *job* that mattered to me. Plus, I had a damn good partner."

Battery shook her head. "Society saw to that, too. Just by doing my job, I ended up on their hit list, and they took away my precinct, my partner, and my ability to be a detective. My badge is nothing more than a paperweight, a reminder of those years I wasted enduring the ire of others just because we didn't share the same amount of melanin."

She met eyes with Bomber. "I didn't live in Canada, but I know the world as a whole wasn't as supportive of the LGBTQ community a decade or two ago, especially in regards to the stereotypes surrounding gay men."

Bomber nodded. He whispered, "I know what you mean about isolation. As an adult, I was capable of choosing the kind of people I could spend my time with. But being gay, and *knowing* it at such an early age, formed a wedge between my parents, my peers, and myself. I'm still quite young, so I know it sounds silly, but Sam was my first love, and I was so lucky to find that man. Now he's gone, thanks to Society. I feel as if I'm back in my childhood home again, coming out to my parents and watching the pain in their faces, as if *I* was somehow hurting *them*."

Aquifer rolled up his sleeves to cover his PAUS implants as he spoke. "See? Life. Isn't. Fair. *Especially* while Society is allowed to run around the world, fucking everything up. But being a cynic won't help you. Instead, learn how to adapt, survive with the ways you *can* succeed, and test the limits of what you're willing to do to accomplish your goals. Can you do that?"

Bomber paused. "I think I can try."

"Good. Because no one is holding our hands here, and one wrong step taken for the sake of pleasing everyone else could spell disaster."

At those words, the group fell into silence. Then, Aquifer added, "Well, that was cathartic. How about we take this gear back to Treehouse and go save Fiji?"

**Honshû, Japan
March 10, 2012-B**

The sun breached the horizon, welcoming the icy mountains and the rolling valleys and the budding trees to a new day. Its light floated over the farmlands of Oide, which surrounded a cluster of rural homes, the tattered Shinto Shrine, and the well-kept blue-and-white Tonohayachinefurusato Schoolhouse. Though most of the town seemed inactive, a cluster of children no more than ten years old squealed as they played outside the school.

Bomber breathed in the cold air, absorbing this little slice of the world as he stepped from his Bogeyman point in the Shinto Shrine. He straightened his backpack and adjusted his winter gear, taking a moment to heat the air around him to further protect him from the elements.

Nice and toasty, he thought, amused with himself.

Battery and Aquifer joined him on his left and right, similarly bundled and weighed down with necessary equipment. Bomber looked behind him and smirked at Shadow, who was brooding in the doorway of the shrine. Because of the conditions here, she had traded in her black outfit for a winterized white one, and she seemed incredibly uncomfortable.

Always the practical one, even when you hate it.

Aquifer peered through the balaclava wrapped around his face at the handheld GPS device in his palm. While they waited, Bomber and the others glanced in the direction of the youthful joviality coming from the schoolyard.

"Alright, we need to be heading that way . . ." Aquifer pointed in a direction over the trees. "Proxy tried to get us as close as possible to Mount Hayachine, but there were limited destinations in such a rural area. The hike ahead of us will be at least eight hours, not accounting for the climb."

"Don't forget," Battery piped up, addressing the rest of the team. "Millipede based his estimation for the attack using Universal

Time, but Japan is nine hours faster. Assuming the attack is based on local time, we've already lost another half of a day. We were given a generous seventy-two hours, and if all goes well, we'll reach the summit by hour thirty."

"That's if our activities in America didn't accelerate their timetable," Bomber added.

"Exactly. It would be foolish to believe we'll be given another forty hours to disable the machine. We need to move quickly, but carefully; such a powerful, valuable device will surely be well-guarded. I don't expect our trek through the forest to be a peaceful one."

[Only one way to find out,] Shadow signed, then turned toward Mount Hayachine and began walking. The rest of the group followed the huntress.

As they found a stable path into the thicket of barren trees, they crossed near the Tonohayachinefurusato Schoolhouse, and Bomber caught a glimpse of the laughing children. They were all quite young, close to the same age, and there were at least two dozen of them enjoying themselves on the schoolyard. It was strange to see so many, considering how small and isolated Oide seemed to be. Nonetheless, the students paid no attention to the four outsiders who disappeared into the woods.

The Treehouse team pressed forward, crunching their boots atop dying foliage. As all signs of civilization faded behind them, the leafless trees gave the area a haunted appearance. A chill wind blew, fluttering the group's various coats, cloaks and jackets.

After several minutes of silence, Bomber said, "I don't suppose anyone brought an iPod with them?"

"SHHH!" the other three members responded.

"Bomber, Society take on all forms," Aquifer whispered. "We can't afford to be distracted when we're in such a dangerous area. Especially considering that we won't be close to any Bogeyman points, so Proxy isn't going to be able to communicate with us or retrieve us while we're out here."

Bomber fell silent, opting to activate his Atomic Vision and scan the area. As he did, tiny footsteps crunched along the woods behind them, followed by a giggle. The others spun to face the noise. Battery dialed her Charge Belt, Aquifer raised a water cannonball with his PAUS, and Shadow took aim with a green, serpentine rifle cradled in her arms. When Bomber turned, he only saw carbon, oxygen, hydrogen . . . after a closer examination, he noticed some of those patterns included sulfur, calcium and nitrogen, not present in most foliage. Blinking away his Vision, he pointed at a nearby tree on their left.

While Shadow and Aquifer took aim at the tree, Battery stepped forward, her voice already warped by the electricity. "Come out. Now."

One of the schoolchildren poked his head around the trunk, giggling as if he were playing a game of hide-and-seek with them. Battery looked to Aquifer.

"Koko ni kite kudasai!" the scientist commanded.

The boy giggled again and ran up to the party, stopping a few feet from Aquifer, standing just a little taller than the scientist's waist.

"Watashitachi wa anata to issho ni i raremasu ka?" The boy asked, staring up at him.

"What does he want?" Bomber inquired.

"Watashitachi wa anata to issho ni i raremasu ka?" The boy inquired again, maintaining eye contact.

"He wants . . . he wants to 'stay with us,' " Aquifer replied. "I guess he wants to come with us?"

[Well, send him away,] Shadow signed, lowering her rifle. [He's either a trap or a liability, and neither of those are acceptable.]

"Right," Aquifer nodded, turning to the boy. "Anata wa ienikaeru hitsuyô ga arimasu."

"Watashitachi wa anata to issho ni i raremasu ka?" The boy repeated, unfazed by Aquifer's statement.

The scientist shook his head. "Îe, ienikaeru hitsuyô ga arimasu."

Behind the team, more leaves crackled, and Bomber spun to see two more schoolchildren step into view.

"How many followed us out here?" Battery exclaimed.

"Watashitachi wa anata to issho ni i raremasu ka?" The three children repeated the first boy's question, their voices harmonizing.

More footsteps, and five more children appeared from behind the trees around them, adding to the choir, chanting, breathing fervor into the words.

"Watashitachi wa anata to issho ni i raremasu ka?"

"Watashitachi wa anata to issho ni i raremasu ka?"

"Watashitachi wa anata to issho ni i raremasu ka?"

Ten more children appeared, maybe more; Bomber couldn't keep count anymore. They encircled The Faction members, laughing at them, demanding an answer to their question.

"Watashitachi wa anata to issho ni i raremasu ka?"

"Watashitachi wa anata to issho ni i raremasu ka?"

"Watashitachi wa anata to issho ni i raremasu ka?"

Step by step, the team backed into each other, aiming their weapons at the approaching children. Aquifer in particular seemed panicked by the intrusion. Once the children closed a formidable amount of distance, he cried out in desperation.

"NO, NO YOU CAN'T STAY WITH US!"

The chanting schoolchildren fell still and silent, staring at the armed adults, waiting for something. Then, the original boy sneezed, lowering his head in the process. One by one, the other children sneezed into their hands, sniffling, their heads down.

The original boy moaned, his head still lowered. It wasn't a sad or sick moan. No, this was more like the angry growl of a house cat whose territory had been encroached. He raised his head, the others around him still sneezing, and stared at Aquifer.

The boy's eyes were jet-black.

More than that, they shimmered, as if whatever substance composing the organs was gelatinous in nature. Bomber couldn't tell if or how he was still able to see, but the boy maintained a flat expression, black eyes affixed on the man.

The other children raised their heads, too, revealing black eyes of their own. Bomber noticed one who raised his head a few seconds too early, revealing that some kind of viscous fluid was rushing in from beneath the eyelids and pushing itself over their eyes. Despite their transformation, they were just as still and calm as the first boy to arrive.

Then, the original boy's nose began to run. Just a droplet trickled down from his nostril, though he did not address it; instead, he remained entranced by Aquifer's visage. The droplet, black and tarlike, reached the young boy's lip and fell to the dying grass below. It struck grass with a faint hiss, followed by a thin line of acrid smoke, and the foliage melted away.

"Watashitachi . . . wa anata . . . to issho ni . . . i raremasu ka?"

The boy asked alone, forcing the words through a mouthful of that acidic tar leaking around his eyes and nose. It bubbled in his mouth, running down his chin and escaping to the ground in fat blobs. He took a step toward Aquifer, his body language now more hunched and menacing than before. The others did the same, dribbling black, burning fluid from their mouths as they spoke.

"Watashitachi wa anata to issho ni i raremasu ka?"

Bomber saw Shadow shake her head and raised her rifle at the closest Black-Eyed Child to her, aiming between the little girl's eyes. The huntress seemed to hesitate, and he remembered her stories of Sofía from Colombia, and the farmhand from Peru. *This is different, Catalina. These aren't human. Or, they aren't anymore.*

"Ow! Fuck!"

One of the Black-Eyed Children closest to Battery had spit at her. The fluid landed on her left wrist and made short work of her coat, her body armor, and even her skin before it started regenerating.

"So, uh, don't let them spit on you," she said, trying to shake the acid off her arm.

"Watashitachi wa anata to issho ni i raremasu ka?"

The air filled with horrific, nauseating retching sounds as the children coughed and hacked. They aimed their faces at the group and vomited streams of the tar-like substance, silencing their question for now.

As soon as the tar sprayed in his direction, Bomber Atomic-Dashed high into the air, far from their acidic reach. While waiting for gravity to catch up with him, he surveyed the scene below. On one side, Aquifer created a water shield for Shadow, who was systematically burning through most of the attackers with her machine gun, leaving the small, acid-covered bodies to decay and melt into the dirt. On the other side, Battery was using trees and rocks as shields from the tar until she could get close enough to strike. Her strategy was not going as well, so he Dashed down toward her, raising both hands to fire his Atomic Guns.

Battery threw away a large stone in her arms, and Bomber was amazed by how little time it took for the Black-Eyed Children to eat away at it. The remainder crumbled apart, flaking away into ash. As she sought out new cover, working her way around the mob of Children, Bomber showered the area with a cluster of orange lasers. Smiling, she rolled behind a nearby tree and gave him a thumbs-up.

Beams of his light streaked throughout the area, piercing the

Children and searing holes into them before bursting into flames. Some of the lasers incapacitated them in one hit, while others required two or three shots to finish off the Child. As he finished his volley, Bomber glided back to earth, cigarette-ember eyes aglow, softening his landing by resisting against the atoms beneath his feet. When he touched the ground, he noticed his fingers reddened and smoking.

I need a second to cool off, he thought, looking toward Battery.

"Tag?" she asked him.

"You're it!" he responded, pointing at another five growling Children approaching them.

In one fluid spin, Battery produced a Muay Thai Kick. Her shin connected with the tree trunk she had hidden behind, passed through it, and ripped the entire tree from the ground, flipping it into the air. Before it could go far, she clutched the end closest to her and arrested its motion, pulling the entire plant behind her. As the five Children drew within range, Battery swiped her makeshift baseball bat into them, causing them to explode against the trunk in sprays of black tar. Her weapon now eroding, Battery released it, rejoining Bomber. Together, they rushed to help the others.

Not one Black-Eyed Child had managed to penetrate Aquifer's shields, nor could they overcome Shadow's oppressive gunfire. The ground around them was blackened and smoking, pulsating with acidic masses that once were the bodies of dozens of Black-Eyed Children. Aquifer looked back to and noticed Battery and Bomber close by, so he closed the semi-circle of water into a complete ringed barrier.

"Society sending creepy Japanese children seems a little on the nose, don't you think?" he yelled to them over Shadow's gunfire.

"For all we know, this insanity *caused* that media trend," Bomber replied.

Battery leaned in. "Bomber, if you don't start helping Shadow, I think she's going to save a bullet for you."

"Right. Open up!"

Aquifer created new portholes in the wall, and Bomber's eyes glowed orange. He lifted the index and middle fingers of both hands and rested his wrists near the openings. Beams of light appeared, rushing into the remaining horde of Black-Eyed Children and piercing through their bodies. The Children wailed and spewed acid as they were felled, melting into the earth. In less than a minute, he saw the last Black-Eyed Child fall.

The forest around them grew quiet as Bomber and Shadow stopped firing, their respective hands and gun barrels smoking. Aquifer snapped his fingers, and the water wall turned into mist, floating off past trees pockmarked by bullets. Shadow turned to the rest of the group as she slung her rifle over her shoulder.

[You aren't tired already, are you? We still have a long way to go.]

Once again, she turned and continued down their path, opting not to wait for a response from the team. Battery dialed down her belt, keeping some energy trickling just in case; Aquifer queued up PAUS commands for a quick defensive response; Bomber allowed his Vision to fade, shaking and blowing on his hands to cool them down. Now content, he joined their impatient compatriot, the other two Faction fighters close behind.

The next two hours were uneventful. Few forest animals called out, though Bomber knew life should have filled the area. On occasion, the trees would rustle around them, though a quick survey with his Vision would rule out foul play. He became more anxious with each passing moment, expectant of a surprise attack but receiving none. His anxiety seemed to be contagious, because Shadow, the most nonplussed of the group, had a worried expression, too. The closer they grew to Mount Hayachine, the more often she would check her rifle, presumably to ensure its viability. After a while, she carried it in her arms, finger wrapped around its trigger guard.

Society, however, was not one to disappoint.

Near the halfway-mark of their journey, Bomber screeched to a halt. "STOP!"

His voice echoed through the woods, and distant birds replied with their own sounds. Everyone else froze in place, reaching for their weapons and equipment.

"What's wrong?" Battery asked.

Something doesn't seem right. "Just . . . just wait a second," he said.

The group took a step back as he scanned the area in front of them. He walked forward, looking at the tree back, then crouched down, staring at the grass and leaves. Glancing to the left, then to the right, he rubbed his eyes. When his hands fell from his face, the starfield appeared, revealing to him the source of his unease.

"We're in a minefield," he said, standing back up.

"How do you know?" Aquifer asked.

Bomber shot him a burning look.

"Oh. Carry on."

"There are wires strung along the ground, low enough to be unseen in the grass," Bomber continued. "Each string connects to two trees, with claymore mines hidden beneath the bark at each end. Were one of us to trip it, we'd be hit by a spray of ball bearings from opposite sides."

[Just this tree?] signed Shadow.

"No," he replied. "It looks like . . . about half the trees near us are wired."

[What's your strategy?]

"Well, the buried IEDs in the Middle East weren't 'disarmed,' as much as they were given a controlled detonation. I'd suggest it here, but . . ."

"But we don't know if that will alert the Mount Hayachine base to our presence," interrupted Battery.

He nodded. "That, but also . . . consider what we're all carrying right now. One stray bearing could make them useless, or worse; it could activate them prematurely."

"Then what's Plan B?" Aquifer asked.

"You trust me. A lot."

Battery raised her palms in a submissive gesture. "You're the one with the career experience. You're the one who can see the bombs. I don't think we could be in better hands."

"Follow me, then."

They moved out, Bomber heading the group. He took them on a weaving, dizzying journey as he mapped out a maze in his head which allowed them to move forward without crossing between claymore-infested trees. The next hour was far more tiring than the last four, as he made constant course corrections and circular routes, dancing around wired explosives with forced gentleness and precision.

While they navigated the treacherous path, he focused so intently on avoiding the mines he almost overlooked the forest's transition from a moderate climate to a snowy one. The dirt and bark dusted with white, their winter boots soon crunched across a blanket of fresh powder. Chilled wind blew into their faces. Bomber's legs burned as their path inclined.

Near the maw of the forest's climate change, he turned to them. "We're out. I don't see any more mines ahead, but I'll keep looking."

They all breathed a collective sigh of relief, and the four Faction fighters drove their boots into the earth, scaling the base of Mount Yakushi and the ridge that separated them from their destination. The dead trees and grass of the woods faded into scarcity behind them, leaving them to face stony crags decorated with tufts of snow. Bomber's skin glowed a faint orange, shielding him from the elements, while the other three pulled their winter clothes close to their bodies, shivering.

On occasion, they would stop to rest and remain hydrated. Bomber would scan the path ahead with his Atomic Vision, while Shadow would use the scope on her rifle to scout out distant dangers. Despite avoiding a messy death at the hands of the minefield, Bomber could not shake the feeling that something worse than the Black-Eyed Children waited around the corner. His concerns continually met silence, though, and before long, they were beyond Mount Yakushi, wading through the snowy valley in the shadow of Mount Hayachine.

Trees returned, and they were back in the wilderness, though this one was buried under softened ice. Gaps in the treetops revealed the peak of their destination, but they had only reached hour seven of their journey, and at least another hour of walking would befall them before they were at its base. On occasion, they would pass piles of straw scattered around the visible woods, but Bomber saw no one placing them there. Gone was any semblance of life, and there were no sounds other than . . .

Heh-heh-heh-heh-heh.

Distant laughter.

Heh-heh-heh-heh-heh.

The team scrambled for their weapons; turbines spun, speakers hummed, rifles racked, and energy manifested. Forming a tight circle, Bomber scrutinized their surroundings.

Heh-heh-heh-heh-heh.

Whatever was producing the laughter, it didn't sound sincere. It was high-pitched, more of a maniacal cackle than a genuine laugh, but there was a dryness to the sound. There was no connection between the laugh and any human emotion, the apathetic difference between a living duck and a hunter's duck call.

Heh-heh-heh-heh-heh.

The laughter grew louder. Snow fell on the team as something rustled the tree branches overhead, but when Bomber turned to see it, the culprit had vanished. He looked behind him and noticed two piles of straw on the path they had already passed. He was certain they weren't there before.

Heh-heh-heh-heh-heh.

He looked to his left, and a pile of straw he'd seen earlier moved a considerable distance closer to them, seemingly of its own volition.

What's going on? he thought, his heartbeat pounding in his chest.

Heh-heh-heh-heh-heh.

Footsteps pattered across the snow to their right, vanishing into the barren trees before he could get a good look at it. He may have noticed the flash of steel.

Heh-heh-heh-heh-heh.

"Bomber," Battery said. "Straw piles?"

Oh, right. Duh.

His eyes glowed orange, and he swept the area. Organic matter curled beneath the moving objects. "Yup."

As the words left his lips, Shadow squeezed the trigger of her rifle, sending a volley of bullets into the closest straw pile to her. Bomber blinked. The pile *had* been in her line of sight, but the bullets only touched stray grass and a few loose pieces of straw. The pile itself disappeared entirely.

Heh-heh-heh-heh-heh.

More crashing resounded overhead. Bomber heard the singing of a blade cutting through empty air, and he ducked in time to avoid something swiping through the space where his head had been. Shadow turned upwards toward the attacker and fired her rifle, but her bullets only shattered tree bark.

Heh-heh-heh-heh-heh.

Thunk.

Bomber turned to see a straw pile appear near him. Something laid on top of it, poking out from the dull yellow stalks . . .

Heh-heh-heh-heh-heh.

Thunk. Thunk. Thunk.

Three new piles appeared around them, in addition to the ones already present. Each pile had something lying at its peak. Curious, Bomber reached for the object closest to him.

"Heh-heh-heh-heh-heh," laughed the straw pile, its tone almost mocking.

Bomber jerked his hand back and watched as the object lifted itself to face him. What he saw was a crude, wooden mask, painted bright red. A scowling mouth with curved, elongated canines were carved into the mask, as were angry, white eyes and furrowed brows. The design of the face was quite ogre-like.

The mask atop the straw rose up, carrying the pile into a standing form. What Bomber now faced was some kind of person in a cloak made of straw, the ends of the arms and legs obscured in shadow, staring through eye holes in its mask. Its laughter never ceased.

Heh-heh-heh-heh-heh.

The others rose, too, forming a circle around The Faction. There were six straw-men in total, each with their own mask varying in design and color. In addition to the red mask, there was a blue, green, purple, black, and yellow one. Each one held out an arm, donned in white, furry sleeves and black, leathery gloves, and revealed what Bomber recognized to be a saya, or Japanese scabbard.

Heh-heh-heh-heh-heh.

He looked to his side and saw Shadow was laughing too, though it escaped her mouth as little more than a wisp of air. Bomber widened his eyes in surprise as she lifted her rifle and speared it into the snow next to her, barrel-down. There it quivered, a green-and-black post of metal and bullets.

"What are you doing?" he whispered.

The others turned to her, and she signed one word. [Namahage.] Shadow reached into her white cloak, retrieved two silver hatchets wrapped in red cord, and charged at the yellow-masked thing in front of her.

The Yellow Namahage did not even flinch; drawing a katana from its sheath, it sprinted to her, legs carrying it forward at an inhuman speed. Snow sprayed into the air along its path, and the swing of its sword was a nigh-invisible whisper in the air.

The other five Namahages rustled and drew their katanas, tensing up to attack the rest of the team. While the Red and Green Namahages approached Battery, the Blue and Purple ones crept up to Aquifer. To his left, Bomber saw the Black Namahage bending its knees to jump.

All the while . . .

Heh-heh-heh-heh-heh.

The Black Namahage raced to Bomber, and the soldier returned in kind. An orange aura surrounded him, and he Atomic-Dashed above and behind the Namahage, his eyes leaving twin trails of light in his wake. While in the air, Bomber spun and fired a blast at his assailant with his Atomic Gun; the orange beam raced toward the center of its straw cloak. Peering over its shoulder, the Black Namahage cartwheeled past the laser with ease, circling around to re-engage with Bomber with a flying leap. Carried aloft by their own devices, the two speedsters began their midair tête-à-tête.

Heh-heh-heh-heh-heh.

He rushed at the Namahage, kicking it in the stomach and pirouetting away, creating distance between them. In his brief respite, he surveyed the battlefield, ensuring the others were handling their own fights without him.

Heh-heh-heh-heh-heh.

Shadow had buried her hatchets into the nearby trees and engaged with the Yellow Namahage using her small scythes. What did she call them again? Bomber couldn't remember.

Heh-heh-heh-heh-heh.

Aquifer had formed a water shield, but the Blue and Purple Namahages were approaching him from both sides. Their katana blades bounced away from the pressurized liquid barrier, vibrating in their hands, and they cocked their masked heads at him, curious. In short, deft movements, Aquifer expanded the domain of his namesake, flooding the area around their feet. Before he could contain or attack the Namahages, they were airborne, scaling the trees and watching him at a distance. His response was to lob water cannonballs at them, but they leapt from branch to branch around him, circling like bothersome mosquitoes.

Heh-heh-heh-heh-heh.

Battery apparently decided to go toe-to-toe with the creatures, ducking and weaving as she lashed out with a flurry of punches and kicks. They tried to stab her, to cut her, but her toughened skin made it impossible.

Heh-heh-heh-heh-heh.

Bomber turned away from his examination to see the Black Namahage centimeters from his face, katana raised. He moved to push it away, but something caught the corner of his eye: A second object rushing toward his face. At the last moment he ducked, spinning in the air to see what had attacked him.

Spooling out behind the Namahage, poking from beneath its straw cloak, was a white-furred, prehensile tail. The appendage was long and sinewy, its movements serpentine, like a trained cobra dancing from within its basket. The tip of the Namahage's tail curled around the wooden handle of what appeared to be some kind of stylized kitchen knife. Cold steel aimed itself at his face, almost independent of the movements of the katana-wielding Namahage. He Dashed backward, raising his fingers.

He wasn't expecting *that*.

Heh-heh-heh-heh-heh.

Bomber fired his Atomic Gun, aiming for the Namahage's heart, but it flipped away, dancing across the treetops. The two grappled back and forth along the tree line a dozen meters above the rest of the action, the former bouncing against the atoms in the air and the latter ricocheting from one tree trunk to the next. On occasion, they met it midair, trading a flurry of speedy punches, kicks, stabs, and energy bolts. When gravity caught up with them, they parted ways, rebounding around the wooded arena and preparing their next strike.

"Bomber! The blades!" Battery called out from below.

"Yeah," he replied, "I caught that."

"No, *scan* the blades!"

Resting on the uppermost branches of the nearest tree, Bomber's eyes winked to life, and he swayed back and forth while surveying the Namahages. Their katanas were structured in a predictable way, folds upon folds of iron and a little bit of carbon, pressed and thinned into steel blades. He turned his attention to the others. Shadow and Battery's opponents also sported tails, which in turn wielded long knives.

Distracted, Bomber almost missed the Black Namahage racing toward him with vengeance. He Atomic-Dashed across the trees, distancing himself from his opponent with a series of orange laser blasts before examining the knives below. Carbon and steel, just like the swords . . . except there was something else. Another layer of carbon, triple-bonded to nitrogen.

"Battery! Their knives are laced with cyanide!" he screamed, amplifying his warning above the clamor so everyone would hear.

Heh-heh-heh-heh-heh.

"Wait, they have knives, too?" Aquifer responded, continuing his waves of water projectiles against the speedy Blue and Purple Namahages. One of the projectiles struck the Blue Namahage in the face, knocking away the mask, but Bomber Dashed away before he could see what was beneath.

Heh-heh-heh-heh-heh.

"What the hell?" he heard Aquifer say, but he was too entrenched in his melee to investigate further.

Heh-heh-heh-heh-heh.

In the center of the excitement, Bomber felt his body temperature rising with the continued use of his powers. Still, the Black Namahage avoided all debilitating attacks, and each pass of the sword was another slice of Bomber's borrowed time. If he were to act, he needed to act soon.

Pressing his back against tree bark, the soldier waited for another attempt at dismemberment by his enemy. He didn't wait long; the wind whipped around him, preceding the appearance of the ogre-masked Namahage. Metal sliced into wood, almost hitting Bomber as he ducked. His hand left the bark, and he Dashed into the sky. Where he had touched the tree, an orange light expanded until it burst outward, melting the buried sword and launching the splinter-covered Black Namahage upward.

Atomic-Dashing beneath the creature in free-fall, Bomber raised his fingers and took aim. A line of atomic bonds formed in front of him, guiding the explosive force he prepared to unleash. Orange energy erupted from between the tips of the index and middle fingers of his Atomic Gun, and a single laser streaked into the air, burning a clean hole through the Black Namahage's mask and head. It went limp; they fell toward the earth, but its body became entangled in the trees, releasing its melted katana and venomous knife to the floor below.

As Bomber glided down with his Atomic Parachute, his speed

reduced again by his repulsion against the atoms around him, he saw the Purple Namahage hacking away at Aquifer's defenses. The creature, so distracted by its attacks, didn't notice—until it was too late—Bomber firing a second shot in its direction. A beam of light and energy drove into the Purple Namahage, burning through its chest and stopping it in its tracks. Bomber completed his descent to Aquifer while the Purple Namahage teetered and fell.

Heh-heh-heh-heh-heh.

Shadow was still sparring with the Yellow Namahage, and in the process she knocked its mask from its face. When Bomber saw what lay beneath, he stepped back, horrified.

Heh-heh-heh-heh-heh.

What stared back was the pink, laughing visage of a deformed macaque monkey. Such an animal should only be a fraction of a human's size, but it appeared this monkey's face was stretched thin across an oversized skeleton to account for the discrepancy. Sewed and stapled scars littered the pink flesh of the macaque, and metal plating gleamed from beneath the incisions, creating a Franken-stein-like appearance.

Worse still, the creature's mind seemed altered by whatever Society had done to it. Though exposed, the monkey's mouth remained open, laughing in a fit of monotone hysterics. Its eyes were wide and watery, but they weren't filled with malice like the Reptiles, with glee like the Bellhops, or with apathy like the Trig-gers.

No, this animal was terrified.

Heh-heh-heh-heh-heh.

Before he could move to assist, the Yellow Namahage lashed out at Shadow with its feet, and when she moved to dodge it, the crea-ture climbed the cluster of trees she had backed it into. Sheathing the scythes, Shadow drew one of her automatic pistols and unleashed a hailstorm of gunfire on the macaque, driving it higher. When it ran out of space, the Namahage flipped over her head, dodging her bullets along the way, and landed near the base of another tree.

A tree with a cord-wrapped hatchet buried in the bark.

Bomber watched the huntress's free hand press a small remote, detonating the weapon. The fire, force, and shards of wood disem-boweled the creature, tossing its remains at least ten meters across the battlefield. A short-lived shower of blood sprinkled across Shadow, leaving red droplet stains in her white, winterized armor and cloak.

Heh-heh-heh-heh-heh.

He heard the buzz of flying sparks and turned to see the Green Namahage chopping at Battery's arms, each strike cutting into her jacket and armor, lifting streaks of electricity from her skin. Every responding punch or kick was dodged or blocked, though Bomber noticed her Red enemy had already been dispatched, lying at her feet with its own katana buried in its neck.

"*Heh-heh-heh-heh-heh.*"

"Yeah, I get it!" Battery yelled, digging her foot into the earth and kicking a spray of dirt and snow into the Namahage's face.

Blinded, it stepped back, sword lowered. It was then that Bomber heard another blade whipping through the air behind him; he ducked, ready to address another attacker. Instead, the blade he heard was Shadow's scythe, spinning past Battery and himself and burying itself into the green ogre mask. The Namahage halted, still for a moment; then, a trickle of blood exited the point of penetration, winding down the grooves of the wooden covering.

"*Heh . . . heh . . .*"

The final Namahage toppled over, landing face-first into the ground and releasing its weapons.

Silence filled the woods, excepting a quiet sizzle from Bomber's contact with the snow. Battery looked around, dialing down her Charge Belt. "Anyone hurt?"

Aquifer sighed. "Just my feelings."

"Yeah, what was that?" Bomber interjected. "I don't think these things wanted to be here."

"That's Society for you." Battery shook her head. "We had to do what we had to do."

Shadow attracted everyone's attention. [Again, is anyone injured?]

Bomber turned and surveyed the group, who seemed a little tired and frayed, but otherwise healthy.

"It looks like everyone's good," he said.

"Let's hope so," Battery replied. "Because we aren't even *inside* the damn facility yet."

**Honshû, Japan
March 10, 2012-B**

Aquifer whistled. "I don't like this anymore."

Shadow looked at him, annoyed. [This part was your idea.]

"I can change my mind, can't I?" he retorted.

Interjecting, Battery said, "So, what's our situation, exactly?"

"According to the schematics we retrieved from Gold Hill . . ." Aquifer checked his notes. "The official entrance to the Mount Hayachine facility is a wide set of camouflaged doors along the base of the mountain. They're sturdy, difficult to pinpoint, and well-guarded. From there, we would have to weave through dozens of manned corridors, stairs, and elevators to reach a control room with direct access to the earthquake machine."

"Not an ideal route," Bomber commented.

"No. *But* . . . this machine's sheer size and power causes it to produce a great deal of heat. Without taking that into consideration, everyone inside the facility would be baked alive whenever it was used. They circumvented this by building a giant ventilation duct around the top half of the machine, carrying the excess heat diagonally through the mountain and releasing it about three-quarters of the way from the peak, right above our heads."

Shadow looked at the snow-covered mountain looming over them, shivering as another stiff breeze blew past her.

"There's *our* entrance," Aquifer said.

"Then let's do this," Battery responded, removing her bag. The others followed suit, emptying their contents: Ropes and harnesses, belays and pulleys, ice axes and pitons, and cleated crampons to tie around their boots.

Once they were wrapped in climbing gear and ready to head out, they began to wind up the navigable face of the mountain. At first, they simply walked along the steep incline, the spikes of their crampons maintaining traction in the snow. Soon, though, the sheer face of the mountain halted their progress, and they hammered long metal piton spikes into the rock, crawling upward like a colony of ants.

Shadow and Bomber, the two lighter and more agile members, climbed ahead of Battery and Aquifer. They used their ice axes to chip away at the slippery accumulations along the rock, anchoring fresh climbing ropes and footholds at regular intervals. The occasional wind would blow, stronger with each measured ascent, and Shadow would find herself clinging to the face of the mountain to avoid being carried away.

Each person's strength and energy levels differed, so she was unsurprised to find them staggered below her after a while. She continued ahead, outpacing Bomber, while Battery kept slowing down to account for Aquifer's languidness. When they were almost halfway to their destination, Shadow heard him slip a little, and she glanced past her shoulder to see him looking down, his face contorted in terror. He covered his mouth and pressed his face against the rock, shuddering.

"I *really* don't like this anymore," he said.

Again, this was your idea, Shadow thought, rolling her eyes.

Battery leaned over, affixing a short climbing rope to her harness and dropping the other end to him. At her gesture, he connected the rope to his own harness.

"You trust me, right?" she asked him. "I won't let you fall."

Shadow smiled. *Always the protector.*

Aquifer nodded a weak thank-you and gritted his teeth, continuing the climb.

Shadow turned and continued ahead of the group, huffing in and out, aligning her handholds and footholds with the pace of her breath. Even the cold wind whipping her white cloak around her body couldn't slow her down. Puffs of chilled breath exited her mouth, sailing away in the same way a low-hanging fog escapes the sky. Above, she saw some sort of lip or overhang, and signaled to the team.

"Is it the vent?" Bomber asked.

She turned to answer and saw him step onto a new piton that he had nailed into the rock.

The piton angled downward, a thin crack preventing it from holding securely, and Bomber's foot slipped. He must have placed too much of his weight on the support, and his fingers lost their grip on the crevices above. The rope he was connected to yanked itself from its supports, plinking out of the rock and failing to offer any reprieve from gravity's uncaring embrace.

"BOMBER!" Battery yelled, reaching out, but she was not close enough to catch him as he dropped past her.

Grasping around him, Bomber squeezed his eyes shut and reached for the wall. Much to Shadow's surprise, his descent slowed, his hand sliding across the mountain face surrounded by a buffer of heat. She squinted her eyes and noticed that his hands were glowing orange and adhered to the rock, shooing away any surrounding snow or ice.

"Hmm," she heard Aquifer say, but she could barely make out his words over the howling wind.

"Well, I suppose it makes sense," Aquifer continued, his body flat against the mountain as he studied Bomber. "If your Atomic Dash is accomplished by some kind of magnetic *repulsion*, then an Atomic . . . Cling . . . would only be natural in the opposite sense, by magnetic attraction."

Bomber looked at his hands again, then down at his dangling legs. "The opposite . . . magnetic attraction . . ."

He held a hand toward the rock above his head, and Shadow saw it snap against it with the force of two powerful magnets joining together. Just like that, his hands and knees were snug against Mount Hayachine, and he resumed the climb upward. Sighing with relief, Shadow completed her climb, happy to be standing on a horizontal surface once more.

What loomed above the lip was a round, mesh wall, large enough to fit a helicopter through. It was tilted so the shaft below dropped at a steep sixty-degree angle, and a light mist strained through the mesh. Bomber, Battery and Aquifer joined her, teetering on the edge of a small overhang at the bottom of the vent, and Aquifer whistled.

[Would you do the honors?] Shadow signed to Bomber, gesturing at the mesh.

The young man's eyes became pinpoints of orange light, the sleeve of his winter coat rustling a little as his index and middle fingers began to glow. He took two short strides to the shaft entrance and drew an arc with his Atomic Scissors, separating the molecules that held the mesh together. His speed had improved after the trial run in Centralia, and an entrance wide enough for the team to fit through appeared in under a minute. Bomber stepped back, sweating, and Shadow admired his handiwork.

Aquifer gathered the team together, leaning against the hollowed tunnel falling into the mountain. "The machine is almost completely underground, with a small torquing engine monitored and connected to the vent to release the heat. We don't have the length of rope necessary to rappel down to that motor, so we'll need to slide. It's steep, but we'll be okay."

"And when we reach the bottom?" Battery asked.

"I'll try to catch us all, but my main priority is a safe landing for Shadow. Should the worst occur, you and Bomber can make your own way down the vent."

Shadow nodded in agreement, unslung her Steyr AUG HBAR-T rifle, and removed her cleats, readying for indoor terrain. The rest of the team did the same, packing away their winter gear. Once they were armed and presumably comfortable, Aquifer stepped up to the crude entrance made by Bomber's Atomic Scissors.

"It's now or never, Treehouse," he announced. "The sooner we get back home, the sooner we convince Proxy to make us some of his lemon tarts."

Those encouraging words were all the convincing Shadow needed. She lined up with her team and plunged into the abyss.

Silver walls surrounded them, dimming to blackness as they slid further from the entrance. Each member was on their back, propping their head and shoulders to face what was below. Shadow's cloak whipped around her, and some of the weapons strapped to her back ground against the metal shaft. She felt a knife at her hip shatter from the friction and send metal shards flying through the air, almost cutting into Bomber nearby.

The ventilation shaft echoed with the sounds of their clothing and backpacks and equipment slipping against thin metal, amplifying as they picked up speed. Aquifer maintained a steady verbal count of their falling rate, and he seemed to be preparing his PAUS to catch them once they reached the machine at the bottom of the mountain.

Shadow saw Battery notice this, too, and the detective leaned over toward her. "How much longer do you think—"

THWACK.

A wide panel of the shaft floor flew open in front of them, and Shadow collided against it along with Battery and Aquifer, rebounding through the new hole and falling into a crumpled heap in the middle of a pearl-white hallway. A dull pain spread along Shadow's body as she lay prone, surprised to be alive.

Striking metal at that speed and angle should have shattered every bone in my body. I must be the luckiest woman in the world.

Shadow finally raised her head to see what had happened.

Surrounding them were eight men in black body armor and masks, much like the ones who raided Aquifer's lab in his pre-Faction days. The men leveled assault rifles at the dazed Faction members, and one lifted his mask to speak, revealing the yellow eyes, blood-stained cheeks and needle teeth of a Reptile.

"Did you think we wouldn't exssspect you?" he hissed, but his gloating was short-lived as his eyes swept across bodies on the floor. *"Who'sss missssing?"*

As the panel opened, Aquifer acted on instinct, flipping his palms behind him. A film of water appeared beneath him and burst upward, launching him over the gap his friends had fallen through. He landed on the other side, but his slide devolved into a violent roll, with no surface on which he could gain traction. Tumbling across his chest, then backpack, then face, then legs, the scientist careened down the shaft.

Equipment loosened and flung free from the centrifugal force, and Aquifer fumbled to hold his bag closer to his body. Too late, a briefcase-sized box launched past an open flap, smashing into the shaft wall before showering the darkness below with its contents.

"NO!"

His outcry did little, and after what seemed an eternity, the tumbling ceased. He was thrown into open air, revealing a straight drop down onto a giant drill-bit-shaped object that could only be the earthquake machine's torquing engine. Moving his arms in a violent, hurried gesture, he materialized a pool right above the machine, but he hesitated. How much momentum had he accumulated along his fall? Something wasn't right.

Still falling, Aquifer slapped his forehead. Surface tension! Striking undisturbed water as this speed would be no softer than striking concrete. Now seconds from impact, he generated a series of ultra-sound bursts, bubbling the water and breaking apart the surface tension. Satisfied, he dove into his pool, allowing the liquid to shear away gravity's pull until he reached a complete stop and floated to the surface.

The scientist snapped his fingers, vaporizing the water and freeing himself of moisture. Back under gravity's thrall, he fell on top of the machine. There were a series of wide openings spiraling along the torquing engine, and through them he could see a bridge and an unmanned control panel, two or three stories below.

Aquifer slipped through the holes, climbing down the machine toward the bridge, and spoke into his radio. "Team, I'm at the machine, but I've lost my dirty bomb. I repeat, I've lost my dirty bomb. Does anyone else still have an intact one?"

───────────────

Aquifer repeated his message in Shadow's ear, but her attention was transfixed on the barrels of the guns aimed at her and the rest of her team. The Reptile commander leaned forward, smiling at Battery.

"Don't even think about touching that belt. We know that you're powerlesss without your electricity. Everyone, ssstand up. Missss Zala would like a word."

Shadow rose, as did Battery and Bomber, and the men in black reached for their bags. Suddenly, Battery shifted her weight, connected the studs in the knuckles of her gloves to the closest enemy. Something crunched, and he fell backward. The commander and three other men lit up the hallway with their machine-gun fire, peppering Battery's body, but she pressed forward, yanking away one of their rifles and beating its owner across the skull with it.

During the chaos of Battery's attack, Shadow leapt at the three remaining men, but Bomber was faster. Two fired upon him, and he vanished, twin lines of orange light fading behind him as he moved. Burning ozone filled Shadow's nostrils, and orange lasers seared through each of their foreheads from behind. They fell to the floor, revealing Bomber standing there with glowing eyes and smoking fingertips.

Shadow, on the other hand, was a little insulted by the relaxed security reserved for her. Her single assailant fired his rifle, and she dodged the first spray of bullets, shielding herself from the second spray with her armored cloak. All the while, her distance between herself and the man in black drew closer, and he panicked, lowering the rifle to back away.

Big mistake.

In the moment of weakness, Shadow allowed her arm to extend, and a knife released from her hand. It twirled through the air and buried into her opponent's chest, the blade sinking in deep. He reached for it, but she, a white phantom, was upon him, clutching the handle before he could. She pulled the trigger, and her WASP knife released a thin stream of pressurized air, blowing an icy, basketball-sized hole into his torso. He seized in shock and fell over. Shadow retrieved her knife and turned toward the sounds of continued gunfire.

The commander and two remaining men emptied their magazines, working with a fury to reload them. Battery approached with a hungry look in her eyes, shoulders swaying. The closest man dropped his rifle and pulled out a knife, stabbing it toward her. She caught his wrist and arm, snapped the appendage at the joint, and used his own hand to slice the blade across his throat. He gurgled and collapsed.

That's my girl, Shadow proudly thought.

Both the commander and his last subordinate drew their sidearms and opened fire on the detective. She held up her arms, deflecting the bullets, and sprinted toward them. When she was close enough, she dropped and swept out a leg, sending them both crashing to the ground. The subordinate reached for his firearm again, but Battery brought her boot down on his head with a decisive stomp, crushing it beneath the mask.

"How? You didn't use powersss . . ." the commander exclaimed, hissing through his rows of teeth.

"It's called body armor. I'm not a one-trick pony," Battery replied, driving her heel into his face.

The pearl-white hallway fell silent.

"What now?" Bomber asked.

Shadow answered by racking the slide on her AUG rifle. [Now we go find Aquifer.]

"More than that," Battery added, activating her Charge Belt. Energy flowed across her suit and body, wiping away the cuts and bruises accrued during her hand-to-hand combat. "Now we get ready for one hell of a fight."

The shrill cry of a Klaxon alarm blared above Aquifer's head while he examined the control panel at the bridge. Doors to his left and his right slid open, and a small army of men in black armor marched into the room, approaching him from either side with rifles raised. A casual flick of his hands formed thick walls of water on each side of the bridge, separating him from his attackers. Gunfire filled the cavern of the earthquake machine as the men attempted to tear apart the volatile liquid structures with their bullets. The projectiles bounced away, causing no harm to Aquifer's defenses, and he continued examining the console in front of him.

He was a chemist, a physicist, and an engineer, but he was no expert programmer. The symbols on the keys and the interface on the screen seemed foreign—not just unfamiliar, but *alien*. Characters swirled into each other, and there didn't seem to be any form of accessible menu. Without some sort of key to this Society device, Aquifer would have no way of understanding the machine—or how to shut it down without a bomb.

The gunfire ceased, and Aquifer turned to see the men examining ways around the barriers. Before they had an opportunity to make an attempt, he lowered his hands and flooded the areas beyond the walls, bringing water rising to the attackers' knees on the bridge platforms. They started to wade away, but he overturned his hands; the waters flipped with them, catapulting the armed men over the railing and screaming into the cavern far below.

Alone again.

"Team, I can't access the machine's controls," he said into his radio. "I need one of your bombs. Can anyone hear me?"

"We got you, Aquifer," Battery replied into her transmitter from behind Shadow, raising her voice over the alarm and the chattering of machine guns. "Sit tight."

Shadow pushed down the hallway, spewing bullets from her AUG rifle into waves of armed men in black. Orange light intermittently flashed against her back as Bomber burned holes into those unfortunate enough to attempt a surprise attack from behind.

Shadow looked over her shoulder and saw Battery reviewing the portable tracker affixed to Aquifer.

"Let's find an elevator or stairwell," the detective said. "He's at least six stories below us."

Shadow nodded and shifted her aim, shredding through a few men in black as they ran around the corner. She held up her hand and gestured for the other two to follow. They continued for a moment before reaching an intersection, with a pair of swinging double-doors in front of them.

Battery consulted her tracker again. "I think we can reach a stairwell in this direction."

Heavy boots approached from the intersection, announcing the imminent arrival of more troops. Shadow led the team forward, bursting through the double-doors and preparing herself for anything.

A wide, pearl-white cafeteria full of people spread out before them. The benches of the cafeteria tables and the lines for the steaming food were swarming with at least a hundred chatting men and women. Some were in military gear, others in lab coats, and still others in construction outfits. As Shadow and her companions entered, they all fell silent, turning to stare.

Well, shit, Shadow thought. *This can't be good.* She aimed her weapon into the crowd, waiting for a reaction.

One by one, the men and women in the cafeteria tensed, shaking with enough violence to rattle the silverware on the tabletops. A wet, ripping sound filled the room, and the strangers' eyes leaked tears of blood as they rolled back, revealing yellow slit lizard eyes. Human teeth retracted, replaced with rows and rows of organic hypodermic needles.

Shadow sighed as she felt her pupils switch, and time slowed down around her.

Yeah, that's what I figured.

Transformed, the Reptiles crawled across the tables, hissing at the unwelcome guests. Those strapped with weapons stood and took aim over the heads of their comrades. Dishes clattered to the floor while inhuman, yellow-eyed creatures slithered between the gaps of the furniture, mouths open and waiting.

"The interferersss . . ."

"Yesss, they've come to stop usss . . ."

"We mussst bring them to Missss Zala . . ."

Battery, Shadow and Bomber looked at one another, and the detective said, "See you on the other side?"

Shadow nodded, and all three split up, rushing toward the horde of Reptiles as they opened fire on the intruders. She ducked low, thinning the herd with a steady stream of armor-piercing rounds from her AUG. Bomber Dashed high, careening into the Reptiles with a series of explosive Atomic Punches, detonating craters into their chests and sending them flying away. To her left, Battery rushed down the middle of the room, bowling over her attackers as she kicked and elbowed a path to the other side of the cafeteria.

Reptiles closed in toward Shadow, and she tried to follow Battery, rotating her hips as she expended hot ammunition into the mountains of slithering bodies around her. There was a moment of reprieve as she separated herself from the attackers by the length of a few cafeteria tables. That reprieve was short-lived when rifles and pistols cracked in her direction, sending bullets flying past her. One struck the shoulder of her body armor, spinning her to her knees, and she gritted her teeth, flipping the closest table to form a protective wall between herself and the Reptile shooters.

Leaning over the edge of the table, Shadow pressed the butt of her rifle into her shoulder and squeezed the trigger. The AUG spat its sleek projectiles across the room, tearing into the least-guarded Reptiles with firearms. They seized as the rounds pierced them, falling to the cafeteria floor in pools of blood. Despite the attack, the remaining shooters circled the tables separating them from Shadow, bearing down on her with their own gunfire as they drew closer.

Diving below the overturned table, Shadow ejected the AUG's empty magazine and reached for a fresh one, but she found her pouch empty. She shook her head and laid the heavy rifle on the ground, bullets flying above her. Reaching into her cloak with both hands, she withdrew her twin automatic Glock pistols, checked them, and raised them to her shoulders, waiting for an opportunity to strike.

Orange light flashed beside her, and she jerked her head. Bomber was sitting behind the table, smoking. He gestured to himself and the ceiling before he signed a few words to Shadow. Her lips curled into a smirk, and she nodded. The two waited for a moment, and then he leapt into action.

An aura surrounded the soldier before he launched into the air, flipping upside-down. His boots glowed as they pulled toward the ceiling in his second attempt at an Atomic Cling. Now magnetized above everyone's heads, Bomber Dashed toward the Reptile shooters, an orange trail of light following him as he zipped around the room like a rocket-propelled firefly. The Reptiles fired up at him, but his chaotic movements made it difficult for them to line up a clear shot.

While the Reptiles were distracted, Shadow vaulted over her makeshift barrier, pounding her boots against the pearl-white floors as she unloaded her pair of Glocks into the armed creatures. As tough as they were, the repetitious beating of automatic gunfire wore them down, crippling their ability to fight back. She ran out of bullets and kicked over the nearest table, crouching to reload, while Bomber Dashed away, likely to cool down.

Elsewhere in the room, Shadow heard a loud series of snaps and crunches, and a few mangled Reptile bodies flew past her table, striking the far wall of the cafeteria. With a low *thunk*, half-dozen more of the creatures pattered against the ceiling before bouncing back down to the cafeteria floor.

I'm glad you're on our side, Battery, she thought, sliding new magazines into her Glocks. She was about to return to the battle, but movement caught the corner of her eye. A new figure slipped into the room, obscured by the chaos. The only notable feature from this distance was a gold-and-black-patterned dress.

Now what?

**Honshû, Japan
March 10, 2012-B**

Aquifer leaned against the console, careful to keep his hands away from the controls. He was watching more and more Reptiles pile up on the other side of the water barriers, leering at him with their yellow eyes and snapping jaws. When enough had appeared to fill the walkways, they climbed each other to vault the walls, and he repeated his previous tactic to catapult them to their deaths.

This time, a *click-clack* emanated from beneath the bridge, and Aquifer backed away from the noise. More skittering sounds, and then a soaking-wet Reptile swung up from the bridge's underside, landing within reach of the scientist. It kicked him with an inhuman strength, and Aquifer sprawled to the floor, winded. Wasting no time, the Reptile sprung upon him, biting at his face.

Aquifer created an uppercut motion at the last moment, forming a full-length barrier of water between the Reptile and his fragile self. The creature bounced from the pressurized liquid and rolled to the side. Scrambling to his feet, Aquifer maintained the shield, swinging it so the Reptile could not get through.

Swaying back and forth, the Reptile maintained eye contact with its twitchy prey, craning its head for a way past the shield. Then, Aquifer lowered his guard, loosening the shield into droplets of water. The Reptile raced at him, mouth open and hungry, but the scientist raised his other hand, completing a new PAUS command. An egg-shaped prison of water surrounded the Reptile. The creature attempted to escape, but the swirling pressure kept pulling it to the center of the trap.

The Reptile's captor turned and approached the railing of the bridge, looking at the endless cavern below. Raising his arm, he floated the water egg out into the center of the opening, surrounded by empty space. Aquifer made eye contact with the creature, who grimaced in anticipation. Not one to build suspense, the scientist released the Reptile, and it plummeted into darkness without saying a word.

Aquifer backed away, searching for other hidden enemies, but he was interrupted by a low, loud whirring noise. His head swiveled in the direction of the towering earthquake machine, then up to the torquing engine. The motor began to swivel, grinding against itself and picking up speed. In front of Aquifer, the control panel came to life, flashing a perplexing series of lights. The scientist moved toward the console, helpless.

"We're running out of time!" he yelled into the radio.

Keeping an eye on the slowly approaching newcomer, Shadow laid down her pistols and withdrew a fragmentation "pineapple" grenade, pulling the pin. When she was sure that the orange and blue blurs of strength and violence that were her teammates were clear of her blast radius, she chucked it into a cluster of Reptiles approaching her table.

The pineapple grenade detonated, tearing through the Reptiles' bodies and sending them tumbling apart. In response to their moment of weakness, Shadow poked her head and arms above the overturned table and emptied another pair of magazines from her machine pistols. The buzzing projectiles carved a swathe into the horde of retreating Reptiles, felling them before they returned to their feet. She ejected her magazines, reloading before rolling over the makeshift shield, and sprinted toward her targets. More gunfire erupted from her hands, the Reptiles' faces imploding under her onslaught.

Her white cloak carried aloft by her speed, Shadow ducked and dodged, sending strategic bursts of gunfire into her enemies. Around her, lasers and bullets and bodies and tables flew together in a visual symphony.

Shadow's Glock ammunition was running low, largely due to the number of bullets required to take down each Reptile. She holstered her machine pistols and withdrew new weapons, opting for a more hands-on approach. She ducked, ran headlong into a cluster of Reptiles, and raised her hands.

Her left arm bent across her chest, gripping her WASP knife so that the point of the blade faced her opponents. Nestled against her wrist, she curled her right arm, holding a silver Mateba Autorevolver. The hefty pistol bore more of a resemblance to it traditional semiautomatic counterparts, but the streamlined upside-down revolving chamber fired six powerful .357 slugs with relative ease. Shadow utilized this advantage, squeezing the trigger in the direction of a nearby Reptile; the released slug bore between the center of the creature's eyes, cracking its head open in a spray of red.

The recoil of the Autorevolver hurt Shadow's wrist, but she found it more bearable than that of the Grizzly and other large-caliber handguns she had used in prior hunts. She shifted her aim and fired a second time, bursting apart another Reptile's head.

Footsteps approached her from behind, barely audible over the gunfire. When the shadows of the would-be attackers were close enough to fill her peripheral vision, she separated her arms. The WASP knife found a home buried into one Reptile's neck, while the Autorevolver was more comfortable jammed beneath the chin of the other Reptile. Both triggers were pulled at once; both Reptiles' heads exploded. She flicked the blood from her knife as the single newcomer finally entered her field of view.

The figure approaching was a dark-skinned woman in a black-and-gold-patterned dress. A headband of gold beads encircled her head, creating the impression of an impromptu tiara. She practically sashayed into the carnage, large brown eyes focused on Shadow. Her lips curled upward into a delighted, welcoming smile, and she beckoned for Shadow to join her.

In a flash, Bomber and Battery appeared shoulder-to-shoulder with Shadow, facing the approaching woman with arms raised, crackling with heat and electricity. Shadow prepared to strike with her revolver when the woman stopped, staring at them from a few paces away. Raising one hand, the woman revealed a black remote with a flashing red light.

"Did you think we wouldn't have redundancies for interference?" she called out.

More reptiles encircled them, and they turned away from the woman to re-engage with the more imminent threat. The woman made an annoyed face, raising her other hand. With the gesture, all fighting ceased, leaving them in the middle of a group of frozen Reptiles. Shadow took advantage of this display to eject the shells from her smoking Autorevolver, loading fresh bullets into the chambers.

"Miss Zala, I presume?" Battery called, her voice echoing around the now-quiet cafeteria walls. "Aquifer said he used to like you. At least, until you turned out to be a mass-murderer."

Zala bowed, slipping her remote back into the folds of her dress. Her other hand clenched, and the remaining Reptiles turned to face the three outsiders. Shadow tensed for another attack. Instead, the Reptiles clutched their heads in their hands, snapping their own necks in one swift motion. Their bodies fell to the floor, leaving only Zala and the three observers on their feet.

"*Much* better. Sometimes you have to tell yourself that there's only one, you know?" Zala laughed to herself, then stopped when she saw them staring. "No, I suppose you don't."

"We already have a man at your controls," Bomber said. "It won't be long before he takes your earthquake machine offline."

"Acharya? A brilliant man, but it seems you may not be so brilliant, Mister . . ."

"It's just Bomber now."

"Well, *Bomber*, I'm sure you know there's no permanent way of shutting down our Disaster Relief project here in Japan outside of physical force. The machine is spinning to life as we speak, so I assume Mister Acharya was not able to provide such a force?"

"Why are you doing this?" Battery asked. "Why the Indian Ocean before, and why Fiji now? What's the point?"

"The point?" Zala almost looked offended. "Look around you. Look at the world. We're filled to the brim with humans, polluting the earth and raping the wildlife and destroying the ozone layer. It's called 'Disaster Relief,' electric girl. What do you think is the biggest disaster for our planet?"

"Wow." Battery shook her head. "Come down from your cross for two seconds, Zala. The world is so much more come complicated than the picture you're painting."

"Consider the technology you wield," Bomber added. "Rather than cutting a swathe through our population, why don't you use it to improve our quality of life so the planet can repair itself?"

Smiling, Zala wagged her finger. "It's not *our* population. It's *your* population. And *your* people are impossible to work with. Always fighting, and arguing, and splitting off into cliques with your inane popularity contests. No, working with your people is just simply not feasible. My approach is far more utilitarian."

This bitch sounds like a James Bond villain, Shadow thought. She slowly took aim at Zala's head with her revolver, waiting for the moment that she suspected would be coming soon.

Battery grimaced. "So, you won't even hear us out? You're insistent about all of this death and destruction?"

Zala stood still, her smile telegraphing her answer.

"Fine." The detective leaned into her radio transmitter. "Aquifer, your friend is boring us. We'll be down soon."

The three moved toward the cafeteria doors, but Zala blocked their exit. "No, no you won't."

Her eyes rolled back, snapping apart the tendons in her skull, leaking droplets of blood as they revealed Reptile eyes. These, however, were not the same color as the others; swirling around the slits that passed for pupils was a luminescent green cloud, a smoky substance quite distinct from the solid yellow eyes of the previous Reptiles. Teeth retreated and then grew back into bundles of thin bone spikes, and her exposed skin rippled as a scaly subdermal layer formed beneath it.

"This isss where you die, interferersss."

"Aquifer? Scratch that. We're busy. Can you do anything about the machine?"

The scientist watched the earthquake machine rattle, building up enough tectonic energy to broadcast itself all the way to the unsuspecting citizens of Fiji. Engine blades rotated at a dizzying speed, grinding clockwise against the cavern walls. Aquifer took a step closer, observing.

It's only spinning clockwise.

"Do me a favor, then, okay?" he asked into the radio. "Kick her ass. And remind her why."

With that, he began to create complex gestures with his arms . . .

Shadow smiled at the reply and pulled the trigger of her Autorevolver. The green-eyed Reptile extended her arms, and a long, curved jile dagger slipped from each of her sleeves, the ivory handles settling into her hands. As fast as a striking rattlesnake, the Reptile crossed the blades in front of her face, deflecting the bullet.

Shadow's smile faded.

Zala lifted her twin blades in a fighting stance, waiting for their next move. Shadow responded by distancing herself, gliding backward while unloading her Autorevolver into the Reptile. Moving in a fluid, dance-like motion, Zala tilted out of the way of each bullet, almost as if she shared Shadow's Gaze.

Shadow stopped to reload, and Battery and Bomber rushed the toothy, grinning Reptile woman. The latter reached her first via Atomic Dash. Appearing a meter in front of her, he clasped both hands together and fired an orange beam at her face. Zala dodged the laser with ease, replying with a vicious jab of her daggers. His eyes widened, but Battery shoved him out of the way, deflecting the blades with her electricity-reinforced skin and armor.

Shadow finished collapsing the cylinder of her pistol, but Zala had changed her target, now rushing toward the huntress. She had to tuck and roll away from the Reptile's attack, but when she completed her maneuver, Shadow took aim and fired several more times. Much to her dismay, each round was wasted on empty air. Despite Shadow's Gaze, Zala remained too fast to shoot at from a distance.

Battery charged past Shadow toward the Reptile, shoulders low and fist cocked back. Zala ducked, but at the last moment, Battery changed tactics, throwing her body into the fight feet-first, implementing a flying double-kick. Her heels collided with her opponent and propelled the Reptile across the cafeteria, collapsing her against one of the tables.

"So, you're, like, the original Reptile, then?" The detective queried.

" 'Reptile?' How quaint. Am I the original? Yesss and no, I sssuppose. Though I wouldn't feel too confident, Mississippi girl. No outcome today will ssstop Sssociety and our goalsss."

Bomber appeared near Zala, skin smoking and eyes glowing a furious orange. "Maybe. Maybe not. But I know *I'll* feel a lot better."

He raised both hands and carved gaps into the air, sending burning pillars toward Zala. The Reptile woman rolled away from the attacks, but Shadow intercepted her escape with a rolling pineapple grenade. Zala leapt into the air, nearly touching the ceiling, and the explosive detonated, sending fragmented metal across the space she had just vacated. Before Zala was able to return to the ground, Shadow saw a silhouette pass overhead as a cafeteria table collided with the Reptile's body, pinning her while it flew across the room.

"Today isn't just about Society," Battery announced as Zala fell and collapsed beneath the rubble. "It's about the innocent people whose lives you've ruined. Those who've been butchered, eaten, tortured, just to fit your twisted needs."

The detective flung another table at Zala, who scrambled away, her movements slower now after the beating. Bomber zipped into her path, stomping against the floor; orange light exploded from beneath his foot, sending bits of tile and concrete spraying. Battery strode toward Zala while she backed away, swinging her daggers to clear the aerial debris.

Shadow lowered her gun and withdrew a hatchet.

Battery said, "It's about Indra, and Aarav, and Priya. It's about Reyansh, and Ananya, and every other Karnataka scientist you murdered."

Shadow hurled the hatchet at Zala, but the Reptile ducked just into time to avoid it. It lodged into the table behind her, right where Shadow wanted it to be. The huntress smiled and detonated the weapon, the shock wave shoving Zala to the ground. Bomber Dashed above her, fingers raised, beams forming. Orange light seared pearl-white tile as Zala slithered away, attempting an escape.

No. You're mine.

Shadow vaulted the table separating herself from the Reptile, Autorevolver raised and spouting bullets. Zala repeated her earlier maneuver, dodging and deflecting the bullets, but Shadow was upon her. Blades clashed as the downward swing of Shadow's WASP knife was halted by one of Zala's jile daggers, the point of the blade centimeters from the Reptile's face. Her other dagger collided with the barrel of Shadow's pistol, pushing it to the side just as Shadow squeezed the trigger again, expending another round. The Reptile flashed her needle-teeth at the huntress.

"That makesss sssix ssshots."

Shadow's reply was to compress her hand around the WASP knife handle. The knife's tip, still hovering above Zala's face, dispersed a blast of pressurized air, flash-freezing the outer layer of the creature's skin. Wailing, Zala stepped back, reaching for her steaming head.

"It's about Nancy, and Jeff, and *Phil!*" Battery cried as she approached, slamming her electrified, metal-studded fist into the Reptile's frozen face.

The flesh broke away in shards, tinkling across the tiled cafeteria floor as if they were pieces of glass. Revealed beneath the surface was Zala's green, scaly form, giving her an appearance similar to the fish-man from *The Creature from The Black Lagoon.* The creature devolved in its ability to communicate, crouching and hissing at her three attackers.

"It's about everyone at my precinct whose lives you stole. For what? FOR WHAT?" Battery seethed, embroiled in blue energy, her arms and legs creating crisp snaps in the empty air as Zala dodged her incoming strikes.

Shadow circled the melee and rose from behind their opponent, sliding her WASP knife into the spine of the distracted Reptile. Before she depressed its trigger, the creature backhanded her to the floor.

The moment Zala turned her attention toward Shadow, Battery stepped forward and kicked her in the chest. The green-eyed creature blurred, and she launched into the far wall of the cafeteria. Crippled, the Reptile slid to the floor. Battery called to her.

"And this? *This?*"

Something moved above Shadow, and her eyes tilted to see Bomber release himself from the ceiling, dropping upside-down until his face met Zala's. Beneath Shadow's Gaze, time slowed to a crawl during his fall, and he reached out to touch the center of Zala's forehead with his index and middle fingers.

"*This* is for Sam," he finished.

The orange light began at his fingertips, but it spread along Zala's lizard scales, illuminating her visage in a speckled starfield. By the time Bomber Dashed away, arresting his own fall, her entire head was glowing. Seemingly aware of her fate, swirling green Reptile eyes turned to the three Faction fighters. That smug, toothy grin returned, and one hand raised, as if to wave good-bye.

POP.

Zala's head exploded in a flash of flame and charred viscera. The decapitated corpse spurted blood from the stump, splashing the white wall behind it. Once the muscles relaxed, it curled onto the floor, lifeless. More blood poured across the floor, mingling with the dozens of other bodies strewn around the cafeteria.

Shadow snapped her fingers, drawing the others from their trance.

"Right. Bombs," Battery said, and they all dug into their bags.

Bomber found his first, lifting the melted and deformed device with a defeated look.

"I got too hot, I guess," he murmured.

The bomb Shadow removed from her bag was torn apart, riddled with stray bullets. She shook her head and set it on a nearby table.

"Well, at least we have . . ." Battery stopped as she located her own device—also been filled with enemy rifle rounds. "Christ on a bike, we are bad at this."

Shadow rubbed her temples while Bomber crossed his arms, glancing toward the exit.

"Maybe Aquifer found a solution?"

Aquifer found a solution.

PAUS didn't like it, though. The machine clicked and chirped, and he felt resistant feedback in the metal of his armor, rattling his bones. Still, he persisted, maintaining and reinforcing his creation.

Surrounding and enveloping the giant earthquake machine was a slanted column of clear water. Through the liquid, the torquing engine spun so fast that the individual gears were hardly visible. At the moment, the water amplified its vibrational effect, disrupting Aquifer's ultrasound field. He focused on building up a layer of subsonic barriers, mitigating the engine's distortion.

The scientist curved his arms, and the column around the machine began to swirl counterclockwise, forming a whirlpool across its entire length. At first, there was no response, and the water shimmered as its spinning was disrupted by the superior strength of the torquing engine. Quickly, though, the whirlpool increased in speed, outpacing the clockwise motion of the earthquake machine. A powerful current tugged against the gears and cylinders, and a horrific, mechanical wail filled the caverns.

Over the screeching of resisting metal, Aquifer heard familiar voices. Sweating, he turned his head to the right and spied his three teammates yelling through the water barrier that still protected the bridge. The scientist strained not to lose focus on his whirlpool tower as he dropped the wall, and his blue, white and orange-clad comrades approached.

"Any bombs still intact?" he yelled over the machine, teeth chattering from the feedback in his armor.

They shook their heads.

"Why are we so bad at this?"

They shrugged, and Shadow approached. [What are you doing?]

"RC cars."

[. . .what?]

"RC cars, they have a little engine inside their body that spins the wheel. If you try to spin the wheel while you hold it, though, that engine still keeps trying to move. Too much force with too little give, and eventually the whole machine breaks. All that pent-up torque has to go somewhere." His eyes drifted to the whirlpool tower surrounding the ever-slowing earthquake machine. "Why not right here?"

New vibrations shuddered up the walls of the cavern, forming hairline cracks in the rock. The bridge beneath their feet shook and groaned, throwing everyone off-balance.

"If that's the case, we need to get out of here!" Bomber yelled.

"No. I must maintain the whirlpool until the engine breaks." He met their eyes. "No half-measures."

Battery nodded, looking at Bomber and Shadow. "Then we stay here, with you."

A slab of rock fell and piled in front of the door they had come through.

"We're out of time, anyway," she added.

The others moved close, embracing the scientist, resisting the vibrations of his armor. Above their heads, the mechanisms in the earthquake machine slowed to a stop, its cries loud and shrill. Little by little, it bent and warped, tearing itself apart. Boulders fell around the team, and the machine fell with it, a dying behemoth collapsing into the abyss. As it passed their level, it swiped at the bridge, shredding it, and all four members of Treehouse plummeted to the darkness below.

———————————

Aquifer spent what felt like forever under a dark pressure, half-conscious. He regained his bearings and looked around, but everything was pitch-black.

"Shadow? Battery? Bomber?" he asked, his voice strained and weak.

In the distance Bomber replied, "Yo."

The space around Aquifer lit up a bright orange, revealing Bomber and Battery. Shadow was barely visible in the space beyond the light, but she appeared to be unconscious. Above them were piles and piles of rock, pressing down a few meters from their faces. Somehow, through chance or fate, a pocket of free space was left open where the four had fallen, protecting them within its stony tomb.

Aquifer felt an unbelievably sharp pain stir in his stomach, and he leaned away from his team, vomiting blood.

"Oh my God!" Battery cried, crawling toward him. "Are you okay?"

"It's . . . PAUS . . ." he said, wincing. "The vibrations . . . I think . . . I ruptured something."

Bomber's eyes glowed orange for a moment, and he nodded. "Yeah, you need medical attention."

"Okay." Aquifer thought for a moment. "How far below the ground are we?"

Bomber scanned the surface above and whistled. "Very."

"Well, what is the range of your Atomic Scissors?"

Bomber put a finger to his chin. "Well, I guess there isn't one, as long as the surface I'm touching is all connected."

"Good. Start cutting a circle into the rock above us all the way to the surface, big enough for everyone to fit through."

"Wait," Bomber frowned, "that'll cause it to collapse on us."

Aquifer offered a faint smile. "I'll take care of that."

He turned to Battery. "Get Shadow and hold her tight. This'll be a bumpy ride."

As Bomber cut into the stone above, Aquifer formed a column of water around everyone, following the line that the soldier was tracing. When Bomber was almost finished, Aquifer held out a hand. "Stop!"

Bomber paused. Above him, the outline began to crack, and silt rained upon their heads.

"Get down here, quick," Aquifer continued.

The soldier dropped to the ground while Aquifer completed his hollow column, the outer edges thick enough to hold up the sliding circle of earth. He left just enough space to fit his three teammates and himself. Grimacing, he lifted his hands into the air.

This is going to hurt so, so incredibly bad.

He pushed the column upward, lifting the cut stone like a jack lifting a car. Shifting a little, he filled the space beneath their feet with water so that they rose in tandem with the rock. Pain filled Aquifer's world, and it took every ounce of willpower not to double over and just give up.

No. They're counting on me.

What felt like hours passed by as they ascended, sliding through the vertical tunnel like a Basilisk slithering from its cave. Finally, daylight shone through the cracks above, and Aquifer shoved the remaining earth from its hole, propelling the team to the side and sending everyone tumbling onto the grass. Around them was a ring piled high with rock and dirt that Aquifer had forced from the ground, towering above them like a miniature mountain range.

Free of his responsibility, Aquifer collapsed, writhing in pain.

"Bomber," Battery commanded, still holding Shadow in her arms. "Help him. Let's get him somewhere we can fix him up."

Bomber stooped down and lifted Aquifer to his feet, wrapping one of the scientist's arms around his shoulders. Together, they stumbled forward, back into the forest, Battery and Shadow close behind.

Hours passed them by as they struggled their way back to the shrine. Aquifer's body felt like one giant bruise, and every small movement sent waves of pain rippling through him, forcing tears from his eyes.

The town in which they had begun finally poked through the trees ahead, and Proxy's transmissions were within range once more.

"Treehouse? Treehouse!"

"We're here, Proxy," Battery replied.

"Fiji's still safe. There were reports of an earthquake in your area, though. Is everyone okay? Did you find the machine?"

"We're okay, and the machine is gone," Bomber said. "Thanks to Aquifer."

Proxy paused for a moment before speaking. "Team, I have to tell you something. I'm getting reports from the coastal prefectures about the earthquake. It really took a toll on Tokyo, Miyagi, Fukushima and Ibaraki. A lot of people just lost their lives and homes in Japan."

Bomber stopped moving. "Are you serious?"

Battery walked past the two men, her jaw clenched, and they strode forward to catch up with her.

"Mutually-assured destruction," she growled.

"Listen, team," Proxy interrupted. "I want to make this very clear. The outcome of your mission is not lost on me. As far as I understand, the lives lost in Japan today were likely in the thousands. But Fiji is home to over a million people. Like it or not, Aquifer made a choice, and that choice saved far more lives than it ended."

Bomber turned to the man in his arms. "Did you hear that? You can't say your invention never brought peace. Look at the bigger picture. You're a hero, Nadi."

Aquifer's eyes welled up, and tears leaked down his face. He tried to wipe them away, but the movement caused spasms of pain, and he coughed up more blood. Ahead of the party, an old wooden shrine loomed, their gateway back home. Aquifer sniffled as they climbed its rickety stairs. Cut away from the world, light faded and noises dulled. In the ether, he felt Bogeyman's pull.

"That's . . . that's all I ever wanted," he whispered. "To *help* people."

Treehouse
December 21, 2012-B

The tinkling of laughter bounded along the dim halls and rooms of a house trapped in time and space. Treehouse was espoused with an amalgam of the more traditional Feliz Navidad and Pancha Ganapati decorations, along with the casual festivities of both Noël en France and the multinational Christmas. In lieu of choosing a specific holiday to celebrate during such a festive time, Treehouse chose to pick out their favorite parts of their customs, creating a new celebration amongst themselves. After much lighthearted debate, they referred to their holiday as "Giving Treehouse."

Sitting cross-legged in a circle along the floor, Quentin watched the team exchange their gifts. They had agreed each person received one item, given to them by another randomly chosen member of the team. Catalina went first, unwrapping a tubular package resembling an umbrella stand. Once the paper was torn away, she uncapped the tube and squinted inside.

"Don't keep us waiting, then!" Quentin insisted.

Catalina slid a short sword from its insulated package, a stubby katana in a black sheath with a black handle containing the word "Shadow" monogrammed in silver. Her face lit up in surprise, and she leapt to her feet, slipping the blade from its sheathe in one clean swipe. The metal glistened in the light, and Catalina looked around the room, expectant.

"Okay, okay, you caught me," Zen said. "I saw how excited you were fighting those 'demons' in Japan, and I noticed you didn't have any swords of your own. I did some research, finding this . . . 'wakazashi?' I'm not sure if I'm pronouncing it right. It's not practical, sure, but . . ."

She was interrupted as the small, black-clad woman jumped into her lap and kissed her on the mouth. Both women seemed surprised by the sudden display of affection, but they leaned into it, collapsing half-drunk onto the floor together. As they continued to kiss,

Quentin averted his eyes, and Nadi coughed uncomfortably.

"I suppose we can come back around to Zen's gift?" Quentin asked with a smile.

Nadi looked to Stacey. "You should go next."

Beaming, Stacey picked up a cube in the size and shape often used to hold small pieces of jewelry. He began to unwrap it, discovering a hinged black box inside. Before opening the box, he winked at Nadi.

"I'm sorry to hurt your feelings on Giving Treehouse. I like you, but I don't *like* you like you."

Nadi laughed and took another sip of wine. "Shut up and open it, Fields."

Stacey snapped open the box and removed its contents, a confused expression on his face. He held to the light a pair of silver mesh caps welded together, almost as if two thimbles had been fused side-by-side. One side of the strange device had a ring-shaped switch and a currently darkened LED light bulb. It took him a moment before his eyes grew wide. Holding up his middle and index fingers, he slipped the welded caps onto them. It was a snug, but comfortable, fit.

"Huh. Not to be rude, but I *am* curious . . . what is it?"

Nadi leaned in and looked at Quentin. "The two of us ended up working together on this one, just to be sure it was done right. Quentin was the one who noticed your difficulty engaging in long-distance combat with tougher Society enemies like the Coal Golems in Centralia. He and I enjoyed the prospect of giving you something stronger to use, rather than always having to rush into danger."

"It's just like Zen's belt, oui?" added Quentin. "She could subsist on a single charge in most cases before a mission, but being given a variable energy source to augment her abilities on the battlefield was much safer and more useful to the team. We wanted to give you your own Charge Belt, or rather . . ." He looked back at Nadi.

With a grand gesture, the scientist finished the sentence. "The Splitter."

Stacey looked at the thimble-like mechanism on his fingers. "The Splitter?"

Nadi nodded. "I won't dive too much into the specifics, since your abilities operate wholly on instinct and don't require an instruction manual. To be concise, The Splitter acts as a miniature particle accelerator, attracting a wider array of particles to your location, powered by those bonds you can tap into. When you activate that switch there—not right now!—The Splitter will accumulate and accelerate the mass around you at a much more proficient rate than you're currently capable of obtaining yourself. When the funnel wall is created, you should simply tap into your abilities and break apart the weakened atoms at the apex of The Splitter. The result, though it has yet to be tested live, should be a *far* more powerful version of your Atomic Gun. An Atomic Cannon, if you will."

Stacey slipped The Splitter from his fingers and into a zipped pocket of Sam's bomber jacket. "Are there any dangers? What about the overheating issue?"

Trading a glance with Nadi, Quentin said, "It's a possibility, as is any attempt to augment your powers. I would recommend reserving The Splitter for emergencies, if you can. We don't know the exact measure of damage it can cause, anyway."

Stacey laughed and shook his head. "This is incredible, guys. Really. I appreciate it so much. More than the gift, just having . . ."

He gestured to the circle, where Zen and Shadow were concluding their display of affection and sitting up again. "Just having my own dysfunctional family to be a part of during the holidays."

Everyone cheered to his comment and clinked their glasses.

[Who's next?] Catalina asked.

"Oh," Quentin said, chuckling to himself, "I think we're good."

Catalina glared at him. [I meant, who's next to open their gift.]

"I'll go!" Nadi exclaimed with a childlike eagerness.

He tore into an envelope addressed to his name and pulled out a booklet. Leafing through it, he looked up at the group, grinning. "Who did this? How did you know?"

Catalina raised her hand. [I pulled your private records using Quentin's computer. You used to be quite the fútbol fan back in Kerala, didn't you? Before Society pulled you into the Karnataka facility. That kind of passion doesn't disappear overnight.]

"You're damn right it doesn't. Blasters for life!"

[Of anyone in Treehouse, you've proven yourself to be the most competent in keeping yourself safe should you slip away to one of those games in that season pass booklet. Considering our busy schedule, you'll be able to make it to . . . what? Three games?]

Nadi laughed. "If that." He leaned it to hug her, and she stood still, allowing it for a few seconds. "Thank you, Catalina."

Quentin smiled. *I'm so happy to have people to celebrate with. People to care about. Other than Maddie, of course.*

"Two left," Bomber stated. "Zen and Quentin."

"I'll go," Quentin responded, grabbing his gift. "I'd like Zen to go last."

"Fine by me!" Zen said.

Quentin shook the small, rectangular box, frowning. *Not much noise. Something soft, or perhaps well-insulated . . . it isn't heavy, so likely clothing of some kind? What kind of clothing would—*He looked around the room, eliminating those who had already received their gifts. "What kind of clothing would Stacey get me?"

The group laughed, and Stacey reached for the box. "Just open it before I do!"

Quentin offered a sheepish shrug and tore apart the wrapping, slipping the lid from the container. When he saw the items inside, his pulse quickened with joy.

"I noticed you liked wearing them," Stacey began, "So I thought—"

"Maddie!" Quentin interrupted in his excitement. *"Here, girl!"*

Nails clacked against hard flooring, and the half-blind Dutch Shepherd emerged from the main bedroom, wagging her question-mark tail. When she was within reach, he lifted a small purple scarf tailored for dogs, wrapping it around her neck. Once he was satis-fied with how it looked, Quentin retrieved a second scarf from the box for himself, donning and adjusting it until it was snug against his skin.

"Beau! Magnifique!" he exclaimed, before turning to Stacey. "Thank you, mon amie."

Maddie turned to walk away, tired of the attention, but Quentin drew her in for a final hug and kiss on the forehead before releasing her. Sighing, he twirled his purple scarf in an absent manner.

"One more," Nadi whispered as a quiet reminder.

"Ah! Yes! From me to you, Zen," Quentin said, broken from his trance. He gestured to a large rectangular box in front of her.

Zen leaned over and lifted it, huffing at its weight. "Finally, my very own brick collection!" she said with a twinge of playful sarcasm.

Paper ripped as she pulled the wrapping from the box, and she stopped, frozen, when she saw the top half of what lay beneath. In a slow, cautious movement, Zen continued to pull apart the gift until it was fully exposed.

Before her was a wooden display case with a glass lid designed to illustrate its contents. Within the case were a variety of metal badges and counterfeit law enforcement IDs, all in different shapes and designs and languages. Opening the case, Zen lifted a counterfeit FBI badge with a fake name and a photograph of her on it.

"I know how much being a detective meant to you," Quentin explained in hushed tones. "I can't give that back to you, but I *can* give you something that allows you to continue the path when undercover and on long missions. Before you are a series of law enforcement badges tailored to you, retrieved with the help of most of our friendly Faction cells. They span every major country and will help you do what you do so well when duty calls."

Zen looked at Quentin with tears in her eyes. "Quentin . . . I have no words. This means so much. You even . . . you even . . ."

She couldn't finish her sentence. Instead, she stood and went downstairs, to the basement. A moment later, Zen returned with her beat-up NYPD detective badge. Holding it above the display case, she set it down in the one empty space between the other U.S. badges and IDs. Her fingers released the badge, leaving it in its new home. "Perfect."

Games and more drinking ensued, and by three o'clock, Quentin was exhausted. They cleaned up and staggered to sleep, Shadow leading Battery back into her room.

It's about damn time, he thought.

A moment later, Bomber came up to Quentin and tapped his shoulder. He hadn't held his alcohol as well, and it seemed to be taking every ounce of willpower for him to just stand and speak.

"Hey . . . I mean it . . . you guys're the best family I could ask for." He wrapped Sam's jacket tighter around his lean body and sniffled. "Almost two years now . . . it never gets easier . . ."

Quentin embraced the young man, pulling their forms together. "It may never go away completely. Just keep doing what would make Sam proud of you. That includes making sure *you* stay happy, doesn't it?"

Stacey nodded and backed away. "I . . . I love you guys."

"We love you too, Stacey. Get some rest, okay?"

The former soldier staggered off to his room. As he entered, Quentin saw Nadi sitting on the kitchen counter, swirling his wine glass.

"Yes?" Quentin said.

"It's been nine months since Japan, Quentin. I know we've kept busy since then, but nothing has been so pressing that we should ignore the threat under our noses."

Quentin sighed. "The hotel. I know. But it isn't a simple decision to make."

"Simple? I risked drowning dozens of coworkers just to guarantee saving six. I sacrificed tens of thousands of lives in Japan to save hundreds of thousands in Fiji. I may not have known the exact outcome of my decisions each time, but I sure as hell knew the risks. And I don't regret it for one moment, not after this accumulation of failures we've experienced at Society's hands."

"Still, Nadi." Quentin shook his head, sitting down on the living room couch. "We know the hotel houses real, human people at any given time, as do the surrounding buildings. No amount of control given to a demolition would guarantee citizen safety, not with such a tall structure. How many lives are we willing to sacrifice to take out a target?"

"How many people has it already eaten, whose bodies it repurposed into killing machines and terrorists? It's not just about destroying a building. It's about stopping this body-swapping madness."

Quentin held up a hand to stop the scientist's heated commentary. "Okay. I get it. We'll convene after the holidays and set up a game plan. One that *minimizes* the loss of civilian life."

"Of course, Quentin. Of course."

California, United States
January 31, 2013-B

Rats skittered across the moist, grimy pipes running along the sewer tunnels beneath the streets of Los Angeles, creating small pattering noises in Proxy's speakers. In his monitors, four pairs of boots splashed along the presumably foul-smelling sewage, highlighted by thin flashlight beams that swept the concrete tunnels.

"Okay, here," Aquifer said, referring to the device in his hands. "We're right below."

They stood beneath a four-way intersection of tunnels, their cameras aiming at the walls and ceiling. Aquifer gestured with his hands, and a clear film of fresh water rose from the sludge, its pressure creating a solid platform for them to stand on. Each person lifted into the air high enough to reach the concrete above their heads. The scientist pointed at three spots along the ceiling, and they began to fasten their satchels to those areas.

"How many?" Bomber whispered into his transmitter while he worked.

Proxy sighed. "Between sixty to a hundred. We tried choosing a slow night, but it's difficult when we don't know how many residents are already Bellhops."

"Yeah, it's just . . . I don't like how *deliberate* this feels."

[That's because it *is* deliberate,] Shadow signed through her button camera. [We have a target and we need to take it out. There is no better night for minimal casualties than tonight.]

"Tough choices, remember?" Aquifer asked, his video feed backing away from his completed device.

"Tough choices," Bomber replied with uncertainty, connecting a final wire.

"Can we clear the area around the building before we detonate?" Battery asked. "A small panic could minimize losses."

Through Battery's camera, Shadow shook her head. [It's too risky. If Society catches on, they might disarm the bombs and heighten security before we can detonate. This is much safer.]

Battery completed her explosive and pulled her hands away from the ceiling. "In that case, how far away should we . . ."

Like a low-magnitude earthquake, a rumbling sound emanated from the sewer tunnels, filling Proxy's speaker so loudly that they rattled against his desk. He heard a distant voice in their microphones, a voice that grew louder and closer with each passing second. The disembodied sound washed across them, rattling his speakers once more.

OHHHMMMMMMMMMMM . . .

Proxy leaned into the monitors, eyes wide. Part of Aquifer's camera swept the ceiling, where black, hair-like tendrils burrowed through the concrete and wrapped around the four mounted explosives. Within seconds, the grey rocked peeled away, and the bombs were sucked upward and out of sight.

"Aquifer, shield!" Battery commanded. *"Shadow, detonate!"*

They acted as a unit, drawing together into a huddle. Proxy saw Shadow press a button on her remote, while Aquifer formed a protective water dome around them to block them from the explosion and debris. His shield proved unnecessary, however; the sounds of bombs igniting was distant and muffled, failing to produce even a vibration in the tunnels.

There was, however, a different reaction from the tunnels. Where the explosives had been swallowed, streams of fire fled from the holes, tracing a branching pattern into the ceiling, reminiscent of a tree's root system. The lines continued down every direction of the intersection until they were out of sight.

"No . . . No, no, no," Aquifer said, dropping the shield. "The hotel doesn't extend that far."

OHHHMMMMMMMMMMMM . . .

More black tendrils appeared, each forming from an opening behind The Faction members. Chunks of living hair wrapped around arms and legs, necks and mouths, pulling them apart and into the walls of the sewer tunnels. As they were pulled upward, dragging along the rock, the craters in the walls sealed shut and blackened Proxy's monitors, aligning their fate with that of *The Cask of Amontillado*'s poor Fortunato.

Proxy rushed to pull up as many security cameras aimed at the Hotel Cecil's windows as he could access, trying to find alternative perspectives of the team. From his speakers—creaking and grinding and cracking. He donned a headset, opting to focus on one teammate at a time.

Bomber's monitor was the first to produce an image as he escaped his attacker. The screen flashed a fiery orange, and the darkness exploded, jettisoning the soldier and his camera out into a carpeted hallway. The hotel groaned and cried, and Proxy's ears filled with terrified screams and horrific wet, slurping sounds.

"Where is that coming from?" he asked.

In the monitor, Bomber's arm appeared, pointing toward guest room doors. "I'm expecting company."

Bomber climbed to his feet and turned to the other side of the hallway, where a sign indicated he was on the fifth floor of the hotel. Approaching him, face plastered with a fearful and cautious expression, was a young woman with Cantonese features wearing a red zippered hoodie, black shorts, and sandals.

The distant screaming in Proxy's ears faded away as the woman reached Bomber.

"What's wrong with everyone?" she whispered, gesturing to the rooms.

Bare footsteps approached the hotel room doors, marching in unison. Bomber gripped the young woman and pulled her around the hallway corner, blocking Quentin's line of sight of any rooms. Beyond their vision, door handles twisted, pulling the barriers apart, and bodies shuffled out. Voices whispered at first, then grew in volume, sharing in unholy hunger.

"Who are they?" the woman squeaked, visibly frightened.

The camera angled toward her face as Bomber looked down. "No one for you to worry about if I can help it, Miss . . ."

"Lam. My name is Elisa Lam."

Just then, there was a blue flash of light in Battery's monitors, and the woman burst through the wall, thudding to the floor. Proxy pulled away from Bomber to watch her.

"Treehouse, I'm inside the Cecil Hotel, somewhere around floor ten," she said. "What's your status? Is anyone in immediate danger?"

Proxy switched his headset to her earpiece. "Bomber's fine. The others are still in the walls. I'm working on finding—"

"Ever the protector, aren't you, Detective?" a gravelly voice interrupted.

Battery's camera spun, her arms rising in a defensive stance. At the other end of the hall was a man with grey, fuzzy skin, hidden by jeans, a loose white shirt, and a grey knit cap. His eyes were round and black, a shark's eyes, and he had the teeth to match. The man flexed his fingers; they were also grey and fuzzy, but Proxy knew from Battery's stories what dangers they posed.

"Now, why on earth are you hurting our beloved Cecil?" he demanded.

Beneath the Chimera's shirt, something twitched and stirred.

"Battery, get out of there," Proxy commanded. "Don't engage the Chimera alone."

Shadow's monitor flickered into view, and Proxy glanced at it in the corner of his eye. Where she landed was a group of nude men and women, their ages and ethnicities varied, all smiling that insane Bellhop smile Proxy had become—unfortunately—accustomed to. They clustered at the other end of the hallway, aiming a mixture of rifles and pistols in Shadow's direction. Where the weapons came from, Proxy couldn't imagine. Perhaps the hotel had weapon and equipment caches for new Bellhops?

As one unit, the naked Bellhops stepped forward, fingers on the triggers of their weapons. They were at least ten long strides from Shadow's reach, and she was armed with nothing more than her wakizashi.

Proxy returned his attention to Battery's monitor, nonplussed. *She can handle that.*

". . . need to understand the mistake you're making," the Chimera was saying. "If you hurt our darling Cecil, she's going to hurt a lot of people. See, the way she's built . . ."

Water splashed in Proxy's speaker, and he turned toward Aquifer's monitor. The scientist had broken out, but he was facing a man in a navy-blue suit smiling from ear-to-ear, his eyes widened like a maniac.

"Mr. Singh?" Proxy heard Aquifer ask.

The man's smile grew wider. "Mother welcomes you, Mr. Acharya."

Proxy glanced toward Bomber and Shadow's monitors, but they were both locked in combat with the naked, gun-wielding Bellhops. He turned back to Aquifer's conversation.

"Cecil asks that we put aside our differences and cohabitate," Singh said. "Let me show you why."

"No!" Battery cried into her transmitter, distracting Proxy. "You fucking monster. All of you, monsters."

"What? What did the Chimera say?" Proxy asked, but she didn't respond.

". . . are you talking about?" Aquifer was saying to Singh.

Raising one hand, Singh splayed his fingers toward the wall. Blood began to dribble from beneath his fingernails and cuticles, announcing the eruption of more of those hair-like tendrils the hotel produced. The strands whipped out from his fingertips, tracing an image against the plaster as if it were an Etch-A-Sketch. The first object to form was a miniature model of the Cecil Hotel. "We are here, see? You see?"

Using the hair-tendrils, Singh drew wiggly lines out from the base of the hotel, fanning them in all directions. Around the hotel and lines, he sketched an outline of Los Angeles, California, the entire West Coast. Those wiggly lines persisted, branching along the map like the root system of a tree.

"Do you see, Mr. Acharya?"

Aquifer stepped away from the image. "No . . . that's impossible. How could no one know?"

"No one stays alive long enough to tell."

Proxy squinted at the map. "What am I seeing?"

"The creature that composes this hotel set out roots along the West Coast," Aquifer explained. "Those roots serve a purpose; I assume that purpose is structural in nature?"

"Now you see, Mr. Acharya," replied Singh. "Mother will never die, but should she be . . . weakened . . . by your pathetic attacks, she only needs to release her roots. If that was her wish, twenty percent of this country would find themselves collapsing into a sinkhole, a mass grave for millions . . . in an instant."

"Mutually-assured destruction," Aquifer muttered.

"Yes, Mr. Acharya." Singh's grin grew impossibly wider.

The scientist raised his hand, a water orb hovering in the air. "Okay. I'll settle for you, Singh."

Proxy shook his head and turned away from Aquifer's monitor. *More fighting. Always more fighting.*

"Elisa, right?" Bomber said. He turned to look through the soldier's camera, where a dozen Bellhop bodies were smoking on the floor.

The woman nodded.

"They're gone for the moment. But you aren't safe inside this hotel."

"How do you know?" she asked.

"Just trust me, for now. I want you to move quickly, but calmly, so as not to draw attention to yourself. Try to be as casual as possible."

Elisa looked around. "Where am I going?"

"Take the elevator straight to the roof. Once I find my team, we'll meet you there and take you somewhere safer. But *be careful.* There are, quite literally, eyes everywhere."

Elisa looked above the camera, presumably at Bomber's face, then glanced back down the empty hall, toward the elevator. Bomber nudged her. "See you soon, Elisa."

Gunfire ceased in Shadow's speaker. Her Bellhops were dead, too, covered in bullet holes and stab wounds. From what he could tell, she had stolen several of her enemies' firearms during her battle, and she was heading toward the stairwell.

"Where are you going?" Proxy asked.

Shadow stopped for a moment to sign into the camera. [Battery's on floor ten.]

Proxy glanced through Battery's camera to check up on her. The detective seemed to have finished her conversation with the Chimera, because they were now engaged in super-powered hand-to-hand combat. He peeked at Aquifer; a similar confrontation was taking place.

This is getting exhausting, and I'm not even there.

More Bellhops appeared in Bomber's monitor, and the soldier traded their bullets with his lasers in the hallway, Dashing around so his video feed was just a blur.

Proxy closed his eyes and rubbed his temples. "Team, this is a nightmare. Disengage and move to the closest exit for Bogeyman recall. We aren't gleaning anything from this experience."

Metal clacked simultaneously in two speakers—Shadow was joining Battery's fight. The huntress fired a machine pistol at the Chimera, and Proxy sat back, watching the evolved conflict unfold.

The stream of bullets disappeared into the Chimera's feathers, not damaging him. Shadow dropped her pistol and gripped the handle of an assault rifle slung around her shoulder, firing it from the hip. As he avoided the attack, Battery kicked him in the back of the knee, and he collapsed. The detective wrapped the man into a headlock and pulled him to his feet, giving Shadow an easier target. Before the rifle rounds could connect, his wings flexed, breaking them apart, and he dove low, allowing Shadow's attack to bounce along Battery's torso.

The huntress sprinted at the winged man, finishing her volley of machine-gun fire. As she drew closer, she unslung the rifle and swung it like a baseball bat at his knees. He moved to stop her, but Battery darted behind him and clapped her hands against his ears, her super-strength producing a shock wave loud enough to ring Proxy's eardrums.

God, that must have hurt a lot.

The Chimera reached for his head, and Shadow's attack continued unabated, cracking against his kneecap. Howling, the winged man fell to his injured knee as Shadow dropped her rifle, sliding another pistol from the waistband of her jeans. She jammed the barrel into his bare chest and pulled the trigger multiple times, but something black hardened where her gun touched him, deflecting the bullets and warping the pistol. He swiped at Shadow, who flew away and crumpled into a heap against the nearest wall, turning Proxy's view of the battle through her camera sideways.

"Shadow!" Battery cried, wrapping her hands around the man's face and driving her knee into his spine.

Something cracked, but he just smirked, biting into one of her fingers with razor-sharp teeth. He didn't seem to break the skin, but she cried out in pain and released him. Stretching, the man stood, re-aligning his spine in the process with a series of hollow pops.

"Cecil?" he asked, looking upward.

OHHHMMMMMMMMMMMM . . .

A hole opened in the ceiling, then in the ceiling above it, then the one above *it*, creating a straight line all the way to the night sky a hundred feet above their heads. With one flap of his wings, the man was airborne, travelling through the holes. Battery leapt to intercept, but he kicked her onto her back before blasting through the hotel and into the open air.

"Damn it!" Proxy yelled, slapping the table. "You almost had him."

Battery finally replied to him, her voice raspy and her breathing heavy. "At least, that's what he wanted us to think."

Okay. That accounts for Shadow and Battery. So, Bomber . . .

Proxy looked at Bomber's monitor. The man was alone again, sprinting up the stairwell toward the roof, just as he had promised Elisa.

He's good. Aquifer . . .

He glanced for a second then performed a double take, horrified. Aquifer had pinned Singh to the wall with a vibrating slab of suspended water and was . . . *sanding* him? The pressure must have been incredibly high, because the water was eating away at Singh's body. Bits of muscle and bone flew away from the Bellhop's arms while he tried to shove the wall away, but he was no match for Aquifer's invention.

The scientist lifted his arms in front of his camera and maintained a hold on the wall, adding pressure to grind down the body of the hive-mind creature before him. Singh's arms were stumps now, the hair-like tendrils lifeless, and the wall was eating into his chest and face. He turned one skinned cheek to Aquifer, still smiling, his cheekbones exposed.

"Praise her, Mr. Acharya. Praise to Mother Cipactli." And then he was gone, a bloody paste pressurized into the red-stained wall.

Proxy felt a little sick. "Team, Bomber's headed to the roof. Join him there and jump toward a nearby Bogeyman point. We need to reconvene." He watched Shadow, Battery and Aquifer run to the nearest stairwells, beginning their climb.

Bomber was already on the roof now, and he appeared to be searching around. Proxy leaned toward the soldier's monitor and squinted. There was nothing on-screen other than pipes, water towers, and a bunch of empty space. Elisa was nowhere to be found.

"Elisa?" Bomber yelled. *"Elisa!"*

No response.

Proxy switched to Bomber's earpiece. "Maybe use your Atomic vis—"

"Already did. She's not here."

Proxy sighed and ran his fingers through his hair. "Where could she have gone?"

He heard wood tearing and rolled his chair back, observing all four monitors at once. The other three operatives burst through the rooftop entrance and joined Bomber, stopping to catch their breaths.

"Did you hear what the Chimera said about the hotel?" Battery panted into her transmitter. "About Cecil?"

"You mean the root system?" asked Proxy. "Singh was talking to Aquifer about it—"

"Wait, Singh's here?" she interrupted. "No, never mind. I'm talking about the other thing."

"I'm sorry," Proxy said, furrowing his brow. "This mission was particularly difficult to parse. What did he say?"

"He said Cecil used to be a person. This building used to be a *human.*"

Proxy laughed. "You're messing with me."

"Why would he lie?" Aquifer asked, shrugging.

"Good point." Proxy frowned. "That's very disconcerting."

Bomber was still staggering around the rooftop, his head on a swivel.

"Who are you looking for?" Battery asked.

"I met a civilian trying to escape," the soldier replied. "I sent her to the roof so we could extract her, but she isn't here. I don't think she made it."

The rooftop creaked, and the team turned their cameras toward the water towers. The structures peeled back and opened, launching black tendrils their way.

"No time to look now!" Battery yelled.

She took a running leap and jumped off the roof, Shadow clasped tightly around her neck. Bomber followed them, Dashing to the neighboring roof below. Battery and Shadow weren't far behind him, colliding with the new building with a thunderous *crash*. Seconds later, it began to rain, and then Aquifer was with them, carried aloft by a leaking water platform. He collapsed next to the other three.

"What a waste," the scientist murmured. "We'll never stop Cecil."

"Not without ending millions of lives in the process," Battery lamented.

"Hell, I couldn't save *one* life," Bomber said, glancing at the hotel above them.

[Not a total waste, though,] Shadow signed, holding out a handheld device where Proxy could see it. The GPS tracker flickered, revealing a red dot bouncing away from their location at a high speed, leaving the U.S. and crossing the ocean.

"What is that?" Aquifer asked.

Shadow responded by forming the symbol for "bird" with her hands in front of her camera.

Proxy laughed and shook his head. "You're crazy, Shadow. You got close to him for *that*? I love it."

I'm just happy you all made it out alive, he thought to himself.

"Well, team," he continued, "I suppose it's obvious what we're doing next. Go gear up and knock on this fucker's front door."

Manta, Ecuador
February 10, 2013-B

Water lapped against the bay of the Autoridad Portuaria de Manta, half-hearted in its tidal force; the loudness of the wet slaps was odd, considering how little effort the Pacific Ocean seemed to exert. Birds cawed overhead, seeking food, shelter, and mates. The sun shone with its natural confidence, and there wasn't a cloud in sight.

This would be a great spot to relax today, Battery thought. *Well, if it weren't for him.*

She directed her attention to a young Ecuadorian, red-faced and arguing in Spanish with Aquifer, who was waving a stack of cash in the man's face. From what little she could pick up, the man didn't seem comfortable selling one of his boats to Treehouse, as the team was unfamiliar to him. Aquifer attempted to erode his stubbornness, but it only angered the man more.

Bomber huffed next to her. "We need that boat. It's the only quiet way onto the island."

The island he referred to was Isla Isabela, the largest of the Galápagos Islands. In the last ten days, the winged man had spent the most time at this location, making it a natural target for Treehouse. Whether it was a home, a military base, or something else, Proxy was confident they would find something valuable on the island.

If they could just obtain a goddamn boat.

Battery stepped over to Aquifer and the young man, tapping the latter on the shoulder. He turned to her, annoyed, and she flashed her new Policía Nacional del Ecuador badge in his face. Aquifer said something else in Spanish, and the other man finally caved, accepting the scientist's money. Proxy spoke up in their radio earpieces as they made their exchange.

"Don't forget to get one with a below-deck cabin. I want to be able to get you home in a pinch."

The man rolled his eyes at Aquifer's additional request, but obliged. Treehouse loaded their duffel bags of equipment onto the white, cuddy cabin cruiser, thanking the seller as they migrated aboard. It wasn't long before they pushed themselves out to sea and were on their way.

The Pacific Ocean
February 11, 2013-B

Bomber whistled, blocking the sun from his eyes despite already wearing sunglasses. "One day down, one to go."

Battery nodded, sharing his impatience. Since Proxy could not locate a Bogeyman transport point on the island, he had to identify the simplest path to their destination. The only commercial route to Isla Isabela was by airplane or helicopter, but such a vessel would be difficult to obtain and impossible to use in a stealthy manner. Their next choice was by boat, but no official paths were marked between Ecuador and the Galapagos Islands by sea, so they planned their own journey.

Their long, boring, forty-eight-hour journey.

Battery turned to Shadow, who nodded, and they lined up in front of each other, fists raised. Battery clipped her Charge Belt around her waist and activated it, feeling the blue ecstasy wash over her body. She gritted her teeth and reminded herself to stay grounded.

"I'll always have my shadow," she reminded herself aloud. Shadow smiled and winked.

Bomber frowned. "Uh, what's about to happen?"

"Don't worry about it," Aquifer replied. "Come, play chess with me."

The soldier wandered out of Battery's field of vision, and she turned back to Shadow. The huntress had already closed the gap between them and was extending her arms for a palm strike. Battery tried to block it, but she was too late. Shadow's palm slammed into her windpipe, and for a moment, Battery felt as if she had swallowed rocks.

"Not this time," she choked, spinning to the deck of the boat with a leg sweep. Shadow effortlessly hopped over the attack as if were a playful game of jump rope, smiling.

Battery tumbled forward, shoving her hands into Shadow's midsection before her opponent reached the ground. Shadow flew across the boat, catching herself at the last moment to avoid going overboard. The huntress made a face Battery had never seen before.

Is that . . . respect? As if to respond, Shadow dove toward her bags of equipment and withdrew a sawed-off double-barreled shotgun, rushing toward the detective. *Oh, that's how you're gonna play.*

Repeating her trick in Hotel Cecil, she waited until Shadow was within range and slammed her hands together, creating a thunderclap loud enough to leave her own ears ringing. Shadow backed away, the sonic affecting her balance on the swaying boat, and Battery went in for the kill.

She moved to tackle Shadow into submission, but she was too slow. Her partner flattened herself on her back as Battery loomed over her, and when Battery tried to pin her, she shoved the shotgun under Battery's chin and pulled the trigger.

Everything went white, and Battery found herself staggering, unable to hear anything. Soon, blue sparks filled her vision and her mind returned to the boat. The repairs from her attack flooded her senses, and she fell to the deck, digging her fingers into the wood.

Hurt her . . . Destroy her . . .

"Yo, chill out!" she heard Bomber yell. The voice sounded miles away. "We're playing a game over here."

Battery glanced behind her and saw the two men embroiled in a game of chess. Bomber was losing, badly; Aquifer wasn't pulling any punches. Amused, Battery snorted.

No. Your shadow's always beside you. She took a deep breath, closing her eyes, and allowed her mind to settle. *That's it. You're in control.*

Nearby footsteps attracted her attention, and she looked up to see Shadow standing over her, extending a hand. Battery grabbed it and stood, noticing the huntress's other hand hosted her still-smoking shotgun. She made eye contact with Shadow. "That's not really—"

A small wave washed over the bow of the boat, drenching them, and they screamed at the cold seawater sticking to their clothes. Chess pieces floating past Battery's feet, and she turned toward Aquifer and Bomber's dismayed faces. Suddenly, Bomber perked up and extended his arm for a handshake.

"Why don't we just call it a tie?" he asked.

Aquifer rolled his eyes and gestured with his hands, sending a tickling ultrasound pulse to wipe away the unexpected moisture. "Sure, whatever."

Battery sat cross-legged on the deck, Shadow lying down with her head in Battery's lap. The detective played with the huntress's hair absently as she watched the stars, admiring the smog-free night sky.

"It's a shame Quentin can't see this," she said.

Her partner met her eyes. [He's a strong man. The strongest I know. He manages. Plus, he always has Maddie.]

"Still . . ."

"Hey," Bomber interrupted, "I just wanted to say good night. We have a big day tomorrow."

The soldier made a "peace" sign with his fingers, crawling into his orange sleeping bag.

Aquifer backed away from the stern, a steaming cup of coffee in his hands. "I guess I shouldn't caffeinate right now, then."

Battery squinted at him. "Where on earth did you get—you know what, I don't care."

He chuckled. "Anyway, sleep is for the—"

His voice faded as a ringing filled Battery's ears—a distant, high-pitched whine, like the noise that old-fashioned television sets emit when they first power on. She looked around, and saw Shadow and Aquifer doing the same. Bomber crawled out of his sleeping bag, rubbing his eyes, and he said something Battery couldn't hear.

The boat seemed to flip upside-down, and the team grabbed the edges of the vessel, steadying themselves. An afterimage of their boat appeared over their heads, complete with ghostly copies of the Treehouse operatives. Battery reached her right arm above her head, and her duplicate did the same, stretching back in her direction. They were now no more than a meter apart. Battery tensed her legs, closing her eyes.

Why not?

She jumped, and their fingers touched.

A prickling numbness traveled down her hand in an instant, spreading past her wrist and forearm and bicep and shoulder, stretching for her neck before she separated from her doppelgänger. Now lightheaded, Battery crashed to the deck of the ship, landing on her back. She blinked the stars from her eyes and looked back at the afterimage, whose right arm was disintegrating. Much to her surprise, her phantom twin looked away, staring at her arm in horror.

The apparition vanished.

Silence filled the night once more. Aquifer and Bomber stood still, staring up at the stars, and Shadow moved to Battery's side, helping her to her feet. Bomber finally looked at the women, a dazed expression on his face.

"What the hell was that?" he asked.

Battery shook her head. The sensation was returning to her arm, and she flexed her fingers, feeling the pins and needles fade away. "We don't really know."

"It's not the first time it's happened, though," Aquifer explained. "It happened back in Gold Hill, too."

[And Abottabad,] added Shadow. [And New York. And Guatapé. It's followed us for at least thirteen years.]

"The thing is, no one else seems to notice or care," Aquifer said. "But the phenomenon keeps happening. Sometimes it helps us find things, sometimes it makes missions difficult, and sometimes . . . it's just weird. Neutral. Like tonight."

"Do you think it's . . . dangerous?" Bomber asked. "Some kind of Society attack?"

Aquifer emitted a low chuckle. "Spending my time with The Faction has led me to assume *everything's* dangerous."

"Especially something that seems so harmless," Battery commented. "We should study this when it happens again, and we'll try to understand it better. If we know what it is, we can use it to our advantage in the future."

At that, the group fell silent, gathering to one side of boat to appreciate the warm air and ocean spray.

The Pacific Ocean
February 12, 2013-B

"Pssst. Hey. Wake up."

Battery unfurled her arms from around Shadow's slender form as Bomber whispered. When her eyes opened, she saw him move to return Aquifer to the land of the conscious. She leaned over and whispered in Shadow's ear for her to wake, and the huntress stirred.

"What is it?" Aquifer asked.

"We're here already!" was Bomber's reply.

The team scrambled up the steps of the cabin, rushing to the boat's bow. There, still almost a speck in the distance, was the tall mountain composing most of Isla Isabela. It was hardly visible in the night sky, but Battery's attention was drawn to a swiveling red light atop the mountain.

Some kind of lighthouse, perhaps?

She squinted. The light was far too narrow to be a spotlight or lighthouse beam. No, it was far more similar to a laser-light or pointer.

"I think we should keep our own lights off for now," Battery said, and the others agreed, snuffing out the cabin light below deck and sitting above-deck in total darkness, waiting.

[I'd feel more comfortable suited up. I suggest you do the same,] Shadow signed to the others as she headed to her duffel bags.

Battery followed suit, shrugging the blue and copper padding over her body and clasping her Charge Belt around her waist. Around her, the team prepared, donning their pearl-white machinery and flowing phantasmal attire and sentimental orange outerwear.

Shadow retrieved a long tube-like container that caught Battery's eye.

"What's that for?" Battery asked.

Shadow smiled as she signed. [Something special I made for a mutual friend of ours.]

Battery shrugged, and Shadow collected the contents of yet another duffel bag and assembled its pieces. Soon she had put together a humongous rifle with a series of straps and handles she connected to herself as a means to support its weight. Once secured, Shadow inserted a lunchbox-sized magazine into the ammunition receptacle, locking it in place.

"You sure your gun is big enough?" Battery grinned. "I think we could score a couple rocket launchers if you want."

[Maybe next time.]

Now prepared, Battery and her teammates stood at the bow of the boat, watching Isla Isabela draw closer and closer. Small waves tilted the vessel back and forth, and Battery felt herself having to grip the edge of the bow to keep herself from stumbling. Finally, the shifting stopped, and she stood straight, tightening her studded gloves.

"We'll be docking at Puerto Villamil," she announced. "The city's been abandoned for years for no apparent reason, and incomplete data about the location made it an untrustworthy Bogeyman target. We'll want to stay sharp at the port. I'm assuming the entire island will be against us."

As if to address her assumption, something red filled her peripheral vision, blinding her for a moment. She looked up to see the light at the top of the island's mountain focused on their boat, flickering as if it were processing information. The team tensed, and it maintained its scan for a moment before disappearing, plunging them back into total darkness. Waves lapped the boat over their heavy breathing, breaking the stillness.

There were a series of hollow explosions, as if someone had fired an air cannon at them. Tufts of smoke rose from each launch point near the island shore facing their boat, and three small objects arced across the sky at them.

"INCOMING!" Bomber cried, and they dove to the deck.

Three objects plunked into the water in a triangular formation around their boat, the entry so smooth and slight the surface was barely disrupted. Battery and the rest of Treehouse scrambled to the side of the boat, but the objects were below the line of visible light now, sinking fast.

Before she could relax, bubbles rose to their level, fizzing like Alka-Seltzer tablets. Aquifer made a confused face, then stepped back and groaned.

"Oh, no . . ."

A silhouette the length and width of a city bus bumped the underside of the boat, rocking the vehicle. Aquifer was already gesturing to his PAUS, creating an unnatural tide toward the island and away from the creatures hiding just out of sight. The boat moved a few extra meters before their progress halted, held in place by a sticky, white proboscis attached to the stern of the boat.

Shadow leaned over the railing and fired her giant machine gun at the proboscis, shredding its root-like ends to pieces and relinquishing the thing's grip on their vessel. They sped forward, away from the trio of charging giant worms, but the creatures gained ground with every heartbeat. Shadow and Bomber unleashed a volley of bullets and laser beams into the water, but the worms were unfazed, swirling around the attacks without losing traction.

In the corner of her eye, Battery caught a sharp obstacle jutting from the water's surface ahead. "AQUIFER! ROCK!" she cried.

Aquifer steered them around it, rocking and slowing the boat. The three purple worms emerged from the water, attempting to crawl onto the deck toward its crew. Battery joined Shadow and Bomber's assault on the creatures, but their heavy, slimy bodies absorbed the punishment with ease, and they stuck to the boat. Aquifer picked up speed, and the drag against the water pulled the worms free, dropping them beneath the ocean's surface once more.

Bomber turned to the de facto captain and reached into his jacket pocket. "Aquifer, do that again. Let them try to jump at us another time."

He raised the Splitter for the scientist to see, pinching the device between his thumb and forefinger. Aquifer nodded, slowing down once more. With Shadow, Battery retreated from the bow, while Bomber slipped the Splitter over his middle and index fingers, activating its ring switch. The tiny LED bulb turned green, illuminating his hand as his made a "finger gun" gesture toward the incoming worms. Battery held her breath.

Bomber's body began to glow orange, but the aura quickly faded to a dark green. A speck of green light formed in the air in front of his outstretched Splitter, growing in size. It started as a grain of sand, then a marble, then a golf ball, baseball, and basketball, settling at beach-ball-size. All sound in the immediate area was sucked into the green ball of light. Energy reverberated back in pulses, blowing the rest of the Treehouse team backward and whipping the tails of Sam's jacket around Bomber's slender frame. Heat from the ball expanded outward, and steam rose from the water around the boat.

Beyond the stern, the three ribbon worms jumped as a single cluster once more, aiming at the boat. Bomber's finger twitched, and the beach ball expanded into a column of green energy, rushing to meet the attackers. The thick beam punched through each worm, and they blackened into flakes of ash in a second. The water around them burst into steam, and the beam curved up, piercing a cloud in the sky with enough power to puff it out into a doughnut shape. It continued out into space, exploding beyond the atmosphere in a crack of green light, illuminating the ocean around them.

Then, night returned.

Bomber collapsed to the deck, his entire body surrounded with black smoke. He clutched at his lungs and wheezed, each breath pushing out more and more of the stuff. The red-hot Splitter fell from his blistering hand and sizzled against the deck, and he fell with it, hacking and trembling from what appeared to be a sudden fever. The rest of the team surrounded him, but Aquifer pushed the women away, wrapping the soldier in a cocoon of water that boiled away in little time; he repeated the process several times until Bomber seemed coherent again.

"Thanks for the rescue, but let's maybe exchange your Giving Treehouse present for something that won't kill you, okay?" Aquifer joked, though concern strained his voice. "Did you keep the receipt?"

Bomber laughed once, and a little bit of smoke puffed from his nostrils. "No, I threw the darn thing away."

"Ah," Aquifer shook his head and clucked his tongue. "What a shame."

Bomber grinned, but it was a weak, weary expression. "I knew I shouldn't have let you go to Bed, Bath and Beyond."

Nodding, Aquifer wiped a tear from his eye. "It's always the 'Beyond' part that allures me."

A splashing sound from the north interrupted them. Aquifer, Battery and Shadow turned toward the noise, leaving Bomber to rest on the deck for the moment. Ahead of them, a dorsal fin the size of a sailboat emerged, gliding toward them with a silent menace. The scientist used his PAUS to steer the boat away from the incomer.

"Is that a shark?" asked Battery. "I *hate* sharks."

The dorsal fin made a U-turn and followed them, swishing back and forth with its lithe power. From its silhouette, the shark-creature appeared to be at least five time bigger than their boat, approaching the size of a humpback whale. Shadow responded to it with a volley of bullets, chattering them into the dorsal fin, causing dozens of small geysers as each round struck the ocean's surface. Most bullets bounced away from the fin, leaving just a thin gash, but a few lodged into it, drawing blood. Still silent, the shark-creature dove below the surface.

All the while, Aquifer beelined the boat toward Isla Isabela.

The shark-creature moved back and forth beneath the water in a smooth, zigzag motion, trailing a cloud of blood as it caught up to the boat. Shadow spat more bullets at it, but the transition to an underwater environment slowed and distorted their progress, preventing any notable damage to their pursuer.

Battery looked away from the stern, toward Aquifer. The shoreline grew closer.

With the gun's barrel leaning against the stern, Shadow took a moment to chain a new box magazine into the machine gun, capping the first round into the breech. As she leaned across the stern to resume fire, the shark-creature leapt from the depths, revealing its face.

Rather than a head, mouth and eyes, the sea monster attacking them had only a stump for the front half of its body. The stump ended in jagged rows of teeth, not unlike those of a normal shark. These spun, however, as if attached to the motor of a buzz saw. Bits of sharp bone rotated around the mouth in a wet, sliding motion, like the sound of chewing gelatin.

This buzz saw mouth clamped onto the front half of Shadow's rifle, as well as a bit of the upper stern, severing everything it touched. Before it could wiggle itself further onto the boat, Battery joined her partner, punching the creature in its "nose" with an electrified fist. Teeth still rotating, the shark-creature fell back into the ocean, leaving behind a trail of loose bullets from Shadow's ruined machine gun.

"Get ready to jump!" Aquifer called, PAUS still raised, watching the beach for imminent impact.

The two women helped Bomber to his feet, and Battery tensed, waiting. Aquifer created a small wave to glide the boat several meters into the sand, but the collision was still rough. Everyone launched from their positions, rolling onto the dry, coarse earth beyond. The shark was still a few dozen meters out in the water, rushing toward them.

Aquifer made a rude gesture at the creature that was *not* meant to control his PAUS. "HA!"

Without stopping, the shark dove below the surface, sending up a cloud of wet silt and sand as it disappeared. The earth rumbled around them, and the dorsal fin exploded from the ground, maintaining course toward Treehouse on land with as much ease as it had in the water. Most of its body remained concealed by sand, but Battery could hear the wet, glassy chewing noise that could only be its method of burrowing through solid ground.

Bomber turned to Aquifer, brows raised and arms outstretched. "Really?"

They scattered into four different directions, splitting the fin's attention. It circled once before following Shadow as she searched through her bandolier. Battery ran after the huntress and the creature, trying to attract the latter's attention.

The land-shark emerged from the earth, spewing clouds of sand and knocking Shadow to the ground. Under its belly were millions of tiny, crustaceous legs, similar to shrimp or krill legs. These little legs skittered the massive beast across the sand, chomping toward Shadow, blood from its dorsal fin mixing with the dirt cloud to create a red haze. Shadow rolled onto her back, presenting some kind of stumpy gun with a drum magazine strapped near her hip.

Just as Battery reached Shadow, the woman scorched the air between herself and the mutant shark, blasting what looked like clusters of ball bearings into its open and hungry mouth. Sharp teeth smashed apart and moist gums split open, and the creature dove once more into the sand.

Aquifer and Bomber joined Battery at Shadow's side as the huntress released the shotgun back to its hanging strap and unpinned two canisters, keeping the triggers compressed.

"What are you—?" Battery began, but Shadow shook her head, signaling for them to back away.

The earth trembled once more, and the land-shark's mouth formed a gigantic ring in the sand around Shadow's feet. She released the canisters, and they plummeted to the ground while the mouth began to snap shut. Before it could close, Shadow wriggled away from the mesh of jagged teeth, escaping. The grenades detonated, coating the sand still piled inside the shark's jaws with some kind of burning liquid.

Napalm? Battery guessed.

Melting and re-forming the silicate at an unnatural rate, the napalm lit up the night, making quick work of converting sand into a sharp chunk of glass. The land-shark attempted to choke down the burning crystal, reverberating the earth with a reflexive gagging noise, but it was no use. Struggling, it returned below ground, smoldering as it made its way back to sea.

And on the horizon, dawn appeared with the rising sun.

**Isla Isabela
February 12, 2013-B**

The team shielded their eyes as they returned to the boat, checking their equipment. Everything seemed intact, so they loaded up. Shadow took a moment to reload her shotgun while Aquifer set up a special homing beacon in the below-deck cabin for Bogeyman to map while they were gone. When everyone was comfortable, they began their trek into Puerto Villamil, toward the mountain stretching before them.

"We won't have to travel as far as we did in Japan," Aquifer said, reviewing the portable GPS. "Since there's no special vent or back-door entrance according to the Gold Hill records, we'll just be bursting through the front door and accepting the consequences."

They continued into the town, looking around for potential dangers. Everything was moldy and decrepit, with tools and toys strewn about the yards.

"What *happened* to this place?" Battery asked in her electronic voice.

As if to answer, an old man poked his grizzled face around the corner of a distant house before pulling away.

"Hey! You!" Battery called to him, reaching for her badge.

She saw him crawl across the street, barging through the front doors of an abandoned storefront. He skittered like an insect, moving across the dirt on his palms and toes with inverted elbows and knees. His pale face stayed low to the ground the entire way, eyes widened as if surprised.

More movement, closer this time, and Battery turned to the left in time to see two small children crawl up the sheer surface of a nearby home in the same manner as the old man. They perched atop the roof, watching Treehouse and twittering to each other with swift, creaky sounds.

Battery shivered with a sudden chill.

A trash can fell to her right, and a young woman skittered out of sight. Inside the receptacle was moldy food swarming with small, black bugs. Bomber leaned closer, but Shadow put a hand to his shoulder, so he stopped, activating his Atomic Vision instead.

"They're just . . . beetles," he said. "Regular picnic beetles."

"And the people?" Aquifer asked.

Bomber turned his vision toward the newcomers, but all had vanished. "No idea."

The team advanced, drawing closer together. Aquifer led the way with his GPS, while Shadow stood behind him to his left with her shotgun drawn. Bomber flanked his right, eyes aglow and watching, an orange aura around his fingers. At the rear, Battery kept pace with the others while walking backwards, blue sparks flowing through the copper paths of her suit and cascading off her studded knuckles.

They reached the edge of the town with no interruptions, other than the occasional peeking of those human-insects around various alleyways and street corners. When the team stepped onto a dirt path leading toward the mountain, Aquifer pointed northwest. The sun rose above them, blazing down while they ventured forward.

An hour passed, then two, as they wandered through barren dirt roads, passing sparse trees and patches of empty land. Aquifer signed to them, indicating that they were nearing the main entrance of the facility.

Something passed between them and the sun, casting a tremendous circular shadow around them, bringing some kind of unexpected eclipse. Battery looked up to see a massive creature carried aloft by black, feathered wings, crying down at them with the shrillness of a hawk. A closer passage as it circled them revealed a green, reptilian body and a thick outer shell.

"Is that—" Battery began.

"No way," Aquifer answered. "I refuse to believe it."

Despite his beliefs, the ground rocked beneath their feet when a two-story-tall snapping turtle dropped in front of them, sporting airplane-sized raven-like wings and shrieking the cry of a hunting hawk. The green-beaked creature eyed them with a ravenous hunger before elongating its neck, snapping at Battery. She curled down and punched upward, holding the creature's mouth open while standing inside of the orifice.

Something hot blew her way, and Battery rolled from the turtle's maw in time to avoid a searing blast of flame from within. The spray scorched nearby grass, dirt and trees, leaving a wave of fire along the ground. Aquifer jumped to the rescue, firing water orbs at the creature, but it flapped its wings, blowing him backward and propelling itself into the air, out of reach.

More flame dumped on the modern-day knights as they huddled away from the strange dragon, seeking solace beneath a water dome erected by Aquifer. The creature circled them, seeing that it was causing no harm against the steaming construct, and it drew closer, preparing to snap at them for a second time. Seizing the opportunity, Aquifer opened two portholes in the barrier, allowing Shadow and Bomber to unleash their varied ranged attacks on the target. The turtle was driven back into the sky, but its shell prevented it from receiving any damage.

The turtle creature flattened its feathered wings against its shell and fell from the sky, dive-bombing Aquifer's shield. The scientist let his construct dissipate, and Treehouse fanned out in time to avoid collision with the beast. A massive shock wave, powerful enough to ripple the air, splayed in a circle around the point of impact, carrying the four fighters off their feet and rolling them into the dying grass. They scrambled to their feet, now a considerable distance from each other.

A column of flame erupted in Aquifer's direction, but he dove low, avoiding fatal burns. Without stopping its tirade, the turtle craned its neck, targeting Battery. Caught off-guard, the detective crossed her forearms in front of her face before blowing into the air, as if she had been standing in front of a space shuttle's engine. Fire ripped around her, and she slammed into a nearby tree, ablaze.

Battery's skin was melting and re-forming, scarring and healing, though her suit was moderately flame-retardant. Her belt, however, was white-hot, and she felt the turbine blades puttering out as metal and wires fused together. Moving with swift purpose, she cranked the burning dial to its highest setting, flooding her body with the last vestiges of her Charge Belt's energy before the device died. Sighing, she unclipped the metal belt and dropped its useless form to the grass.

She and Bomber darted at the turtle, pounding against its shell with electrified and explosive fists, but their collisions caused little damage to the behemoth. It screeched and flung them back, away from its body. Shadow strode forward as her teammates flew over her head, sending round after round of shotgun blasts into the creature's eyes and mouth, but the attacks were simply ineffective. Sparks flew as wasted ammunition bounced away from its armor.

"Shadow!" Aquifer yelled, pausing from a series of complex hand gestures. "Flashbang?"

Shadow reached to her bandolier, retrieved a canister, and tossed it to him.

Battery backed away. *When it comes to Aquifer's plans, you should always keep your distance, Zen.*

Aquifer held up the canister. "Timer?"

[Three seconds,] the huntress replied.

The scientist pulled the pin, keeping the trigger squeezed tight, waiting for something. The moment the turtle opened its mouth to blast fire at Battery and Bomber, he encased the grenade in a water orb and launched the entire thing into the back of the creature's throat. The beast coughed and choked, but Aquifer stepped forward, triggering some kind of PAUS command.

In the same moment the flashbang detonated, filling the turtle's stomach with light, Aquifer's PAUS chittered, and water began pouring from the creature's throat. It turned and leapt at the scientist, but something held it in place, as if there were a ball of lead in its stomach. Hunger and aggression turned to fear and confusion, and it tried to screech again, but more water bubbled from its mouth.

Before the creature could react further, Bomber Dashed along the turtle's shell, drawing an orange line across the hardened surface. Once his snip from his Atomic Scissors was complete, he lifted his hand, jumping away. The turtle creature sizzled, then split in half horizontally, releasing an overabundance of water, blood, guts, and digested fish into the dirt and grass. A sickening smell like seaweed filled the air as it died, and the team backed away, covering their faces as they coughed.

Battery looked to her waist, lamenting the loss of her belt. Despite its absence, errant blue arcs still encircled her body.

I'll just have to make do with the energy I've got left, she told herself.

———————

The team's journey progressed with little conflict. On occasion, Battery caught a glimpse of one of the picnic-beetle-villagers skittering across a plain or hiding in the tree branches, but those sightings were rare.

Eventually, they reached the base of the mountain spanning along Isla Isabela, brushing apart shrubbery to reveal a large silver door, like a garage door. Bomber used his Scissors to make quick work of the barrier, and they slipped inside, noting no sign of an alarm or any kind of guards.

Empty, pearl-white hallways led them through a maze of corridors, and the team backtracked several times in the process of finding a path toward the winged man's GPS signal. They moved further into the hidden base, illuminated by artificial lights and the glistening decor. Aquifer still led the way, flanked by the respective armed and glowing Shadow and Bomber, with a crackling Battery keeping an eye on the rear.

Their pathway yielded no information about the purpose or design of the facility, and any rooms they stopped to explore were barren. In one instance, there was a single pearl-white table in a small space, splattered with droplets of dried blood. Another room seemed to be a smaller version of the cafeteria from the earthquake machine facility, though no one inhabited it.

The quiet was causing Battery unrest.

"Here," Aquifer whispered, pointing at a pair of heavy metal double-doors at the end of their current hallway. "We're close."

"Okay, Treehouse," Battery said, straightening her gloves. "Be careful. Kick ass, but don't forget to take names, too."

As if on cue, the doors Aquifer had gestured toward glided open, the sound so quiet Battery almost failed to notice.

"Names, detective?" A gravelly voice boomed from the room. "What names do you want?"

She spun to peer into the new chamber, stepping closer to its entrance.

The mountain of Isla Isabela possessed a massive concave crater at its peak, flattening the structure a little. Under the crater the room had been built, creating a large circular warehouse of sorts. The ceiling was some kind of screen or multi-way surface, because they could see through the stone and grass of the mountaintop and into the blue sky above. In the room's center, surrounding by an array of consoles and screens, was the shirtless, winged man.

He looked and them and smiled, stretching his arms and his grey wings to the sky. "Welcome to our Galapagos base."

Treehouse traded glances, and everyone drifted their attention to Battery. She furrowed her brow. "I don't like this. I don't like *you*. What's the point of this production?"

The man shrugged. "Maybe I'm feeling chatty. Don't you want your answers? All the secrets to the universe?"

Shadow placed a hand on her waist before signing. [Put up or shut up, asshole.]

"Now, now," he chided. "No need to be rude. I didn't have to leave the tracker on myself. I brought you here of my own free will."

"Why?" asked Aquifer. "What do you want?"

The man sighed. "It's not really about what *I* want anymore, Acharya. We're a collective. We have a goal, and we each strive toward that goal with different approaches."

"Wait," Battery held up a hand, looking around. "Why are you telling us this? Are you waiting for something?"

A gravelly laugh filled the room. "Kipper, don't insult my intelligence, and I won't insult yours, okay? We both know you four are too smart to walk into a trap unprepared. I won't waste my resources on this."

"Then why?" she pressed.

"Well, that's *my* way reaching our goal. But maybe I should back up for a moment and introduce myself before I explain." He extended a hand, though it was too far away from their reach. "My name is Strix."

Bomber frowned. "Okay."

[What is this goal?] Shadow signed. [Why are you killing people? Why are you spreading terror?]

"Well," replied Strix, "We certainly don't *intend* to do that. We genuinely have good intentions, despite all appearances to the contrary. But our experiment extends beyond your desire to eke out your own existences, and that makes us disliked. So, please forgive our sometimes-callous attitudes."

"You didn't quite answer her, though," Aquifer said. "What 'experiment' is this? What's your point?"

"Well, we're running a . . . a science project of sorts. A project on the evolution of humanity, and its ability to dominate. In our opinion, as long as inferior strands of human DNA remain so easy to kill, they haven't earned the right to stay alive. Our steps are logical, and they're in your best interest, even if you can't see the bigger picture."

"What about ethics?" Aquifer demanded. "Humanity can evolve on its own—without your involvement. You violate the ethics of science when you interfere and harm others to further your personal experimentation."

The winged man laughed. "Those are *your* ethics, and quite frankly, you have not done well to abide by them. Where were your ethics when the Tuskegee camp allowed hundreds to suffer and die to abate the effects of syphilis today? Where were your ethics when Henrietta Lacks's identity was violated in the hopes of fighting future concerns like polio, cancer, and AIDS? How about human radiation tests, or Operation Top Hat, or the Holmesburg Prison? Even Hitler's eugenics programs had major benefits."

Strix shook his head. "You sound so superior when you look at a piece of the picture, now that the world you're in is *our* Tuskegee camp and the disease we're fighting is your own inability to return to your once-superior status. You've been watered down and made ineffective by your emotions and your sensitivities and your 'ethics.' But the moment something you've deemed unethical suits your emotional needs, you forget everything you ever moralized." He paused. "The purity of science will forever outlive the flawed ethics of humanity."

Aquifer sighed, and Battery stepped forward. "What you've described doesn't fit everyone in the world. If you wanted to experiment on humanity, find volunteers. Join the world leaders. Create structure in what you do."

Bomber laughed. "Right? You want to help 'humanity,' but I'm over here fighting coal-powered robots and giant turtles. That's supposed to help us somehow?"

Strix grimaced. "Like I said, each of us pursues this plan in our own, unique way. It's what we agreed upon when this endeavor first began. Kalt and Xiao and Zala and Cecil and even your precious Noam, or whatever they call themselves now, do things differently. Some experiment on wildlife. Some on technology. Some on biology. Some simply seek to keep a stable global population size."

"Yeah, we know," Aquifer replied. "Disaster Relief."

"Right. Your survival, as a species, *is* our top priority. The problem is, you're terrible at doing it on your own." Strix sighed. "Ultimately, it doesn't matter. I'm monologuing like a campy supervillain because that's *my* approach. I'm a psychologist. I studied with the best. Pavlov, Piaget, Skinner. They all helped build me into the man I am today."

"So?" Battery asked impatiently.

"I study human behavior during moments of crisis. Without knowing how you'll adapt to new challenges, I believe you have no way of acting as a group to move past tragedy in a constructive way. Just look at how often you're at each other's throats after a couple buildings fall, or a man in a car gets his head blown off."

Battery looked at Shadow, who shrugged. [Fair enough.]

"Oof," he continued. "I apologize for my long-windedness. I just wanted to set a precedent so you can understand what I want from you."

"And that is?" Bomber extended his hands, waiting for a response.

"I want you to succeed. See, even Society can stagnate. Our goals are pure, and our methods are logical, but we don't face enough resistance. I want you to understand who we are. We're trying to help *you* evolve, but Society needs to evolve, too."

Battery raised an eyebrow. "And Society is alright with this."

"Well," he winked at her, "what they don't know won't hurt them."

His black eyes shifted to Bomber. "Fields, right? You seem skeptical of my intentions. But don't you feel like you've learned so much about your Refinement since your partner was taken from you? Look at how much you're able to evolve and grow with just a small push in the right direction."

The soldier took a step back. "You? That was . . . you?"

He fell to his knees, and Strix just smiled at him.

Okay, that's enough. Battery raised her energy-laced fists. "Strix, you can fuck right off with your kind gestures."

She rushed the man, knuckles pulled back to strike, not noticing the vapor escaping her chilled mouth until it was too late. Strix sidestepped her attack, revealing the Fireman's outstretched hand. As she touched his fingertips, her momentum was sucked from her body, freezing her in midair. He pulled away, and gravity reappeared, dropping her frosted form to the ground.

Strix stepped in and kicked her onto her back, pressing a command on a nearby console at the same time. "You thought I wouldn't be more prepared? I'm disappointed."

Battery turned to see two chambers rising from the floor, releasing their contents. Static filled her head.

"Come to me."

"Stay with me."

"Kill for me."

"Love me."

Two tall, thin men in suits stepped from the chambers, their faces empty and white.

No, not men. But not all monster, either. What did Shadow call them again?

In the distance, the huntress raised her shotgun and signed three words to Aquifer, whose hands were at his temples.

[The Slender Men.]

The two creatures stepped forward, growing more arms from their back with unnatural, cracking motions. On the floor, Bomber remained on his knees, dazed by grief and anger.

"Come to me."

"Stay with me."

"Kill for me."

"Love me."

Then the Slender Men attacked, battling with the woman in black and the man in white. Battery tried to pull herself to her feet to assist, but Strix kicked her back down.

"Just like old times, isn't it?" he said. "Before your fancy equipment."

The Fireman stood to the side, motionless.

Battery reached out, punching into the bottom panel of the nearest console. Squeezing and pulling, she disconnected a handful of wires, drinking their energy. Strix kicked at her again, but she grabbed his foot, punching his kneecap with her free hand, producing a resounding *crunch*.

Strix wailed, pulling back to heal, and the Fireman punched her with a flaming hand. Battery sped across the circular room, crashing into the far wall, feeling her bones shatter from the force. She lay still, giving herself the opportunity to recover. Nearby, a black figure darkened her light. She looked up, greeted by Shadow's wry grin and outstretched hand.

[Trade?]

"Trade."

Battery rose to her feet, assisted by her partner, and they stood together. Aquifer was battling the two speedy Slender Men, Bomber was still recovering, and the Fireman was watching Strix rejuvenate his broken knee. In one deft move, she grabbed the huntress by her waist and flung her upward, toward the ceiling. Shadow's cloak ruffled behind her like the cape of a comic-book superhero, and she was soon scrambling among the rafters in the ceiling.

The detective turned her attention to Aquifer, bounding over to him. Over her shoulder, she saw Strix flap his wings, his face twisted into an ugly glare. "Hey, water guy!" Battery yelled. "Switch with me!"

He turned, glanced at the approaching winged man, and nodded. Battery tackled the Slender Men, slamming them to the ground. In the corner of her eye, Aquifer launched a volley of water cannonballs at Strix. The grey man dodged the attacks with ease, drawing ever closer.

Then a young man in an orange-and-green jacket stepped between them.

"You sick freak," Bomber said, his tone low.

Metal glinted on the soldier's right index and middle fingers. "Bomber, wait!"

A green aura encircled the man as his hand raised, pointing his Atomic Cannon at the incoming flyer. The ball of energy before him began as a speck and grew into a thick column of light, tearing apart the air and cascading toward Strix. Smoke and the smell of burning hair surrounded Bomber, whose eyes glowed a furious orange.

Just as the light beam seemed to hit its target, Strix dodged to the side, and it continued up into the ceiling, carving a tunnel through the metal and rock and shaking the room as it depleted. The hole it left smoked, and slabs of magma filled its walls. The exposed space whistled as wind blew into the tunnel.

Bomber teetered, coughed once, and collapsed to the floor, unconscious.

"Thanks for the quick exit, boy," Strix snarled, circling above them like a vulture, zooming for the new hole.

Water encircled him, and he was dragged back to the ground by Aquifer's outstretched hand. Bubbles escaped as he struggled, but the pressurized force kept dragging him to the center of his aquatic prison. The Fireman ran toward him to assist, but was interrupted by an object whistling at him through the air.

Battery rolled to the side, still engaged with the Slender Men, and saw a black arrow headed toward the axe-wielding enemy. He raised a hand to halt it, but it never reached him. When it was about a half-meter away, the strange-looking arrowhead exploded, spattering the Fireman with a clear fluid. Acrid smoke rose from his left glove and sleeve, dissolving his clothes.

The closest Slender Man drew her attention away from the other battles, striking her in the back of the head with an outstretched claw.

"Come to me."

"Stay with me."

"Kill for me."

"Love me."

"Sorry, I'm taken," Battery growled, tearing the first Slender Man's head from its body in a gush of cottony fluid.

One of two voices in her brain quieted.

The other Man wrapped its many arms around her, ejecting its rhino-horn injection spike from its vertical mouth. It bent down and attempted to impregnate her, but the spike shattered against her skin, spilling a thick, white fluid with the smell and consistency of spoiled milk across her body armor.

A buzzing filled her head—and immense pain.

"Serves you right," Battery said, and slapped her hands together between its ears as if she were clapping to kill a mosquito. White fluid exploded over the floor as the Slender Man's head was flattened into paste, and the corpse released her, falling to join its brother on the ground.

Gasping, Battery returned to her feet, admiring her teammates at work.

Shadow reloaded her compound bow, pulling another home-made acid-arrow from the tubular quiver on her back and notching it. She winked at Battery from the rafters and let loose, striking the center of the Fireman's chest with more corrosive chemicals. More frantic than they'd ever seen him, the Fireman stripped away his outer jacket and gloves, revealing tan, muscled arms and a maroon t-shirt. His mask and helmet still hid his face.

Battery turned toward Aquifer, who was watching his prey. Strix had first fought to escape his prison, but now he was clutching his stomach and chest as his skin rippled around him.

"Funny, isn't it?" Aquifer called to him. "You spent all this time learning to adapt and to survive, but most don't take into consideration rarer, harder-to-obtain illnesses. Take decompression sickness, or 'the bends,' for instance. It was so easy to recreate with my PAUS. As a fellow scientist, I'm sure I don't have to spell it out to you. How long will it take your body to heal from the change in pressure, from one embolism after another?"

Strix's eyes were wide as he coughed into the swirling waters, but the Fireman was too preoccupied with Shadow's acid attack to assist. With a furious underwater roar, the winged man expanded his wings, bursting the capsule. He fell to the floor, sputtering something under his breath before Aquifer had a chance to recreate his compression chamber.

"One hundred . . . and fifty . . . million . . . people."

"Excuse me?" Aquifer asked.

Battery joined Aquifer's side as Strix continued. "My heart . . . is wired . . . with a dead man's switch. Should it stop beating for more than a few seconds, a signal is sent to six different nuclear bombs buried at the center of six different major cities around the world. One hundred and fifty million people. Are their lives worth mine?"

Battery snarled. "You coward."

"No, detective. I'm a survivor. And I will allow my partner to kill me if we are not permitted to leave this instant."

He gestured to the Fireman dancing around Shadow's acid arrows.

Battery looked at Aquifer, who sighed, lowering his hands.

"This isn't over, Strix," she said through gritted teeth.

"I certainly hope not. Put my knowledge to good use, lab rat."

With that, he picked up the Fireman by the waist, and they vanished into the hole Bomber had created. While leaving, he yelled, "Expergiscimini ab intus!"

The moment Strix was gone, Shadow, Battery and Aquifer rushed to Bomber's side, and the latter doused him with water to cool him down. After a moment, the soldier coughed and awoke, turning over to see their concerned faces. "Did I get him?"

Battery sighed. "No. You didn't. But you almost killed yourself trying. Don't do that again. Do you understand?"

He weakly nodded.

Shadow looked around the open room, turning her attention to the consoles, then to the Slender Men on the floor. [What do we do about this place?]

Aquifer walked toward the consoles. "I have an idea."

He punched at the controls, releasing more chambers filled with grotesque, shadowy creatures, though he did not open their doors. Instead, once he was satisfied with the presence of what appeared to be at least three dozen genetic experiments, he drew the rest of the team close.

"Stand still," he commanded.

Water filled the room, rippling beneath their feet so, as it rose, they stayed on the surface as if it were solid ground. The ceiling soon approached, drawing them closer to the hole Strix and the Fireman had used to exit. The flooding ceased, and they crawled into the tunnel. When they no longer touched the water, Aquifer stopped them.

"Shadow," Aquifer said, extending his hand. "Knife?"

The huntress drew her combat knife and handed it to him, who then handed it to Battery.

"What's your charge feel like right now?" he asked.

She grimaced, understanding what he was trying to do. "Just a moment."

The detective slid back into the water until she was waist-deep, floating at the edge of their exit tunnel. Bending over, she stabbed herself in the thighs with the knife, wincing as she tore gashes into herself with super-strength. Each hole closed with a burning blue light, producing ample amperes of energy that crackled through the conductive water, colliding with the consoles and chambers. Sparks flew and bodies writhed as Society's work in the Galapagos was fried and electrocuted into uselessness.

Battery handed the bloody knife back to Shadow, who wiped it off.

"That's most of what I had in me," she said. "Let's hope it was enough."

Treehouse
February 12, 2013-B

Proxy hunched over the computer, listening to the recording of their time spent at Isla Isabela. He was quiet for the most part, nodding or scribbling some notes at specific moments in the conversation with Strix. While he worked, Battery, Bomber, and Aquifer loitered around him, slouched and exhausted from their trek. Shadow had disappeared into her room to change into more casual clothes.

After several minutes, Proxy removed his headphones. "First, I want to tell you how proud I am for having a team like you with me. I didn't think I would survive creating my own Faction cell, but despite my best efforts at self-sabotage along the way, you four have contributed more to Faction efforts in the last decade than everyone else has in the last three."

There were awkward murmurs of gratefulness.

"So," he continued, "What do you think about Strix?"

"He's telling the truth," Aquifer said. "At least, he thinks he is. He has a degree of conviction in him that only an honest man of science can portray, in my experience."

"I don't care about his convictions," added Bomber. "How pure his goals are doesn't excuse his actions taken to reach them. And I mean *beyond* what he did to Sam. There must be better ways. We're right to be trying to shut down Society."

Proxy looked to Battery. "You seem quiet."

Yeah, no shit. An enemy who believes they're the good guys are the hardest ones to fight. We've lost entire Faction cells and stood by while hundreds of thousands of innocent people died. For what? So we could kill a few 'bad guys?' That's just the ones who we can kill at all. No, this a nightmare, and every step forward feels like ten steps back.

She sat up and smiled a little. "Just tired. I agree with Bomber."

Shadow re-entered the basement, still in her cloak and armor. Battery glanced at her, surprised. "Couldn't find something to wear?"

The young woman ignored her, sitting down next to Proxy at a different computer. He smiled and returned to his notes, tapping a phrase near the bottom.

"Now *this* was something that interested me. 'Expergiscimini ab intus.' Do you recognize this, Mr. Acharya?"

Aquifer shook his head. "I think it's Latin? That's the most I know, though."

Proxy spun in his chair to pull up a virtual translator. As he selected the "Latin" option, Battery saw Shadow slip her hand beneath the desk and flip a switch.

Wait, isn't that the one for . . .

The program ran, producing words Proxy read aloud.

"Expergiscimini ab intus: 'Rise from within.' "

He frowned. "What on earth does that have to do with—"

His words were interrupted by an unflattering, hollow *crack*.

Blood, skin, and bits of skull splattered Battery's face, temporarily blinding her. She gagged, hastily wiping away the viscera to see what had happened. To her horror, Proxy teetered in his chair, the top half of his head missing. Blood gurgled from the stump, where it let out a final gasp before the body fell to the floor, twitching.

Behind him with an outstretched hand, wrist-shotgun still smoking, stood Shadow.

Location & Date Redacted

I suppose it's appropriate to pause and point out the obvious: Our world is one of many.

Each world is defined by the choices of its inhabitants; the shifting of the tides; the flapping of butterfly wings. Some worlds contain mostly terror, while others contain mostly hope. The average world, of course, lies somewhere between the two. This is the case for your world, dear reader, as it is for many others.

There are even worlds where a cheap flashlight wasn't left lying on the floor of a police precinct in New York City in 2001.

This is not that world.

ERROR

ERROR

ERROR

<u>UNAUTHORIZED REPORT</u>

Treehouse
September 10, 2001-B

Catalina leaned over the bathroom sink, shirtless, applying iodine to the thin punctures left behind in her shoulder by that Reptile in New York, wincing and grimacing until her private show of weakness evaporated. There was no reason to be so childish about such a minor wound.

Something burned in her shoulder, down into her bone and muscle, and she wiped away the brown iodine fluid, inspecting her bite. The holes pulsated, closing at an unnatural rate. Alarmed, she rushed to the bathroom door to alert Quentin and the cute new detective. A sense of calm washed over her as her hand touched the doorknob, and she stopped.

Why was she here again?

She looked around. There was iodine and blood in the sink, but *she* wasn't injured. She was fine.

Everything was fine.

Everything issss fine, a voice whispered in the back of her head.

Treehouse
July 8, 2002-B

Catalina hovered above Quentin as he slept, kitchen knife in hand. She felt dazed, like a sleepwalker. A name whispered in her ear, and she raised her arm.

Ssstab.

The huntress shook her head.

What? No. Who is this?

Ssstab.

No.

Ssserve usss.

No.

You will, ssslave.

She awoke in the morning, sweating. What had she been dreaming about? The memory was fading, and it was fading fast. Many years had passed since Catalina last had a nightmare. Not since her mother died.

A voice whispered the same name into her ear.

Catalina despised nightmares.

Kerguelen Islands
March 20, 2005-B

The dripping of a moist cave was drowned out by the buzzing of heavy machinery. Catalina looked around, finding herself naked and strapped to a table. Lizard-faced people surrounded her, studying her, baring their needle teeth. She looked at her arm, an IV bag drawing her blood. Despite her situation, she only felt calm in the presence of these creatures.

"It will take time to develop," one of them hissed.

"Think of how happy Cccecil will be," another replied.

"And thossse of usss lucky enough to reccceive it," a third spoke. *"Like the one we call Zala."*

"What ssshould we call it?" A fourth asked, holding a vial of green, cloudy fluid into the light, studying it.

It was the same color as Catalina's eyes.

They pondered for a moment, and Catalina found herself saddened their stares were no longer on her. Finally, the first one spoke again.

"Ssshroud. We'll call it ssshroud."

Berlin, Germany
April 22, 2006-B

The name whispered in the back of Catalina's head. She lay against the window, watching Kalt the polar-bear-man explode, pondering its meaning. Who was this person? This thing?

She stood and signaled for Quentin to retrieve her. Traveling from a nearby storage closet to the Bogeyman chamber, she slipped a dog-laxative from one of her belt pouches. When Quentin and Maddie greeted her, she smiled. The moment the former turned away, she kneeled and fed the laxative to the latter.

Quentin spoke about the mission while Catalina changed clothes, but she wasn't listening; her attention was on the Dutch Shepherd. The moment the dog seemed uncomfortable, she signed to the analyst. [I think she has to use the restroom.]

Maddie whimpered, swishing her tail a little, and ran out of the basement. Quentin jumped to his feet, a worried expression on his face.

"Watch Bogeyman while I'm gone, please?"

The moment they left, Catalina retrieved a flash drive from her pocket, plugging it into one of the central computers at Quentin's station. Operation files appeared on-screen, and she copied them to the drive.

Koshasth . . .

Obelisk . . .

Tai Sui . . .

She reached for Péndulo, but Zen's announcement that she was ready to transport stopped her. Quickly snatching out the drive and pocketing it, Catalina brought the detective back into Treehouse. The woman emerged, brushing plaster dust from her hair. Admiring her, even blushing a little, Catalina looked away, forgetting about the drive.

Wasn't she just watching Bogeyman for Quentin, anyway?

Arizona, United States
November 12, 2008-B

Catalina perused the aisles of the Casas Adobes Safeway, looking for fresh produce for the week. Zen came with her, but she had wandered off toward the processed foods. Alone, a familiar voice spoke in her head, saying a name.

Reaching into her pocket, Catalina was surprised to find a black, nondescript flash drive waiting for her. She looked around before shoving it behind the bananas. As she walked away, she found herself texting a mysterious contact named "S" in her burner cellphone.

Casas Adobes Safeway in AZ. Behind the bananas. Acharya shops here often.

Treehouse
May 4, 2011-B

Stacey Fields is Refined. Husband is in Alberta. Hurry.

Catalina looked down into her empty hand.

Was her phone out before?

Quentin strode forward and spoke, interrupting her confused thoughts. "For now, you may call me Quentin. Welcome to The Faction, mon amie."

Treehouse
March 11, 2012-B

Catalina was brushing her teeth in the bathroom when something snagged the bristles. Stopping, she reached into her mouth, feeling around her gums. Something pricked her finger, and she pulled away, watching a bead of blood form on the skin.

More carefully, the huntress felt behind her teeth. Lurking just past the point of visibility was an extra row. Except they weren't flat; they were pointy and sharp.

Reptile teeth.

Catalina rushed to the bathroom door, just as she had a decade ago, and just as she had done dozens of times since. As with each other instance, a voice spoke its name in her head, and her muscles relaxed, slowing her to a halt. She shuddered, wrapping her arms around herself, feeling violated.

It'sss almossst time.

Treehouse
February 12, 2013-B

Zen, Nadi, and Stacey took a step away from a terrified Catalina and her headless victim. The huntress shook, doe-eyed, tears streaming down her face, staring at her smoking shotgun contraption.

What had she done?

Something's wrong.

It'sss time . . .

NO. SOMETHING IS WRONG.

Catalina bent her arm, forcing the unused shotgun barrel past her teeth, willing herself to squeeze the lever. Her fingers didn't respond. The only sound was the chattering of her mouth against the hot metal.

Zen moved toward her, tears in her eyes. "Not you, Cat . . ."

The cloaked woman lifted her other hand, willing Zen to stop, and the detective did. Catalina tried to squeeze the lever again, but her body wouldn't cooperate. Slipping the barrel from her lips, shaking, crying uncontrollably, she mouthed two words to her friends.

[Rule Three.]

"Rule three?" Stacey asked.

"Maintain your identity," Nadi whispered.

A name whispered into Catalina's brain, and she twitched and spasmed, her muscles tense. The urge to vomit—to purge—flooded her brain, spreading throughout her body rather than staying in her throat or stomach. Her eyes rolled back, beyond her control, and she felt the tendons controlling them straining to stay intact.

As the first of the muscles tore, her clear tears ran red with blood. The ripping, like wet paper, filled her skull, and her loosened eyes slipped further backward, darkening her sight. Her vision soon returned, though it was now tinted a jaundiced yellow color, inter-rupted by cloudy swirls of green.

Blood filled her mouth, tasting like pennies, and her bones ached as her human teeth retracted, revealing rows of protruding, needle-like teeth. In pain, she attempted to hiss, but her vocal cords remained severed, so only a squeak emitted. Her skin crawled and pulled taut against her body while a subdermal layer of scales grew to protect her.

The name spoke again, and she reached within her cloak.

The detective is the ssstrongest. Her firssst.

The scientist is the sssmartest. Him sssecond.

The soldier is the fassstest. Him lassst.

Catalina's pupils twitched, and time slowed.

RECONNECTING . . .

RECONNECTING . . .

UNAUTHORIZED REPORT PURGED

Stacey stood, sickened and saddened, as he watched his friend transform into a yellow-and-green-eyed Reptile. She was covered in her own blood and the blood of her long-time teammate. Behind him, he heard Maddie run into the basement, hurtling toward Quentin's corpse, barking. Something sharp and metal glinted beneath Catalina's cloak, and she swung it at the dog.

"No!" Zen cried, jumping between them.

Catalina's wakizashi sliced through the air, burying into Zen's right bicep. A spray of blood obscured Stacey's view of the fight, and he moved with Nadi to assist. The red cleared, revealing a one-armed Zen standing still with a horrified expression on her face. Before anyone could react, Catalina spun and made a horizontal slash, cutting deep into Zen's neck and releasing another stream of arterial blood. Finishing her spin, Catalina back-kicked Zen in the stomach, sending the detective sliding across the floor. Zen sprawled, unmoving, her blood expanding across the concrete floor.

Nadi raised an arm, but so did Catalina; before he could gesture, she squeezed the trigger of the automatic pistol in her other hand. Bullets spewed at the unarmored man, riddling his abdomen and extremities. He fell hard, collapsing in a pool of blood, silent and still.

"Zen! Nadi!" Stacey cried, Dashing away from Catalina's bullet-spray.

He dove behind the Bogeyman chamber and returned fire at Catalina, who twirled around his lasers with ease. Dropping her pistol, she unhinged the shotgun still clipped to her waist, launching a burst of ball bearings toward the soldier. They flew past his face, almost hitting him, and he scrambled from the basement in an attempt to lure her into a more open area.

As Stacey rolled into the garage, a tiny machine-gun turret popped down from the ceiling, drawn to his movements. It unloaded its small-caliber rounds at the man, who dodged them in a series of Atomic Dash zigzags. When it paused to reload, Stacey melted it with a well-timed Atomic Gunshot. Thanks to Bogeyman's effect, though, the turret began to re-form, cooling and building itself back to its former status. Rather than stay in an endless fight, the soldier continued into the main house.

Stepping foot into the front hallway, Stacey felt a series of mechanisms shifting beneath the floorboards. Using his Atomic Vision, he scanned below himself to see a grid of metal tubes. One-by-one they ignited, blasting shotgun pellets up through the floor in spaces where his feet created pressure. He Atomic-Clinged to the ceiling, but the first few sent metal buckshot through his shoes and into the fleshy soles of his feet. Gritting his teeth in pain, Stacey crawled across the ceiling, avoiding the hallway floor.

As he passed from the hallway to the living room, scanning his surroundings, something clicked above his head. Metal spikes jutted from the top and bottom of the entryway, dedicated to skewering the injured soldier. He Dashed forward in time to avoid further harm, but one spike caught the bottom corner of Sam's jacket, tearing off a small chunk of the fabric.

Landing in the center of the living room, he grabbed his feet in agony; a second later, Stacey heard footsteps behind him. He turned. Catalina, in her phantom outfit, exited the garage, running along the hallway wall parkour-style above the self-repairing shotguns in the floor. When she flew through the entryway, the metal spikes caught her by the cloak; in one fluid motion, Catalina unclasped it, revealing her body armor and the unbelievable amount of weaponry strapped to it.

Thunder filled the small space as her shotgun fired in quick succession, emptying the remaining ball bearing rounds from its cylindrical magazine in Stacey's direction. He rolled away from the blasts, but the floor fell away from him, dropping him into a small pit. The walls began to close like some kind of hydraulic press, so he Dashed up to the ceiling.

As he landed, he must have triggered another sensor, because a new grid of barrels ejected from the kitchen wall, firing a wave of small-caliber bullets toward him. This time, frustrated, he glowed orange, swatting his hands outward. The incoming bullets matched his hue and exploded into harmless fragments midair, showering his skin and clothes with pinpricks of warmth.

Below him, Catalina unloaded her second automatic pistol at the ceiling, raining plaster dust onto the floor as he darted around, avoiding the gunfire. With a full-body ricochet more luck than cunning, Stacey flew toward her, melting the gun in her hand with an orange laser burst. Unfazed, she spun into another back-kick, catching him in the gut with her heel mid-Dash. Stacey saw stars and rolled to the ground, separating himself from her with the living room couch. Coughing, he spat up blood, worried her kick ruptured something internal.

The sound of unsheathed metal caught his attention, and he crawled away just in time to avoid being skewered by Catalina's WASP knife jutting through the fabric of the couch. Lizard-like, she skittered across the furniture, knife in one hand and some kind of metal rod in the other. Stacey rose to his feet, took a deep breath to quell the fear and pain, and raised his fists, summoning the skills obtained via Zen's—and Catalina's—trainings.

The wind whistled, signaling the slice of a blade toward his face. He ducked, augmenting the action with a gentle push from his Atomic Dash, enhancing his speed. As the WASP knife passed over him, her other arm slipped upward, striking his chest with the tip of the rod. Almost too late, he noticed a trigger on the rod handle, so he fell backward, narrowly avoiding the spike that launched from the rod with a hydraulic hiss. His foot closest to that hand shot up, kicking the rod from her grasp.

[U . . . R . . .]

Stacey noticed the now-free hand signing something, previously masked by the weapon. As he fought her, he tried to watch the hand. Was the real Catalina communicating to him?

[I . . . A . . . Stop . . .]

Gears and ratchets clacked around them, and all visible Proxy traps retreated into the walls, floors and ceiling. Over an intercom, Stacey heard Nadi's voice, weak from blood loss.

"Bogeyman . . . now . . ."

Stacey understood. This was a sensitive base of operations, and Catalina could no longer stay here without compromising the entire Faction.

The knife jabbed out once more, this time releasing cold, compressed air toward Stacey. His eyes glowed orange, heating the air back to room temperature before it caused nerve damage to his skin. Beside him, the couch was reversing its condition, sewing itself back together from the knife wound. Likewise, the holes in the ceiling from the automatic gunfire were closing, the plaster dust on the floor absorbing into the wood.

Distracted by her WASP knife, Stacey missed a shin-kick to his leg, knocking him to his knees. Catalina's signing hand ceased for a moment, drawing a small-caliber .22 pistol from her ankle holster. The barrel pressed against his forehead, but before she could pull the trigger, he ripped away the weapon's atoms through the physical contact. The gun exploded in her hand, and the shock wave knocked the two combatants apart. When Catalina landed on her back, her gun hand went limp, and her knife hand dropped the diving blade.

With not a moment to waste, Stacey Dashed three times: Once to Catalina, grabbing her by the torso; once across the house, carrying her; then a final time through the garage, the basement, and into the waiting Bogeyman chamber. There, he released her, and she slammed into the back of the metal tube with a resounding *clang*. The doors shut behind them, and they were in darkness, her lizard-face leering at him with those glowing yellow-and-green eyes.

Still, in view of his Atomic Vision, her other hand signed.

[E . . . M . . .]

Bogeyman hummed to life as she pounced, drawing a black combat knife. Resuming his aura of enhanced speed via Atomic Dash, Stacey sparred with her, matching her quick, deadly strikes with blocks and punches of his own. The walls fell away, and they were falling and continually grappling. Her blade slashed at his shirt, tearing into his flesh, but he batted her arm away, cauterizing the wound with his free hand.

The empty, windless fall swallowed them in black silence, yet they grunted and whispered, trading a flurry of blows. Knees met abdomens, fists met faces, and elbows met each other. During the fall, she drew another pistol. He kept her close, and the darkness filled with missed gunshots and laser beams, the projectiles disappearing into nothingness. When Catalina's magazine emptied, she emitted a silent hiss before flinging it away. The other hand whipped forward, releasing her unused wrist-shotgun barrels.

Just then, their descent slowed, and they were thrown off-balance, landing in a supply closet. Hovering all around them, frozen in the air, were their bullets and lasers, still mid-flight. They stayed that way for a second, a suspended snowfall of violence, but then momentum caught up with them, and the inside of the space was burned and shredded by a tidal wave of energy and projectiles. Wood and plaster and shelving collapsed, and in the chaos, Stacey slipped outside.

He found himself in the back of a closed pottery store, limping through the dark aisles, seeking guidance from the night stars outside the distant industrial windows. Rushing through the store, he sought an exit, when quiet steps nearby alerted him to an incoming attack. Stacey turned in time to hear an unflattering, hollow *crack*.

Shotgun pellets spread toward him, and he repeated his earlier swipe, disintegrating the bits of metal. Two grenades landed at his feet, and he Dashed up to the ceiling before their fiery explosion could dismember him. As they detonated, sending a shock wave through the store and shattering its merchandise, Catalina grinned up at him, eyes glowing and hand signing.

[A . . . Stop . . . L . . . E . . .]

He dropped, and they resumed their melee. Punches and kicks battered them about the store, and soon they were near one of the plate-glass windows leading outside. When he tried hit her, hoping for incapacitation, she grabbed his arm and used his momentum to flip him over her shoulder, crashing him through the window. He landed on sidewalk, covered in deep cuts and bits of glass, staring up at a sign.

WELCOME TO HISTORIC TROLLEY SQUARE.

A shadow . . . *the* Shadow . . . darkened his view, standing over him in triumph, a kama scythe in each hand ready to strike. This time, he remembered its name. Her blood-streaked cheeks highlighted her lizard stare and needle teeth, an ensemble Stacey suspected would haunt him for years to come—if he survived. The metal blades glinted off the moonlight as they began to slice toward him.

"Stop," he said, raising his hand.

She froze, looking down. At the tip of his extended index and middle fingers was a small, silver device with a glowing LED light. Around him, the air began to turn green.

"Don't make me."

To his surprise, Catalina's right hand trembled and dropped its kama.

"You can't avoid this."

Stacey watched her free hand sign those seven letters one last time. Then it changed its message, repeating two words.

[Do ... It ... Do ... It ...]

Sighing, Stacey raised his hand. The Reptile in Catalina tried to run, but something else held her frozen in place.

[Do ... It ... Do ... It ...]

The energy before him swelled into a ball, closing the gap between them. What else could he do? Lock her up? Tear her apart to "fix" her, like Society? It was too dangerous, especially after the heavy blows The Faction had already taken.

This was his call. He'd have to live with it.

[Do ... It ... Do ... It ...]

"I'm so sorry, Catalina."

The Reptile regained control and lunged at him.

Stacey turned his head, tears in his eyes, and fired.

The night went silent.

And with a roar, green energy whipping out and enveloping Catalina. Waves of it rippled around her, blackening the walls of the pottery store, screaming through the air as ozone burned away and fresh oxygen rushed in. Stacey immediately redirected his blast, sending the excess nuclear power up into the air like a firework before tossing the Splitter from his hand, smoke curling around him.

On the wall before him, where he had fired, were Catalina's remains. Not her body, nor her clothes, nor even her weapons. No, all of it disintegrated by the blast. Only a silhouette of ash remained, ingrained against the wall—a nuclear afterimage.

In her final act of bravery, she embodied her chosen name.

––––––––––––––––––

Zen, Nadi, and Stacey huddled around the repaired living room. Maddie refused to join them. Instead, she was lying in the basement, whimpering and licking her diseased owner's hand. Stacey couldn't bear to go back in there, to face Quentin's corpse. Not right now.

"What are we going to do?" Nadi finally asked, wincing and clutching at one of the many bandaged bullet holes along his body. Stacey had no idea how the man continued to survive such major injuries.

Zen looked away from the two men, silent, her eyes widened in a thousand-yard-stare. Her left hand reached over and clutched at the stump where her right arm used to be.

Apparently, she isn't completely invincible, Stacey thought, shaking his head.

Zen shuddered, a reaction that Stacey recognized well. It was the onset of phantom pain.

Likely the first of many.

Since Zen refused to talk, Stacey coughed, grabbing at the amateur cauterization across his torso. He had returned to Treehouse and worked out Catalina's message. A piece of paper in his hand revealed, in blocky letters, the name their fallen comrade had tried so desperately to share.

"What are we going to do?" Stacey said, repeating Nadi's words. "What else can we do? We rebuild Treehouse, just like Millipede rebuilt Koshasth."

Nadi nodded, satisfied but still somber. "I'll check Proxy . . . *Quentin's* personnel records. We can rebuild."

Zen didn't bother to respond.

Stacey looked down at the name on the paper in his hand.

LEMURIA

"We rebuild," he growled, crushing the paper into a ball, "and then we *hunt*."

9 781952 706233